ALL ALONG THE WATCHTOWER

WAYWARD SONS
BOOK 2

HARPER JACKSON

TAKE THE LEAP PUBLISHING

PROLOGUE
FORD

"Dude, it wasn't your fault."

Sawyer wouldn't stop pacing, looking like he was gonna puke. "How is it not my fault? If I hadn't helped her sneak out..." He raked his hands through his hair. "She almost died, Ford. If Willa had—God. Jace is never gonna forgive me."

"Bullshit." Rios wasn't having any of it. "Willa was gonna find a way to that party no matter what. If you hadn't brought her, hadn't noticed she was missing..." He didn't finish the thought. Didn't have to.

Yeah, Sawyer had helped Jace's little sister sneak past her helicopter parents to get to the beach party, but he'd also saved her life. He was the one who realized she was gone, spotted her in the water, and went in after her like some crazy action hero during the storm. Did CPR until she started breathing again. Got her help. She was alive because of him, even if she was stuck in the hospital on the mainland right now. Jace had gone with his parents, and we'd been waiting to hear something—anything—for hours.

Sawyer was still in his wet clothes from the party, looking like a half-drowned rat. Mom and Mimi had tried to get him to change, but he wouldn't listen. If Jace hadn't told us to keep an eye on him, Sawyer would probably still be out there on the beach, storm or no storm.

Nobody had any clue how Willa ended up in the water. She grew up here—she wasn't some tourist who didn't know better. She'd been swimming since before she could walk. Something about it felt wrong. Thank God Sawyer had spotted her at all. It had been a damned miracle he hadn't drowned trying to save her. Life would seriously suck without Sawyer Malone. He wasn't just my best friend—he was my brother. All the Wayward Sons were.

None of us had slept. My moms went up hours ago, but they kept checking in like we were little kids again. Sawyer wasn't gonna crash until we knew Willa was okay, so here we were, keeping watch with him. I tried not to think about what would happen if she wasn't okay.

The storm finally died down around sunrise. Still no text from Jace. He had to be just as wrecked as we were.

I could hang here with Sawyer as long as he needed, but we were gonna need fuel to keep our eyes open. I looked at Rios. "Coffee?"

"Hell yes. And maybe raid Mimi's cookie jar?"

"She'll kill you if she catches you eating cookies for breakfast."

The shadow of Rios's usual smartass grin appeared. "Please. I'm her favorite, and you know it."

"You wish." But before I could make it to the kitchen, someone pounded on the front door. We all froze.

"Who the hell?" Rios muttered.

"Maybe it's Jace." The hope in Sawyer's voice made my chest hurt.

But when I yanked open the door, it was Bree standing there looking like she hadn't slept either. She had that look she got when everything was going sideways—all pale and tense, arms wrapped around herself like she was holding something in.

"I know it's crazy early," she said, "but I saw the lights on. I'd have texted, but..."

"What's wrong?"

"Gwen's missing."

Gwen Busby was one of Willa's besties. She and Rios's younger sister, Gabi, were their own tight friend group. The three of them were a few classes under all of us, so we didn't exactly hang out, but we kept an eye on them. They'd absolutely been together last night at the party, before everything had gone to shit.

"What do you mean, missing?" Rios demanded.

"No one has seen her since the party last night. Her parents raised the alarm when she didn't come home. They're putting together an island-wide search. I figured y'all would want to be there."

Rios shook his head. "But that's impossible. I saw her myself when we were clearing out right before the storm hit."

"Chief Carson will want to hear about that, for sure. All I know is, she didn't make it home last night."

I scooped a hand through my hair. "Could she have gone home with somebody else?"

"Who?" Sawyer asked. "Willa's still in the hospital, and she didn't go home with Gabi."

"I mean... maybe a guy?" I suggested. "There was a lot of hooking up at that party."

"She's not that girl," Bree argued. "I mean, first time for everything, and it's not like I'm exactly an expert on normal teenage girl behavior since I spend all my time hanging out with you yahoos, but

I don't see her willingly staying out all night with some guy."

She let the implication hang until we were all moving to grab our shoes.

My moms came downstairs, both in their bathrobes, eyes heavy from sleep.

Mom's eyes cleared when she spotted the four of us. "Is there news about Willa?"

"Not yet. Gwen Busby never made it home last night. They're organizing a search," I explained.

Mom and Mimi exchanged a look.

Mimi clutched the lapels of her robe together, her dark eyes full of worry. "We'll go dress."

Forty minutes later, we were spread out near Osprey Beach, where the party had been held last night. In the wake of the storm, there was no sign of the hundred or so teens who'd been here, except for the blackened pile of wood that was all that remained of the bonfire. Seaweed and driftwood were scattered all across the beach, along with the usual mess following a storm. If there'd ever been any footprints or other obvious signs to follow, they were definitely gone now.

An incident command tent had been set up at the edge of the boardwalk. The officer running things had organized all the searchers into a line to begin walking the area in a grid pattern. Hatterwick Island was only thirteen miles long and three miles across at its widest point. While it wasn't a big is-land, there were still plenty of places for someone to disappear, like the woods that occupied the center of the island going north. Maybe Gwen had tried to find shelter from the storm and injured herself. Sprained an ankle or something and hadn't been able to make it out.

"Gwen!" I shouted her name, my voice dying out in the heavy, humid air.

We made our way into the woods, continuing forward in our grid pattern. The morning ticked slowly by with her name becoming a chorus from all the searchers. I wondered again if she'd gone off with some guy. Had anybody been creeping on her? Was there some asshole out there who'd pressured her to do something she hadn't wanted to? I tried to think back to last night, to whether I'd seen any-thing. But the truth was, Gwen was someone at my periphery. Friend of a friend. I knew her, but she was younger. Only fifteen to our eighteen. She wasn't a direct part of our group, and all I'd been concerned with last night was enjoying myself and the start of the last summer I'd spend on the island with all the Wayward Sons before we split up in the fall.

Up ahead, someone bolted through the trees. "Gwen? Gwen! Where are you?"

I recognized that panicked voice as belonging to Miles Busby, Gwen's college-age older brother.

I picked up my pace and caught up with him. "Hey, man."

Miles whirled on me, his eyes almost feral with panic.

I lifted my hands in peace. "You okay? You need some water?"

"I need my sister."

"I get it. We're all looking. But maybe you should drink down some water. If you keel over from dehydration, you won't do her any good." I offered him some of my own water.

After a long hesitation, he took it, drinking down half the bottle. His eyes closed on a defeated sigh. "I'm her big brother. I was supposed to look out for her. And now she's..." His voice choked off.

"Hey, you don't know that. She might be fine."

But I could see he didn't believe that. And as the day progressed, and the search continued, with no word, no sign of her whatsoever, I was starting to get a really bad feeling that something terrible had happened to Gwen Busby.

CHAPTER 1
FORD

Present

MISSING

The word caught my attention, as it always did, though I already knew every word of the poster by heart. I'd been seeing variations of it all over Sutter's Ferry for years. This summer would be the fourteenth anniversary.

Gwen Busby. Brown hair. Hazel eyes. Age at time of disappearance: 15. Age now: 28.

This poster was a newer one, with a computer-rendered, aged-up photo of what she might look like now next to the original smiling image that had come to haunt everyone on Hatterwick Island. The open question of what had happened to her had irrevocably marked our community. No trace of her had ever been found, and all had gone quiet—until last summer, when Willa had inadvertently blown things open again.

She'd never been the same after that summer, after her drowning. She'd had no memory of how she'd ended up in the water. We'd all chalked it up to very real trauma, but the truth had turned out to be far more chilling.

It turned out she'd been the last person to see Gwen alive. The two of them had left the bonfire together. They'd been nabbed in the woods. But only Gwen had been the target. Willa was a mistake. Wrong place, wrong time. Or so they'd said. They'd rectified the situation by throwing her overboard and leaving her to drown. It would've worked, if not for Sawyer.

When Willa didn't die, the man behind the kidnapping had gone to incredible lengths to make absolutely certain she wouldn't remember a thing. I didn't know the full details of the additional trauma she'd endured, only that once she'd found the courage to face her demons and started to remember, she'd nearly been killed for her trouble.

Chief Carson hadn't found corroborating evidence to back up what Willa remembered. Not surprising. After all this time, the likelihood of there being anything to find was so incredibly slim.

Roland O'Shea, the man who might've been able to answer some of those questions, was dead. He'd been some kind of middleman—though, in what, it wasn't clear. Drug running? Human trafficking? Something else? The community was still reeling from the revelation that one of its most trusted members had carried such a dark secret. That he'd had something to do with Gwen's disappearance. No matter the particulars, the heartbreaking and tragic reality was that Gwen Busby had probably met a horrible end. But the people of Hatterwick— especially the Busby family—still wanted answers. Closure, at the very least.

I didn't know if we'd ever get it.

Shaking off that grim thought, I tugged open the door to the Pelican Point Bistro and stepped inside. I automatically scanned the space, looking for my brothers. We'd kept in close touch all these years since we'd joined the Navy, and we got together as often as possible. But it had become an increasing rarity for all of us to be on-island at the same time anymore. The planets had aligned such that we'd all made it home for a delayed holiday celebration with the family that remained on Hatterwick. There'd been parties and dinners, lots of celebration about Elian Sebastian McNamara—Eli for short—Rios's newest nephew, who'd arrived just days before Thanksgiving. My moms had done their utmost to spoil us all, as if Mimi's cookies were sufficient blackmail to get us home more often. And hell, they really were. But tonight was just us guys.

The Bistro wouldn't have been my first choice. It was... fine. But it had never been our place. That had always been the Tidewater Tavern. Of course, the tavern wasn't the tavern anymore. It had been renamed even before the fire that had burned the original structure to the ground three years after Gwen's disappearance, the summer we'd all joined the Navy. Now it was the OBX Brewhouse, and Bree had built it into an impressive microbrewery with its own devoted following and award-winning reputation. I wished we'd been able to meet there. Not only because it was hands down the best bar on the island, but because I just... wanted to see her.

But that wasn't an option. Because we weren't friends anymore. I'd fucked things up with her.

So that meant we dealt with either the pretension of the Bistro or the threat of a bar fight at Home Port, the dive bar frequented by the fishermen and other locals on the island. I'd have been more comfortable with the peanut-shells and old country music at Home Port, but that had been one of Sawyer's dad's favorite haunts. The last thing I wanted to do was remind my pal of all those times he'd had to scrape his dad off a bar stool to get him home, so I'd suffer the discomfort of mood lighting and tablecloths.

Maybe a bourbon would make it better.

Jace clearly had the same idea. I found him tucked into one of the curved booths on the far side of the restaurant, positioned so he could see every entrance and exit of the place, in addition to the panoramic views of Pamlico Sound that were one of the biggest draws for diners. Not that there was much to be seen in January. His button-down shirt was open at the collar, and in that moment, with one arm stretched along the top of the booth and a glass of what was probably single-malt in his hand, he looked exactly like what his parents had raised him to be—the island prince. As the current generation of the founding family of Sutter's Ferry, they'd thought he'd take over everything. But he'd been bucking their expectations for years now, winding up in naval intelligence rather than going on to Ivy League law the way they'd wanted.

"Getting started without us?" I asked.

He flashed a welcoming smile. "Sawyer's outside, calling home to check in with Willa. I find a couple of fingers of Glen Morangie make the fact that one of my best friends married my sister a little less weird."

"Sorry. Not sorry." Sawyer didn't bother to hide the contented grin as he joined us at the table.

"Lucky bastard." But I pulled him in for a back-thumping hug.

"Yeah, I damned well am."

He adored Willa. Always had. But truth be told, I'd never expected him to actually *do* anything about it. He'd had hangups about not being good enough for her. But after a medical discharge landed him back on Hatterwick last summer, the two of them had been through some serious shit. It was good to see him happy. Good to know that the two of them had found a deep and abiding love. Even if the sight of them together filled me with just a bit of envy.

I didn't get that kind of satisfaction from my career. I liked my job. I was good at it. I'd done well in the Navy. We all had. But that was all it was. Work. A job. I was a man who came from rock solid family ties, and I'd always imagined I'd be building my own by now. Yet I was still alone.

And whose fault is that?

Oblivious to the direction of my thoughts, Sawyer slid into the booth. "We gettin' food or just drinks?"

"We can eat here, or we can dig into the mountain of leftovers Caroline foisted on me before I managed to get out the door." Rios shrugged out of his coat and moved toward my end of the U-shaped booth. "Move over, asshole."

I scooted deeper into the booth. "Dude, she just had a baby. How does she have the energy to cook?"

"Oh, she's got Hoyt well-trained after all these years. He makes a surprisingly good pozole for a white guy. There's enough for each of you to take home and then some."

"Do we actually have time to get through all that before you and I leave for Norfolk?" We had only two more days before we headed out for the naval station in Virginia. Me for a training exercise and Rios to update some certifications.

He arched one dark brow. "I sure as hell won't be the one to tell her if we don't."

The server approached our table. "Welcome to Pelican Point Bistro. My name is Nadia, and I'll be your server tonight. Can I get the rest of you gentlemen something to drink?"

We placed our orders, along with a request for a seafood appetizer platter. When she'd left, Sawyer leaned back in his seat, taking us in. "Man, it's been so good to have all y'all on-island again. Even if it's just for a matter of days."

"Wish it could be longer," Jace conceded. "Weirdness of you sleeping with my sister aside, it was good to spend time with both of you. Good to see her so happy. She wouldn't have healed this much without you."

One corner of Sawyer's mouth kicked up, and

unmistakable pride shone in his eyes. "She's worked her ass off at it. And I know it does her good to see you. Any idea when you might shake loose again?"

"Nah. They're sending me under for another one of those if-I-tell-you-I'd-have-to-kill-you kind of classified missions. I may be out of contact for a while. It makes me rest easier knowing you've got her back."

"Always." He spread his arms and grinned. "Marriage is good, fellas. Y'all should try it."

"There's the matter of the rest of our contracts," I pointed out. We still had a year-and-a-half of service to go. And that was assuming none of us re-upped.

Sawyer waved a hand in dismissal. "There are ways around that for good reasons."

Rios huffed a laugh. "You do know you're the only one of us with a woman, right? Jace and I have... friends at various ports of call, but nothing serious. And I'm not sure Ford has even had *that* in the past ten years."

All eyes turned to me.

"What? Because I don't talk about my love life, you assume I don't have one?"

"Yes," they all chorused.

"Jackasses," I muttered. Though they weren't entirely wrong. I'd been a serial monogamist throughout college before I'd finally called it quits with my on-again-off-again girlfriend, Emily. Since then, I'd tried the casual thing occasionally, but those kinds of hookups left me feeling hollow. There were women I knew in the service who'd have been fine with a friends-with-benefits sort of arrangement, but I couldn't do that, either. I wanted permanence, and until I met a woman who made me see the potential for that, I didn't see the point of wasting everyone's time.

My friends were all grinning as Nadia returned with our drinks. I took a deeper swallow of the bourbon than I probably should have. It burned its way down my throat, dissolving the knot that seemed permanently lodged there whenever I came home.

Rios pinned me with a look. "Have you tried to talk to her on this trip?"

Though I'd never confessed to any of them what had gone down that terrible summer, I knew they meant Bree. There wasn't any hiding the fact that she loathed me now. Glancing down into the warm golden liquid in my glass, I shook my head. "No. She made her position about me very clear, and I have to respect that."

I'd fucked up the best thing in my life, and I wasn't sure I'd ever be able to outrun that regret.

It was something I was still trying to figure out how to live with.

CHAPTER 2
BREE

I rolled silverware into napkins while Monty waved his hands with his customary dramatic flair, nearly knocking over the flight of experimental brews lined up between us.

"Darlin', you haven't lived until you've tried a sour with blood orange and hibiscus. It's absolutely divine." He lifted one of the small glasses, holding it up to the pendant lights like he was examining a precious gem. "Though I suppose we should probably give it a more marketable name than 'Divine.'"

"Your last divine creation was that chocolate porter that tasted like burnt tires." I snatched the glass before he could spill it. The brew had a lovely rose-gold color, and the aroma wasn't half bad.

"That porter was ahead of its time." Monty pressed a hand to his chest. "And Peter loved it."

"Peter loves you. He'd drink motor oil if you served it to him." What I wouldn't give for a partner with that kind of devotion. I credited my brewmaster and his husband for the fact that I hadn't one hundred percent given up on true love. I'd only given up about eighty-five percent.

"True." A dreamy smile crossed Monty's fine-boned face. "That man is a saint. Unlike my mother, who still can't believe her only son is 'wasting his degree' making beer instead of practicing law in Charleston."

"And God love you for it." I took a sip of the sour. The tartness hit first, followed by citrus notes and a subtle floral finish. "Okay, you might be onto something with this one."

"Of course I am. When are you going to learn to trust my genius?" He leaned against the bar, waggling his perfectly groomed eyebrows. "Now, what shall we call it?"

As it was January and the slow season, the Tuesday night crowd was thin—just a few regulars at the far end of the bar and a couple of tourists sharing a pizza in the corner. I had time to play this game. "Island Sunset?"

"Too basic." Monty wrinkled his nose. "This is

art in a glass, sugar. It needs something with more punch."

"Hibiscus Hurricane?"

"Better, but still not quite there." He grabbed a cocktail napkin and started scribbling. "What about... Blood Orange Bombshell?"

A gravelly laugh erupted from the end of the bar. "Sounds like what Duck's ex-wife used to call herself," Wally called out.

"Watch it, Briggs." Duck shifted on his barstool. "That woman was a natural redhead."

"What?" Milt cupped his ear. "Who's dead?"

"Nobody's dead," Pop shouted, then turned to me. "How about calling it 'Sunset Strip?'"

I poured them each a taster. "Pop, that sounds like a gentleman's club."

"What's wrong with that?" Cliff grabbed his glass. "Might boost sales."

"Lord help me." I dropped my forehead into my palm. These guys were impossible, but they were my impossible.

"Orange You Glad?" Duck offered.

Monty gasped. "I will not have my creation subjected to puns."

"What about 'Island Time?'" Pop raised his glass. "Because one sip of this, and you'll want to slow down and stay awhile."

"That's..." Monty paused mid-protest. "Actually, not terrible."

"Ed's still got it." Wally clinked glasses with my grandfather. "Unlike some people around here."

"Who's got it?" Milt squinted.

"Island Time it is." I started writing it on the specials board. "See what happens when you old coots put your heads together?"

"Who you calling old?" Duck protested. "I've still got all my own teeth."

"Half of them anyway," Cliff muttered into his beer.

The Gray Beards dissolved into their usual bickering, and I caught Pop's eye. He winked at me, and I felt a surge of gratitude and affection. These men might drive me crazy, but they'd been my family's backbone since the day Pop had brought me back to Hatterwick, when I was just a skinny, scared eight-year-old, who'd half wondered if social services had handed me over to a pirate instead of my ostensible grandfather. With his booming captain's voice and scruffy beard, Pop had absolutely given off that vibe. But it turned out that crusty exterior hid a heart of absolute gold, and I'd do anything for the man who'd given me roots, a home, and a purpose.

I grabbed fresh silverware rolls and headed out to check on my tables. With two servers out—one with the flu, one at her kid's basketball game—I'd picked up the slack. Didn't bother me. I'd done every job in this place since I was tall enough to reach the industrial sink. Moving between tables felt as natural as breathing. I'd learned to balance plates on my forearm before I could drive. Pop had insisted I learn the business from the ground up, even though I'd practically grown up in the original building.

For a split second, I saw the charred beams of the old tavern, smelled the acrid smoke that had lingered for weeks. Marv the marlin, Pop's pride and joy, nothing but ashes. We'd thought we'd lost everything. And in the face of that devastating grief, I thought I'd finally gained the one thing I'd always wanted.

Nope. Not going there.

We'd rebuilt bigger and better. The new OBX Brewhouse had risen from those ashes like a phoenix, transforming from Pop's casual tavern into something that drew craft beer enthusiasts from up and down the coast. The exposed brick walls and reclaimed wood gave the space an industrial-meets-coastal vibe that perfectly balanced modern and rustic. Floor-to-ceiling windows looked out over the sound, and the deck offered prime sunset views back toward the distant mainland.

I'd spent countless nights poring over business

plans, researching equipment, studying brewing techniques. Pop had backed my vision one hundred percent, even when the bank turned up their noses at a woman, who hadn't yet been old enough to even drink, wanting to open a brewery. But I'd done my homework. Craft beer was exploding, and the Outer Banks had been ready for something beyond mass-produced lagers.

Hiring Monty had been the last piece of the puzzle. His experimental nature and classical training had elevated our offerings beyond typical beach brews. We now distributed to restaurants across three states, and our seasonal releases drew lines around the block.

I traced my fingers over the smooth bar top—reclaimed heart pine that Pop and I had salvaged ourselves. The fire had destroyed so much, but we'd managed to incorporate pieces of the original building into the new space. The old sign hung in the entry. Brass railings now lined the stairs to the second floor. And behind the bar, I'd mounted a shadow box containing Marv's partially melted brass nameplate—the only piece of Pop's prized catch we'd recovered.

Over a decade of blood, sweat, and more than a few tears had built this place into something extraordinary. Something that was mine. Sure, technically Pop still owned controlling interest, but he'd stepped back years ago, content to hold court with his buddies while I ran the show. This was my home, my legacy, everything I'd worked for.

The register dinged as another order came through from the kitchen. I grabbed fresh plates and headed that way, ready to tackle whatever came next.

I dropped off a fresh round of IPAs to the Masons—third generation shrimpers who'd been coming here since before I could see over the bar—when Lindsay Messina waved me over to her table. She sat with Astrid Thompson, both of them sharing what looked like our fish tacos.

"Hey stranger." I slid into the empty chair. "Haven't seen you in here this week."

Lindsay pushed her dark hair behind her ear. "Been crazy at the office. Boss fired one of our seasonal workers today, which is always ugly. And you wouldn't believe the paperwork involved in getting ready for Corbin to come back."

"Corbin O'Connell?" The name caught me off guard. "Didn't know he was coming home."

"His dad's knee surgery isn't healing right." Lindsay's cheeks flushed slightly. "He's taking leave to help run things for a few months."

Astrid grinned over her Corona. "And Lindsay

here hasn't stopped talking about it since she found out."

"Oh my God, stop." Lindsay threw a napkin at her friend.

"What? You only had the biggest crush on him all through high school." Astrid turned to me. "She used to find excuses to walk past the lifeguard station."

"That was one summer!" Lindsay buried her face in her hands. "And he totally saved me from drowning at that beach party."

"You mean when you 'accidentally' got caught in that tiny riptide?" I arched an eyebrow. I hadn't known these women well during high school, but even I remembered that incident.

"I hate you both." Lindsay peeked through her fingers. "Besides, that was forever ago. I'm sure he doesn't even remember."

"Uh-huh." Astrid's knowing look said everything. "And you volunteering to handle all his onboarding paperwork has nothing to do with those memories."

Lindsay's blush deepened. "I'm being professional."

"Professionally thirsty maybe," Astrid muttered.

"Speaking of thirsty," Lindsay dabbed her

napkin at the corner of her mouth, "did you see all the Wayward Sons are home?"

My hand tightened on the edge of the table. I forced my fingers to relax.

"God, yes." Astrid fanned herself. "Whatever the Navy's doing, it's working. Did you see Rios's arms?"

"Please, Ford is where it's at." Lindsay sighed. "Those tattoos."

My chest squeezed in a familiar vise grip. I pushed back from the table, pasting on what I hoped passed for a neutral expression. "I should check on the Gray Beards before they start arm wrestling again."

"Oh, come on, stay." Lindsay caught my wrist. "When was the last time we just sat and dished?"

I extracted myself as gently as possible. Years of practice had taught me how to dodge these conversations with surgical precision. "Some of us have to work. Rain check?"

The truth was, I couldn't bear to hear his name, let alone discuss how good he looked. No one had ever cut me as deep as Ford Donoghue. Not my father, who'd dropped my mom and me, and disappeared. Not the mom who'd chosen drugs and addiction over me.

That was why I kept my relationships light, casual, and firmly time-limited these days. Three months max, no exceptions. No one got close enough to see past my walls. No one got the chance to break what I'd spent years carefully piecing back together. And, so far as I was concerned, no one ever would again.

CHAPTER 3

FORD

The aroma of Mimi's famous French toast filled our kitchen, mixed with the sharp scent of coffee and the salt breeze drifting through the open windows. Didn't matter how cold it was, we were gonna get fresh ocean air to start the day. I slouched at the counter, watching my moms move around each other in their usual morning dance.

"You're sure you can't stay another day?" Mimi flipped the bread on the griddle, her halo of natural curls bouncing as she turned to face me. "I barely got to show you my new pottery pieces."

"Those training exercises wait for no man." Mom grabbed her travel mug, briefcase already by the door for court. "Though I wish they would."

"I know, I know." I snagged a piece of bacon

from the plate—a blue and gray swirled glaze that was also one of Mimi's creations. "Trust me, if I could stretch these days out longer, I would."

Mom leaned in to kiss Mimi, and I felt a glow in my chest. Their open affection had never been a source of discomfort for me. The fact that my moms loved and adored each other had always been a gift in my book. They were an odd couple, the statuesque Viking of a woman with the curvy, pint-sized hippie artist she'd met in the French Quarter years ago. But they worked. They'd not only given me a rock-solid foundation growing up, but they'd frequently served as the same for my friends who weren't so fortunate in their parentage. I didn't mind sharing. In this house, it was always the more the merrier.

Mom pressed a kiss to my temple on her way past. "Just try to swing back through before you ship out again?"

"I'll do my best." The words caught in my throat, thick with everything I couldn't quite express. We all knew 'best' might not be enough, but they never made me feel guilty about the duty that so often took me far from home. That unconditional support was just one more way they showed their love.

Mimi slid a plate in front of me, the French toast artfully arranged with fresh berries and dusted with powdered sugar, just like she'd done since I was a kid. "Eat up, baby. You've got a long drive ahead." Her warm brown eyes crinkled at the corners as she watched me, probably remembering all the other breakfasts we'd shared in this kitchen over the years.

"Thanks, Mimi." I dug in, savoring each bite. No one made it quite like her, with that hint of vanilla and nutmeg she'd never reveal the ratio of. Even after all my years in the Navy, tasting food from ports around the world, nothing compared to her French toast. It was home on a plate.

"Your mama and I worry, you know." She settled across from me with her own coffee, wrapping her hands around the pot-bellied mug that was one of her most popular styles.

"I know you do." I reached across to squeeze her arm. "But I'm good at what I do. And I've got the best team watching my back. Plus, nobody's coming after the supply guy." My role as a supply corps officer was a little more complicated than that, but nothing for them to be concerned about.

Mom checked her watch and grabbed the worn leather briefcase she'd been carrying to court for as long as I could remember. "I've got to run. Court waits for no woman either."

I shoved back from the table and rose to pull her in for a squeeze.

She hugged me tight. Though I was a full head taller these days, sometimes I still felt like the gangly teenager who'd shot up six inches in one summer. "Drive safe. Call when you get there."

"Yes, ma'am." I held on an extra moment, breathing in her signature scent of lavender and sandalwood and imprinting it on my memory to last until I came home again. "Love you, Mom."

"Love you too, sweetheart."

Through the kitchen windows, morning sun glinted off the whitewashed lighthouse walls. The old beacon hadn't guided ships in decades, but it still stood sentinel over our piece of coastline. A watchtower. When my moms bought the property, the tower and caretaker's cottage had been falling apart. Now the expanded cottage wrapped around the base of the lighthouse in a horseshoe of weathered cedar shingles and bright window boxes overflowing with Mimi's herbs and the sturdy pansies that could weather winter on the Outer Banks.

"How's the new studio working out?" I nodded toward the glass-walled space they'd added last fall, jutting out toward the water like the prow of a ship.

Mimi's face lit up. "Perfect light, perfect view. Though your mom keeps saying I'm going to fall right through the floor with all my pottery wheels and kilns."

"You did reinforce it, right?"

"Of course! I may be an artist, but I'm not completely impractical." She topped off my coffee. "Though I did have to promise no glass-blowing experiments."

I choked on my coffee. "Please tell me you weren't actually considering that."

"A girl can dream." She winked. "Besides, the attic workshop has plenty of room for new ventures."

The attic had been their pet project—expanding what had once been a cramped attic into a workshop that ran the full length of the house. They'd done most of the work themselves, cursing and covered in sawdust for months. I'd helped when I could, hauling lumber up the narrow stairs and installing the skylights that now flooded the space with natural light. Mom and Mimi had insisted on doing the bulk of the renovation though, determined to create exactly the studio space they'd always dreamed about. Even now, years later, I could still hear Mimi's excited chatter about proper ventilation and the way Mom had fretted over every measurement three times before making a single cut.

"Speaking of ventures." Mimi retrieved a wrapped package from beside the fridge. "A little something for you to take with you."

Inside was one of her signature potbelly coffee

mugs, glazed in deep blues and greens that swirled like the ocean. My throat tightened. "It's perfect, Mimi. Thank you."

"Well, you need something civilized to drink from. Can't have my boy using those awful Navy mess cups all the time."

I ran my thumb over the smooth surface, re-membering all the mornings I'd watched her throw pots in her old workshop, the wheel spinning hyp-notic circles while she shaped wet clay with sure hands. I missed those mornings. Missed, too, the meditative nature of simply watching her work. Hell, I missed everything about the island. I had for a long time, but something about this trip had really brought it into sharp focus.

Well, not something. Sawyer. Seeing him building a life with Willa had me actually thinking about retirement when my contract was up. The way they'd settled in together, making something real and permanent, stirred up feelings I'd been fighting since the day I enlisted.

I set the mug down carefully, tracing the spiral pattern with one finger. Could I really come back here? Make a life on this tiny strip of sand where every other corner held memories of Bree? The thought of running into her at the market or the post office made my chest ache, but maybe that was exactly why I needed to come home. Some wounds didn't heal with distance, and Lord knew I'd tried that route for long enough.

The boardwalk where we'd spent summer nights watching stars, sharing secrets and dreams while the waves crashed below. The dunes where we'd hidden from the world, building sandcastles as kids. The cove on the north end of the island where everything had changed, right before it all went straight to hell. That night still haunted me—the fire's glow reflecting off the water, the taste of whiskey, and the way she'd looked at me with such raw hope in her eyes.

Bree's walls were titanium-reinforced these days. The few times we crossed paths, her eyes skated past me like I was a stranger. Worse than a stranger—someone who didn't even register as worth acknowledging. Each time it happened was a fresh punch to the gut, a reminder of how spectacularly I'd managed to destroy twenty years of friendship in one alcohol-fueled night and its aftermath.

"You're thinking awful hard for this early in the morning." Mimi's voice cut through my spiral, her knowing tone making me wince. She'd always been able to read me.

"Just... future stuff." I tried to brush it off, but my other mother had the tenacity of a bloodhound when she caught the scent of something bothering me.

"Ah." She nodded sagely, her curls catching the morning light. "Would this have anything to do with a certain blonde brewery owner?"

I groaned, slumping back in my chair. "You're worse than Mom with the interrogations." Mom was an environmental rights attorney now, but she'd started her career as a prosecutor, and those instincts had never quite gone away. Between the two of them, keeping secrets had been impossible growing up.

"Please. Your mama taught me everything I know about extracting information." Mimi gathered our plates with practiced efficiency, the ceramic clinking together. "You know, sometimes the hardest wounds to heal are the ones we keep picking at." Her warm brown eyes held mine, full of warmth and acceptance.

"I'm not picking." But the protest died on my lips. Who was I kidding? "Okay, maybe I am. But seeing Sawyer and Willa so happy... it just hits different now." Seeing them together since I'd been back, the way they'd looked at each other like they were the only two people in the world, had twisted something in my chest.

"Because you want what they have? Or because you had a shot at it once, and you blew it?"

My gaze shot to hers. I'd never told either of my moms what had gone down with Bree. But neither of them were stupid women. Maybe they'd guessed. Hell, they'd seen the way everything changed after that night, the way Bree stopped coming around, stopped answering my calls. I appreciated the fact that they'd never pressed.

"Doesn't matter." I shrugged, fidgeting with my coffee mug to avoid those knowing eyes. "My retirement is a long way off. Plenty of time to figure my life out."

"Or plenty of time to keep running." Mimi's voice held no judgment, just that quiet wisdom that had guided me through more than one crisis growing up. The same tone she'd used when I'd crashed my first car, when I'd bombed my AP chemistry final, when I'd told them I was enlisting.

I stood and pulled her into a hug, pressing a kiss to the top of her head, breathing in the faint scent of turpentine and clay that always clung to her clothes from her studio. "I love you, Mimi. But please stop meddling."

"Love you too, baby. So, of course, I won't." She squeezed tight, her slight frame somehow managing to envelop me the way she had since I was a kid, even though I towered over her now. "Just re-member—sometimes the right words aren't nearly as important as just showing up and being present."

My presence was exactly the thing I hadn't been able to do a damned thing about from the moment I'd enlisted. The irony of that wasn't lost on me. Over ten years of service to my country had cost me the one person I'd never meant to hurt. But I filed that wisdom away for some future point when maybe, just maybe, I'd find the right way to get Bree to hear my apology.

CHAPTER 4
PEYTON

"I want to see!"

Before the tiny terror before me could boost himself up on the ferry rail and fall overboard, I snagged the back of his coat. "Hold it."

"But I want to see!" Jamie whined, his lip jutting out in a pout I just knew was going to precede an epic tantrum, because he was four and that's how that worked.

"Let's do it from over here."

I tugged him over to one of the benches lining the exterior of the ferry and helped him climb up. I kept a tight arm around his waist, stabilizing him against the rock of the boat on the waves. The overhang of the second level did almost nothing to block the drizzling rain or the spray that splashed up as we cut through each swell, but Jamie didn't seem to care, and I was certainly no stranger to the rain. We were both riveted by the view of the island rising out of the gloom ahead.

Hatterwick Island. The very bottom of the chain of barrier islands known as the Outer Banks. I'd read about it online and seen pictures. But they'd all been taken on bright, sunny summer days, not in the middle of a January rain, beneath a sky so gray it was hard to tell where it stopped and the ocean started, save for the wink of lights from Sutter's Ferry, the only village on the island. I couldn't quite wrap my head around the idea of a place so small it only had one town.

As we neared, I could make out what were probably sandy beaches. The island itself was long and low, with the faintest hint of what might've been trees off to the north, beyond the buildings that made up the village. So different from the rocky beaches where I was from.

The ferry's horn blasted a long, low note, signaling we were about to dock. The big engines roared, and the boat shook as we began to slow. Jamie vibrated against me as the pilot—was it called a pilot on boats?—neatly slid the vessel into place at the ferry terminal. He clapped in excitement as staff began to move around us, tossing ropes and doing whatever was necessary to secure the boat.

"C'mon. Let's go find your mom."

Taking a firm grip on his hand, I led him back inside the main cabin. Rachel was in the back, juggling a diaper bag that probably weighed more than I did, along with her two-year-old, Marianne, and the baby, Rosie.

"Oh, my gosh. Thank you for keeping an eye on him, Peyton."

"Of course. Can I help you get everybody back to the car?"

"I think we're going into the terminal first for a mandatory potty break."

We joined the line of people filing off down the ramp into the ferry terminal. My shoulders began to itch in a sensation that was becoming all too familiar. I lifted my gaze to one of the big concave mirrors in the corner of the cabin, studying the people behind us in line.

Some guy a half-dozen people back was staring at us. Tall, skinny, with that ropey kind of muscle. Dark hair. Scruff on his jaw. Did I recognize him? Hard to say without getting a better look.

The line moved forward, propelling me out of the cabin and away from the mirror. I didn't turn around as I helped Jamie down the ramp. Gangplank? Was it still called that when it wasn't a pirate ship?

Rachel heaved a sigh of relief as we stepped into the terminal. "Do you see your dad?"

I flashed a confident smile. "I texted right before we arrived. He's waiting in the parking lot. Thanks for letting me tag along with you. It made me feel better on the crossing."

She beamed. "Absolutely. You were a godsend helping me with the kids."

"You're so welcome." I took the opportunity to look back now, scanning the other passengers, but I didn't see the dude who'd been behind us.

"Do you want me to walk out with you to the car?" Rachel's voice pulled me back.

Jamie tugged at her sleeve. "Mama, I gotta pee."

"No, no. It's fine. It's a small island, and you've got enough on your plate. Thanks again. You guys enjoy your trip here." With a little wave, I left the little family by the bathrooms and ducked through the doors of the terminal out to the village.

No one was waiting for me. No one had been waiting for me for three months. The foster family who'd taken me in didn't exactly count. I mean, they were... fine. There were two other foster kids. Both girls. They were okay. And the parents were nice enough. But they weren't my mom.

That hadn't been why I'd left.

Was it crazy to think somebody had been watching me? Maybe. But over the past few months, I'd just had a feeling. That creepy, crawly feeling of eyes on me. I never saw anybody. Not for sure. There'd been a few times I thought... maybe. Like the guy in line to get off the ferry just now. Then I told myself I was being ridiculous. That I just felt alone and squirrelly in my new circumstances. Unsettled. That's what the therapist had told me.

But Mom had always said to trust my instincts. If my gut said something was wrong, it was telling me that for a reason, and I should listen.

So I had. I'd made this crazy plan, taken this desperate trip across thousands of miles. Doing exactly what I'd done today and attaching myself to a series of moms with little kids. Because Mom had been that mom who helped out other kids, other women. Which meant I knew the look of good moms who would help. And they had. So no one had realized that I was traveling entirely on my own, and I'd avoided creepers and cops alike as I switched from bus to bus.

Was anyone looking for me yet? Probably. But not here. No one would have expected me to come so far. No one knew I had any connection here. Not when I'd only found the evidence myself a few weeks ago when going through Mom's things.

I paused just outside the door of the ferry terminal, tugging the hood of my jacket up over my hair. Not that it did a thing to stop the fuzzing and curling from the wet. Out on the street, a car rolled by, its brake lights one of the few pops of color in the gray. I'd studied the map of this place before I came, trying to figure out where to go. I had a few places in mind to ask, but before I tried any of them, I needed to scope out some places where I could take shelter for the night in case this went badly. I'd been on the move for days now, so I'd mostly dozed on busses as we'd rumbled across the country. That wouldn't be an option here on this tiny island. It struck me as the kind of place where they rolled up the sidewalks at night. No 24-hour Walmarts here. I had some money left, but a night at a motel or something would take a big chunk of it, so I wanted to avoid that option if I could.

I set off in the rain, ducking down side streets in case Rachel saw me and worried. For nearly an hour, I wandered, checking alleys and overhangs. I'd need something more than that. It wasn't as cold here as a lot of places this time of year, but it was still January, and hypothermia was still a thing. I might be dipping into my limited funds after all. I had enough for two nights, maybe three, if I was careful about my food. After that, I'd need to get creative.

In the end, I found myself down near the marina. Boats bobbed in their slips, and I had the ridiculous thought that they'd been tucked in for the night. Light and a faint twang of country music spilled out of a building ahead. A bar?

I moved closer, trying to see the sign.

Home Port.

Through the window, I could see the building was pretty full. This seemed like the kind of place locals would hang out. Maybe I should go inside and ask here.

As I was trying to make up my mind, my skin prickled. Careful not to make any sudden moves, I casually glanced around, searching for the eyes I knew were on me.

A man stood near the entrance to the bar, a cigarette in hand as he watched me. Its tip glowed orange as he inhaled. Then he blew a stream of smoke out of one side of his mouth. Gross.

He wasn't *doing* anything. Just looking. But he gave me the heebie jeebies.

A truck passed me, pulling into the lot beside the bar. Its headlights swept over the man's face, causing him to squint.

It was the guy from the ferry. And there was no question this time that he was looking *at me.*

I quickly stepped back into the shadow of the nearest building. Maybe he was staring because he recognized me from earlier. Or maybe it was something else. I wasn't sticking around to find out.

It was time to head back up into the main part of the village to find the person I'd come all this way looking for.

CHAPTER 5

BREE

I wiped down the bar for the third time in ten minutes, more to keep my hands busy than from any real need. Cleaning was meditative for me. Based on how the Brewhouse sparkled, I ought to be a frigging Zen master by now. The steady patter of rain against the windows matched my mood—gray and subdued. But at least I could breathe again, now that Ford had left the island. Not that he'd notified me of his comings and goings. We had the island grapevine for that. Or, in this case, Lindsay, who'd texted that she'd seen both Ford and Rios driving onto the morning's ferry when she'd been on the way to work this morning.

My gaze drifted to Willa, typing away in her usual booth. Roy Kent, her massive black pit bull, sprawled at her feet, his gigantic head resting on his paws. No doubt he'd appreciate a play date with my own pup, Keeley, who was hanging with Pop today at his place and being spoiled within an inch of her life. I knew that extra bulk she'd picked up around her middle was a hundred percent due to the fact that he had zero ability to say no to her begging face. Maybe once the rain had passed, Willa and I could take the pair of them down to the beach for a romp, and we could have a good catch up.

I missed having her as a roommate. She'd been my first friend after everything had imploded with Ford. Hell, she'd been my first truly close female friend ever, given I'd always been a fifth wheel to the rest of the Wayward Sons. She was the only one I'd actually told about what had happened—and that had only been under the influence of a pitcher of margaritas during a particularly low moment. I wasn't worried that she'd blab the details to anyone, even Sawyer.

Willa understood secrets. She'd had a boatload of her own, including the fact that she'd been in love with Sawyer since she was thirteen. When they'd up and eloped last year, I hadn't been at all surprised. Anyone with eyes in their head could see he was crazy about her. And even my romantically jaded heart sighed when I saw how they looked at each other. No, I didn't resent him for taking her away. If anyone deserved their happily ever after, it was her. She'd been through hell and lived to tell the tale.

The front doors opened again, letting in a gust of wind, and I tensed before I could stop myself. But it was just Drew and Kelly McNamara and their tiny daughter, Isabelle, seeking refuge from the weather.

"Hey, y'all." As our hostess, Carly, was currently rolling silverware at the other end of the bar, I grabbed menus and met them at the hostess station. "Your usual booth?"

Kelly smoothed a hand over her baby bump. "Please. This one's demanding curly fries."

"Gotta appease the bump."

I led them to their table, sneaking another peek at Willa as we passed. She hadn't even looked up, lost in whatever grant proposal had captured her attention today. The woman was a machine when she got into the zone. Between the grants she'd landed for the betterment of the island and the work she was doing to turn the land she'd inherited from her grandparents into a protected wildlife refuge, she had plenty to keep herself busy.

Back behind the bar, I started a fresh pot of coffee, breathing in the rich aroma that would forever remind me of early mornings with Pop. The afternoon lull wouldn't last much longer. The rain would drive the locals in early tonight, looking for warmth and company and probably more than a few orders of our famous fish and chips. I welcomed the coming rush. Keeping busy helped quiet the endless parade of memories scrolling through my head about the man I put in so much effort to avoid.

Ten years shouldn't feel like yesterday. Ten years should be enough time to forget the big boom of his laugh, and the way his eyes crinkled at the corners when he smiled. Or how I'd believed him when he'd held me after the fire and said everything would be okay, though my whole world lay in ashes around us.

I shook my head, banishing the memories as I grabbed a rag to wipe down the already spotless counter. He'd made his choice. And I'd made mine. The Navy had been more important to him than anything we might have had, and I'd rebuilt my life brick by brick without him.

The coffee maker sputtered its last drops, and I grabbed the carafe, grateful for the distraction of refills.

The door opened again, and this time it was Sawyer, shaking rain from his jacket. He strode in, bringing the scent of sea air and storm as he headed straight for Willa's booth. His whole face lit up at the sight of her, his gray eyes warming. Despite her habitual Airpods—her shield against unwanted social interaction—she glanced up at his approach, as if he were her true north. The way they looked at each other filled my chest with a hollow ache I refused to examine too closely.

Returning the carafe to the warmer, I busied myself with wiping down glasses, trying not to watch their reunion. But it was like a car wreck. I couldn't look away as she slid out of the booth and straight into his arms. The easy way they fit together, the natural intimacy of their hello kiss. It was the kind of effortless connection I'd dreamed about having once upon a time, before reality had shattered those hopes. I scrubbed harder at an already spotless glass, pretending the burn behind my eyes was from the cleaning solution rather than anything so complicated as *feelings*. I didn't do feelings. Not when I could help it.

Not that I begrudged my friends a moment of their happiness. God knew they'd both been through enough to earn it, with everything Willa had endured with her family and Sawyer's own rough start in life. But sometimes, watching them together reminded me of everything I'd lost. The easy affection, the way they looked at each other like nothing else in the world mattered. Because I'd long ago learned that, other than Pop, no one would ever put me first. Not my parents, who'd left me behind without a backward glance, and certainly not the one person I'd been foolish enough to trust with my heart.

When the pair of them started getting a little too cozy, I cleared my throat. "Okay, you two. I've got no problem with Willa setting up a mobile office here, but I draw the line at y'all making it a second bedroom."

Willa eased back from him, pink-cheeked and fighting a smile. "Sorry, Bree. We're celebrating."

I arched a brow. "Oh? There an announcement you want to make?" My gaze slid down to her belly. Were they already jumping ahead on their happily ever after and starting a family?

"Not *that* kind of announcement." Her blush deepened. "Sawyer just got his contractor's license. He's all official."

"No shit? Congratulations, Sawyer." I offered him a fist bump. Finally, something good was happening to someone who deserved it. "You want a celebratory drink?"

"Let's have a couple glasses of whatever y'all's latest creation is."

"You got it." I headed back behind the bar to pull their pints, giving them a moment of privacy. Monty's Island Time was the perfect thing for a celebration.

As I reached for the tap, the door opened again, and I glanced up out of habit, the way I'd done thousands of times over the years since taking over the Brewhouse.

A teenage girl stepped inside, shoving back the hood of her jacket and shaking raindrops from dirty blonde hair that curled in wisps around a sharp-featured face. Something about the way she moved caught my attention. A familiar swagger in her stride that I couldn't quite place, like a half-remembered song. She had to be new to the island—I knew all the local kids, especially the ones who hung around during off-season. Being one of the few year-round businesses that welcomed teens, I made it my business to keep track.

I set a pint glass beneath the tap. "Can I help you, hon?"

The girl approached the bar and leaned forward on her elbows, her posture radiating a confidence that seemed both natural and practiced. "I hope so. I'm looking for somebody."

Those green eyes. Where had I seen them before? They sparked something in my memory, making my stomach do an uncomfortable flip as my brain tried to connect dots it didn't want to acknowledge.

"You meeting your party here?" I scanned the room, trying to match her with one of our current customers. But I knew everyone here, and she didn't belong to them. At this time of year, I knew pretty much every face that walked through my door, and hers was new.

"No, not like that. I'm looking for my father. He lives here on the island. I thought, this being such a small place, that maybe someone here would know him."

Red flags went up. A kid looking for her daddy who lived here? In January? Why didn't she know exactly where to find him? And where was her mother? I recognized bravado in her posture and a knowing in her eyes that made her seem older at first glance, but up close, I'd put her at thirteen, maybe fourteen tops. I bet she easily fooled others, though. This kid had seen some shit. I recognized the look, having seen it in the mirror for most of my life. That particular blend of defiance and vulnerability brought back memories of the day Pop first took me in—memories I usually tried my best to keep buried.

"We can sure give it our best go. Who's your daddy, hon?" Surely I could find the kid's dad to make sure she wasn't running around here on her own. It wasn't safe for a kid by herself. Not even on an island this small. We had the legacy of Gwen Busby to remind us of that. Even after all these years, that wound in our community had never truly healed.

The girl straightened her spine, chin lifting in a

gesture that sent a chill down my spine because I knew where I'd seen it before, even before she spoke. That particular tilt of the head, the set of those shoulders.

"Ford Donoghue."

The room tilted sideways. My fingers went numb where they gripped the tap handle, and I was dimly aware that beer was overflowing the glass beneath it. The roaring in my ears drowned out everything but the echo of those two words, pounding through my head like waves against the shore.

Ford Donoghue.

Holy shit.

Ford had a daughter. The man who'd walked away from everything—from me—had a child standing right here in my bar, looking at me with eyes that held shadows I recognized all too well.

CHAPTER 6

FORD

I drummed my fingers on the steering wheel as I took the exit toward Norfolk. The rain that had chased us from the Outer Banks had finally given up, leaving puddles and wet asphalt in our wake. Through the rearview mirror, dark clouds stretched across the southern horizon like an angry bruise.

"You thinking what I'm thinking?" Rios shifted in the passenger seat, killing the classic rock station we'd been arguing about for the last hour.

"Mario's?" The hole-in-the-wall Italian joint had been our go-to whenever we passed through Norfolk.

"Read my mind." He checked his phone. "We've got time before check-in."

I navigated through the streets on muscle memory, though it had been years since I'd been stationed here. The drive had been exactly what I needed after leaving the island—easy silence punctuated by bullshit arguments about Zeppelin versus Floyd and whether pineapple belonged on pizza. It did not. After so many years in the Navy, these moments of normalcy with any of my brothers felt like anchors, keeping me steady.

"You ever notice how Mario's wife always calls you 'too skinny'?" Rios grinned as I pulled into the cramped parking lot. "Even though you're built like a brick shithouse?"

"Says the guy she force-feeds three plates of pasta." I killed the engine, stretching my legs as best I could in the confined space. My six-foot-three frame never quite fit comfortably in these compact spaces. "Remember when she wouldn't let Jace leave until he finished that entire tiramisu?"

"Man looked green for days." Rios chuckled, shaking his head at the memory. "Swore off Italian food for a month after that."

The neon 'Open' sign flickered in the window, and the smell of garlic hit us before we even reached the door. Some things never changed, and Mario's was one of those constants—red checkered tablecloths, photos of Italy yellowing on the walls, and Mario's wife, Lucia, ready to scold us for not visiting sooner. It was exactly the kind of pre-dictable comfort I needed right now.

It felt good having this slice of normal with Rios. The kind of easy friendship where you didn't need to fill every silence or dance around difficult topics. Where you could just be. After everything that had happened lately, I needed this familiar rhythm, this connection to simpler times.

"Ford! Rios! My boys!" Lucia's thick accent carried across the restaurant as she bustled toward us, arms spread wide. "Where you been? Too long, too long!"

I'd long since stopped marveling at the fact that she seemed to know the name and face of every sailor who walked through her door.

She wrapped me in a hug that smelled of basil and warmth, then moved to Rios. "Both so thin! Navy no feed you?" Her weathered hands patted my cheeks like I was still that green recruit who'd demolish three plates of her spaghetti after a day's training.

"We eat fine, Lucia." I slid into our usual booth by the window, the vinyl seat creaking in welcome. "Just can't compete with your cooking."

She clucked her tongue, already scribbling on her notepad. "The usual? Extra meatballs for my hungry boys?"

"You know us too well." Rios settled across from

me, relaxing into the expected routine. "When you gonna leave Mario and come marry me instead?"

Lucia cackled, her dark eyes crinkling in a face that had seen decades more than we had. "You gonna have to do more to tempt me than that." She swatted at him with her order pad, the gesture full of motherly affection.

She disappeared into the kitchen, returning moments later with two frosted glasses and bottles of Peroni. The scents of garlic and oregano followed in her wake, making my stomach growl.

Rios took a long pull from his bottle. "Remember that time Jace tried to convince Mario to give him the marinara recipe?"

I tipped my beer into one of the frosted glasses, watching it foam. "Got about as far as you did trying to sweet talk Lucia into sharing her tiramisu secrets." Even back then, Rios had been smooth as silk, but Lucia was immune to his charms.

"Worth a shot." He shrugged, his dark eyes dancing with amusement. "What about that road trip to Pensacola? When Sawyer's piece of shit Chevy broke down outside Atlanta?"

I grinned and sipped. The beer was cold and crisp, washing away the last traces of highway dust. "We ended up sleeping in that sketchy motel with the neon cowboy sign?" The memory hit like a warm wave, taking me back to simpler times. "Place had magic fingers beds that ate quarters."

"You and Jace spent twenty bucks making those beds shake."

"Best waste of money ever." I traced a ring of condensation on the table, remembering how we'd laughed until our sides hurt that night. "Think we hit every dive bar between here and Florida that summer."

"Back when gas was cheap, and we were dumb enough to think we could live on beef jerky and Red Bull." His voice held a note of nostalgia that echoed my own thoughts about those carefree days.

Lucia returned with bread still steaming from the oven, and the rich smell of garlic butter filled our corner of the restaurant. The aroma mingled with the scent of marinara and fresh herbs, reminding me of a hundred other nights in a hundred other places just like this. Some memories were better shared over carbs and beer, in places that felt like waypoints between the lives we'd built and the ones we'd left behind.

"It's been forever since we had a real road trip with all the Wayward Sons. We should do that again next time we get the chance." Because I felt more anchored after these past days with my brothers than I had in a long time. Something about having Jace, Rios, and Sawyer around made the world make more sense, like puzzle pieces clicking into place.

Rios huffed a laugh and shook his head, his beer bottle dangling loosely between his fingers. "Not sure that's ever gonna happen again, bro. Not now that Sawyer's married."

I plucked up a slice of bread and slathered butter over it, savoring the way it melted instantly into the warm surface. "Willa would never stop Sawyer from doing anything he wanted to do."

"It's not that. He doesn't want to get that far from her for that long. You saw how he was this week."

"You don't think that's just the newlywed talking?" Damn, if the pair of them didn't have the glow. It was probably the regular mind-blowing orgasms. Hard not to be a little jealous of that, especially given how long it'd been since I'd had anything resembling a real relationship.

"Some of that, sure. But that break-in at O'Shea's old office has Sawyer and Willa both rattled."

I paused. "It's not his office anymore. That new guy was appointed by the state to take over all O'Shea's cases. Are they even called cases with family law? Anyway, what's his name?"

"Matthew Alward. Yeah, he was. And if the police found anything to suggest this was related to what happened last summer, they aren't sharing." Rios grabbed his own hunk of bread, ripping off a piece. "But I think, for all his good humor about it, Sawyer's still playing guard dog. Can't really blame him after everything that went down."

That sobered me up right quick. "You don't think there's somebody else out there who wants to kidnap her, do you?" It had been more than six months since Roland O'Shea had tried to silence Willa, who still didn't remember everything that happened that night. More than six months since he'd been killed in the process. The memory of that night still gave me cold sweats sometimes, and I hadn't even been directly involved.

"I hope to God not." Rios's jaw tightened, and I recognized the look of a man ready to throw down if necessary. "But O'Shea wasn't working alone. By his own admission, he was a middleman. There are still the other folks who were involved out there somewhere. What if something about the operation was hidden in that office?"

"It's been six months. Why would somebody wait that long to try to retrieve it?"

"Police presence for a lot of it. Then renovations. That new security system. There could be reasons. Either way, I think Sawyer's right to stick close. Just in case. If for nothing else than her peace of mind." He took another bite of bread, chewing thoughtfully. "Hell, if it were me, I probably wouldn't let her out of my sight, either."

Now that we were off island, I dared to breach the subject I'd been wondering about the whole time we'd been back in the States. The question had been eating at me since we'd left Hatterwick behind, but I hadn't wanted to bring it up where the wrong ears might hear. "Did it make a difference?"

Rios sipped his beer and arched a brow, his expression carefully neutral in that way that had been drilled into all of us during our time in the Navy. "Did what make a difference?"

"What Willa remembered about being the last person to see Gwen alive." I kept my voice low, though we were the only ones in this corner of the restaurant. Some habits died hard, especially when it came to a case that had haunted our island for over a decade.

That long ago summer, Rios had gone to Chief Carson and reported everything he remembered about seeing Gwen Busby at the end of that party. When no other trace of her was found, he'd turned Rios into a scapegoat, implying that Rios had done something to Gwen. There had never been a shred of evidence, but the implication had been enough for an island of people who'd been desperate for answers. Rios had been convicted in the court of public opinion. He and his sisters had suffered from those accusations for years. Another man might have fled, but Rios had stuck it out, in order to look after his sisters against their abusive father. But after Gabi had left for college and Caroline had found Hoyt, Rios had joined us when we all enlisted in the Navy. He'd wanted the chance to start a new life out from under the shadow of those false opinions. It had worked. He'd thrived in the Navy, and as such, he'd come home the least of all of us.

One shoulder lifted in a shrug. "Nobody said anything to my face this time. But people still eye me with distrust. Wondering if I'm cut from the same cloth as my father."

He said it easily. As if he weren't bothered by the fact that people thought he could murder someone the way Hector Carrera had murdered their mother and covered it up for years before coming after Caroline when she'd dared to move out and start her own life. The casual way he spoke about it made my gut clench. I'd seen what that kind of suspicion had done to him over the years, and I knew this careful neutrality masked deeper hurts.

Anger rose quick and hot, as it always did when this subject came up. "Man, fuck them all. No one who knows you believes any of that." He'd been one of my brothers since childhood. The idea that anyone could think him capable of hurting Gwen was ridiculous.

"Most of that island never knew me to begin with. That was the problem." He glanced toward the water, jaw tightening. "So it's going to take a lot more to clear me than the memories of someone a lot of folks believe is an unreliable witness because of her own trauma. For some people, the only thing that's going to change their mind would be Gwen showing up in the flesh to tell the story of what actually happened that night. I don't see that happening after all these years."

Because Gwen Busby was dead. If she'd been able to contact her family, she would have by now. After more than thirteen years of silence, that was the only logical conclusion, even if no one had ever found a body to prove it.

I hated all of this. Not only because my friend had suffered enough at the hands of prejudiced assholes, but because I was starting to grasp the fact that he truly might never come home. And under the circumstances, I couldn't blame him. Hell, if I'd been treated the way Rios had, accused of something so heinous, with nothing but whispers and sideways glances to back it up, I probably wouldn't come back either. The whole situation made my gut churn with guilt and anger.

Lucia sashayed over, carrying two bowls of

spaghetti topped with enormous meatballs. "For my starving boys!" she declared, presenting our plates with dramatic flair.

Her infectious enthusiasm and incredible cooking made it hard to hang on to a dark mood.

"God, this looks incredible, Lucia."

Rios speared one of the giant meatballs and took a huge bite, his eyes drifting shut in exaggerated bliss. "I'm telling you, you should just marry me. I'll do anything for these meatballs."

"You visit me again before you go, then maybe we discuss." She gave another playful wink before bustling off.

"Pretty sure I'm wearing her down," Rios commented.

I grinned, happy to see him back on an even keel, and dug into my food. "You keep telling yourself that, pal."

CHAPTER 7
BREE

My heart had stopped dead in my chest. Those sea-green eyes, the high cheekbones, even the way she held herself. She was a gangly, adolescent version of Mama Flo. The longer I stared at the girl in front of me, the more I saw Ford.

Her father.

Jesus.

"Do you know him?" The kid's voice wavered, uncertainty creeping in to replace that brief show of bravado. Her fingers twisted in the hem of her jacket, and I watched her swallow hard, like she was fighting back tears.

"Yeah. Yeah, I know him." The words came out rough, like I'd swallowed sand. My tongue felt thick and useless in my mouth as I tried to process what I was seeing—this living, breathing piece of Ford standing right in front of me.

The usual buzz of conversation in the bar died. Heads turned our way—because everyone knew Ford Donoghue. He might have been gone for years, but his shadow still lingered here, especially at the bar where we'd practically grown up. And if I didn't want this news spreading like wildfire across the island, making it to Ford's moms before the kid could blink, I needed to get her the hell out of the public eye.

Swallowing hard against a throat that had gone dry as dust, I waved the girl around the end of the bar. "C'mon. Let's go somewhere a little more private to talk." My heart hammered against my ribs as I tried to maintain an outward calm I definitely wasn't feeling.

The kid was about to balk. I could see it in the way she rocked slightly in her black Chucks, her fingers fidgeting with the strap of her backpack like she was ready to bolt for the door at any second.

I lowered my voice, leaning in just enough to keep the conversation between us. "I'm guessing you don't come from a small town. If you don't want all your business all over the island before sunset, you'll want to take this back to my office." God knew how fast gossip traveled here—especially anything that had even the remotest hint of scandal. A daughter no one knew existed definitely qualified as that.

Sawyer materialized at my elbow, protective as always. "Everything okay here?" His steady presence was both reassuring and complicated, given how close he and Ford had always been.

I cut my eyes toward him, a silent plea. His gaze shifted to the girl, and I watched understanding dawn across his features. The same shock I felt was written all over his face—this kid was unmistakably Ford's.

"She's looking for Ford?" Willa's voice was barely a whisper behind him, thick with the same disbelief I was struggling with.

"Yeah." I touched the girl's shoulder, gentle, not wanting to spook her more than she already was. "Let's head back to my office." Where I could figure out what the hell I was supposed to do with this bomb that had just been dropped in my lap.

The kid's gaze darted between the three of us, wariness creeping into her expression. Smart girl. I'd have been suspicious too, walking into a bar full of strangers, looking for someone who might not even want to be found.

"I'm Bree Cartwright. I own the place." I gestured to the others, keeping my movements slow and deliberate. "This is Sawyer Malone and his wife, Willa. They're old friends of your—of

Ford's." The word caught in my throat, but I pushed past it.

Her shoulders relaxed a fraction, some of the tension easing from her jaw. Good. Trust was important right now, especially given how young and vulnerable she looked standing there in her wrinkled hoodie and scuffed sneakers.

I guided her around the bar and through the door that led past the shiny row of brewing tanks toward my office, Sawyer and Willa trailing behind us like a protective detail. The weight of a dozen pairs of eyes pressed against my back, making my skin crawl with remembered anxiety. I knew what it was to be stared at. To be the unexpected surprise, the girl who showed up out of nowhere with a story no one quite believed. No matter what my beef with Ford, I'd do whatever I could to protect this kid from that.

My office wasn't much—just a cramped space with a desk covered in invoices and a couple of chairs that had seen better days—but it beat having this conversation on the floor. I clicked the door shut behind us, blocking out the noise and curious eyes, grateful for even this small refuge from the weight of speculation I knew was already circulating through the bar.

The girl perched on the edge of one chair like a sparrow ready to take flight at the first sign of danger, while Willa claimed the other, Roy settling at her feet with a heavy sigh. The girl eyed him, and the dog gave a hopeful thump of his tail as he gazed up at her.

"He's a big love muffin," Willa explained.

The girl reached out a tentative hand toward Roy, letting him sniff her before he butted her hand for pets. The barest hint of a smile tugged at the corners of her mouth as she scritched behind his ears.

Sawyer leaned against the wall, arms crossed over his broad chest, his presence oddly reassuring. I settled behind my desk, shuffling some papers to buy time to get my racing thoughts under control and tamp down the memories threatening to surface.

"What's your name?" I kept my voice gentle, the way I used to speak to the scared strays that would show up behind Pop's bar.

"Peyton Walsh." The name came out barely above a whisper, her fingers twisting the frayed hem of her hoodie.

My chest tightened as I studied those features that were at once familiar and strange. "How old are you?"

"Fourteen."

I arched a brow, calling bullshit. The defiance in those sea-green eyes—so like Ford's—flared, reminding me of another teenager who used to sit in my grandfather's kitchen, full of that same stubborn pride.

"Well, I will be in two months," she amended, lifting her chin in a gesture that was pure Donoghue.

My heart stuttered as I did the math. March. That meant... Jesus. That summer before Ford left for college. The summer Gwen Busby had disappeared. But who was her mother? I wracked my brain, trying to remember any girls Ford had been seeing then.

Had he known about this? The question rose like bile in my throat.

No. The answer came with absolute certainty, settling like a stone in my gut. Whatever Ford had done to me, whatever anger and hurt I still carried—and there sure as hell was plenty—I knew him down to his bones. If he'd known about this girl, she wouldn't be standing here looking for him. He'd have been there, probably coaching tee ball and chaperoning school dances. It wasn't in him to walk away from responsibility. That had been drilled into him by both his moms.

"Okay, you're here to see your dad." If I kept repeating it, it would get less weird. Right? "Where's your mom?"

Pain flashed across Peyton's face, raw and fresh,

like a wound that hadn't had time to scab over. "Gone."

The single word had me pushing away from my desk and crouching down in front of her chair until we were at eye level. My knees protested the position, but I ignored them. "She left you?"

"Sort of." Again Peyton's fingers twisted in the hem of her oversized hoodie. "She died."

Oh God. The words struck me like a physical blow, stealing the air from my lungs. This child. This poor child. No wonder she had that haunted look in her eyes.

"Oh, honey." The words came out rough, choked with memories I usually kept locked away. "I'm so sorry."

My hand moved of its own accord, covering her trembling fingers. She didn't pull away, and something in my chest loosened at the tiny victory.

"I was eight when my mom died." The admission slipped out before I could stop it, drawn from that deep well of shared pain. "I know what it feels like. That... emptiness. Like someone reached in and scooped out everything that made sense in the world. Like you're just... drifting."

Peyton's eyes locked with mine, something desperate and hungry in their depths. The same look I'd had when social services was trying to figure out what to do with me. "What happened to you?"

"I ended up here. With my grandfather." I squeezed her hand, feeling the slight tremors running through her willowy frame. "Pop—Ed—he took me in. Gave me a home. A family. Saved me, really."

"Did you know him before?"

"No." A sad smile tugged at my lips as I remembered that first awkward meeting, both of us terrified but trying not to show it. "Never even met him. But he chose me anyway." And I'd never stop being grateful for that. Pop had been my anchor when everything else was chaos.

Tears welled in her eyes. "I don't have any other family. That's why I came looking for... for him."

The weight of what she wasn't saying pressed against my chest. No other family meant foster care. Group homes. The system. Christ. I remembered that, too.

"How long?" I asked softly.

"Three months." Her voice cracked. "I couldn't... I couldn't stay there anymore."

The desperate need to run. To find something—someone—to hold on to. God, I remembered that feeling. It had driven me to try running away twice before social services found Ed.

"You're safe here." The promise came from somewhere deep in my soul, bypassing every single one of my carefully constructed walls. "Whatever happens next, we'll figure it out together. Okay?"

A single tear tracked down her cheek. Impatient and faintly embarrassed, she swiped at it with her sleeve, but nodded.

Behind me, I heard Willa's quiet sniffle. But I kept my focus on Peyton, on this girl who'd had her whole world ripped away, just like I had.

"Where are you from?" I kept my voice gentle, not wanting to spook her.

"Oregon."

Shit. That was the other side of the continent. My stomach churned. "Who brought you here?"

Peyton's gaze skittered away, fixing on the wall behind me. Her fingers twisted harder in her hoodie. The evasion spoke volumes.

"Did you come here on your own? All the way across the country?"

A bare nod.

Jesus Christ. My mind filled with every horrible scenario that could've befallen a thirteen-year-old girl traveling alone. Human trafficking. Assault. Robbery. The fact that she'd made it here in one piece was nothing short of miraculous.

"You're very smart and brave to have managed that." I congratulated myself for saying that instead of putting my head between my knees to wheeze through the what-if anxiety still coursing through my veins.

"Are you going to tell me where my dad is or not?" Steel crept back into her voice, that earlier vulnerability vanishing beneath a fresh shield of teenage bravado.

"He's not here." The words felt like rocks in my mouth.

The color drained from her face, leaving her already fair complexion ghostly pale. "Not here? Where is he?"

"He's in the Navy. He just left the island this morning to go back." I hated being the one to deliver this news, watching hope die in those eyes that were so much like Ford's.

Pure panic flashed across her features. Her chest rose and fell in sharp, quick movements, and I recognized the early stages of hyperventilation. Her hands trembled at her sides, and she swayed slightly in the chair as if the floor had suddenly become unstable.

"It's going to be okay." I grabbed both her hands in mine. "We're going to get him back for you. We've just got to let him know you're here." *That you exist.* The words echoed in my head. Ford had a daughter. A beautiful, brave, terrified daughter who'd crossed the country alone to find him.

"You're friends?" Hope and desperation mingled in her voice.

"We used to be. A long time ago." The words tasted like ashes in my mouth. "Just... give me a little bit."

I jerked my head toward the hall, urging Willa and Sawyer out ahead of me. Quietly, I shut the door behind me, not wanting to spook the terrified teenager I'd left in my office. My heart was still hammering against my ribs, trying to process what was happening.

"Are we sure this is real?" Sawyer's voice was low. "I mean, how do we know she's really Ford's kid?"

I fixed him with a look. "Take one good look at that kid and tell me she doesn't look just like him."

He scrubbed a hand down his face. "Yeah, okay. She's like a teenage, female version of him." Even his stance shifted uncomfortably as the reality fully sank in.

Willa's brow furrowed, her analytical mind already working through the implications. "If her mother's dead, someone had custody of her. They're probably missing her right now."

I could see where she was going with this, and I held up a hand, protective instincts I didn't even know I had surging to the surface. "We aren't contacting the police. Not yet. Not before Ford knows.

By rights, this is his to deal with." And something in the girl's eyes told me there was more to her story than she was letting on.

Sawyer ran a hand through his sandy hair. "Want me to call him?"

Bless him. I could let him do it. I could offload this whole thing onto someone else's shoulders. But then I thought of Peyton, of the fear and desperation in her eyes. I'd been where she was, lost and alone and aching for someone to give a damn. Doing anything else felt like abandoning her.

And I wouldn't do that. Couldn't do that.

I shook my head. "No. I'll do it. Y'all want to head on back out front? See if you can do anything to head off the gossip train?"

"Yeah. Sure." Willa squeezed my shoulder, her eyes full of empathy and warmth.

To buy myself another few minutes, I grabbed a Coke from the cooler and took it in to Peyton. The can was cold and slick against my palm, condensation already beading on the surface.

"Thanks." Peyton's voice was barely more than a whisper as she wrapped her fingers around the can.

"I'm just gonna go call your dad." I hesitated for a moment, wanting to say more, to somehow reassure her that everything would be okay. But I didn't make promises I couldn't keep, so I just gave her a small smile and turned away.

I closed myself into Monty's office down the hall. Unlike my own shoebox of a space, his was twice as large, with neat rows of filing cabinets and framed black and white prints of the island decorating the walls. A sleek computer perched atop the desk beside an ancient rotary phone that he'd picked up in an antique store to use as a paperweight. Weird, wonderful man.

I slumped back against his desk, took a deep breath, and pulled out my phone to dial a number I should have deleted years ago in order to break ten years of silence.

CHAPTER 8

FORD

I rolled my shoulders as I headed down the hall toward the conference room, satisfied with how the afternoon's exercises had gone. The new protocols we'd been testing showed promise, though there were definitely some rough spots to iron out. Nothing we couldn't handle. My muscles ached pleasantly from the physical demands of the training—a comforting sensation that reminded me of my track and field days at UGA.

"Lieutenant Commander." Captain Patton nodded as I fell into step beside him. "Good work out there today." His weathered face showed approval.

"Thank you, sir." I straightened instinctively,

falling naturally into the posture that had become second nature after all these years in service.

The rhythms of base life settled around me like a well-worn uniform. Here, I knew exactly who I was and what was expected. No complicated history. No ghosts of past mistakes haunting every corner like back home. The Navy had given me structure, purpose, and most importantly, distance from the mess I'd left behind with Emily when I'd called it quits with her for good—though sometimes, late at night, I still found myself thinking about that summer, about Bree, about all the things I'd run from.

We entered the conference room where the rest of the team was already gathering. The smell of stale coffee lingered in the air as everyone took their seats, notebooks open and ready for the debrief. Lieutenant Rodriguez was sketching something on the whiteboard—probably that tricky maneuver we'd attempted during the third run of the drill. Chief Warren had already claimed his usual spot near the window, methodically arranging his pens in perfect parallel lines.

"Alright people, let's break this down," Captain Patton called out as he moved to the front of the room. "Starting with the morning exercises..."

The fluorescent lights hummed overhead as we dove into the analysis. My pen moved across the page, taking notes on improvements needed for to-morrow's runs. Here in this sterile conference room, surrounded by the structured routine of military life, I felt centered again. Ready to face whatever challenges tomorrow's exercises might bring.

My phone buzzed against my thigh, inter-rupting Captain Patton's analysis of our formation issues. I shifted to pull it from my pocket, ready to send it to voicemail. I could call Mom or Mimi back when we finished—they were probably just checking in like they did every week, Mimi eager to share the latest island gossip while Mom fretted about whether I was eating enough. They could hardly be expected to know when I was through for the day. But the name on the screen stopped my heart.

Bree Cartwright.

The same Bree who'd excised me from her life a decade ago with surgical precision, cutting away every trace of our friendship like it was diseased tissue. The Bree whose number I couldn't bring myself to delete from my contacts, even though she'd made it crystal clear she never wanted to hear from me again.

Bree did not call me. She did not text or email. She'd said nothing at all to me in ten years, main-taining a silence so complete it felt like we'd never existed in the same universe. This could not be anything good. My gut twisted with a combination of dread and something that felt dangerously like hope.

"Sir," I cut in, already pushing back from the table, metal chair legs scraping against the floor. "I apologize, but I need to take this call. It's urgent." My heart hammered against my ribs like it was trying to escape.

The captain's eyebrows rose, but he nodded, probably reading the tension in my face. I was out the door before anyone could question it, my hands shaking so badly I nearly dropped the phone as I swiped to answer. The hallway suddenly felt too narrow, too confining for whatever was about to happen.

"Bree? Is everything okay?" My voice came out rougher than intended, heart hammering against my ribs. A decade of silence broken had to mean disaster. Because I wasn't remotely delusional enough to think a miracle had occurred and she'd somehow decided to forgive me.

"You need to get back to Hatterwick immediately."

Ice flooded my veins as I recognized that flat tone she used to cover up great emotion. That careful control had always been her tell—the more even her voice became, the bigger the storm brewing underneath. Bree didn't do upset. She locked it down, determined she could out-think feeling, just like she had since we were kids. "Did something happen to Mom? Or Mimi?" My mind raced through terrible scenarios, remembering how Mom had mentioned some chest pain last month.

"Shit. No." She dragged in a breath, the sound shaky even through the phone line. "No one is injured. It's not your moms." The pause that followed felt loaded with something I couldn't quite grasp, something that made my stomach clench with dread.

My own breath shuddered out as I sagged against the wall outside the conference room, grateful for the empty hallway. "Okay... What's going on then?" The fluorescent lights buzzed overhead, a steady drone that only highlighted the thundering of my pulse in my ears.

The silence stretched so long I pulled the phone away to check if the call had dropped, the screen's glow confirming we were still connected. "Bree?"

She took another audible breath that crackled through the connection, the sound so achingly familiar it transported me back a decade. "I have your daughter sitting in my office."

The words didn't compute, like they were being spoken in a language I'd never learned. "My what now?"

"Your daughter, Ford." Her voice was uncharacteristically gentle.

"But... I don't have a daughter." My free hand pressed against the wall, steadying myself as the floor seemed to shift beneath my feet. The conference room behind me felt a million miles away, along with the stack of reports I'd just presented and everything else that had made sense in my life five minutes ago.

"Yeah, turns out you do. She's thirteen—nearly fourteen—and looks just like you."

"I don't... I... That's..." The words tangled in my throat as my mind raced backward through time, searching. My pulse whoosh wooshed in my ears so hard I could barely hear anything else. Sweat broke out across my forehead.

"I did the math. It would have been the summer before you left for college."

There'd only been the one girl. Casey Walsh. Long, curly brown hair, big brown eyes. She'd been on-island for three weeks of vacation with her parents. We'd bonded over running, spent endless hours walking the beach, making out under the pier. Then more. I remembered how she'd cried when they had to leave, promising to write, to call, to stay in touch somehow.

She never had. Not one letter. Not one call.

Nothing but silence and memories that had faded like footprints in the sand.

Suddenly, I couldn't get enough air into my lungs. I slid down the wall until I hit the floor, my knees giving out. But this wasn't possible. We'd used protection. If she'd gotten pregnant... Surely she would have told me? I'd given her my number, my email. Hell, she knew my home address. She'd been to my house. I'd even written it all down on that little scrap of paper from her dad's hotel notepad, watching as she carefully tucked it into her wallet.

"I don't understand. Where is her mother?"

Bree made a small sound, something between sympathy and pain. "Dead, apparently."

"Oh, my God." The air left my lungs in a rush. Now I understood why Bree had been the one to make this call. She knew this story. She'd lived it. She'd been just a kid herself when she'd landed on Ed's doorstep, scared and alone.

I had a thousand and one questions about how this girl had ended up with her, of all people, but I held them all back. My free hand pressed against my eyes, trying to block out the fluorescent lights that suddenly seemed too bright. The irony wasn't lost on me. Here I was, sitting on the floor of my office at the Naval Station, learning I had a daughter from the one person who had every right to never speak to me again.

A daughter. I had a daughter, and I'd missed thirteen years of her life. A daughter who'd lost her mother and somehow found her way to Hatterwick looking for me. And I hadn't been there. Hadn't been around to protect her or her mother. What the hell kind of man did that make me?

"Look, Ford, she came all the way across the country to find you entirely on her own. No doubt someone is looking for her." Bree's voice vibrated with tension. "I haven't contacted anyone because I didn't want to involve the authorities before you even knew about her. But I won't be able to keep this quiet forever. You need to come home to deal with this."

"I... Yeah." My head spun. The implications hit like waves—a child, alone, crossing the country. If I hadn't already slid to the floor, the idea of that would've taken me out at the knees. My stomach churned at the thought of what could have happened to her out there. What kind of desperation drove a move like that? "I'll get emergency leave. I don't know how long it'll take." What the hell was my CO going to say? How could I possibly explain this situation when I barely understood it myself?

"She'll stay with me until you get back."

It was a big fucking ask. One I wouldn't have

made of Bree. Not after all these years, not with our history hanging between us like a storm cloud. But she was offering nonetheless, and the gesture meant so much more to me than I wanted to admit.

The knot in my chest loosened just a fraction. "Are you sure? My moms..."

"Your moms will be beside themselves with enthusiasm and will overwhelm the poor kid. She shouldn't meet them before she meets you." The way she said it, so matter-of-fact, so... *Bree*... made my throat tight.

A part of me wanted to laugh because, no matter what had happened between us, what walls we'd built, she knew my family.

"Okay. Okay, yeah, you're right." I shoved to my feet, already planning what I needed to do. The chain of command. The paperwork. The protocols. My mind clicked into military mode, because that was easier than processing everything else. "I'll go do what I need to do and let you know as soon as I can head back."

"Okay. I need to get back to her."

"Bree?"

"Yeah?"

"What's her name?"

A pause stretched through the line, heavy with meaning I couldn't decode. "Peyton. Peyton Walsh."

"Peyton." The name felt strange on my tongue, foreign yet somehow precious. A daughter. My daughter. The words echoed in my head like a bell tolling, each repetition making it more real.

Jesus Christ. Everything I thought I knew about my life had just been blown sideways. Thirteen years of memories suddenly had a shadow version playing alongside them. All the moments I'd missed, all the firsts I hadn't known existed.

"Thank you." The words felt entirely inadequate for what she was doing, for being the one to reach out when I knew exactly how much it must have cost her.

Another long pause filled the line, crackling with unspoken history. "Just hurry, okay?"

"As fast as I can." I was already reaching for my keys, my body thrumming with urgency even as my mind struggled to process this seismic shift in my world.

CHAPTER 9

BREE

I stood in my office doorway, watching Peyton nurse her Coke. The set of her shoulders reminded me so much of Ford it made my chest ache. But there wasn't time to unpack that particular emotional landmine. This whole situation had me *feeling* more than I usually allowed myself to feel in a month. My capacity for continuing to function through all of it was rapidly running out. So I did the only thing I could. I shut it all down and shoved it deep into a mental closet to pull out when things didn't feel so much like a crisis.

"I spoke with your dad." Not a sentence I'd ever thought I'd be uttering. "He's working on getting home as soon as he can. Thankfully, he's just up in Virginia for a training instead of shipped off to who knows where." It seemed prudent not to mention he'd been stationed in Japan the past few years.

Peyton seemed relieved by that news.

"You're going to stay with me until he gets back. Is that okay?" I wasn't sure what the hell I'd do with her if it wasn't, but a kid in her circumstances had few enough choices. I knew how important it was for her to feel like she had some control.

"That'd be okay."

"All right. I've got to square a few more things away here, then we'll go."

No way was I keeping the kid at the Brewhouse tonight. We needed to be out of the public eye. I'd be lucky if Mama Flo and Mimi didn't show up on my doorstep later, as it was.

Whipping out my phone, I texted Monty.

BREE:

I need you to come in and cover for me tonight.

MONTY:

Ooo, did we find some sexy young thing to break your dry spell with? :eyebrow waggle GIF:

BREE:

Not even a little bit.

MONTY:

:pouty face GIF: Hope springs eternal.

BREE:

It's an emergency. I'll explain later. Just please get here as soon as you can.

MONTY:

Is Ed okay?

BREE:

He's fine.

MONTY:

On my way.

That sorted, I pulled my mental armor into place and headed back out to the floor to check on customers. Drew McNamara and his family were already gone. So were two of the other tables. Willa and Sawyer were still at their booth. I crossed over, automatically checking every other table. A few more patrons had wandered in while I'd been in the back.

Willa arched both brows. "Well?"

I kept my voice low. "He's working on getting back. I'm taking her home with me in the meantime. Did anyone say anything?"

Sawyer shook his head. "No. Drew and Kelly will keep mum. I think the other tables might have been too far to hear for sure." He leaned forward, gaze intent on me. "You okay?"

"Fine."

When he only looked at me, I blew out a breath. "I'm taking this one minute at a time. Right now, my focus is on Peyton."

He and Willa exchanged one of those married-people-telepathy looks.

I wagged my finger between them. "Just no. I want no part of whatever silent conversation you're having about me right now."

Willa reached out to squeeze my hand. "Fair enough. But we're here if you need us. For anything."

I unbent enough to squeeze back. "Thanks, Wills."

I went back to check on Peyton. She'd just about finished her Coke.

I was on the verge of asking if she wanted food, when Monty burst through the kitchen doors in a whirl of color and energy. "Your knight in fabulous armor has arrived, darling."

"Thank God." I pulled him into a quick hug. "I need you to handle things tonight."

His gaze slid past me to where Peyton sat. Questions blazed in his eyes, but bless him, he didn't ask them. Instead, he straightened his bow tie and gave me a small nod.

"Peter's popping by for dinner later. We'll keep the ship sailing smooth as silk." He squeezed my hand. "Go do what you need to do."

I grabbed my keys and gestured to Peyton, who eyed Monty with equal curiosity. "Come on, sweetie. Let's get out of here."

She slung her worn backpack—the only thing she had with her—over one shoulder. My throat tightened at the sight. I remembered what it felt like to have next to nothing of my own beyond a broken heart and what fit into a trash bag. We slipped out through the kitchen's back door. The rain had finally stopped, and the evening air had turned crisp, carrying the salt-tang of the ocean. My Jeep sat in its usual spot in the small back lot, and I unlocked it with trembling fingers.

Peyton climbed in without a word. The silence stretched between us as I drove through the village streets toward my cottage. I caught glimpses of her in my peripheral vision, the way she kept her backpack clutched tight against her chest like a shield.

The drive was mercifully short. As I pulled into

my driveway, I realized I had no idea what to say to this girl who'd traveled across the country alone, searching for a father who didn't know she existed.

The lights inside were on. I'd texted Pop to go ahead and drop Keeley home. I hadn't explained why, just said I'd be home early tonight. If he'd wondered why I hadn't been by to pick her up myself, he hadn't asked. We both slid out of the Jeep and trudged up the walk to the front door of the cottage. The moment I opened the door, my sweetheart of a mutt began to bark and dance, turning excited circles as she realized we had company.

Too late, it occurred to me that Peyton might not be okay with dogs. Sure, she'd seemed okay with Roy, but he hadn't been in total crackhead mode like Keeley was. As I turned to grab for her collar, Peyton made a noise of delight and dropped to her knees. My pup yipped and immediately began bathing her face with kisses. The giggle snort that followed relieved at least a little of the anxiety coursing through me.

"Peyton, meet Keeley. Keeley, please do not feel the need to bathe our guest."

Keeley barked and bounced, her blue eyes sparkling with joy and mischief.

"Cookie?"

Her floppy ears perked.

"Assume the position."

She raced into the kitchen and plopped her butt to the floor, tail swishing. I crossed over and dug out a biscuit. "Good girl."

She nipped it out of my hand.

I realized Peyton still stood in the open door. "Come on in. Let me feed her, and I'll sort out what we're gonna have." Maybe I should've had my kitchen staff prep something for us, but I'd been in too big a hurry to get her out.

Peyton shut the door, and I pretended not to notice her looking everywhere at once, taking in my space while I scooped kibble into a bowl. I wondered what she saw. I wasn't exactly a decorator. My place was a hodgepodge of furniture that was more about comfort than cohesion. I spent so much of my time at the Brewhouse that I didn't concern myself overmuch with how things looked here.

Eventually, the girl came into the kitchen while I was poking around the fridge and freezer in search of something for dinner. I didn't have much. Owning a restaurant, I usually had most of my meals there. Other than breakfast.

"How do you feel about breakfast for dinner?"

Peyton slid onto one of the barstools at the counter, easing the backpack to the floor by her feet. "Pancakes?"

"I can do pancakes." It wasn't precisely nutritious, but I wasn't aiming for parent of the year here. I just wanted to see the kid got fed. I wondered when her last meal had been.

I began pulling out ingredients.

"Why are you helping me?"

Eggs in hand, I glanced back at her. "As I said before, I've been where you are. I never knew my dad, either. My mom died when I was eight, and I got put into the system until they found my grandfather, and he brought me here." I began measuring out pancake mix, keeping my voice casual. "It's a scary place to be."

I doubted I'd earned enough trust to get her to talk about whether she'd had any problematic experiences in the foster system, but I wanted to open the door in case she had.

Peyton shrugged. "It wasn't so bad. They weren't mean or anything."

Nothing in her posture or expression suggested she was hiding anything. For her sake, I hoped like hell it was true.

I couldn't resist satisfying at least some of my curiosity as I mixed the pancake batter. "How did you even know to come here? Did your mom tell you about Ford?"

"No. Never." Peyton traced patterns on my counter with her finger. "But after she... after she died, I was going through her stuff, and I found some letters she wrote him. She never sent them."

My hand stilled on the whisk. "Letters?"

"I guess maybe she felt guilty about never telling him about me, and every year she wrote him a letter talking about me. She talked about vacationing here on Hatterwick and meeting him. I took a chance that he was still here."

My stomach turned at how differently this could have played out. What if she'd arrived after Ford had left the Navy and moved somewhere else? What if she'd run into someone who didn't know him? The possibilities made me ill.

I forced myself to pour batter into the heated skillet, keeping my voice steady. "Smart and resourceful. That's something else you have in common with your dad."

"You said you were friends." There was a question in her voice.

"Growing up, yes." I focused on the forming bubbles in the pancake. "He's been in the Navy for a long time now."

"What's he like?"

This was absolutely the last thing I wanted to talk about, but I knew the girl was hungry for any scrap of information. I understood what that was like.

I flipped the pancakes, buying time to organize my thoughts. "He's... kind. Always has been. The sort who'd drop everything to help someone in need." Like he was doing now. "He was a track star in high school. Got a scholarship to Georgia for it."

The spatula trembled in my hand as memories flooded back. Ford helping Pop repair the old sign back when the Brewhouse had been the Tidewater Tavern. Ford teaching the younger kids to swim at the community pool. Ford defending kids getting picked on. It was how we'd met. When he'd intervened with a bully getting up in my face about my lack of parents. He'd handed that kid his ass and become my shield, my confidant, my everything.

I squeezed my eyes shut and breathed through the pain. When I was sure my voice would be steady, I kept going. "He's funny too. Quick with a joke, but never mean ones." I slid the first stack of pancakes onto a plate. "And loyal. To his family, his friends."

Until he wasn't.

I pushed that thought away. This wasn't about me or my issues.

"Do you have any pictures of him?" Peyton's voice was small, hesitant.

"Not here." I hadn't been able to look at them in years. "But Pop has albums full of photos from when we were growing up. I can ask him tomorrow." If she stayed that long. If she didn't bolt like I'd wanted to so many times before Ed became my anchor.

My phone buzzed. A text from Ford.

FORD:

Got emergency leave. Coming
home tomorrow.

Relief washed through me. I showed Peyton the message.

"Tomorrow?" Her eyes went wide.

"Yeah. Which means you should eat and get some rest. I expect you're tired after all the travel it took to get here."

God knew, I was exhausted simply from the past couple of hours of trying to process the reality of her existence.

She poured a small ocean of syrup on her pancakes. "It has been a minute since I had a bed." Her eyes flicked up to mine. "Or a sofa's good, too."

Had she managed any sleep at all since she left Oregon? Or had she stayed in that faintly dozing state, ready to bolt in case someone invaded her personal space or threatened her? Either way, tonight she'd have a room of her own, with a proper bed.

"I've got a guest room, kid. I'll make it up after we finish dinner."

CHAPTER 10
FORD

I stood on the front porch of Bree's cottage, staring at the bright turquoise blue door. My hand hovered over the brushed nickel knocker, heart pounding like I'd just run ten miles at a sprint. The last twenty-four hours felt like a fever dream, reality bending and shifting around me with each new revelation. A daughter. I had a daughter. And Bree had finally broken her silence. The weight of both those things pressed down on my chest.

The door swung open before I could knock, making me jump slightly. Bree filled the frame, dressed in well-worn jeans and a faded OBX Brewhouse t-shirt that had seen better days, blonde hair pulled back into a tail that caught the morning light. Those gray eyes I remembered so well watched me with careful wariness, like she was trying to decide if letting me in was a mistake.

"You made it." She stepped back, gesturing me inside, her bare feet silent on the weathered wooden floors.

I ducked through the doorway, too aware of how small the entry felt with both of us in it. The cottage smelled like coffee and something sweet. Maybe cinnamon. A quick glance told me the place was homey. Lived-in. There were books stacked on every surface and a mess of colorful throw pillows piled on a weathered leather couch. An array of dog toys were scattered across the floor, some bearing the battle scars of enthusiastic chewing. It was nothing like the stark military quarters I'd left behind, with their regulation corners and institutional feel.

"Yeah, finally. Had to call in every favor I had." My voice came out rough from lack of sleep, and I could feel the fatigue settling deep in my bones. "The paperwork alone... I swear the Navy was easier to join than getting emergency leave approved."

"You look exhausted." There was no judgment in her tone, only casual observation, and something else—maybe concern—that she quickly masked.

"Haven't slept." I scrubbed a hand down my face, feeling the rasp of stubble against my palm. "I keep thinking I'm going to wake up and this will all be some weird dream. Like maybe I imagined having a thirteen-year-old daughter show up out of nowhere."

Bree crossed her arms, maintaining a careful distance between us. "It's real. She's real. She's sleeping in my guest room right now."

The weight of that hit me again, a sucker punch to the gut that drove most of the air from my lungs. A daughter. Here. Under this roof. Not some far-off concept anymore, but flesh and blood. "How is she?"

"Scared. Trying not to show it." Bree's expression softened slightly, the mask she usually wore around me cracking just a bit. "She's got your eyes. Even does that thing where she narrows them when she's thinking hard."

That simple statement made my heart stutter in my chest. I sank onto the worn wooden bench by the door, legs suddenly unsteady beneath me. "I can't believe Casey never told me. All these years... Christ, I missed everything."

"Ford." Bree's voice was gentle in a way I hadn't heard in a decade, since before everything fell apart between us. "Take a breath. We'll figure this out."

We, not me. The distinction wasn't lost on me, even through my exhaustion.

It had been so damned long since Bree and I

had been any kind of "we." I lifted my gaze to hers, then couldn't make myself look away. This was as close as we'd been in years, and I took the opportunity to just drink her in. The morning light streaming through her front windows caught the gold in her hair, and for a moment I was twenty again, watching her laugh on the beach. The air between us crackled with the tension of unspoken words, regrets, and possibilities that had died because I'd been careless and had taken her for granted. More than ten years of distance, of pretending the other didn't exist, and now here we were, forced back into each other's orbit by circumstances I never could have imagined.

A floorboard creaked down the hall.

My head jerked in that direction, and the world promptly tilted on its axis. The sudden movement sent a wave of dizziness through me, a reminder that I hadn't slept since getting that first message about my daughter.

The girl standing there was unmistakably mine. It was like looking in a time machine. Those were my eyes staring back at me, wide and uncertain. My nose. My jaw. Even the way she held herself, shoulders slightly hunched as if trying to take up less space, mirrored my own teenage awkwardness, when I hadn't quite learned how to navigate the world in a body with limbs that seemed to have grown a mile overnight. I remembered all too well what that felt like, the constant awareness of taking up too much space, of accidentally knocking things over in the school hallways.

Bree moved toward her with an easy grace, as if the kid wasn't staring at me like she'd seen a ghost. "Morning. There's breakfast, if you want."

But Peyton's attention was locked on me, her fingers twisting in the hem of her oversized sweater as Keeley pressed against her legs with a quiet whine. The silence stretched between us like a living thing, heavy with thirteen years of missed moments and conversations we should have had. My heart hammered thumped heavily in my chest, as if it wasn't quite sure how to keep doing its job. I fought the urge to look away from that penetrating gaze that was so like my own.

"Peyton, this is Ford Donoghue," Bree said softly. "Ford, this is Peyton."

Every drop of moisture in my mouth had evaporated, and I swallowed as I stood, trying to get past the sensation of cotton to speak. "Hi." The word came out rough, inadequate for the weight of this moment, for all the things I needed to say to this child I hadn't known existed until yesterday.

Peyton still didn't speak, her shoulders tense as she stared at me.

Bree's gaze bounced between us, her expression

a mix of concern and understanding. "Does any-body want coffee?"

"Yes." We spoke at once, and I tried a hesitant smile because apparently we had at least one thing in common. Though, wasn't thirteen young to be drinking coffee? How would I know? I had a decade of parenting experience to catch up on, and the weight of that knowledge pressed against my chest like a physical weight.

With one last look at me, Peyton trailed Bree into the kitchen. After a moment's hesitation, I fol-lowed, giving both of them plenty of space, not wanting to spook my daughter any more than she already was. Bree pulled two mugs from the cabi-net, then glanced at the kid. "How do you take yours?"

"Half milk, half coffee, two sugars." Peyton's voice was quiet but sure, like she'd ordered this drink plenty of times before.

With the ease of long practice, Bree filled the mugs from the carafe on the counter. She prepped Peyton's mug as asked, and added a spoonful of sugar and a splash of milk to the other, her move-ments quick and efficient.

She still remembered how I took my coffee after all these years? It was a reminder of everything we'd once been to each other, everything I'd walked away from that summer so long ago. Or maybe it was simply one of those details that stuck in her mind because of all her years in the food service industry.

"Thanks." But her eyes slid away from mine after she handed over the mug.

"Right. You two probably want some privacy to talk. I'll just head on to the Brewhouse." She paused to glance back at Peyton. "Unless you want me to stay? I will, if that will make you more comfortable."

I appreciated her looking out for Peyton, even if it was against me. For all that we apparently shared blood, this child didn't know me. I couldn't even imagine what she'd been through just to get here. The thought of her traveling alone, seeking out a stranger she'd only known about from whatever her mother had told her, made my chest tight with a mix of guilt and concern.

"I'm okay." Peyton managed a small smile. "Thanks."

"Right. I'll be at work. Just... lock up behind yourselves if you leave. Keeley will be okay inside." Bree lingered a moment longer, her hand on the doorframe, before she moved on into the hall.

The front door clicked shut behind her, leaving a heavy silence in her wake. I gripped my coffee mug like a lifeline, watching Peyton trace circles on the kitchen table with her finger.

"Should we sit?" I gestured at the chairs,

fighting the urge to pace the kitchen like a caged animal. My palms were sweating, and I wiped them against my jeans.

She nodded, sliding into the seat across from me. Keeley flopped at her feet with a sigh. The dog's presence seemed to provide more comfort than I could manage right now.

My mind raced with a thousand questions, each one competing to burst out first, but I forced myself to start with the obvious. "Your mom is Casey Walsh." The name felt strange on my tongue, dredging up hazy memories of a brief relationship that now held life-altering consequences.

"Was." The word fell like a stone between us, and pain flashed across her face, making her look even younger and more vulnerable.

My chest tightened with a surge of grief—not just for Casey, but for this girl who'd lost her mother, for all the years I hadn't known about her. "I'm so, so sorry. Can you tell me what happened?" I leaned forward, trying to project a calmness I didn't feel.

"Brain aneurysm." Her voice cracked, and she stared down at her hands. "She was fine one minute, then..." She shrugged, but I saw the tremor in her shoulders, the way she curled in on herself. "The doctors said it was quick. That she didn't suffer." Her words carried the hollow tone of someone who'd heard that reassurance too many times to find comfort in it anymore.

I wanted to reach across the table, to offer some comfort, but I didn't know if I had that right yet. My fingers twitched against my mug, every new parental instinct screaming to do something, any-thing, to ease her pain. "And your grandparents?"

Her eyes narrowed, a flash of defiance burning through the grief. "Already looking for someone to pawn me off on?"

The defensive tone, the way her chin lifted—I'd seen that exact look on Bree's face so many times as a kid. So determined not to show weakness. Not to need anyone. It was like looking at a ghost from my past.

"No. Just trying to put together a picture here. Were you staying with them after your mom passed?" I kept my voice steady, gentle, trying to project the same calm Bree had shown earlier.

"My grandparents died before I was born." She took a sip of coffee, avoiding my eyes. "It was always just Mom and me. Until it wasn't."

My exhausted brain tried to work through the implications of that. If they'd died before Peyton was born, that meant somehow Casey had lost both her parents less than a year after leaving Hatter-wick. She'd been on her own in the world with a baby at eighteen. That had to have been incredibly difficult. So why the hell hadn't she reached out? I would've been there. I would have done the right thing.

But I said none of that to this child who had no reason to believe me.

"When did she die?" I fought to keep my voice steady despite the storm of emotions churning inside me.

"Three months ago."

"And since then? Who have you been living with? Who's been responsible for you?" The questions tumbled out before I could stop them, each one weighted with the guilt of not having been there.

Those green eyes shuttered, and her fingers tightened on the mug until her knuckles went white. "A foster family."

I bit back the eleven thousand questions I wanted to ask about that. If something had been going on there that had prompted her to run away to find me, she sure as fuck wouldn't be going back. The protective instinct that had slammed into me the moment I'd learned she was mine roared to life. We'd have time to address... whatever might have happened. Right now, she needed to know she was safe, that she wouldn't have to run again.

I drew a steadying breath. Time to be practical about this situation. If she'd been in foster care, then she'd have a caseworker at social services. No doubt they'd be looking for her. We'd need to notify them she was safe while we started the process of testing to prove paternity.

"Peyton, we need to contact your case worker. Let them know you're safe while we sort out—"

She shot up from the table so fast her chair clattered to the floor. Before I could blink, she'd yanked open the back door and bolted. The flash of her dark blonde hair whipping around the door frame sent my heart into overdrive.

"Shit!" I jumped up to follow, but Keeley had the same idea. The dog's scrambling paws tangled with my feet, and I stumbled, catching myself on the kitchen counter. The edge bit into my palm as I pushed off, losing precious seconds. By the time I righted myself and made it to the door, Peyton had vanished into the crisp morning air.

"Peyton!" My shout echoed off the neighboring houses, desperation clawing at my throat.

The late morning sun beat down on a maze of backyard fences and garden plots. No sign of which direction she'd gone. Bree's cottage sat in the middle of the village, surrounded by other homes, making it impossible to guess which route she might have taken. My mind raced with possibilities. She could have ducked between any of the houses, taken one of the footpaths to the beach, or headed toward the commercial district. Ten years of military training, and I couldn't even keep track of one scared teenager.

The dull thud of my heart turned into a desperate pounding. Less than twenty minutes. I'd had my daughter in front of me for less than twenty minutes, and I'd already screwed up. Made her run. Just like her mother had apparently run all those years ago, taking any chance of me knowing Peyton with her.

CHAPTER 11

BREE

Morning sun streamed through the windows of the Brewhouse, casting long shadows across the empty tables. It was too early for customers, too early even for me to be here, normally. Running a bar meant I kept late hours, which meant I usually slept in.

Not today.

My phone sat silent on the counter. No texts. No calls. No updates.

The quiet gave me too much space to second-guess the fact that I'd left Peyton and Ford alone. She'd been through so much already. Lost her mom. Traveled across the country alone. And Ford... well, he had about as much experience with kids as I had with deep sea diving. It wasn't like I had a ton, either. But I'd been her, once upon a very long time ago. And I hadn't been willing to trust anyone further than I could spit.

I grabbed a cloth and attacked imaginary water spots on the glasses, arranging and rearranging them behind the bar. The kitchen staff would arrive soon. Mandy always showed up first, usually bursting through those doors like a hurricane of gossip. If word had gotten out about Peyton, she'd know.

The coffee maker gurgled in the corner, filling the air with its rich aroma. I'd already prepped everything for lunch service that could be prepped, short of actual food. As my short-order cook, Bonita, had informed me in no uncertain terms, that wasn't my purview, and I didn't chop correctly. Which meant there was nothing left to do but wait.

I wandered through the building, checking the gauges on all the brewing tanks and chasing imaginary dust bunnies, before ending up back at the bar.

Maybe I should text Ford. Just check in. Make sure everything was okay.

I picked up my phone, then set it back down. No. They needed time to figure this out on their own.

The kitchen door banged open, making me jump.

"Jesus, Mandy. Give me a heart attack, why don't you?"

But it wasn't Mandy. Ford ducked inside, his tall frame filling the doorway. Alone.

My stomach dropped. "Where is she?"

"I fucked things up." He raked his hands through his hair, making it stand on end. "She bolted. I've been looking for the past half hour, but I can't find her."

Of course she'd bolted. Because that was what kids like us did when shit got too real or uncomfortable. Damn it, I shouldn't have left them alone.

The worry etched across his face matched the churning in my gut. "What happened?"

"I started asking questions. She took it wrong, thought I was trying to get rid of her." He slumped against the door frame and squeezed his temples. "I was just trying to work through the logistics." The eyes he lifted to mine were panicked. "Do you have any idea where she might have gone?"

My mind raced through possibilities. If the meeting had gone badly and she was running... "Maybe back to the ferry terminal? She might try to get off-island."

The color drained from Ford's face. "Shit. I didn't even think—"

"Go check there. The last ferry left more than an hour ago, so she couldn't have been on it. I'll get out and look myself." I grabbed my keys from under the bar. "If we don't find her within the next hour, we pull in the others." I couldn't explain why I didn't want to pull them in now. My instincts still shouted at me to keep this secret small and tight in order to protect her.

We split up. I brought up a mental map of the island, thinking about which way she might've gone from my place. I was fairly centrally located, only a mile and a half from the ocean in three directions. If she wasn't immediately trying to get the hell off-island, she'd probably want to be alone. I would.

The route to the sound side of the island would have taken her through the village. Plenty of shops she could duck into, but I didn't think she'd seek out people if she was upset. The south would take her toward the lighthouse and her grandmothers. Not that she'd know that yet. But the stretch of salt marsh between here and there would mean she'd be walking in the open for a lot of the way. Ford would probably have seen her. Which left either the beach on the Atlantic side or the maritime forest. There were plenty of places in the latter to get lost, and if she was from Oregon, maybe she'd seek out woods. But I was banking on beach.

I drove past the marina, following the curve of the shoreline. In the distance I could see the lighthouse, but I didn't make the turn. I kept going, on out toward the far eastern edge of the island. A squat clapboard building came into view. The research station where Astrid Thompson conducted her sea turtle research. No lights on inside. This time of year, she often didn't work at the station. It was well outside breeding season. But I took advantage of the small crushed-shell parking lot to drop my Jeep, because this stretch of beach wasn't accessible by vehicle.

It was exactly why I'd come here myself over the years. Sometimes I craved the isolation and the endless waves. Sometimes I just needed to scream my heart out. The surf was loud enough that no one would hear.

A flash of movement caught my eye. Just a quick shadow ducking behind one of the taller dunes. My heart kicked into higher gear. I'd bet my brewery that was Peyton.

Careful not to move too fast or seem like I was trying to sneak up, I picked my way closer. When I rounded the dune, I found her huddled in the sand, arms wrapped around her knees. Her face was streaked with tears. She was hunched into her sweater, which wasn't strictly warm enough for January on the Outer Banks. Not with the wind gusting as it did on this side of the island.

One thing at a time.

I settled into the sand a few feet away, staring out at the ocean instead of the girl. "This is where I always come when everything feels like it's falling apart. Somehow I can breathe here."

I'd spent what felt like months of my life out here in the years after I'd cut Ford out of my world.

She swiped roughly at her cheeks, but didn't respond.

"The waves help. It's kinda like they're washing everything away. Even if it's just for a little while."

I caught the barest of nods in my periphery.

"You wanna tell me what happened?"

"He wants to send me back." She spat the words.

"Did he actually say that?" I knew he hadn't. He wouldn't.

"He said we needed to contact my case worker. That's the whole point of her."

I fixed the girl with a look. "Peyton, honey, you ran away from the people who are legally responsible for you. I don't know how you thought all this was gonna go down, but functionally, we *do* have to let them know where you are and that you're safe. Because there will be police and other folks out looking for you. It's not fair to tie up those resources when you're not really missing."

"Oh." Her voice was small.

"Yeah. 'Oh.' Listen, I'm not saying Ford handled it perfectly. But maybe consider he's had less than twenty-four hours to adjust to this whole dad thing, what with not knowing you existed. Maybe cut him a little slack. He's got a lot to figure out."

When she said nothing, I continued. "Look, I've known your dad since we were kids. He's one of the most loyal people I've ever met. When he commits to something—or someone—he's all in." The words felt like glass in my throat, but Peyton needed to hear them. "He's the guy who spent three days searching the woods for my dog when she got lost back in high school. The guy who was first in line to help shovel out the rubble when the brewery burned years ago."

Peyton picked up a handful of sand, letting it sift through her fingers. "Why'd you stop being friends?"

My chest tightened. "Who said we weren't?"

"Y'all didn't act like friends back at the house."

No, I don't suppose we did.

"That's... complicated. And not important right now. What matters is that Ford's a good man. He'll do right by you, if you give him the chance."

"But what if he doesn't want me?"

The vulnerability in her voice was a punch to the gut. "Honey, that's not even a possibility. Trust me on this. He's freaking out right now, trying to find you."

She hugged her knees tighter. "I guess shouldn't have run."

"Maybe not. But I get it." I shifted closer, brushing sand off my jeans. "What do you say we go find him? Let him know you're okay?"

She nodded slowly. "Yeah. Okay."

I pulled out my phone and fired off a quick text to Ford.

Bree: Found her. Meet us back at my place.

"Come on." I stood and offered her my hand. "I'll make you some hot chocolate while we wait. The good kind, with the fancy marshmallows I keep for special occasions."

That earned me a small smile as she let me help her up. "Thanks. For coming to find me. And... you know. Everything else."

"Any time, kid." I meant it more than I wanted to admit. "That's what friends are for."

Ford was pacing the driveway when we got back. I saw him start to rush my Jeep, then check himself, waiting until we both got out. "You're okay."

His visible relief seemed to put Peyton more at ease.

She scuffed the toe of her shoe on the driveway. "Yeah. I'm sorry I ran."

"I'm sorry I made you feel like you had to."

We all stared at each other until Peyton finally broke the awkward silence. "So now what?"

"A paternity test. We'll need it so I can establish

a legal claim of parental rights. I don't actually know after that. We have a lot of stuff to figure out. But I promise you, we *will* figure it out. You're not alone anymore."

My heart ached because it was the same promise he'd made me so long ago. The one he'd broken. But my private pain had no place here, because I knew he'd do right by his daughter.

"In the meantime, do you want to meet your grandmothers?"

CHAPTER 12

FORD

After taking some time at Bree's place for hot cocoa and a little more discussion of next steps, Peyton gathered up her stuff—just one stuffed backpack... Jesus, the sight of that single bag about cut me off at the knees—and we headed for home. It was still home, though I hadn't lived here full time in years, just visiting Mom and Mimi during holidays and long breaks. I didn't know whether it would be home again moving forward, whether I'd need to find a place better suited for a teenager, with her own room and space to grow. That was another of those details I hadn't figured out yet, one more item on the ever-growing list of things I needed to sort through.

One step at a time, Donoghue.

My grip on the steering wheel tightened as we passed the marina, and I took the turn onto the road that wound through the salt marsh, toward the far southern tip of the island. The silence in the car was broken only by the crunch of shells under tires as we drew closer. It was still a few hours out from sunset, but the lighthouse itself speared up, a beacon in the afternoon sky. Seabirds wheeled overhead, their cries carrying on the salt-laden breeze that buffeted the car.

Peyton pressed her face to the window. "*That's* where you live?"

"Where I grew up. Yeah." I slowed the car so she could really take in the view of the place. How long had it been since I'd done the same? Looking at it now, I tried to imagine what Peyton saw. A tall, whitewashed tower beside a cozy house that had been expanded every which way in a charming jumble of additions that somehow worked as a whole. Mom and Mimi had painted the shutters a cheerful red last spring, and the flower boxes beneath each window overflowed with the pansies that were tough enough to survive the winter, a riot of color against the weathered shingles.

"The lighthouse itself was decommissioned years ago. My moms bought and renovated it and the attached caretaker's cottage. They're still here." I watched Peyton carefully, trying to gauge her reaction to that particular detail. The last thing I wanted was for her to feel uncomfortable, especially since we were just starting to build some trust.

"You have two moms?"

"Yup. Florence—she's my biological mom—and Delilah, her wife. That's Mimi." I smiled, remembering how Mimi had earned that nickname from all my friends growing up, not just me. Her warm, nurturing presence had made her everyone's second mom.

Her brow furrowed. "What about your bio dad?"

"Never met him." I let out a humorless laugh. "Something we've got in common." The words came out before I could stop them, and I winced. "Sort of." I gripped the steering wheel tighter, cursing my lack of filter. Here I was, trying to be the responsible adult she needed, and I'd just reminded her of exactly how I'd failed her.

My stomach churned as I stared up at the lighthouse windows, the panes glinting in the afternoon sun. By some miracle, word hadn't reached my moms yet about their surprise granddaughter. I knew I'd have heard from them if they had. Probably in the form of about fifty missed calls and concerned text messages. I had Bree to thank for that. She'd moved fast to keep Peyton under wraps until

I could get here, proving once again she was better at handling crises than I was.

I had a lot about this situation to thank Bree for. But it would have to wait. Right now, I had bigger fires to put out.

My palms went sweaty on the steering wheel as I pulled up in front of the house, the tires crunching on the shell-strewn driveway. I had no playbook for this, no training manual on how to tell your parents they had a teenage granddaughter you never knew about. Hell, I barely knew how to process it myself. The Navy had trained me for countless scenarios, but nothing like this. All I could do was stumble forward, hoping each next decision wasn't completely wrong.

A curtain in the front window stirred, the gauzy fabric dancing briefly before falling still. Probably Mimi. She'd have heard the car, always alert to visitors. This time of day, I knew she was liable to be home working on her pottery, or maybe in the attic workshop. I wasn't sure about Mom's court schedule today, and the doors to the garage were down, leaving me guessing whether I'd be facing them both at the same time.

Well, if I had to go through this more than once, so be it. We'd get through it. I'd spent enough years dealing with my moms' particular brand of loving interference to handle whatever came next.

"What if they don't like me?" Peyton's voice was small, with no trace of her earlier bravado. Her fingers twisted the hem of her sweater, a nervous habit I'd noticed over the past couple of hours.

"Not possible." I turned to face her, trying to project more confidence than I felt. "They're going to love you. Fair warning though—Mimi's probably going to try to feed you about twelve different things in the first hour. She shows love through food. Her chocolate chip cookies alone are worth the price of admission."

"What about your other mom?"

"My friends call her Mama Flo. She tends toward more aggressive momming and has been occasionally known to slide into smothering territory. It's all very well intentioned, but boundaries are a thing. Don't worry, I've got you." I fought the urge to reach out and squeeze her shoulder, still unsure how much physical contact she was comfortable with.

She shot me a little side eye that showed she didn't fully believe me. And why should she? She didn't know me. But she would. I had to believe that time would prove my commitment.

"You ready?" I asked.

Peyton took a deep breath, squaring her shoulders like a soldier heading into battle. "I guess we'll find out."

The front door squeaked as I shoved it open, the hinges protesting exactly as they had since I was a kid. The sound of my childhood. "Mom? Mimi?"

Movement from the kitchen caught my eye as Mimi's head poked around the corner, flour dusting her dark curls and the bridge of her pert little nose, standing out like freckles against her dark brown skin. "Ford?" Her eyes went wide, and she wiped her hands on her apron. "What are you doing here? I thought you had training."

"I did. Do, technically." That was a whole other mess I'd have to sort out later. My commanding officer wasn't thrilled about my abrupt departure, and he was gonna be less so about whatever came next, but some things couldn't wait.

Mom's voice carried from upstairs, sharp and concerned. "Is that Ford?" Footsteps thundered down, and she appeared at the landing, case files tucked under one arm, reading glasses shoved up on top of her head where they threatened to fall. Her business suit was wrinkled, which meant she'd been working from home this afternoon. "What's wrong?"

"Nothing's wrong." I cleared my throat, trying to project a calm I definitely didn't feel. "But something called me back early."

Peyton hung back in the doorway, half-hidden behind me like she was using my bulk as a shield.

Anxiety rolled off her in waves, making the air feel thick and heavy between us. Hell, my own heart hammered against my ribs so hard I was sure everyone could hear it.

"There's someone I want you to meet." I turned back and held out my hand, beckoning Peyton forward. My palm was sweaty, and I fought the urge to wipe it on my jeans.

She shuffled into the room, shoulders hunched, looking about as small as she could make herself, despite her height. Her eyes darted between my mothers, then fixed on the floor, her fingers back to twisting the hem of the sweater.

"This is Peyton." I swallowed hard, the words nearly sticking in my throat as the magnitude of what I was about to say crashed over me at full force. "Your granddaughter."

The files hit the floor with a thud, papers spilling out across the hardwood. Mom's mouth fell open, her green eyes wide with shock. Mimi's hand flew to her chest, leaving a floury handprint on her brightly patterned shirt.

"Ford Michael Donoghue, why is this the first we're hearing about this?" Mom's voice cracked like a whip, carrying that sharp tone I remembered all too well from my teenage years. The one that meant I was in serious trouble.

Beside me, Peyton flinched, and I instinctively

shifted closer, wanting to shield her, though I knew Mom's displeasure was absolutely aimed at me instead of her. The protective urge surprised me. It felt both foreign and completely natural at the same time.

Peyton inched a little closer, her shoulder barely brushing against my arm as she shot a worried glance up at me. She whispered, her voice carrying a hint of nervous amusement, "She middle named you." The corner of her mouth twitched, like she was trying not to smile despite her obvious anxiety.

Despite everything, I felt a smile tugging at my lips. "Not remotely for the first time, I can promise you." I reached back and squeezed Peyton's shoulder, grateful she didn't flinch away from my touch. "I only found out yesterday, Mom. That's why I'm back. I came straight here as soon as I could get leave."

Mom's eyes narrowed, her lawyer face firmly in place. The same expression I'd seen her wear in countless courtrooms when she was about to dig into a particularly troublesome witness. "But who?" She paused, and I could see the wheels turning behind those sharp green eyes. "Not Emily."

"No." Thank God for small mercies. My on-again, off-again relationship with my college girlfriend had been volatile enough without throwing a secret baby into the mix. We'd broken up and gotten back together so many times it had made everyone's heads spin. "Her name was Casey."

"Was?" Mimi's voice was soft, gentle, carrying that note of motherly concern that had gotten me through some rough patches growing up.

I glanced down at Peyton, who'd gone still beside me, her gaze fixed on the floor as if she could somehow make herself invisible. My heart ached at the obvious pain in her rigid posture. "She... died."

The words dropped into the silence like stones in still water. Mimi lasted all of three seconds before she'd dropped her kitchen towel and closed the distance, scooping Peyton into a tight, cinnamon-scented hug. Had she been making snickerdoodles when we got here?

"Oh, sweet girl. I'm so, so sorry." She rocked Peyton back and forth, even though Peyton was almost a head taller already.

I braced myself, ready to intervene in case this was all too much too fast for my daughter. But after only a few moments, she melted, returning the embrace. Such was the great power of Mimi.

On the stairs, Mom's face had lost the stern lawyer's set and softened into a warmth and vulnerability few outside of family ever saw. Her eyes held a multitude of questions, but she bit them back for now.

"Right, so I know this is a shock, but we've got a lot to figure out, and not a lot of time to do it in. I thought y'all could help with that." My voice wavered slightly, betraying the nervous energy thrumming through my body.

Mom knelt and gathered up the scattered files, her movements precise and methodical as always. "Well, there are certainly a lot of details that need filling in. I'll put on the kettle." Calm. Practical. Let's do what comes next. These were the traits that had made her the anchor of my childhood.

Mimi kept her arm around Peyton's shoulders and ushered her toward the kitchen, radiating the warmth she was famous for. "You just come right on in here, sugar. I've got snickerdoodles coming out of the oven in ten minutes." The scent of cinnamon and butter was already wafting through the house.

Peyton shot me a cautiously amused glance, the ghost of a smile playing at her lips. I smiled back and mouthed, *Told you.* Already, I could see her shoulders relaxing fractionally under Mimi's gentle guidance.

Mom stopped next to me, fixing me with a meaningful stare. The kind that had always made me feel like she could see straight through to my soul.

"It's real," I murmured.

"Oh, I can see that with my own eyes." She

skimmed a hand through my hair in the way she'd been doing since I was no higher than her knee. She had to reach a lot farther now. "I'm guessing we have to set about proving it before things get messy. And they will get messy, won't they, Ford?"

"You guess correctly." My throat felt tight with everything left unsaid, everything we both knew was coming.

Nodding, she squared her shoulders, and I saw the lawyer in her emerge—the fierce protector who'd fought for environmental justice up and down the coast. "Then let's get to work."

CHAPTER 13

BREE

The benefit of having devoted my every waking minute to the Brewhouse all these years was that I'd pulled together and trained a phenomenal staff. So on the rare occasions I needed to step away, I generally could without much fuss. After the past twenty-four hours, having met Peyton, broken my silence with Ford, and gotten dragged into their little family drama with the search for her this afternoon, I absolutely couldn't deal with the public tonight. There'd been no downtime. No opportunity to process any of this. I was far too raw to be put on the spot, and I inevitably would be if I were there.

The Brewhouse was at the center of village life for the locals. Whether it was anyone's business or not—and I was of the firm opinion that it wasn't—I'd get asked what I knew about Ford's surprise daughter. The two of them deserved the privacy to figure out their new relationship without being at the center of a public soap opera. Until I was capable of calmly saying so, without telling anyone to fuck off, I didn't need to be behind the bar.

I also didn't want to face questions about my own relationship with Ford. What had happened between us was one of the best-kept secrets on Hatterwick. I'd never admitted it to anyone. Neither had Ford. So far as anyone knew, we'd had a falling out over subjects unknown and were no longer friends. People were aware I didn't speak to him, despite the fact that I'd maintained cordial relationships with the rest of the Wayward Sons and even Ford's moms. If there'd been speculation—and I was certain there had been—no one had been fool enough to share it with me directly. That was fine by me.

But now Ford was back on-island, and I really needed to process the implications of that.

I opened my freezer door and grabbed a pint of chocolate chip cookie dough ice cream. I didn't often eat or drink my emotions. Having a mom who'd died as a junkie because of her own addictions meant I kept myself on an extremely short leash for indulgences. But this felt like a reasonable recourse in this situation. Hell, after the day I'd had, I probably deserved a whole damn freezer's worth.

From her spot at the end of the counter, Keeley huffed and stomped a paw as I pried off the top and dug straight in with a spoon. My loyal companion had opinions about everything, including, apparently, my choice of comfort food.

"Don't you judge me. I haven't spoken to the man in ten years. Now he's back, and I have no idea how he's going to work all this shit out, but I know he's not going to abandon that kid with his moms while he goes back out on deployment. Which means he's going to be actually *back*. Which means I have to see him. If that's not an excuse to have ice cream for dinner, I don't know what is." I shoveled another heaping spoonful into my mouth, letting the cold sweetness numb my churning thoughts. "And don't give me that look. You get treats when you're stressed, too."

My pup just stared at me with *Uh-huh* eyes, her golden head tilted in that way that made me feel like she could see straight through my bullshit.

"It's fine. Now that I've handed off Peyton, I can go back to not talking to him again." The words tasted like a lie, even around the mouthful of ice cream.

Keeley looked deeply unimpressed by my logic.

She angled her head and gave me a side eye that would make any teenager proud.

"I can," I insisted, though my heart squeezed tight at the idea of it. It had taken so much out of me to stay away from him all these years. The only reason I'd managed to pull it off was because he'd been gone for most of it. He'd only made it home a handful of days a year, which made avoiding him as easy as checking the calendar for Navy holidays and listening to the town grapevine for when he hit the island. But now? Now he'd be here. Every. Single. Day.

My dog lay down and crossed her front paws with a sigh and an eye roll, as if to say, "Humans." Her whole body language screamed judgment, and I didn't appreciate it one bit.

I scowled. "Nobody asked you." I shoved another big bite of ice cream in my mouth, letting the chocolate chunks crunch between my teeth.

God, it had been so good and so awful to see him up close and personal. I hadn't let myself look when I'd seen him on-island before, but there'd been no avoiding the reality of him in my front entryway. He was... massive. He'd always been tall, but over the past ten years in the Navy, he'd bulked out in a big way. Yet it hadn't been his size that had struck me like a fist in the sternum. It was how he'd looked so lost and overwhelmed just before meeting his daughter. That vulnerability had gotten to me in a way nothing else could have. And then he'd come to me when Peyton had disappeared on him. I knew that had more to do with the fact that I knew who she was and that we had sufficient in common that I was the most likely to think like her. But a part of me had felt really good that he'd known he could count on me in a crisis. Even now.

And that was very dangerous thinking.

Restless and nervy, I ate more ice cream, shoveling in another spoonful of chocolate chip cookie dough, as if the sugar rush might drown out the unwelcome thoughts taking over my brain.

Keeley bounced to her feet moments before my back door opened and Pop strode in. He took one look at the ice cream in my hand and harrumphed. "Good thing I brought dinner." He set a takeout bag on the kitchen table and bent to scratch a wagging Keeley, who'd immediately abandoned me in favor of her second-favorite human. "Can't have you living on dessert alone."

"What are you doing here? I thought you were playing poker with the Gray Beards tonight." I tried not to sound defensive, but Pop had an uncanny way of showing up when I was most unsettled.

"Thought you might want to talk." He gave me that knowing look that always made me feel about eight years old again.

"What on earth gave you that delusion?" I jabbed my spoon back into the carton, avoiding his eyes.

He just arched one bushy eyebrow with the same unimpressed look I'd gotten from my dog. "You really gonna tell me there's nothing to talk about when you were seen with Ford earlier today? After not giving him the time of day for ten years?" His tone held that mix of concern and judgment that only a parent—and let's be honest, grandfather or not, he was the only one I'd ever really had—could master.

"Nothing I want to talk about." I stabbed my spoon deeper into the melting ice cream.

He ignored my annoyance and crossed to pull plates out of the cabinet, the clink of ceramic against ceramic filling the silence between us. "I'm not trying to dig into your business." The gentleness in his voice made it worse somehow.

"Really? What do you call it?" I couldn't keep the edge from my voice, knowing I was being unfair but unable to stop myself.

"I'm just asking what changed." He waited me out like he always did.

"His daughter showed up at the Brewhouse." The words tasted bitter on my tongue, stirring up memories I'd rather leave buried.

The plates rattled as he set them on the

counter. My grandfather had been around. He'd seen and heard a lot in his lifetime. Everything from bar brawls to hurricane evacuations to tourist shenanigans. It took a hell of a lot to surprise him, but at my words, those grizzled caterpillar eyebrows hit his hairline.

"Daughter?" The word came out as more of a croak, and I couldn't blame him. This was exactly the kind of bombshell that made small-town tongues wag.

With a weary sigh, I snatched the plates and moved to the table, needing something to do with my hands. As we spooned out kung pow chicken and beef with broccoli, letting the fragrant steam curl between us, I gave him the overview of what had happened. Better he hear the real version from me instead of the island grapevine. That would be circulating soon enough. Probably already was.

"No wonder you latched onto the girl. She's like an older version of you."

I bit into an egg roll and jerked one shoulder in a shrug, the crispy wrapper crunching between my teeth. "I feel for the kid." The words came out more defensive than I'd intended.

"So you protected her until Ford could get back. And you called him yourself rather than pawn it off on someone else."

I bristled, dropping the rest of my egg roll onto

the plate. "Peyton deserved that. She deserved to know someone gave a damn about doing right by her."

"Not saying you were wrong. It was the kind thing to do."

That edged too close to acknowledging my own history, and my shoulders hunched up toward my ears. "I can pay it forward. That's all it was."

Pop reached out to lay one gnarled hand over mine, his skin weathered from decades of working on the water. "Baby girl, you never owed me a damned thing."

I owed him everything. But that was an old argument I didn't want to rehash right now. Not when the wounds of the past felt so raw and exposed.

"What's she like?"

"She's at that age where she's both really mature and so very young. She's tall, like Ford, so she can get away with people thinking she's older than she is. When I think of all the things that could have happened to her on her way here from Oregon? Christ, it still makes me want to put my head between my knees." I shuddered, thinking of all the true crime podcasts I'd listened to over the years.

"Sounds like she's resourceful."

"Yeah. And scared. She ran away and made it all the way from the West Coast to here in search of a man she didn't even know, rather than stay put. That takes a lot of guts and desperation."

Pop sobered, his weathered face creasing with concern. "You think she was in a bad situation with the foster care?"

"I talked to her about it a little. She didn't show any of the expected signs of abuse, but you and I both know that can be hidden. Whatever she came from, she'll be safe here. Ford and his moms will see to it."

"Reckon that means he's moving home. If not immediately, then as soon as he can manage."

He was fishing, and I knew it. Pop had always been good at that—dropping little hints and waiting to see what kind of reaction he'd get. Usually, I gave him more to work with, but not about this. Not about Ford.

"It doesn't matter. It doesn't change anything. I did my duty by the kid, and now I can get on with my life." The words were too sharp, but I couldn't soften them now.

"Maybe it's finally time for you two to talk about whatever happened."

"Hell has not frozen over, so no, it's not. Drop it, Pop." I stabbed at a hunk of broccoli with more force than necessary.

He lifted his hands in surrender. "Okay." But I

could tell from the way his mouth twisted that he wasn't done with the subject forever.

I poked at the last bite of beef on my plate, not meeting his eyes. The words stuck in my throat for a moment before I could get them out. "Do you still have the photo albums from when we were younger?"

"Of course." His voice gentled, the way it always did when he sensed how close to the surface my emotions were running.

"Could you bring them by? I promised Peyton I'd ask about them."

Pop gave me a long, silent look before finally nodding. "Yeah, I can do that."

CHAPTER 14
FORD

FORD:

:picture of DNA results:

RIOS:

Congratulations! It's a girl!

SAWYER:

:GIF of Deadpool cracking his knuckles: Preparing to be favorite uncle.

UNKNOWN NUMBER:

Kid won the lottery.

FORD:

Thanks, assholes.

Of course the moment the paternity test results had arrived, I'd texted my brothers. The scientific confirmation of what my gut already knew still felt like a brick between the eyes. I was a dad. For real. But there was no time to mentally process that I truly had a kid. A fully formed person, with likes and dislikes and quirks I hadn't even begun to scratch the surface of learning. One I was now the sole parent of. Or would be as soon as all the legalities were sorted. Mom and Mimi had celebrated with pink champagne, sparkling pink lemonade, and a behemoth German chocolate birthday cake—apparently Peyton's favorite.

And I upended my entire world to start making a stable one for my daughter.

The moment I had proof of paternity in hand, I contacted Peyton's caseworker in Oregon and started the process of claiming her. The Amber Alert had been canceled. I'd been granted emergency custody while the rest of the legal machine did its thing to finalize the arrangement. I'd already started dependency paperwork to get her benefits and taken her to get her military ID. My job situation was still up in the air. I was on emergency leave for the next few weeks, and my command was exploring the potential for a remote position. I wasn't sure how fast they'd come back with an answer about that, but for the moment, I was dealing with the problems directly in front of me.

Right this moment, that included a very reluctant teenager.

"We've gotta talk about school, kid."

Peyton immediately pulled into herself, shoulders rising toward her ears, knees tucking into her chest where she sat on the window seat in the kitchen. It was just us for the moment. Mom was in court, and Mimi had a meeting with one of the shops that carried her art.

I settled in across the table with a second cup of coffee. "I know you don't wanna, but that's one of those non-negotiables of the world. If we don't get you enrolled ASAP, the powers that be are gonna come after me, and I kinda don't think that would look great for them letting you stay with me."

Her head snapped toward me, some of the color leeching out of her cheeks. "You think they'll take me away?"

Shit. I was traumatizing her without even trying. Father of the year, right here. "I mean, there's no reason for them to now. But that's one of my jobs as a parent. To make sure you go to school."

She slumped, blowing out a long breath as she stared at the scuffed toes of her Chucks.

"Is it the big catch up you're worried about or being the new kid?"

"Both." Her fingers restlessly picked at a loose thread on her sweater. Mom and Mimi had taken her to pick up a few things, and her foster mom in Oregon was supposed to be making arrangements to send her stuff, but I made a mental note that we needed to order her some new clothes. The climate here was a lot warmer than where she was from.

"Everybody's gonna be talking about me."

I dragged my focus back to the current issue. No reason to blow smoke up her ass. "Yeah, probably so. That's the nature of small towns, and you're big news, here. But that doesn't mean it will all suck."

Peyton shot me a glare. "How would you know? You were never the new kid. You grew up here."

"That's fair. You're right. I wasn't the new kid. Not until college. I was the guy who made friends with the new kid and intervened when she got bullied."

That earned me a look of speculation. "Are you talking about Bree?"

I hadn't actually brought her up over the past several days, though that had been a challenge. I didn't know how much Bree wanted to do with us, now that she'd discharged her duties by uniting us in the first place. But this was relevant.

"Yeah. She had a rough start in life. Came here when she was a good bit younger than you. That would've been third grade for us. Some people weren't kind." I could still remember the first time I'd seen her, all knobby knees and defiance covering up so much hurt, as Zack Pickering made up some nonsensical, bullshit rhyme about her being unwanted by anyone.

"Did you beat them up?"

I blinked. "What?"

"Your hands curled into fists."

Shit, they had. I forced my fingers to relax and bought myself a little time by sipping the coffee. God, I'd missed Mimi's chicory blend. "It's probably bad parenting for me to admit it, but yeah, I did. Violence shouldn't be the first response. I wish I could say it was never the right response, but some people don't respond to anything else." And I'd never been one to stand by when someone needed protecting.

"Did you get in trouble?"

"Oh yeah. I was suspended for a week. So was he. Our schools have a zero-tolerance policy for fighting."

"Did you regret it?"

"Not for a moment. I got an incredible friend out of it." And I'd gone and lost her.

I hadn't seen Bree again in the week I'd been

back on-island, juggling all the details of changing my life. From long experience, I suspected she was hiding. But it would only be a matter of time before our paths crossed again. Hatterwick just wasn't that big. I wanted to believe that her breaking the silence to help with Peyton was the potential start of a thaw between us, one that would allow me to begin to repair what I'd damaged all those years ago. But that was wishful thinking. She'd been there for Peyton because she identified with her. It didn't take a shrink to figure that out. It wasn't about me.

But I couldn't forget how she'd looked at me with something other than loathing or chill fury for the first time in forever when she'd said, *We'll figure this out.*

A slip of the tongue? Or did it mean something?

Peyton huffed. "I guess if I've gotta."

For a moment, I forgot what we'd been talking about. Oh, right. School.

"Unfortunately, you gotta. But there's one more thing we've got to sort out before we go enroll you."

"What's that?"

"Our home address."

"We aren't staying here?"

I couldn't gauge how she felt about the idea of that, but I'd been giving this some thought the past several days. "That's an option. But I was thinking we could get our own place. See, I've been gone from home for a long time, and as you've seen, Mom and Mimi have kinda expanded to take up all the space. They'd clean out to make room for us and be happy to do it, but it might be kinda cramped. I thought you should have a say in where we live." And it would hopefully keep me from leaning too hard on them. They'd disagree with that, but Peyton was my responsibility. I had a lot of missed years to make up for.

She blinked in obvious surprise. "I get an opinion?"

"Of course you do. I mean, we've got a budget to stick to, but I thought we could spend the rest of the day checking out options for places to rent." Being the off season, we ought to have a decent selection. I'd already put a call in to Rene Johnson to set up some showings.

Maybe it was a mistake to rent something. Maybe I ought to wait until my job situation was sorted, then look at actually buying a house. But much as I adored my moms, I wasn't sure if they'd be able to let me be the parent if we were living under their roof. Not that I had a damned clue how to be that parent, but this wouldn't be my first trial-by-fire experience, and I was committed to figuring it out. I felt like Peyton and I needed our own space to do that.

Or maybe I just didn't want my moms to have a front-row seat to my inevitable fuck ups.

Peyton stared at me, a faint line forming between her brows.

"What?"

"It's just..." She trailed off, dropping her gaze.

"Just what?"

"Never mind."

"No really. Say what you're thinking. All of this is a huge change for both of us, and good communication is the only way we're gonna get through it."

She sucked in a breath. "It's just... you're taking all this awfully well."

"All this?"

"I mean... me."

Did that mean her foster family had considered her a problem? One of those "too much" kids? Curling my fingers around my mug, I chose my words carefully. "Peyton, you're my daughter. You may have been the world's biggest surprise, but I'm not upset you exist. I'm only sorry I didn't know about you sooner. So that I could have been there with you growing up. Helped your mom, whether we worked out as a couple or not."

She angled her head, apparently fascinated by that. "You would have done that?"

"Hell yeah, I would have done that."

Her lips pressed together, another clear sign she wasn't sure she could say what she wanted to.

"Communication, remember?" I prodded.

"I just... Mom never talked about you. Ever. And for a long time, I wondered if that was because you were a bad guy."

I had so many questions for Casey. And I'd never get the answers. "Fair question to have, under the circumstances. But you came anyway."

"Yeah. I thought I'd do some recon to find out what you were like, if it was even worth telling you who I was."

"Guess Bree kinda spoiled that." And thank God for it. I may have only had a week of knowing I was a dad, but nothing on earth could make me give this kid up.

Peyton's lips twitched. "Yeah. But it was okay because she insisted you were a good guy. The best guy."

Had she really? That definitely was *not* the assessment I would've expected from Bree Cartwright after all these years.

"What's your verdict?"

She studied me for a long moment with those eyes so like mine. Then her lips quirked up the barest hint. "You're all right."

From a suspicious teenager, that felt like the highest form of praise.

"I can work with that. You're pretty okay yourself."

The quirk turned into a brief flash of an actual smile.

"So how 'bout it? We go look at houses, and then maybe get some lunch while we're out?"

"Sounds like a plan."

CHAPTER 15

BREE

I'd spent the past week getting back to business as usual. There'd been questions about Ford and Peyton. Everyone was talking about his surprise daughter and opining about whether they remembered her mother from that long-ago summer. But I'd managed to redirect most of those. Monty was dying of curiosity, but had recognized that pressing would only result in grumpitude and retribution, neither of which he was interested in dealing with. The rest of my staff had likewise steered clear, which was fine by me.

Pop had brought the photo albums by. I hadn't contacted Ford about it because I didn't want him to think the status quo between us had changed. It hadn't. But they'd be there for the next time I saw

Peyton. If the stack of them in the corner of my living room mocked me, trying to draw me down a dangerous road of nostalgia, I ignored it. I wasn't putting myself in a position to relive the glory days or delude myself into questioning whether I'd been too harsh or, worse, somehow wrong.

Ford had hurt me. Period. Not maliciously, not in any calculated way. That wasn't the kind of guy he was. But his thoughtlessness had been even worse. It had showed me exactly where his priorities lay, and I'd finally given up the foolish hope that they'd ever be with me. No more pining. No more wasted effort dreaming of a future where my best friend ever saw me as anything more than one of the guys. I'd moved on with my life without him at the center.

In a sense, he'd done me a favor. I'd thoroughly learned my lesson that men couldn't be trusted. That they'd never stay. That I'd never be important. So I treated them accordingly. As friends or the occasional plaything for mutual itch scratching. Nothing more. If I had the odd pang of longing when I looked at the likes of Willa and Sawyer or Caroline and Hoyt, well, I was only human. But romantic entanglements simply weren't a priority for me. I cared far more about the family I'd made and the business I'd built.

I needed to get to that business in the next hour.

I was expecting deliveries to come in on the next ferry, including a special order of winter seasonal hops that Monty had been pestering me about for weeks. "C'mon, Keeley. Time to head home."

My pup clamped her ball between her teeth and laid down on the beach, giving me her best sad-pupper face. The same one that had prompted me to bring her home from the shelter when I'd stopped by "just to look." Those big blue eyes and floppy ears had done me in completely, just like they were trying to do now.

"We've already been out here for an hour." The winter wind was picking up, whipping hair across my face.

She dropped her ball between her extended forelegs and barked, obviously determined to nego-tiate. This wasn't a new game. My girl was nothing if not persistent, and she knew exactly how to play me.

"I have to go to work." I planted my hands on my hips, trying to look stern.

Her tail began a hopeful wag, and I knew what she really wanted. The same thing she always wanted when she got like this.

"You wanna go hang with Pop today?" He spoiled her rotten with treats and belly rubs, but I couldn't really blame him. She had that effect on everyone.

Keeley barked and snatched up her ball, shooting past me to head for my Jeep, her nails clicking against the wooden deck boards of the boardwalk as she ran.

Knew that would work. The two of them mutually adored each other. Pop spoiled her shamelessly, but I couldn't bring myself to try to rein him in. Besides, if he was spoiling his granddog, he was less likely to be out doing something strenuous or dangerous, like trying to catch another marlin to replace Marv. He might be in denial of his age, but I was sure as hell aware of it, and of the fact that he couldn't do everything he used to. The last time he'd overdone it, he'd ended up in the ER.

Keeley leapt into the backseat with her usual enthusiasm, and we made the short drive from the beach to home. A delivery van from Beachcomber Bargains was parked in front of the cottage next door, with a couple of guys hauling in a cream-colored sofa through the narrow front door. Huh. I wondered if the owners had decided to shift into the vacation rental market instead of property rental. So many people on the island had because tourism was a big chunk of what kept Hatterwick running. But I hated to see the housing market for locals continuing to shrink. God knew, it was hard enough for the people who actually lived here year round to find affordable places as it was.

As soon as I opened the door, Keeley jumped out and made a beeline for next door, her golden fur a streak of sunshine against the weathered boardwalk.

"No! Keeley! Come. Damn it."

I'd gotten spoiled in the off season, not having to keep her on a leash all the time. With fewer tourists around, she'd had more freedom to roam our stretch of beach. I hurried after her, ready to apologize to the owner or property manager or whoever was overseeing the furniture delivery.

A delighted female laugh told me at least they didn't sound pissed.

I stepped into the house. "I'm so sorry. She got away from me." Then I stopped dead at the sight of my dog giving Peyton a tongue bath. The girl sprawled on the floor, giggling, while my traitor of a dog showed where her true loyalties lay.

"Hey Bree! Hey Keeley. Who's a good girl? You're a good girl."

Keeley's tail went into full helicopter mode.

My brain didn't want to work. "What are you doing here?" A dozen possibilities flashed through my mind, each more unlikely than the last.

"Moving in."

I couldn't have heard her correctly. The words bounced around in my head like a pinball, refusing to make sense.

"I'm sorry?" My voice came out higher than usual, squeaking like a rusty door hinge.

"Hey, neighbor."

Every cell in my body went on high alert at the sound of that voice. The deep rumble of it sent an unwanted shiver down my spine. I forced myself to turn and face Ford, doing my best to maintain a neutral expression despite the way my heart hammered against my ribs. "Neighbor?"

But, of course, I already knew. My mind just didn't want to accept reality. The universe, it seemed, had a twisted sense of humor and an apparent vendetta against my peace of mind.

"We're the new tenants." To his credit, Ford had the good grace to not be cocky or blasé about it. There was a definite look of concern in those familiar green eyes.

"Ah." Points to me for making that a noncommittal noise instead of the scream I'd have preferred. My throat felt tight, like I was trying to swallow sand. I jerked my head toward the backyard. "Talk to you for a minute?"

"Sure."

He beat me to the door that led out to the back patio, opening it like a gentleman and waving me through. I ignored the height and breadth of him as I passed, though it was harder than it should have been. Ignored, too, the fit of the gray henley over the muscles the Navy had apparently honed to perfection. The scent of his soap—something clean and masculine—drifted past as I moved by him. I didn't quite manage to ignore the ink peeking out from the sleeves he'd shoved up to his elbows, revealing muscular forearms that spoke of years of physical labor. When had he gotten all those tattoos?

Focus!

Ford shut the door and placed himself between me and the house. Deliberately blocking Peyton's view of us because he thought I was going to lose my shit on him? It wasn't the worst idea in the world, considering the way my blood pressure had just spiked through the roof.

I kept my voice low, though my fingers itched to grab his stupidly broad shoulders and shake him. "Here? You're telling me that of all the rental property available on the island, you had to choose *here?* Next door to me?"

"Peyton chose. I figure she's had few enough choices the past several months. It was something I could give her. And she likes you." His voice was maddeningly reasonable, those eyes watching me with an intensity that made my skin prickle.

Well, what the hell could I say to that? Her situation tugged at something deep inside me that I didn't want to examine too closely.

"Though, to be completely fair, it may also be

because she loves your dog, and she hasn't managed to wear me down enough in a week to get her one." His mouth quirked up on one side in that half-smile that used to make my heart flip. Still did, damn it.

I felt my lips twitch. No. *No.* I was not going to smile. The kid was a little operator. I had to respect that about her, the way she'd managed to get exactly what she wanted without actually asking for it directly. But this was a fucking disaster. It put the man I'd done my level best to forget *right here,* in my space, where I couldn't avoid him or the memories that came with him.

Ford folded those massive arms, rocking back on his heels. "Look, I know this isn't what you'd have chosen. I'm sorry about that. I'll try to keep Peyton out of your way."

Any urge to smile evaporated, and I shot him a fulminating glare, anger rising hot and fast in my chest. "Don't you dare. She needs to know she has allies. Whatever... issues there are between us, she can count on me." The words came out fierce and protective, surprising even me with their intensity.

His face softened with gratitude, his eyes warming in a way that made my heart stutter. "Thank you."

I didn't want praise for doing what was simply the bare minimum of being a good human. "I don't want your thanks, Ford. Just do right by that kid."

"I'm doing my best."

I nodded. I knew he would. Family was everything to Ford. It always had been.

He opened his mouth to say something else, but I was already moving past him, reaching for the door. My fingers trembled slightly on the handle as I tried to ignore the gravitational pull of him. "I need to collect Keeley. I've gotta get cleaned up for work."

With one last quick goodbye to Peyton, and an absent, "Good luck with the move," to them both, I made my escape back to my own house, practically running down the wooden steps.

But the moment I shut myself inside, I collapsed back against the door, my heart hammering against my ribs like it was trying to break free.

How the hell was I going to survive having him right next door?

CHAPTER 16
FORD

"I'll be here after school to pick you up." Sutter's Ferry was small enough Peyton could walk home from school, but a lot could happen in a mile and a half. If the day went badly—if some asshat teenager decided to pick on her the way Zack had picked on Bree—I wanted to be there to do damage control. The thought of her getting bullied made my jaw clench. I might be new to this whole parenting thing, but protecting her was an instinct I didn't have to learn.

Did Peyton's massive eye roll mean I was doing something right as a parent? God, I hoped so. Every interaction felt like navigating a minefield.

"Right. Bye." Without actually looking me in the eye, she joined the stream of kids walking into the school. She gripped her backpack straps so tightly her knuckles were white. I watched her disappear into the crowd, fighting the urge to follow her inside like some helicopter parent. Instead, I forced myself to stay put, reminding myself that hovering wouldn't help either of us.

Damn it. I knew she was nervous, and I didn't know how to make that any better. Maybe I could pick up ice cream for post-school therapy? Hell, I should probably look into actual therapy for her. Maybe for us both. This was a huge transition, and we were both feeling our way blind. A professional couldn't be a bad thing. I'd add it to the list that was already a half mile long. For now, I was going to do the first thing I'd done purely for myself in more than a week.

I turned toward the coast road that followed Pamlico Sound all the way to the far north end of the island, past the maritime forest and the intertidal marshes that Willa was turning into a wildlife sanctuary for the wild horses that roamed this end of Hatterwick. A trio of them wheeled away from the road as I approached, trotting back into the woods. This end of the island was otherwise uninhabited, except for Sutter House, the ancestral home of the island's founders. Willa had inherited it from her grandparents when they passed, along with pretty much everything else associated with the Sutter legacy. She and Sawyer had moved in after they eloped last year.

Sawyer had done a lot of work updating the place, and it showed. The three-story shingle-sided house with multiple gabled roofs stood proudly on its perch above the beach. The multitude of windows shone, and the white trim stood out, crisp and bright. It was one of the few structures on the island that had never been wiped out by the hurricanes that frequently battered the Outer Banks. I knew Sawyer would do everything in his power to see that remained true.

I parked in the crushed-shell drive that curved out front and headed for the side door leading into the kitchen. The door opened before I could knock. Sawyer took one look at me and smirked. "You gonna need something stiffer than coffee?"

"Little early for bourbon, so I'll take the coffee and be grateful." I trailed him inside. I'd been out here just once before, for a party they'd thrown when all of us got back on island for our delayed holiday celebration. God, had that just been a couple of weeks ago? "Where's your bride?"

"Went into town for a volunteer day at the animal shelter. She thought you might want some... how did she put it? Quality, one-on-one guy time." He handed over a steaming mug. I recognized it as one of Mimi's.

"She's not wrong." There hadn't been time to update Sawyer and the rest of the guys about more than the basics since I'd gotten Bree's phone call. Rios and Jace were already back at their duty stations, but I had never been more grateful that Sawyer was retired. The whole situation had my head spinning, and I needed someone to talk to who wasn't direct family.

"So. How you doin', Papa?" His voice held equal parts amusement and concern.

Because I finally could, I set the coffee aside and did what I'd been tempted to do from the beginning. I bent and tucked my head between my knees, trying to get my racing thoughts under control. The position reminded me of track meets from a lifetime ago. But the pressure to perform back then had been nothing compared to this.

"That good, huh?" Sawyer's hand landed on my shoulder with a reassuring squeeze.

I blew out a long breath. "I am overwhelmed as fuck. In the span of a week, I found out I have a daughter, broke the news to my moms, proved her paternity, got emergency custody, got all her dependency shit sorted, rented and partially furnished a house..." The list felt endless, and saying it all out loud only emphasized how much my life had changed in such a short time.

"That's next door to Bree. We're coming back to that."

Of course he'd heard.

"—gotten her enrolled in school, and otherwise effectively turned every single aspect of my life entirely upside down. I've made arrangements for my stuff to be packed up and shipped back from Japan, and for all the things that were Peyton's and her mom's that have been in storage to be shipped cross country so she'll have some things that are truly hers. And I just dropped her off at school. Where she's in the eighth fucking grade. I have a kid, and she's almost in *high school*." That nearly had me putting my head between my knees again.

"You sure you don't want something stronger than coffee?" Sawyer gestured toward the bar, where I knew he kept the good bourbon stashed away.

"I already feel like a failure as a parent, so day drinking doesn't seem like quite the thing." My hands tightened around the coffee mug, drawing comfort from its warmth.

Sawyer squeezed my shoulder again, his grip steady and reassuring. "Ford, man, give yourself a break. You've been a dad for barely more than a week. And I'd say you've accomplished a hell of a lot. What are you gonna do about the Navy?"

"I considered a dependency discharge, but my

superiors think they can still use me remotely." I'd gotten word on that yesterday, and the relief had nearly knocked me sideways. "So the rest of my contract will be transitioned to the Reserves. It means I can be here most of the time, and I don't have to worry about unemployment. At least not for a while yet." The thought of trying to navigate a civilian job search on top of everything else had been giving me cold sweats.

"That's good. You're doing what you can to give her stability. I'm sure she needs that after everything she's been through. How did Mama Flo and Mimi take the sudden news of their grandma status? I bet they were shocked as hell."

"Like champs. Because they're rock stars. They've been amazing about the whole thing, actually. They're not exactly thrilled I rented a house instead of staying out with them, but I think, given all the time I need to make up for, it'll be important for Peyton and me to have our own space. Plus, she needs somewhere that feels like it belongs to her, you know? Somewhere she can put down roots."

"Makes sense." He kicked back against the kitchen counter, cradling his own mug, steam curling up into the air between us. "So, are we gonna talk about the fact that Bree finally talked to you for the first time in a decade? That had to make you feel... some kind of way."

He was fishing, I knew. I wasn't about to talk about what went wrong between me and Bree. I never had. I'd simply accepted full responsibility for the dissolution of our friendship. Because it had been my fault. The weight of that knowledge had sat heavy in my gut for a decade.

"It was a shock by itself. A bigger one to find out why she was calling. I don't think my brain has had the chance to really catch up on any of it." The words felt inadequate to describe the earthquake that had rocked my world in the past few days. It was like trying to drink from a fire hose.

"Uh-huh. And now you've moved in next door." He folded his arms. The look on his face said he wasn't buying my attempt to dodge the subject.

I jerked a shrug that was far more nonchalant than I actually felt. My coffee sloshed dangerously close to the rim of my mug. "It was the house Peyton chose. I guess I could have steered her toward one of the others, but she likes Bree. More to the point, she trusts her, and I don't think she has many adults who have that honor right now." And if I was being honest with myself, which I tried to avoid doing too often these days, having Bree next door felt both like torture and coming home.

Sawyer soaked that in, his gray eyes thoughtful as he studied my face. "The two of them have a lot in common."

"Yeah. Yeah, they do. And I'll admit I have a hard time looking at Peyton and not being reminded of Bree when she first came to the island, even with the age difference." The parallel was impossible to ignore, like some cosmic joke the universe was playing on all of us.

"Does that make it easier or harder?"

"Maybe some of both? I hope it means I handle Peyton better because I have some clue what she's been through. But it's definitely had me thinking a lot about the past." I paused, shoving a hand through my hair in frustration. "I fucking miss her, Saw."

"I know you do. You always have. It's gutted you not to have her in your life." He arched an expectant brow. "So what are you gonna do about it now that you're back on-island?"

"I'm not gonna harass her. Bree made her position about me clear a long time ago."

"But?"

"But, I'll admit that my kid just might be the bridge I need to at least get her to hear my apology. Which is honestly more than I ever thought I'd get." A chance to apologize was so much less than what I wanted. I didn't know if I ought to have actual hope now or not, but I was a natural optimist, so it was a struggle not to wish for a second chance to make things right.

Sawyer crossed the kitchen to join me at the table. "Look, man, I've never stuck my nose in about whatever went wrong between you two. As you say, Bree made her position clear, and she's not precisely a forgiving woman. She's had a lot of life experience that made her that way. She doesn't believe what people say. She believes what they do. Seems to me that if you want her back—in any capacity—the only way to earn that is to show her with action the thing she needs to see. Whatever that may be."

His words hit just a little too close to home, and it made me wonder if he suspected what had really gone down all those years ago. But he wasn't wrong. I'd destroyed Bree's trust, broken a promise that had been sacrosanct to her. Action was the only way past those mile-high defenses. And for the first time in forever, I was finally in a place where I could do something about it.

I just had to decide whether I actually should.

CHAPTER 17

PEYTON

I hunched lower in my seat, pretending to read my history textbook while feeling twenty pairs of eyes burning into my back. Second day at Sutter's Ferry Middle School, and I was already the main attraction in this small-town freak show.

"That's her," someone whispered two rows over. "Ford Donoghue's secret kid."

I gripped my pencil tighter, focusing on the page about the Revolutionary War that I wasn't actually reading. The whispers followed me everywhere—hallways, cafeteria, even the bathroom. It was the same song, different verse from what I'd experienced in Oregon. Back there, I'd been the girl with the dead mom. Here I was the secret baby who showed up out of nowhere. The girl whose dad didn't even know she existed until last week.

At least in Oregon, people had waited until I was out of earshot to talk about me. Nobody here had gotten up the nerve to talk to say anything directly to my face, but everywhere I went, I heard conversations starting and stopping abruptly when I came into the room that way that said everyone was for sure talking about you.

I wanted to pull up my hood and hide until the day was over, but that wasn't an option. Hoods weren't allowed up in class. It was part of the dress code.

Stupid rules.

The clock on the wall tick tick ticked, counting down to lunch period. That was a whole other nightmare. I didn't have anybody to sit with, and no part of me wanted to run the gauntlet of finding somewhere to sit that didn't encroach on some pre-existing group's space. Maybe I could go to the library and find a quiet corner to read. I could inhale my sandwich on the way. Would I get in trouble for that?

The bell rang before I'd figured out my plan. Damn it.

I shoved my history textbook and spiral notebook into my backpack, trying to be quick about it. The faster I could get out of here, the better chance

I had of finding some hiding spot before the lunch rush.

"Hey, you're the new girl, Peyton, right?"

I froze, one hand still gripping my math folder. A girl with dark curly hair tied back in a ponytail was looking at me from the next row over. She had freckles scattered across her nose and was wearing a bright yellow sweater that somehow didn't make her look like a walking banana.

I nodded, waiting for whatever was coming next. Probably some nosy question about my dad or why I'd shown up out of nowhere.

"I'm Madison." She smiled, revealing a set of blue braces. "You looked kind of lost yesterday at lunch."

"Yeah, well..." I shrugged, not sure what else to say. Was she making fun of me?

"Why don't you come have lunch with us?" She hitched her own backpack higher on her shoulder. "We sit by the windows in the corner. The table's not super crowded or anything."

I blinked, trying to process what was happening. This girl—Madison—was actually inviting me to sit with her? Not because she wanted dirt on my situation, but just... because?

"For real?" The words slipped out before I could stop them.

Madison laughed, but it wasn't mean. "Yeah, for real. Unless you've already got plans?"

"No, no plans." A warm feeling spread through my chest. "Yeah, thanks. That would be... thanks."

"Cool. Come on, then."

As we walked out of the classroom together, I remembered what Ford—my dad... that was still weird to think about—had said last night about how he was always the guy who befriended the new kid when he was in school. Maybe he wasn't totally wrong about how things worked here.

I followed Madison through the hallway, dodging clusters of students rushing to lunch. She, of course, knew exactly where she was going. She'd probably lived here her whole life. I'd gotten a tour before I started, but I was still getting my bearings.

"So the middle school and high school share a campus." Madison gestured vaguely to our right as we passed a set of double doors. "All their buildings are on that side, and ours are over here. We share common areas, like the cafeteria and gym, though."

"That's... efficient, I guess?" In Oregon, our schools had been completely separate.

Madison shrugged. "Small town. It's cheaper than building two of everything. The high schoolers have different lunch periods than us, so we don't really run into them much. Except sometimes in the gym if PE schedules overlap."

We turned a corner, and I tried to mentally map our route. Yesterday I'd just followed the crowd, but I still felt disoriented. Every hallway looked identical—beige walls, blue lockers, motivational posters about perseverance and teamwork.

"Is it weird having a dad who just... appeared?" Madison immediately clamped her hand over her mouth. "Sorry! My mom says I have no filter. You don't have to answer that."

I almost stopped walking. Here it was—the real reason she'd invited me to lunch. Information mining.

"It's fine," I said, even though it wasn't. "And yeah, it's weird."

Madison nodded earnestly. "I bet. My parents are divorced, and when my dad got remarried, I suddenly had this stepmom I had to deal with. Not the same thing at all, but still weird."

Something about her straightforward admission made me relax a little. "Does your stepmom suck?"

"Nah, she's actually pretty cool. Makes amazing cookies." Madison pushed through a set of double doors, and we entered the cafeteria. The noise hit me like a wall—hundreds of voices all talking at once, the clatter of trays, chairs scraping against floors.

I thought of Mimi's snickerdoodles. "My... grandma makes really good cookies." That felt so weird to say. I'd never had a grandparent before. Mom's parents had died in a car crash before I was born. Now I had two grandmas. That was pretty cool. Maybe. Probably.

"Our table's over there." Madison pointed to the far corner where three other kids were already sitting. "Come on, I'll introduce you."

Madison led me to the table where three kids were already sitting. My stomach clenched with new-kid anxiety. Would they be nice? Would they care that I was Ford Donoghue's surprise daughter?

"Guys, this is Peyton. She's new." Madison slid onto the bench. "Peyton, this is Trevor, Sarah, and Jake."

Trevor was a lanky boy with sandy hair who barely looked up from his phone. "Hey."

Sarah waved enthusiastically. She had a pixie cut and bright blue glasses. "Hi! Where'd you move from?"

"Oregon." I hovered awkwardly, my hand clenching my backpack strap for dear life, until Madison patted the empty space beside her.

Jake, a stocky kid with dark hair, nodded at me. "Cool. That's like, super far."

"Yeah." I sat down, grateful for the spot Madison had saved me. From here, I could see through the windows to the grassy area outside.

The view of open space made the crowded cafeteria feel a little less suffocating.

I pulled out my lunch—a brown paper bag that Ford had packed this morning. He'd stood in the kitchen looking completely lost, asking if I preferred turkey or ham. It was weird watching a grown man so completely out of his element.

I unfolded the top of the bag and pulled out my sandwich. That's when I saw it—a bright yellow Post-it note stuck to the plastic wrap. In messy handwriting: "Have a good day, kid. :)"

A smiley face. He'd actually drawn a smiley face.

I quickly flipped the note over before anyone could see it. What kind of goofy person put notes in a middle schooler's lunch? My new dad, apparently. I should have been mortified—I was thirteen, not six—but something warm unfurled in my chest instead.

Mom used to leave notes in my lunch too, when I was little. She'd draw little cartoons or write silly jokes. I hadn't thought about that in ages.

I slipped the note into my pocket while the others weren't looking. It was totally childish, and I was definitely too old for lunch notes with smiley faces, but... it felt kind of good that he'd thought to do it.

Movement beyond the window caught my attention. I expected to see another student or a teacher walking by. Instead, I saw *him*. The guy who'd been on the ferry. The one I'd seen later that night outside of Home Port. He was talking to someone. A woman. I couldn't see her face, but her body language was rigid, like they were having an argument. They stood in the shadow of one of the high school building across the green space. Mystery dude didn't seem too happy with how the conversation was going, either.

As I watched, the woman waved a dramatic arm. Telling him to go? Must have been because dude broke away and began walking in the direction of the cafeteria. The sidewalk he followed went right by the window where I was sitting. As he passed, he glanced inside. Our eyes met, and again, I felt that shiver of *ook*. Then he *winked* at me.

I jerked back.

Madison leaned toward me, frowning. "Hey, are you okay? Something wrong?"

I blinked, pulling my attention back to the lunch table. "No, I'm fine."

"You look like you saw a ghost." She followed my gaze toward the window. "What were you looking at?"

"Do you know that guy?" I pointed, but when I looked back, the sidewalk was empty. The man had vanished like he'd never been there at all.

Madison squinted through the glass. "What guy?"

"Never mind." I took a bite of my sandwich to avoid saying anything else. My appetite had disappeared, but I needed something to do with my mouth besides talk.

What was I going to say, anyway? That some random creepy dude I'd spotted on the ferry had just winked at me through the window? That would sound completely paranoid. Or worse, like I was making stuff up for attention. The last thing I needed was for people to think I was some weirdo who invented stories about strange men to seem interesting. If I started talking about mysterious men following me around, I'd cement my reputation as the school freak before my second day was even over.

I looked back out at the green space. The woman was still there, looking in the direction the guy had disappeared. I couldn't tell if she was annoyed or upset or what. Didn't matter. I didn't know her. I didn't know him. There was no reason to think any of this had anything to do with me, and I had friends to make.

CHAPTER 18

BREE

The sun had set, cloaking my little cottage in darkness. Damn, I hated winter hours. It felt like time for bed by six PM. Considering I owned a bar that stayed open late, nights didn't usually bother me, but they just stretched out so long this time of year. Temperatures had dipped into the thirties, and all I wanted to do was curl up with Keeley and a movie. Something with a lot of action. Maybe *The Old Guard*. That one was always good for some quality female-led ass kicking.

I'd just pulled a pizza from the freezer when someone knocked at my front door. My shoulders tensed. What if it was Peyton? Or worse, Ford? I wasn't prepared for unplanned drop-bys. There hadn't actually been any yet, but I figured it was only a matter of time. Tonight might be the night. Peyton had started school a couple days ago. Which I knew only because everyone on the island was talking about it, not because Ford had told me.

What if she wanted to talk about it?

Damn it. I was in my comfiest, frumpiest sweatshirt and yoga pants. Which shouldn't actually matter. I wasn't trying to impress either of them. But I needed more armor before our next encounter, because the kid got under my skin. And her dad... Her dad was a complication I wanted to go back to avoiding.

Keeley's tail thumped against the floor as she lifted her head.

"If that's Ford, you're fired as a guard dog." I padded to the door in sock feet.

But instead of my new neighbors, I found Willa and Gabi on my doorstep, loaded down with bags that clinked ominously. Roy's massive black form crowded behind them, his tail wagging ninety to nothing as he strained toward the door and Keeley.

"No." I crossed my arms, planting my feet in what was probably a futile attempt to block their entry. "Whatever this is, no."

Gabi shouldered past me anyway, hauling what looked suspiciously like several bottles of wine and a canvas bag that smelled divine. "You've skipped the last two girls' nights, and we're staging an intervention."

"Because I've been busy. And we finished our rewatch of *Ted Lasso*." That had been our excuse for the last couple months of girls' nights, our collective obsession with the show giving us a perfect reason to gather weekly. "We're between shows."

Willa followed her inside, Roy darting around her to greet Keeley with enthusiastic sniffs. "We all know you're not busy. You're in prime avoidance mode, and we're your friends, so we're not letting you wallow alone."

"I'm not avoiding anything." The protest sounded weak even to my own ears, and the knowing looks they both shot me made it clear they weren't buying it either.

"Sure you're not." Gabi started unpacking containers of what smelled like Caroline's famous lasagna. Damn it, I had a real weakness for her sister's lasagna. The aroma of garlic and herbs filled my kitchen, making my stomach growl in betrayal. "Which is why you're about to eat frozen pizza alone."

I crossed my arms, trying to ignore the way my mouth was watering. "Maybe I like frozen pizza."

"Nobody likes frozen pizza that much." Willa uncorked the first bottle of wine with practiced efficiency, the pop echoing in my kitchen. "We brought real food and better company. And you're going to tell us everything."

"There's nothing to tell." I watched Roy curl up with Keeley in his favorite spot by the kitchen island, clearly settling in for the duration.

"Bree." Gabi's voice went gentle, taking on that doctor-knows-best tone she'd perfected during her residency. "The guy you've been avoiding for a decade just moved in next door with the teenage daughter no one knew existed. There's plenty to tell."

I accepted the glass Willa handed me, knowing resistance was futile. The rich burgundy promised a temporary escape I desperately needed. "Fine. But I'm not talking about the past."

"We'll start with the present, then." Gabi began dishing up the lasagna. "How are you really handling all this?"

Every instinct I had shouted at me to deflect. I didn't do all this feelings shit. It never solved anything and just left me feeling worse than I did to begin with. I'd done stints in therapy over the years. I knew all this was because I was shit at attachment —what had my therapist called it? An avoidant attachment style?—and had trust issues out the wazoo. Life had done a damned good job presenting me with plenty of evidence justifying the continuation of all those trust issues.

But these women had worked hard to get close to me, and they'd been really good friends. I knew they were doing all of this for what they perceived to be my own good. And considering both of them were in stable, committed relationships, maybe they weren't wrong.

Not that I was looking for one of those.

The reason why was right next door.

"I'm crawling out of my skin." The admission slipped out without my permission, my fingers fidgeting with the stem of my wineglass.

"Because you're afraid of running into Ford, or because Peyton reminds you of you when you were a kid?" Willa asked.

I took a long sip of wine while I tried to organize my thoughts. "Both. I get antsy every time Ford comes home, but I get through it because I know it's never for more than a week at a time. We both know the rules of engagement, so I just have to wait him out. But now? Now he's home. Presumably for good. I know I won't be able to continue to avoid him in the same way. I wouldn't be able to even if they hadn't moved in next door."

"And you won't try because of Peyton." Willa watched me with those observant hazel eyes that always seemed to see straight through my defenses.

I sighed, the sound heavy with resignation. "No."

"Tell me something. That afternoon she showed up at the Brewhouse, Sawyer and I were there. You could have let him call Ford and run interference on all of it. He'd have happily saved you the stress of that."

"I know." The words came out barely above a whisper.

"So why didn't you let him? That's not a criticism. I'm legitimately curious." She leaned forward, elbows propped on her knees, waiting for my answer.

I bought myself some time by forking a bite of lasagna. For a moment, my attention was distracted by the herbed ricotta filling and bright tomato sauce. Was there anything better than homemade pasta? The warmth and comfort of it settled in my stomach, a welcome buffer against the weight of this conversation. But my friends waited with expectant gazes.

"She would have run. She came all this way fueled by desperation, with this idea in her head of finding her dad the only thing keeping the fear at bay. Once she got here and found out that Ford wasn't around, she was getting ready to bolt. I saw it in her eyes. If anything had happened to her because I was too chickenshit to call him after all this time, I would never have forgiven myself."

"Bree, you're many things. Chicken shit isn't one of them," Gabi insisted.

Oh, how wrong she was. But I was in no mood to disabuse her of that opinion.

"So that's why you brought her home with you that first night?" Willa prompted.

"I figured she'd be more likely to trust someone who'd been where she is. I was a lot younger when it happened to me, but I still understand it. It's a shitty thing, not belonging to anyone. Always waiting for the other shoe to drop. If I could keep her safe until he got here, I had to. Even if it meant having to face him again."

Gabi topped off the wine I hadn't even realized I'd drained. "And how did that go?"

"I didn't murder him." *Or throw myself into his arms.* "I'll call that a win."

I could still see him standing in my entryway, taking up all the space, looking exhausted and terrified and more vulnerable than I'd ever seen him. Ford Donoghue had always been a rock. Seeing him like that had left me... weak and wanting to be there for him. The urge to comfort him had been so strong I'd had to dig my nails into my palms to keep from reaching out. But that wasn't who we were to each other. Not anymore. We'd burned those bridges more than a decade ago.

"You helped him look for her when she ran off." Willa's soft voice was a question of its own.

I twitched my shoulders, trying to appear casual even as my wine glass trembled slightly in my grip. "He asked. I was the one most likely to figure out where she'd gone. And I was right. That wasn't for him. It was for Peyton." The words sounded hollow even to my own ears, but I clung to them like a lifeline.

Neither of them looked as if they believed me, but at least they didn't call me out on it. Their shared glance of understanding made me want to crawl under the table.

Willa cut her pasta into small bites, not quite looking at me. "I know he hurt you. But it's been a very long time, and it seems like the two of them are going to be in your life, whether you like it or not. Is there any possibility that this could be a chance for the two of you to start over?"

"No." The answer was instant. Visceral. "I'll be there for Peyton because she needs all the people in her corner she can get, but I'm not opening the door to Ford again." My fingers tightened around my fork until my knuckles went white, and I forced myself to relax my grip.

Letting him back into my life in any capacity was a recipe for heartbreak, because he could never be what I needed him to be. I was safer having no expectations at all.

CHAPTER 19

FORD

"Mr. Donoghue, I appreciate you coming by with Peyton." Police Chief Bill Carson was all easy smiles as he welcomed us to the police station. Given how he'd harassed Rios and Sawyer in our youth, I didn't trust the casual attitude one bit. But when the chief of police asked you to bring your kid by the station, you did it.

"I assure you, this is just a formality."

Beside me, Peyton practically vibrated with jackrabbit energy, clearly anxious about being here. Her case worker hadn't mentioned any kind of delinquent behavior when we'd spoken. Maybe this anxiety was just over the possibility that something might threaten her new place here. I'd just have to do my best to reassure her. Nothing and nobody was going to take her away from me.

"Is this to wrap up some paperwork around the missing persons report that was filed in Oregon?" I asked, keeping my voice carefully neutral despite the tension coiling in my gut.

"Not exactly. Y'all want anything to drink? A Coke or something?" Carson's casual tone only heightened my suspicion that everything was not as it seemed.

I glanced at Peyton, watching as she twisted the hem of her hoodie. Her face had gone a shade paler since we'd walked in.

"No. Sir," she added.

"Alright then. Come on back."

We followed Carson down a short hallway and into a small conference room that was dominated by a table and six chairs. Two other people were already inside. I pegged the woman as late forties, with long dark hair pulled back into a tail, sharp gray eyes, and a suit wrinkled like she'd been in the car for hours. Her companion, a thirty-something black man with wire-rimmed glasses and an equally wrinkled suit, shot a smile that was probably supposed to put us at ease. Instead, every protective instinct I had roared to life.

I edged in front of Peyton. "Who are you?"

Carson shut the door behind us with a decisive click that echoed in the small space, further amping my sense of having been trapped. "Special Agents Olivia Burns and Cedric Langston, both of the FBI."

"Portland office," Agent Burns clarified, her gray eyes sharp and assessing as they moved between me and my daughter.

What the actual fuck did the FBI want with my kid? My heart rate kicked up a notch, and my mind raced through possibilities, none of them good.

Peyton and I were brand new to each other. While Mimi and Mom had initiated hugs with her, I had no idea how she felt about men, so I'd been letting her set the pace on physical contact. But now I reached out, placing an arm around her shoulders and pulling her into my side. She was trembling, barely perceptible, but there. No way did I want her feeling alone in whatever this was. When she didn't pull away, I counted it as a win, even as dread settled like lead in my gut.

"Why are we here?"

"We just have some questions," Langston said.

I didn't trust that casual tone in the least. "Do we need an attorney?"

Burns angled her head. "Do you?"

Oh, hell no. My mom had taught me better than

that. "I want someone to tell me right now exactly what interest you have in my minor child."

Rather than answer, Burns sat. "Mr. Donoghue, did you have any contact with Casey Walsh, the child's mother?"

What the fuck? "Not since we were eighteen. No."

"You weren't a part of your daughter's life?"

It was a fair and reasonable question, but it put my back up, nonetheless. It was probably meant to throw me off my game. "I wasn't aware I had a daughter until two weeks ago. But that sure as hell doesn't mean I'll give you the chance to railroad her." My voice came out harder than intended, but I wasn't about to apologize. Not when it came to protecting Peyton.

Something sparked in the woman's eyes. Annoyance? Approval? Whatever it was, Burns kept it carefully contained behind that professional mask of hers.

Langston spread his hands. "We've gotten off on the wrong foot. Let's all sit down." His tone was conciliatory, but there was a tension in the set of his shoulders that made me wary. "Nobody's in any kind of trouble here."

I doubted that. Federal agents would hardly trek all the way to Hatterwick if something wasn't wrong. But I nudged Peyton toward a chair and took the one beside her, positioning myself slightly forward, a shield between her and whatever was coming. The weight of her fear pressed against my shoulder like a physical thing.

Langston offered a sympathetic smile to Peyton. "You've had a lot of changes the past few months. I'm sorry about your mother. Losing her had to be hard."

The feds were aware of Casey's death? That couldn't be good. Had they been watching her for some reason? My stomach clenched as possibilities, each worse than the last, flashed through my mind.

Peyton shot a glance at me, then back at him before muttering, "Yeah." Her fingers twisted in her lap, worrying at a loose thread on her jeans. The defensive hunch of her shoulders made her look even younger than thirteen.

"Did your mom ever talk about her work?"

Peyton jerked her shoulders. "Sometimes. Mostly complaining about the stupid people who didn't do their paperwork right and made more work for her."

Langston flashed a rueful grin. "We all hate those coworkers." He was doing a good job of making this sound more like a casual conversation than the interrogation it was obviously meant to be.

Burns leaned forward. "Did she ever bring work home?" The sharp edge to his question cut through Langston's carefully crafted atmosphere.

"No. She said work was for work hours and home was for family time." Peyton's chin came up slightly, a touch of pride in her voice.

"Admirable." Langston nodded. "Hard to maintain sometimes, though. Did she ever get calls about work after hours?" He kept his tone light, but I could see the intensity in his eyes as he waited for her answer.

"I don't know." There was an edge to Peyton's voice that was part sarcasm, part belligerence, and all teenager. I wasn't about to call her on it under the circumstances. These two were fishing for something, and she knew it. The way she'd drawn into herself, shoulders hunched, told me she was getting more uncomfortable by the minute.

"Did you ever meet anybody from her work?" Burns pressed. "Any office buddies? Her boss? Maybe at a company picnic or holiday party?"

Were they investigating Casey herself or whoever Casey had worked for? The intensity of their questions made my internal radar ping. This wasn't just about a runaway kid anymore.

"What is this about?" I shifted slightly closer to Peyton. "Why would a thirteen-year-old kid be privy to any knowledge about her mother's work?"

And what information were they so desperate to find that they'd come all the way out here to get it? The hair on the back of my neck stood up as I waited for their answer.

"Kids soak up all kinds of things adults aren't aware of," Langston said smoothly, though his eyes had hardened at my interruption. "Did you have any contact with anybody from her work, Peyton? Even just in passing?"

"No."

"So you haven't seen anybody since she died?" The older agent's tone was deceptively casual. "Maybe at the funeral?"

Peyton frowned, her shoulders hunching inward. "Mom was cremated. And anyway, how would I know? I wasn't involved in any of that."

I really didn't like the direction this was going. Something about their questions and the way they kept circling back made my skin crawl.

Langston leaned forward, bracing his elbows on the table, his posture deliberately non-threatening even as his eyes remained sharp and focused. "Did you ever see anybody harassing your mom? Being rude to her or threatening her in any way? Even something that might have seemed small at the time?"

But Peyton was apparently done answering questions. Her face had gone pale, and her hands trembled slightly where they rested on the table. "Was somebody after my mom?"

Shit. She'd said Casey had died of an aneurism, but what if that hadn't been the truth? Or what if it had been incited rather than natural? There were probably ways to do that.

"We're not aware of anybody."

Which wasn't exactly a no.

My kid stared at them with an impressive degree of teenage disdain that probably should have terrified me for the years to come. "So you just expect me to believe that you followed me all the way across the country for no reason? Seriously, how stupid do you think I am?"

Both agents glanced at me, probably waiting to see if I was going to discipline her for rudeness, but hell, I was right there with her. The kid had a point, and I wasn't about to shut her down for calling out what we were both thinking.

"Neither of us is as stupid as you seem to believe. You're being very careful not to say what any of this is actually about. So let's get down to brass tacks. Is my daughter in some kind of danger?" I wasn't going to accept any more evasive non-answers.

After the barest of hesitations, Burns leaned back in her chair. "We have no reason to believe that she is."

That reply didn't exactly fill me with confidence, but I pressed on. "And she's not in any sort of trouble?"

"No." Another careful, measured response that revealed absolutely nothing.

"Then unless you're going to develop sudden transparency, I think we're done here. If you have any further questions, you can send them through our attorney." I pushed back from the table, the legs of my chair scraping against the floor with finality. "Let's go, Peyton."

She scrambled up beside me, and I kept my body between her and the agents as we headed for the door. Carson didn't try to stop us.

My blood boiled as we walked through the station. These people had no right coming here and interrogating my kid without proper representation. She'd been through enough losing her mom without dealing with some bullshit federal circus.

The afternoon sun hit my face as we stepped outside, making me squint against its harsh glare. I kept my hand protectively on Peyton's shoulder until we reached my car. Only then did I turn to her. "You okay?"

Peyton nodded, wrapping her arms around herself like she was trying to hold herself together. "Yeah."

"You have any idea what all that shit was

about?" I studied her face, looking for any hint of recognition or fear that might tell me more than her words.

"No." She wouldn't quite meet my eyes, but I didn't think it was because she was hiding anything. More like she was still processing the interrogation herself.

"Okay."

Her head snapped up, eyes wide with surprise. "That's it?"

I leaned against the driver's side door, trying to project calm and stability even though my insides were still churning. "That's it. Look, I know we're new to each other, but you're mine, and that means I'm always on your side. Got it?" My voice came out gruff with emotion I hadn't expected to feel quite so soon.

Her lower lip trembled for a long moment that had me wanting to pull her in for a crushing bear hug before she got it under control. The silence stretched out between us as she studied my face, like she was searching for the truth of my words. Finally, she whispered, "Got it. Thanks."

"C'mon. We'll go grab some ice cream to take the sting out of the algebra homework you still have to do."

She tugged open her door. "I didn't say I had algebra homework."

"You didn't have to. You have Mrs. Winslow, who I also had for Algebra I. She always assigns homework."

Peyton's eyes widened—in surprise or horror, I wasn't sure. "You had my algebra teacher?"

"Small town, kid. Small town. C'mon."

CHAPTER 20
BREE

"Why in the ever loving hell did I let you talk me into karaoke night?" I winced as Darren Delaney from the fish market mangled another note of "Sweet Caroline." The entire bar seemed to collectively cringe.

"It brings in business," Monty insisted, though his usual unflappable confidence wavered a bit. "Look at table six. They ordered three rounds just to get through Bob's set."

Darren's predecessor on stage had committed crimes against music I couldn't even talk about.

"And how many customers have we lost permanently?" I tried not to look directly at the makeshift stage area.

"Darling, you wound me. This was a stroke of

genius." Monty flinched as Darren's voice went sharp enough to kill on a particularly ambitious high note. I fought the urge to check the glass wall dividing the dining room from the brewing tanks for cracks. "Though perhaps we should institute some basic qualifying rounds."

I shot him a look. "*Now* you're thinking about quality control?"

"Well..." He gestured expansively with his free hand. "The liquid courage aspect is working beautifully. Just look at all these drink orders. But I may have underestimated the psychological trauma inflicted by prolonged exposure to tone-deaf amateur performers."

"You think?"

"At least the tips are good?" Monty offered weakly. "People seem to feel generous when they're drinking to dull the pain."

I had to laugh at that, even as I shook my head. "Next time you have a brilliant business idea, run it by me more than twenty-four hours in advance?"

"Where's the fun in that?" He grinned, but quickly sobered as Darren launched into an encore. "Though perhaps we should limit performers to one song each."

"Make that a hard rule, and I might forgive you for this nightmare." I grabbed two more beers for a desperate-looking couple at the end of the bar. "Eventually."

"Lord have mercy, my hearing aid's about to commit suicide." Milt cranked down the volume on his device, his weathered face pinched with pain.

"For once, you're the lucky one." Duck took a long pull of his beer. "The rest of us have to suffer through this with full audio."

"What was that?" Milt cupped his ear.

"He said you're lucky to be deaf!" Wally shouted, making me wince.

Pop leaned forward on his barstool. "Now Bree-girl, you know I support all your business decisions, but this..."

"Don't look at me." I held up my hands. "This was all Montgomery's doing."

"Ah, the fancy brewmaster strikes again." Cliff nodded sagely. "Remember when he wanted to do that wine and painting night?"

"That actually worked out fine," I defended.

Duck cackled. "Only 'cause you banned Wally after he painted something that looked like copulating possums instead of a sunset."

"It was abstract!" Wally protested.

"It was obscene," Pop countered. "Nearly gave Mrs. Henderson a heart attack."

"What about Mrs. Henderson?" Milt asked.

"Never mind!" they all chorused.

Monty swept by with fresh pretzels. "I hear you gentlemen critiquing my entertainment choices."

"Entertainment's a strong word for this torture," Duck muttered.

Monty sniffed primly. "I prefer to think of it as community building through shared adversity."

The Gray Beards exchanged looks before bursting into laughter.

"Boy, you could sell ice to an Eskimo." Pop wiped his eyes. "But maybe next time stick to trivia night?"

"Or bingo," Cliff suggested.

"What was that about my lumbago?" Milt asked.

I bit back a smile as I moved down the bar, leaving them to their usual bickering. At least they were having fun, even if it was at Monty's expense.

Half a dozen songs later, I was reasonably sure I was bleeding from the ears. Someone attempted to murder 'Total Eclipse of the Heart,' and the sound system squealed with feedback. I ducked behind the bar, as if that would somehow protect me from the assault to my senses. "Dear God, make it stop."

"Hey, Bree."

I shot to my feet so fast, I almost cracked my head on the counter.

Ford stood on the other side. I could only blame the crimes being perpetrated by microphone for not noticing he'd come in. My mouth dried up. This wasn't how we did things. For ten years, we'd perfected the art of careful avoidance, coordinating our movements through mutual friends to ensure we never had to interact. Those were the unwritten rules. But I supposed I blew those all to hell when I got involved with his kid.

As my heart hammered against my ribs, I fell back on my role as bartender. "What can I get you?"

"Just a beer. Dealer's choice. I've heard good things."

Yeah, he would only have heard because I'd all but banned him from this place. If I felt a little pinch about that behind my breastbone, I ignored it as I pulled him a pint of Island Time. He didn't grab the open stool nearby.

When I slid the glass across the bar, his fingers curled around it. "Can you get away for a bit? Just back to your office for a conversation. It's about Peyton."

Brain trauma from karaoke night had me nodding without hesitation, even though being alone with him was the last thing I wanted. "Monty, Sarah, I'm taking ten. My ears are ringing."

Ford followed me down the bar and into the hall. The moment he stepped into my office, I shut the door and breathed a sigh.

"You okay there?"

"I don't know. Do I have brains leaking out my ears? Because I'm pretty sure they've been liquified."

With a serious expression, he leaned in to check both sides of my head. "All clear. I take it the current performance is the rule rather than the exception?"

"I had no idea we had so many tone deaf people on the island. Never again. I don't care how much it gooses alcohol sales. Never again." Scrubbing both hands over my face, I did my best to focus on Ford. Then I immediately wished I hadn't because I was all too aware of my closet-sized office with his 6' 3" muscled frame taking up more than its fair share.

"Thanks for meeting with me."

Right. As if we'd set up something formal. Fine, if that was how he wanted to play it, I'd roll with it. "What's going on? Is Peyton okay? Is she getting hassled at school?"

"Not so far as I know. She's made a couple of friends, I think. At least some girls who invited her to sit with them at lunch, so that's a win. No, this is about something else." He scrubbed a hand down his own face, and I heard the rasp of his skin against the stubble darkening his jaw. My brain immediately remembered the feel of it beneath my own palms.

Focus.

"Carson called us in to the police station today."

That immediately wiped any memories of the past out of my brain. "What? Why?"

"There were two FBI agents waiting to talk to us. To her."

I blinked. Whatever I'd expected him to say, it hadn't been that. "FBI? What would they want with a child?"

"That's a good damned question. One they didn't answer. They asked her a lot of questions about Casey's work. They didn't clarify, but reading between the lines, it sounded like they might be investigating whoever she worked for. I don't know if they were trying to determine the extent of Casey's involvement or what."

"What did Peyton say?"

"She didn't know anything. Said Casey had a hard line between work and home. She didn't know any of her mom's coworkers, and Casey didn't talk about work. I don't know what they thought Peyton might know that made them come all the way out here."

That wasn't the only thing that struck me as odd. "Why now? Her mom died three months ago, right? They'd have had ample opportunity to ask all these questions of Peyton then."

"I asked her after if she had any idea what all this was about, and she said no."

"Do you believe her? Or do you think she's hiding something?"

Ford spread his hands and leaned back against my desk. "I don't know. I told her I did. That I'm on her side. I have no reason not to be. But I'm not gonna lie, Bree. I'm struggling here. I have no idea how to handle all this. I want to do right by her."

This man. He wanted so desperately to do the right thing, which was so much more than my own dad had ever done. Another few bricks in the wall I'd built between us crumbled, because I couldn't keep lying to myself that he was the callous guy I'd made him out to be in my head.

I found myself leaning back against the desk beside him, close enough that I felt the warmth of his thigh alongside mine. "I don't think there's a chapter in Parenting 101 about how to handle it when federal agents question your middle schooler." I considered the situation. "If they're coming to ask her about all of this now, three months out from Casey's death, that sounds like they're looking for something they think Casey might have had. Information maybe?"

"Seems like coming out and asking directly would've made a lot more sense."

"Do you think Casey was involved in something

shady?" I wasn't judging. My own mom had been a drug addict. She'd done things to support her habit that hadn't been legal.

"I have no idea. I'd have said no, but the truth is we spent two weeks together a million years ago. I really didn't know her. She was on her own with a baby to support. I don't know what she might have done to survive."

I could feel his grief over that, could see how he was struggling with the reality of all those lost years.

I laid a hand on his arm. "Stop it. Stop beating yourself up over all the things you didn't do the past fourteen years. You didn't know. You can't blame yourself for not doing things when you *didn't know*. She chose not to tell you she was pregnant. We may never know the why of that. And that sucks. I know that why is gonna gnaw at you. But you're doing all the things now. That's the only thing anyone can expect of you. Even you."

Ford's gaze shifted from where my hand still rested on his arm to meet mine. There was an openness and question there that I didn't know what to do with.

"Bree—"

I realized the bar had gone eerily silent. I held up my hand. "Wait. Do you hear that?"

"Hear what?"

"Exactly." I shoved away from the desk and

threw open the door, marching back out into the bar, Ford on my heels.

I emerged from the hallway to find the karaoke machine dark and silent. The crowd huddled in small groups, speaking in hushed tones that reminded me of funeral parlors. Even Darren had abandoned his spot on stage.

My skin prickled. The shift in atmosphere was jarring after the earlier cacophony.

I stepped behind the bar where Monty stood frozen, his face drained of color. Gripping him by the arms, I turned him to face me. "What's going on?"

My brewmaster swallowed hard. "We just got the news. Someone found a body on the beach."

CHAPTER 21

FORD

I stirred the pot of chili on the stove, taking a deep inhale of the fragrant scents of cumin, chilies, and tomatoes. It was one of the relatively small repertoire of recipes I could make reliably, and I'd been delighted to find out that my kid shared my affinity for spicy food. We'd invited Mom and Mimi over for family dinner tonight. The first one in our new place. The house still looked a little spartan, as none of my stuff had arrived from my last duty station, and the truck with Peyton's stuff was still working its way across the country. But we had the essentials. A table and chairs we'd also picked out at Beachcomber Bargains, and I'd ordered a full set of new cookware.

Peyton was putting ice in glasses for tea when I

heard the front door open. "Where are my babies?" Mimi sang out.

"Kitchen," I called.

Mimi bustled into the room, a large wrapped box in her arms. "Something smells amazing in here."

Mom was right behind with a second box.

"Chili. The cornbread's just about to come out of the oven." I replaced the lid on the pot. "What's all this?"

Mimi beamed. "Housewarming presents."

Peyton perked up. "Really?"

"Really. Come unwrap."

We all watched as she tore into the paper, revealing a collection of handmade pottery in her signature deep blues and greens. Dinner plates, salad plates, bowls, and mugs, each one unique but clearly part of a set. She must've started on these the day she found out about Peyton.

My throat got tight. "Mimi, you didn't have to do this."

"Of course I did. Every home needs proper dishes." She lifted out a bowl, showing Peyton the wave pattern carved into the rim. "I made these special for you both."

"They're beautiful." Peyton ran her fingers over the glazed surface. "You made all of these yourself?"

"That's what I do, sweet girl. I'm a potter. Well, it's one of my mediums, anyway."

My daughter looked intrigued. "Can you show me sometime?"

She squeezed Peyton's shoulders. "I'd love nothing more."

I had to turn away for a moment, pretending to check the cornbread in the oven while I got myself under control. My moms had always known how to make a house feel like home. Even this sparse rental with its bare walls and empty spaces felt warmer already.

Mom touched my shoulder. "You okay?"

I nodded, not quite trusting my voice. "Yeah. Just... thank you." Clearing my throat, I opened the cabinet. "Well, let's set the bowls on the table and put the rest away."

I began loading plates onto an empty shelf, and the timer went off. "Chili's ready, and there's the cornbread."

"Got it." Mom snagged a potholder off the hook on the side of the fridge and pulled the cast-iron skillet from the oven.

Peyton stood at the door to the backyard, peering out toward the neighboring yard. "Hey, Bree's home. We should invite her to dinner."

Mom and Mimi exchanged a look. I did my best not to react. "You're welcome to walk over and issue the invitation, but it's quite possible she's got plans, or she's just home to let Keeley out before heading back to the Brewhouse."

"I'll go ask." She'd bounced out the door before any of us could blink.

I wondered what excuse Bree would offer, because no way was she going to be up for a family dinner. Not when I was involved.

No one was more surprised than I was when Peyton came back a few minutes later with Bree and Keeley in tow. Judging by the faintly confused expression on Bree's face, she wasn't quite sure how it had happened either.

"Hey." I flashed a smile I hoped she found welcoming rather than manic. "Thanks for joining us."

"Hi." Bree hovered just inside the doorway, looking as if she might bolt at any second, much as my daughter had the day we'd met. Keeley trotted past her to investigate the house.

Mimi swept into the awkward like a welcome breeze, scooping Bree into one of her signature hugs. "It is so good to see you, darlin'. It's been too long."

After only a moment's hesitation, Bree squeezed her back, her face relaxing. "It has. Great to see you, Mimi. You, too, Mama Flo."

"You can sit by me," Peyton announced as she set a fifth place at the table.

The corners of Bree's mouth tipped up. "Sounds good."

A few minutes later, we all settled at the table with our food.

Bree crumbled her cornbread into her chili. "So how's school going?"

"Everybody was talking about the dead guy today," Peyton announced.

Mimi frowned. "I'm not sure this is appropriate dinner conversation, baby girl."

"We're all wondering, though," Mom conceded.

Peyton shrugged. "I mean, I'm sorry somebody died, but I'm not sorry they've got something else to talk about besides me."

Angling her head, Bree added some shredded cheese to her bowl. "Fair point."

I knew the conversation wasn't likely to veer toward anything else. "Did you hear anything at the Brewhouse today?" The bar was such a hub for gossip, I figured there was a solid chance Bree had heard whatever there was to hear.

"It was David Galef and definitely a homicide."

I frowned. "David Galef. Why do I know that name?"

"Few years ahead of us in school. In Caroline's class, I think. He works—worked—in the fishing industry during the season. Odd jobs during the off. He was a grade A douchecanoe."

Bree said it easily, as if she were describing the weather.

But I knew her. "He give you problems?"

Her gaze flicked up to mine. "None I couldn't handle."

Damn if that didn't incite a million more questions.

"They said at school that this was the second body found in the past year. What was the deal with the last one?"

Shit. This really probably wasn't an appropriate topic for a teenager. But I'd rather her talk about this with us than anyone else. "We had a hurricane last year. There were some old remains discovered in the aftermath. Our friend Willa and her husband Sawyer found them. Turned out to be a guy who was involved in... well, some not good things."

"Did the police figure out who killed him?"

"Well, not so much the police as Willa." Bree dipped cornbread into her chili. "The killer came after her."

Peyton's eyes went wide.

"No, no. She's okay. He was killed." Bree winced. "I'm making this worse."

I shook my head. "You're the one who was here." Of course, Mom and Mimi were, as well, but they hadn't been involved. Bree and Willa were tight.

"They also said it had something to do with a girl who disappeared a long time ago," Peyton added.

Mom picked up the conversational baton. "Gwen Busby."

It seemed like the ghost of her was never far away these days.

"She was only fifteen—little bit older than you when she went to the end of school bonfire. It's been a tradition on the island for a long, long time. She disappeared from the party, but nobody realized until morning because a big storm blew in and ended things early. The whole island mobilized to look, but no trace of her was ever found."

Mimi laid a hand over Mom's. "So tragic."

"What do they think happened?"

I was not about to admit to my kid, who wasn't that much younger than Gwen had been, that the current suspicion was that she'd been a victim of human trafficking. "Something bad."

I'd known it was bad at the time, even before that possibility had been raised. But now? Looking at it through the lens of a parent of a teenage girl? I couldn't imagine what I'd do if anything happened to Peyton, and she'd only been mine for a matter of weeks. Now the island I'd always believed was safe had a murderer on the loose. It was nothing to do with us, and there was no reason to believe anyone I cared about was in danger, but the idea of it still made me nervous. Especially as I needed to leave the island for a couple of days.

"Not to change the subject precisely, but I need to go out of town for a couple of days."

Conversation came to a screeching halt, and Peyton immediately froze up.

"I just have to be gone overnight. Two days at the most. I have to head to Norfolk to formalize the arrangements to transfer the remainder of my naval contract to the Reserves instead of active duty. It means I can stay here on Hatterwick and work remotely."

She relaxed at that. "Oh. Okay."

"You'll be staying with your grandmothers for the night until I get back. But under the circumstances, I want someone picking you up and dropping you off from school until this murder is solved, just as a precaution."

"When do you have to go, honey?" Mimi asked.

"Day after tomorrow."

Mom frowned. "I'm gonna be up at Nag's Head for a meeting. Delilah also has a meeting with a distributor up there."

Mimi waved that off. "I can reschedule."

"I can do it." Bree wasn't looking at us when she said it, just continued to eat her chili, and if Peyton hadn't been staring at her in hope, I might've thought I'd imagined the offer.

My daughter immediately turned pleading eyes in my direction, hands folded in supplication. "Can I? Please?"

Oh damn, I was gonna have to work on developing some kind of immunity to this look, or we were gonna end up with a dog sooner rather than later. Was this how she'd convinced my former best friend to come to dinner?

I looked at Bree. "Are you sure?" We definitely weren't at a place where I felt like I could ask her for much of anything. Certainly not to keep my kid.

One shoulder jerked in an easy shrug. "Sure. She can stay with me, and I'll handle pick up and drop off. It won't interfere with my schedule at the Brewhouse. I did my homework in a booth up there growing up. She can, too."

"Well, if you're sure, we'd really appreciate it."

"I'm sure."

Peyton did a fist pump. "Yes! Did you ask your pop about those photo albums?"

Bree's flinch was almost imperceptible. "I did. Have the whole pile of them at home."

"Sweet! Please tell me you have lots of embarrassing photos of my..." Peyton hesitated. "Of Ford."

So far, Peyton had been very careful not to call me anything in particular. I couldn't blame her for not being ready to call me Dad. Still, I felt a vague pang of disappointment.

Bree caught my eye, and I saw the flash of empathy before she smirked. "Oh, his middle school years are going to give you fodder to tease him for years to come."

Taking the olive branch, I adopted a mock stern expression. "That's a dangerous game you're starting, Cartwright. I was there for all of *your* embarrassing moments, too."

She sipped her tea, totally stone faced, but I didn't miss the sparkle in her gray eyes. "Some of us were smart and ruthless enough to destroy the evidence."

"I distinctly remember a certain someone wearing their hair in tiny butterfly clips all through seventh grade." I couldn't help needling her.

"At least I never tried frosted tips." Bree's mouth curved into a wicked smile.

"That was a dare from Sawyer!"

"And you kept them for three months."

"They grew on me."

"Like a fungus." She turned to Peyton. "Your father thought he was going to be the next Justin Timberlake."

"I had moves."

"You had something. Pretty sure it was a medical condition."

Mom snorted into her chili.

"Don't encourage her," I protested. "She pushed me into the pool at my own thirteenth birthday party."

"Because you put a snake in my beach bag!"

"It was rubber!"

"I didn't know that until after I'd already screamed bloody murder in front of half the eighth grade."

The easy back and forth felt so natural, like we'd stepped through time to before everything went wrong. Before I'd screwed everything up. My chest ached with how much I'd missed this. Missed her.

Peyton's head swiveled between us like she was watching a tennis match. "I need to see these pictures."

Bree's eyes danced with mischief. "I've got you, boo."

I groaned, but this was the longest conversation Bree and I had managed without her walls slamming back into place. I didn't want to do anything to break the spell. So I merely dropped my head into my hands and gave a theatrical moan. "I'm doomed."

CHAPTER 22
BREE

I pulled up to the school just as the last bell rang, parking in the visitor's lot alongside other waiting parents. Keeley's tail thumped rhythmically against the backseat as kids began streaming out of the building in noisy clusters. Peyton emerged with her backpack slung over one shoulder, her long legs eating up the ground as she made her way to my Jeep. Even from here, I could see the tension in her shoulders.

"Hey." She slid into the passenger seat, immediately reaching back to scratch Keeley's ears. The dog's happy whine filled the car as she pressed into Peyton's touch.

"How was school?" I tried to keep my tone casual, still learning how to navigate these regular conversations with a teenager.

"Fine." The response came with a restless fidget that I recognized all too well from my own school days—the constant shifting, the way her knee bounced against the dashboard.

"You look like you're about to crawl out of your skin." I watched her from the corner of my eye as I pulled away from the curb.

"Just tired of being inside all day." She pressed her forehead against the window, her breath fogging the glass. "The walls start closing in after a while, you know?"

I made a quick decision, turning toward the beach access road instead of home. "How about we take Keeley for a walk? Get some fresh air before heading to the Brewhouse for a snack?"

Her whole face lit up, tension melting away. "Really?" The way she perked up reminded me of a wilted flower finally getting water.

"Really." Movement and food. It always worked for me. Sometimes the simplest solutions were the best ones.

Ten minutes later, we were strolling along the shoreline at Osprey Beach, Keeley running ahead to chase seagulls. The salty breeze whipped our hair around, and the late afternoon sun painted everything in warm gold, and the temperatures felt more like March than early February. The beach was nearly empty this time of day, just the way I liked it.

"Thanks for this. I needed it." Her voice was soft, almost lost in the sound of breaking waves.

"I remember what it was like, being trapped inside all day." I watched her skip a shell across the incoming waves with perfect form. Just like Ford used to do. The memory flashed through my mind like a sandpiper darting in and out of the waves. "Your dad taught me how to do that." The words slipped out before I could stop them.

"Yeah?" She searched for another suitable shell, her movements precise and deliberate, just like his. "What else did he teach you?" There was a hunger in her voice that made my heart ache.

"How to fish. How to body surf." I smiled at the memories, remembering long summer days when the air was thick with humidity and possibility. "How to hot wire a car, though we never actually did it. Your dad was always better at the theory than the practice when it came to troublemaking."

She laughed, and it was so much like Ford's laugh. "Did you teach him anything?"

"How to make the perfect s'more. How to lie convincingly to his moms." I grinned, thinking of all those nights we'd spent around beach bonfires. "How to sneak out without getting caught. Though honestly, I think Mama Flo and Mimi just pretended not to notice half the time."

"Sounds like you were trouble together."

"The worst." But the best kind of trouble. The kind that had made growing up on this island magical.

I leaned over to bump Peyton's shoulder with mine, noting how she didn't flinch away. "How's it going with you two?"

"It's weird." Peyton kicked at the sand, sending a spray of tiny grains into the air. "He's trying so hard. Like, sometimes I catch him just staring at me like he can't believe I exist. Yesterday, he spent twenty minutes telling me about his high school track medals, then got all flustered when he realized I might not care about that stuff."

"That's probably exactly what he's thinking. Ford's always been the type to overthink everything."

"He asks about Mom a lot." Her voice went quiet, almost lost in the sound of the waves. "I get why, but..."

"But it hurts to talk about her."

She nodded, wrapping her arms around herself like she was trying to hold everything in. "And I feel guilty because I can see it upsets him that he didn't know about me. That Mom never told him. Sometimes he gets this look on his face, like he's trying to do math in his head, probably figuring out where he was when different things happened."

"That's not on you, kiddo. None of it is."

"I know. He says that, too." She bent to pick up another shell, turning it over in her hands and running her fingers along its ridged surface. "He's different than I expected. Better, maybe. I thought he'd be... I don't know. More of a jerk about the whole thing."

"How so?"

"I don't know. From Mom's letters, I thought he'd be... I don't know. More like a kid? But he's so *responsible*. Always checking if I've done my homework, making sure I eat breakfast." Her nose wrinkled. "He tried to give me a curfew. And he's always asking where I'm going and who I'll be with, like some kind of helicopter parent."

I couldn't help laughing. "Welcome to having a parent who gives a damn. Trust me, it's better than the alternative."

"Yeah." She tossed the shell into the waves, watching it disappear beneath the foam. "That's new. Like, really new."

The raw honesty in her voice made my heart ache for this kid who'd clearly been taking care of herself for way too long. "Your mom didn't?"

"She did her best. But she worked a lot. When she was there, she was really present, you know?

But I was on my own a lot of the time." Peyton shrugged, her shoulders hunching slightly, as if trying to make herself smaller. "It's just different with Ford. He's always there. Wanting to know things. Trying to figure out what I like to eat and what shows I watch and stuff. Yesterday he actually sat through three episodes of this stupid reality show I like, just because I was watching it."

"That bothers you?"

"No. Maybe? I don't know." She kicked at the sand again, sending a spray of it toward the water. "It's just a lot sometimes. But I... kind of like it too? Like, sometimes I want to tell him to back off, but then when he's not around, I sort of miss it. Miss him. Is that weird?"

"Not even a little bit."

We lapsed into silence for a bit. I scooped up a piece of driftwood and hurled it for Keeley. As she streaked off after it, Peyton asked, "Did you and my dad ever date?"

The question shouldn't have surprised me, but it still made my stomach twist into a knot. "No. We were only ever friends." Except for one night when I'd believed we'd become more. But I was definitely not thinking about that. I'd spent ten years not thinking about that.

"Sarah said you hated him."

I stopped at that, my hand freezing mid-throw with another piece of driftwood. "What?"

"It was something else I heard at school. That you hadn't talked to him in like a decade." She scuffed her toe in the sand, not quite meeting my eyes. "People talk a lot about everybody around here."

Why the hell was *that* getting talked about by middle schoolers? Small town gossip was one thing, but this felt way too personal to be making the rounds at the local junior high.

I didn't want to lie to this kid. My conscience wouldn't allow it, even if it might've been easier. "I don't hate your dad." That had always been true, even during the darkest moments when I'd wanted to.

"Then why the not talking to him?"

Keeley returned with the stick, dropping it at my feet and looking between us with those soulful eyes.

I had to consider how to answer the question in a way that wasn't going to damage the relationship Peyton was building with her father. The last thing she needed was more reasons to doubt him. "He did something that hurt me deeply."

She frowned, her brows drawing together in that way that made her look so much like Ford it made my chest ache. "On purpose?"

Oh, I wanted to believe it had been, in those dark nights when anger and hurt had been my only companions. But I knew better, had always known better, deep down. "No, not on purpose. But it hurt me all the same."

"Did he apologize?"

Such a simple and obvious question from such a young soul. I'd lost count of the number of times Ford had tried over the years—in person, in texts, in emails that I'd never opened. I could have thrown him under the bus, listed every perceived slight and mistake, but that didn't seem fair. Not now, not to his daughter. "I've never really let him."

Peyton absorbed that, her eyes taking on that analytical gleam I was starting to recognize. "I mean, it sucks that he hurt you. But he was, what, like twenty? Boys are dumb for a *long time*. Testosterone poisoning."

I couldn't stop the snort laugh that burst out of me at her matter-of-fact assessment. "You're not wrong."

"I'm just saying, maybe he regrets being dumb. It doesn't change that he hurt you, but it seems like that would matter. To me it would, anyway. Like, if someone I cared about was really sorry and kept trying to make it right."

Her simple interpretation left me speechless. I'd just been schooled by a thirteen-year-old, who somehow managed to cut straight through all my carefully constructed defenses with the ruthless logic of youth.

Did it matter? I didn't know, but I had to acknowledge—to myself anyway—that I'd missed Ford. Having him back in my life, even in this weird way, was making me realize exactly how much. The timber of his laugh, the way his eyes crinkled at the corners when he smiled, how he still ducked his head when he was uncomfortable. All of those tiny details were at once a comfort and an attack.

I didn't know what to do with that. Didn't want to examine too closely why my ribcage seemed to shrink every time I thought about it.

"C'mon." I shook off the uncomfortable train of thought. "Let's head back to the Jeep. You need anything before we head to the Brewhouse? Water? Snacks? A bathroom break?"

"Maybe a trip to the library, if there's time? We got assigned a paper on piracy in the region, so I figure'd that's the best place to start."

"Not a bad option, but actually you probably want the island museum. Monty's husband, Peter, volunteers there pretty often, and I know they've got a lot of exhibits on local pirate stories."

"Oh, that sounds great."

The island museum was quiet this time of day, the late afternoon sun slanting through the windows. Peter looked up from the desk as we walked in, his face brightening.

"Bree! What brings you by?"

"Hey Peter. This is Peyton. She's doing a paper on local piracy."

His eyes lit up. "Ford's daughter? Monty mentioned you'd just moved to town." He came around the desk to shake her hand. "Welcome. You've come to the right place. We've got quite the collection of artifacts and documents from the colonial period."

I wandered over to the gift shop area while Peter led Peyton toward the exhibits, pointing out specific displays that might help with her research. The rack of maps caught my eye—reproductions of historical charts marked with shipwrecks and supposed treasure locations.

"These are new." I pulled one down to examine it. The artwork was actually pretty impressive, with detailed illustrations of ships and sea creatures. "Way better than the cheesy ones they used to sell. See, look, the paper's even artificially aged."

"Oh, that's a new program we're trying," Peter explained. "A bunch of local artists made their own renditions of local treasure maps. Aren't they cool?"

Peyton joined me, peering at the map in my hand. "Are any of these real?"

"The shipwrecks? Most of them. The treasure... That's more complicated." I handed her the map.

"But if you want the real stories behind them, Pop knows them all. He's covering at the Brewhouse today. He loves telling the tales of Blackbeard and the other pirates who used to hide out in these waters."

"Really? Like, actual historical stories or just tourist stuff?"

This kid wasn't interested in being snowed. Good for her.

"Both. But he knows which is which. He's lived here his whole life, studied all the history. Just maybe don't get him started unless you've got some time to spare. He can talk about this stuff for hours."

"That would actually be perfect for my paper."

"Then let's head over there. I need to check on things, anyway." Noting the way she still stared at the map, I made a snap decision. "Want it?"

She started to put it back. "No, that's okay."

I snatched it back. "Every Hatterwick resident should get her own treasure map. It's a rite of passage."

Peter nodded with a faux serious expression. "She speaks the truth."

"Do you like this one? Or would you rather have one of the others?"

Peyton seriously considered all the selections before making her choice. I hid my smile as I paid for the map, and we headed out to the parking lot.

My skin prickled as I reached for the driver's side door, the hair on the back of my neck standing at attention. I felt weirdly exposed out here in the open. As if someone was watching us from behind one of the scraggly live oaks, or maybe from a parked car. Paranoid, I did a slow sweep of the area but saw no one suspicious lurking in the shadows of the museum's side garden or near the dumpsters.

"Something wrong?" Peyton's question snapped me back to the present.

It was just a case of the heebie jeebies because David Galef's killer hadn't been caught. The whole island was still on edge about it. "Nah. I'm fine. I think I'm just hungry." The excuse was weak, but it was better than admitting I was jumping at shadows.

"Me, too! Can we have fries for a snack?" Her face lit up at the prospect of food, reminding me that teenagers were basically bottomless pits.

"We can have anything you like." I forced myself to relax, focusing on her enthusiasm rather than my paranoia.

"Sweet!"

CHAPTER 23
FORD

My tires bumped down the ramp from the ferry and onto the island. Home for real this time. No more counting down until I had to deploy again. The ferry's horn blasted, signaling to those waiting that boarding for the next crossing to the mainland was about to begin. The sound of my childhood. Now the sound of my future. Some version of it, anyway. My naval career wasn't over, but shifting to the Reserves meant I could put down real roots here. Build a life with my daughter.

My daughter. The words still felt surreal. Every time I looked at Peyton, I saw pieces of myself, pieces of my mom. Thirteen years of her life I'd missed. First steps. First words. First day of school. All those moments I should have been there for.

Casey should have told me.

The anger that bubbled up whenever I thought about it wasn't productive. She was gone now, and Peyton needed me to focus on the present, on being the best father I could be. On not fucking this up.

I turned onto the main road toward the village, weaving my way toward the Brewhouse. My palms were damp on the steering wheel. I'd only gotten a handful of texts from them while I'd been gone. Mostly reports from Bree that she'd picked Peyton up or dropped her off at school, but also one picture of Peyton passed out snuggling with Keeley. Damn it, I really was going to have to get her a dog.

The wall between Bree and me still felt impenetrable, but I thought maybe we were down a few bricks. She'd been amazing with my kid, helping to give Peyton stability when everything in her world had been turned upside down. Bree hadn't been obligated to do that. It was just further proof of the soft, squishy heart she hid beneath that naturally prickly exterior.

Would there ever be a time when she'd let me back into that heart? Before Peyton, I'd have said absolutely not. But now? I didn't know. I wouldn't plan some kind of formal offensive to breach those walls of hers, but maybe sheer exposure would wear her down. I so desperately wanted the chance to prove to her that, if she ever let me in again, I'd be more careful with her. But that was a problem for another day.

The Brewhouse's parking lot came into view, already filling up with the dinner crowd. Time to collect my kid and figure out how to do this whole dad thing right.

My phone rang as I pulled into a space. The number for the shipping company I'd hired to pack up and transport all of Peyton and Casey's things that had been in storage flashed across the screen.

"Mr. Donoghue? This is Mark with Cross Country Moving."

"Hey Mark. Tell me you've got an estimated delivery date for my daughter's things."

The heavy pause that stretched across the line told me that wasn't why he was calling. I tensed, waiting for the other shoe to drop.

"Sir, I'm so sorry. The container was stolen from our facility last night."

The words didn't immediately process. "What do you mean, stolen? How does someone steal an entire shipping container?" I supposed it wasn't an entire shipping container. This company specialized in those smaller pod-type containers. I imagined that several could be moved on one eighteen-wheeler load.

Another pause. "Well, they took the entire truck. Yours was only one of the units lost. Security cameras outside the truck stop show someone breaking into the truck and probably hot-wiring it while the driver was inside. The police are investigating."

I dropped my forehead against the steering wheel. All of Peyton's childhood memories. Her mom's things. Everything she had left of her old life, gone.

"What are the chances of recovery?"

"These thefts are rare, but when they do happen, we often recover at least some of the contents. The thieves usually dump what they don't want. I've already filed the insurance claim and notified local law enforcement."

"Keep me updated. The second you hear anything."

I ended the call and sat there, trying to process. Peyton had been talking non-stop about getting her stuff back. Her favorite blanket. The photo albums. Her mom's jewelry. How was I supposed to tell her this?

As I stepped inside, the scent of hops and fried food wrapped around me like a welcome home hug. The dinner crowd buzzed with conversation, but my eyes went straight to the corner booth where Peyton sat with Ed Cartwright.

My kid leaned forward, elbows on the worn wooden table, completely absorbed in whatever Ed was saying. A weathered looking map lay spread between them, Ed's gnarled finger tracing what looked like a route along the coast.

She looked happy. Settled, even. I couldn't bring myself to destroy that right now. Not until we knew more about whether anything could be recovered.

I'd wait. Just a little while. Just until we had more information. God, I hoped I wasn't making another massive mistake.

"... and that's where they say Blackbeard lost his head." Ed's gravelly voice carried across the bar. "'Course, plenty of folks claim to know where his treasure ended up."

"But nobody's ever found it?" Peyton's eyes were wide.

"Oh, pieces have turned up here and there. But the real treasure?" Ed tapped the map. "That's still out there somewhere, waiting to be found."

I couldn't help grinning. Ed had told me those same stories when I was a kid. The way his eyes lit up hadn't changed a bit. "Still telling tall tales?"

"They're the best kind," Ed insisted.

Peyton grinned, clearly delighted with him. "Mr. Ed knows everything about pirates!"

"That he does." I nodded at the old man. "Thanks for entertaining her."

"Entertaining nothing. This one's got a proper

appreciation for history." Ed winked at Peyton. "You come back anytime you want to hear more stories."

I caught sight of Bree behind the bar, juggling drink orders and looking harried. She gave me a quick wave before turning back to her customers. I lifted my hand in return, mouthing 'thank you.'

"Ready to head home, kiddo?"

Peyton carefully folded up her map. "Can we come back tomorrow? Mr. Ed was going to tell me about the shipwrecks."

"We'll see." I helped her gather her backpack. "Homework first."

"It is homework! I've got a paper on piracy in the area."

"Then I'm sure we can sort something out."

I herded her out to the car and steered us toward home, my headlights cutting through the shadows that shrouded the road. If the silence felt not exactly comfortable, at least it wasn't strained. Progress.

"So you had a good time with Bree while I was gone?"

"Yeah. She's really cool." Peyton fiddled with the edges of the folded map she'd tucked in an outside pocket of her backpack. "You should apologize for whatever dumb boy thing you did all those years ago to hurt her."

I nearly swerved off the road. "What?"

"Whatever you did that made her not want to talk to you. You should apologize. Mom always said a proper apology is the first step to fixing anything."

My throat tightened. "Your mom was really wise." I glanced over. "Did Bree say something about all this?"

"No. But people talk."

That was the damned truth. The island gossip mill was alive and well as ever.

She pinned me with a look that reminded me eerily of my mother. "*Are* you sorry about whatever dumb boy thing you did?"

I couldn't believe we were talking about this. But I could be honest without getting into specifics. "It's my second biggest regret in life."

She studied me for a long moment. "What's the first?"

I sent her a long glance from the driver's seat. "Missing out on the first thirteen years with you."

The words hung between us as I pulled into our driveway. Peyton absorbed that, her fingers still tracing the edges of her map.

"I wish I'd known you then, too."

We headed inside. Peyton immediately disappeared into her room. I heard the door click shut. Maybe she needed a little time to process. I dumped my own bag in my room, then opened the fridge to figure out what was for dinner. I probably should've gotten takeout from the Brewhouse. A casserole dish sat on the top shelf, neatly wrapped, with a note on top from Mimi.

Chicken Broccoli Alfredo. So you don't have to think about dinner when you get back.

God, my moms were awesome.

A few minutes later, Peyton's footsteps padded back down the hall.

"There's something you should probably see."

I looked up from where I'd been setting the oven to preheat. "What is it?"

"You never actually asked how I knew about you."

"I thought your mom told you." But even as I said the words, I remembered Peyton saying her mom had never talked about me. It was a mark of how overwhelmed I'd been with the whole situation that I'd lost that detail.

She shook her head, clutching what looked like a stack of envelopes to her chest. "I found these after she died. They're letters. To you. It seems like she wrote one every year, but she never sent them."

My heart stopped as she held out the bundle. The envelopes were creased and obviously well-read, each one carefully opened. My name and "Hatterwick Island" were written in neat handwriting on the front. Each envelope had a number written in the corner, starting with one.

I stared. Thirteen years of letters. Thirteen years of my daughter's life, captured in her mother's words. Words Casey had wanted to tell me but never did.

I forced myself to reach out and take the stack. "Are you sure you're okay with this?"

One thin shoulder lifted. "I mean, technically, they were addressed to you."

"Thank you."

I sat, carefully extracting the first letter.

Dear Ford,

I hardly know how to start this. I suppose there's no real protocol for sharing news this big—especially when I've kept the secret for so long. I guess there's no other way other than to rip off the bandaid, so here goes.

You're a father.

Before you ask, yes, I'm sure it's you. There was no one else before or since. We have a beautiful baby girl, and I've selfishly kept her from you. There's really no excuse for it. I know you have a right to know, and yet here we are. All I can offer you is the why, though I know it's no excuse.

After I left Hatterwick and you, my parents and I came home to California. Less than a month later, both of them were killed in a car accident. It was devastating, as you might imagine. In all the chaos after, I didn't realize I was pregnant. Not for months. I assumed the missed periods were all from stress. By the time I figured it out, I was already four months pregnant.

I came to Georgia and tracked you down. But by the time I found you, saw you on campus, it was obvious you were already deeply in love and happy with someone else.

I paused, thinking back. That would have been right after Emily and I had gotten together. God, if Casey had only known how wrong she was, how might things have been different?

I'd already lost my entire family, and I

was afraid of what might happen if I told you. That's no excuse. You have a right to know. But I couldn't risk losing this baby. So I didn't approach you, and I left, telling myself I was doing the right thing by letting you be happy in the life you'd chosen.

I know this letter doesn't make up for all the things you've missed because of my selfishness and fear, but maybe it'll help just a little.

She went on to paint a picture of all those firsts from that first year, giving a highlight reel that was full of her own joy in our daughter. My eyes burned with unshed tears by the end, and I had to swallow a few times before I could trust myself to speak.

"Thank you for sharing these with me."

"I thought maybe it would help."

"It does."

She pushed up from the chair. "I've got homework. Let me know when dinner's ready?"

"Yeah."

She disappeared down the hall. I took a moment to pop the casserole in the oven, then I settled in to read the others.

CHAPTER 24
BREE

The moment Keeley and I stepped inside from our morning walk, she made a beeline for her water bowl, and I made a beeline for the coffeepot. Courtesy of the wonders of modern technology, a timer ensured it was ready as soon as we got home. I filled my favorite mug and added a generous splash of hazelnut creamer, inhaling the rich aroma as I soaked up the warmth between my palms. But the ritual didn't have its usual settling effect.

After two days with Peyton, the house felt too big, too empty.

It had felt the same after Willa moved out, which was how I'd ended up with Keeley only a few weeks later. My pup was great company, but she didn't quite make up for the loss of another human in the space. Those years with Willa as my roommate had spoiled me. I'd gotten used to having someone to share coffee with, to bounce ideas off of, to just exist in the same space without pressure to fill the quiet.

Maybe I ought to look for another roommate. The cottage had plenty of space, and the extra income would help cover some upgrades I'd been considering, like a pergola to cover the back patio.

Keeley's tail thumped against her bed, drawing my attention. She gave me that soulful look that always made me feel like she could read my thoughts.

"Don't give me that look. This has nothing to do with getting attached to Ford's kid." I took a long sip of coffee. "I just miss having a roommate."

But I was fond of Peyton. So was Pop. He'd had a grand time telling her pirate stories. He'd never admit it to me, but that man really wanted to be a great-grandpa. Lord knew, it wasn't likely to ever happen through me. If he could have a bit of that relationship with Peyton, I didn't see the harm in it. The two of them enjoyed each other. And the more people she had in her corner, the better off she'd be.

But it also meant that Ford was inevitably becoming part of my life again. I wasn't sure what to do with that. There was a part of me that wanted to just fall back into the way things used to be. Once upon a time, he'd been comfort and safety. And there was no erasing the years of history we shared.

But there was no erasing the pain, either. And it was there, each and every time I saw him.

A soft knock sounded on the kitchen door. Keeley bounded over, wagging, and I glanced up to see the very object of my thoughts standing on the other side, as if I'd summoned him.

What the hell was he doing here?

I crossed over to open the door. "Is Peyton okay?"

Ford blinked. "What? Yeah. I dropped her off at school a couple of hours ago."

"Did she forget something?" I could've sworn I checked the guest room for her stuff.

"No. Can I come in?"

Still worried, I backed up to let him inside.

The house that had felt so big just minutes ago immediately shrank with him in my kitchen. Somehow he just took up so much space, beyond the physical.

"Did you hear something more from the FBI about all that mess? Or find out what the deal was with Casey's job?"

Ford's lips twitched, his green eyes sparking with faint amusement. "No. If you'll let me talk, I'll tell you why I'm here."

Right. I had to actually shut up to get any answers. Still, my nerves spilled out of my mouth again. "You want coffee?"

Wait. Why was I offering him coffee? I didn't actually want him to stay any longer than necessary.

"Coffee would be great."

I filled another mug on auto pilot, waiting for him to speak. But Ford only watched me move around my kitchen, apparently not bothered by the silence.

I handed him the coffee.

"Thanks. Can we sit?"

Oh God. Was this really a sitting conversation?

"Easy. This isn't some kind of bad news. You tense up exactly like Peyton."

"We've both got plenty of reason to." But I sat at the kitchen table.

Ford dragged out a chair opposite me and dropped into it. "She reminds me so much of you."

"She's not as prickly as me. More years with someone who seems like she was a really good mom."

He studied his coffee. "I think she was. And I'm so torn about that because if Casey had lived, I don't know if she'd ever have told me about Peyton. I could've missed out on my kid's entire life without ever even knowing she existed."

I could see how much that idea of that killed

him. "Both of those things can be true. She could have been a great mom and still made a mistake in not telling you. No sense dwelling on could have. You have her now, and I know you'll do everything in your power to make your time together count."

His chin dipped. "It's made me rethink so many things. Really evaluate my priorities and what matters."

Something in his tone had me going stiff again, my fingers tightening on my mug. "Kids will do that."

When he lifted his gaze to mine, my stomach twisted into a cleat hitch knot.

"There are things I need to say to you. That I've needed to say for years. I know you haven't been ready to listen. And I get that. I hurt you. In ways that should have been so fucking obvious to me before I did it. When I left for the Navy, I broke the very first promise I ever made to you—that you wouldn't be alone anymore. I had my reasons for going, but none of them matter. I made the decision without taking you into account, and I ruined the best friendship I ever had. I know it's too little, too late, but I am sorry. I've always been sorry. And I just... I needed you to know that going forward."

The bloom of pain started in my chest and spread outward, overtaking every inch of my body as I closed my eyes and soaked in the apology I hadn't allowed him to make for a decade. He knew. He actually knew and understood why I was upset. Why what he'd done had cut me to the quick. I shouldn't be surprised. No one had ever known me better than Ford. And it mattered that he recognized it. That he owned it. So few people understood that was an essential component of a genuine apology.

Opening my eyes again, I found his gaze steady on my face, waiting, pleading. He'd said his piece. Now it was time to say mine.

I sipped at my now cold coffee to wet the throat that had gone dry. "I appreciate the apology and the acknowledgment. But it's not that simple. That last summer wasn't the first time you hurt me, Ford. There were little slices to my heart for years before that. You were my best friend, but I never felt like yours. It was always your brothers who came first, and I so often felt like I got the scraps of your attention. I took it because I loved you, and I figured anything was better than nothing. Then the tavern was torched, and for the first time ever, you truly put me first. You were there for me, supporting me, making me believe everything was going to be okay, even though the bottom had totally fallen out of my world. I got through it because you were there, and I thought, no matter what happened, I'd keep getting through it because I had you."

A muscle jumped in his jaw, but he didn't interrupt me as I paused for another sip of coffee. "You were my first. Did you know that?"

He jolted, obviously shocked. "I—"

But I didn't want to hear it, so I pressed on. "You changed things between us that night, and I thought—finally, *finally* you saw me. Saw us. What we could be together. I was the idiot who was building castles in the sand in the days after, thinking we were on the same page. And then you announced that you and all the other Wayward Sons had enlisted in the Navy. That you were leaving in a matter of weeks. That the decision had been made before you ever took me to bed. And that was my line, Ford. Because you never discussed it with me. Never even brought up the fact that you were considering it. And it was just more proof that I wasn't a priority for you."

His face twisted as if I'd stabbed him directly in the gut. "Bree—"

I held up a hand to stay whatever protest he might have made. "No. I've spent literally my whole life not being a priority for people. I won't settle for less."

"Nor should you. But Bree, I—"

"Stop, Ford. I know we're both older. And maybe things have changed for you, but even if they have, I can't be a priority for you now, either, because you have Peyton. That's exactly where your priority *should* be. She needs you. All of you. So I appreciate the apology, but it doesn't undo the damage."

He opened his mouth, then closed it again, his face twisting with unfettered grief. Maybe that should've moved me, but I had my own pain to grapple with.

"You should go."

"Bree—"

My control of my emotions had been stretched razor thin, and I didn't want him to be here when I snapped. "If you ever loved me at all, please, just go." I forced the words out past the lump in my throat.

Reluctance in every movement, Ford pushed back from the table and strode to the door. A moment later, it shut quietly behind him.

Keeley padded over, leaning against my leg and whining, and that show of support broke me. All the stress and strain and grief I'd managed to hold back for *years* poured out of me in a torrent of tears.

CHAPTER 25
FORD

If you ever loved me at all.

As if she doubted I ever had.

God, those words made me bleed. I'd wanted to stay and argue, but I knew that would only make Bree dig in deeper. So despite every instinct screaming at me to stay, I'd done as she asked and walked away.

Though I absolutely needed to get to my own work, I hadn't made it further than my sofa.

I'd known for years that I'd fucked up. I'd known I'd hurt her. But somehow I'd never realized that she'd felt so excluded. In my memories, she'd been with me almost as much as the rest of my brothers. I'd thought we'd included her, but maybe she'd just felt like a tagalong. An afterthought.

How the hell had I never noticed?

Probably because I'd never had to fight for my place in the world, in any group. I just accepted I had a right to be there. But Bree had never felt as if she belonged. I'd known that from the beginning, and I'd foolishly assumed that we'd done enough to overcome all that childhood trauma.

More fool me.

Of course she'd felt like I chose my brothers over her when I joined the Navy. To some extent, it was true. That decision had belonged to all of us, and I hadn't consulted her. I hadn't consulted anyone outside the Wayward Sons. Once it was done, I hadn't planned to keep it from her, but I'd been working my way up to finding the right way to tell her. I'd known she'd be upset, but I'd thought it would be like when I'd left for college.

I hadn't planned to sleep with her. Not ever. She was my best friend, and I hadn't wanted to fuck that up, despite the stirrings of attraction I'd been fighting off since my first break with Emily. I'd been afraid it was just some weird rebound thing, and I wasn't about to use Bree like that.

But she'd been so devastated after the fire. I'd wanted to distract her. To comfort her. There'd been alcohol and an unexpected kiss that rocked me to my core. Because it had finally stripped off the blinders I'd been wearing for years. I wasn't just attracted, and it wasn't some reaction to being free of the toxic ties to Emily. I was in love with Bree. Had been for years. And I'd been too fucking stupid to realize. I should have stopped there. Should have immediately admitted that I'd enlisted. But she'd kissed me again, and it had set us both on fire. From there, things had just... gotten out of hand. Gone too far.

You were my first. Did you know that?

Christ, I hadn't known. Somehow that compounded my fuckup to an infinite degree.

And now... now I didn't know what to do. The apology I'd been hanging onto for years hadn't been enough. It hadn't changed anything. As she'd said, it didn't undo the damage I'd done. Nothing could.

The knowledge of that absolutely killed me. I wanted to make things better. I wanted to prove to her she was a priority for me. But I wasn't even sure she wanted to be a priority for me anymore, and I had no idea what to do with that.

I'd told myself I'd be satisfied if I could earn back her friendship, but facing her down today, I had to admit the truth, even if only to myself.

I was still in love with her.

Bree was the unfinished business I'd left behind. The specter that cast a pall over every relationship I'd attempted since.

I wished I had it all to do over again. That I'd

hadn't been blind to the extent of my feelings for her. I would never have enlisted, and maybe we would have finally become exactly what she'd imagined with those castles in the sand she'd talked about. Because, damn it, we were good together. Not just physically—although holy hell, yes—but as friends. We understood each other. And we could have—should have—been each other's everything.

Instead, I'd taken her for granted. I'd been a damned fool. And now I might have lost her for good.

The ringing of my phone dragged me out of my rumination. I didn't recognize the number and almost let it go to voicemail. I wasn't in the mood to speak to anyone. But on the off chance that it was something to do with work, I answered anyway. "Hello?"

"Lieutenant Commander Donoghue?"

The use of my rank had me shoving my emotional turmoil aside. Probably was something related to my new assignment or maybe we'd missed something in connection with my transition. "Speaking."

"This is Special Agent Langston."

Everything in me went on high alert. "What do you want?"

"First off, to apologize. I didn't agree with how we were asked to handle things with you and your daughter. You were right that we weren't being forthcoming about why we came to see you."

Oh fuck. What now? "Has that changed?"

Langston paused. "Officially, no. In fact, my superior would be pissed as hell to know I was talking to you."

I shoved up from the sofa and began to pace. "And yet, here you are."

"Here I am. Against direct orders, because I think you're a man who can handle himself. Out of an abundance of caution, I'm sharing some of the details of our investigation with you. I need a promise of your discretion."

"I'm not sure who you think I'd be sharing with. What's going on, Langston?"

"Casey Walsh was helping us investigate the company she worked for."

"So she wasn't under investigation herself."

"No, no. She came to us, actually, after finding some... inconsistencies in paperwork. It was enough for us to verify that something was going on, but not sufficient to be actionable. She was gathering additional intel."

My brain spun with the implications. So Casey had realized something shady was going on at work, and instead of searching for a new job, she'd gone to the authorities. Then stayed in when they'd asked for more.

"Are you suggesting that someone found out? Is that why she's dead? Was Casey's death something other than natural?" The idea of it turned my stomach. Had she died because she'd tried to do the right thing?

"We have no reason to believe her death was anything but a natural tragedy. But the information she was gathering for us has disappeared. We don't have it, and according to our sources, neither does the company."

"That's why you were asking Peyton all those questions. You thought Casey brought it home."

"We don't know what she did with it. The fact is, neither does anyone else. I'm concerned there is a slim possibility Peyton could be a target because of it."

"Then why in the hell did y'all wait three months to talk to her?" I fought the urge to plow my fist into the nearest wall. If they'd thought she was a target and done nothing all this time...

"As I said, the possibility is remote, and if no one else had thought of it, we didn't want to draw attention to her unnecessarily. We had been monitoring her through her foster family. But when she disappeared, we feared the worst."

That mollified me somewhat. They hadn't completely hung Peyton out to dry. "So when we contacted social services about her being here, y'all were notified."

"We were. At that point, it seemed prudent to try to talk to her, just in case."

"So, what's changed? Why are you concerned enough to be violating direct orders to warn me?"

"Nothing overt. Our meeting just didn't sit well with me. Based on what she said, Peyton probably doesn't know anything. But we simply don't know for sure, and I felt it necessary and reasonable to give you at least this much so that you can effectively protect your daughter."

Appreciation mingled with frustration. "You expect me to be able to protect her when I have insufficient intel on who these people are? I have no idea what I should even be on the lookout for." I could just imagine how well Peyton would react to a full protection detail. As if her classmates needed any further reason to gossip about her.

"I'll be coordinating with local law enforcement, apprising them of the potential threat and the known actors of the organization. It doesn't rule out that they could hire someone, but that's the best I can offer for now."

His best was a long damned way from actually being useful. What good did it do to know there might be a threat if I didn't have any indiction at all about what it might look like? "What the hell am I even supposed to do with this information?"

"Be vigilant. In all probability, this is an overreaction on my part. There's no legitimate reason for anyone to come after Peyton. They had ample time to try while she was still in Oregon. In the weeks and months after Casey's death, no one broke into the storage unit where her mother's things had been stored, which would have been the next logical move if they truly thought she had something."

I stopped pacing. "I had all of Casey and Peyton's things from Oregon packed up and shipped. The truck with the container on it was stolen yesterday."

Langston's voice went sharp. "From where?"

"I don't actually know. A truck stop along the route. I can send you the name and number for the manager of the shipping company. He said a police report was filed and an insurance claim made. Do you think this has something to do with your case?"

He went quiet for several long moments, thinking. "It feels too fucking coincidental for my taste. But the good news is that if it *is* connected, they went after the things, not your daughter. They may not even know where Peyton is, now that she's all the way out there with you."

"That's not nearly the comfort I think you want it to be."

"I'm sorry for that. Send me the contact info for the shipping company. I'll follow up. If we find out anything else relevant to you, I'll be sure to reach out again."

"And if anything happens here?"

"You can reach me at this number."

I supposed that was the best I was going to get. "Langston?"

"Yeah?"

"Do us a favor and catch these assholes. I'd like a chance to just get to know my daughter in peace."

"We're doing our best."

But as I hung up the phone, I wondered if their best would be good enough. On the chance that it wasn't, I had to be at *my* best, and that meant circling the wagons and bringing everyone in my circle up to speed so we could make a plan.

CHAPTER 26
BREE

I didn't want to see Ford. I still felt too raw from our encounter yesterday, and there hadn't been time to rebuild any of my defenses. All through my shift at the Brewhouse last night, I'd felt like a giant exposed nerve, to the point that I'd shut myself into my office to work on tax shit rather than risk facing any actual people.

But Ford had invoked the one thing that would unequivocally override my reservations—Peyton. I might have thought he was abusing that fact, except that the 911 request had come via group text. If he'd tagged in Sawyer and Willa, Gabi and Daniel, both his moms, *and* me, something was up. I thought of what he'd told me about the FBI's interest in Peyton and wondered if something else had happened there. I couldn't imagine what other reason he'd have for bringing us all together without the girl herself. She was currently up at the Brewhouse, head to head with Pop, talking pirates again for her school project.

If Peyton was in some kind of trouble or danger, I wasn't going to let my own complicated feelings for her father stop me from being there to help. That was the only thing that sent me across the patch of lawn separating our houses barely twenty-four hours after I'd banished Ford from my kitchen. Keeley trotted at my heels, tail a cheerful metronome.

Everyone else had already arrived. I'd waited until I'd seen the crowd of cars in the driveway to ensure I wouldn't be stuck alone with him. I didn't know what else he might try to say to me, and I wasn't prepared for any more emotional upheaval.

I hesitated at the door before finally just opening it and walking inside. We weren't that kind of friends anymore, but if everyone was talking, it was possible nobody would hear my knock. My dog bolted inside, making a beeline for Willa and Roy.

Gabi pulled me into a hug. "Hey, girl."

"Sorry I'm late." I squeezed back, grateful for her steadying presence.

Willa waved from where she sat on the floor with both dogs. "You're right on time."

Sawyer stood beside her, arms crossed, his usual easy smile nowhere in sight. Whatever was going on had him worried. Or maybe that was lingering worry over the fact that David Galef's killer was still on the loose.

"Bree, honey." Mimi swept over to hug me, and I fought the urge to melt into her maternal warmth the way I had when I was younger.

Mama Flo lifted the coffeepot in silent question.

"Yes, please." I'd do better if I had something to do with my hands.

Daniel, Gabi's Coast Guardsman boyfriend, nodded from his spot by the window. He and I weren't close, but I appreciated how good he was for her. He'd taken an apartment on the island to be closer to her, though his posting at Nags Head had him gone a lot.

And then there was Ford.

My breath caught at the sight of him, echoes of yesterday's conversation hitting me like a punch to the gut. Dark circles shadowed his eyes, and scruff darkened his tight jaw. When our gazes met, the weight of everything said and unsaid between us felt like an elephant sinking down on my chest.

"Thanks for coming." His voice was rough.

The mix of grief and gratitude in his expression

made me want to look away, but I forced myself to hold his gaze. "You said it was about Peyton."

That was all I needed to know. That would always be enough to bring me running, and we both knew it.

His shoulders relaxed a fraction. "Yeah. We need to talk about keeping her safe."

"What's going on?" I settled into the remaining chair, purposefully not looking at him. "Did something else happen with the feds?"

Daniel's brow winged up. "The feds?"

I listened as Ford gave us the update. The varying degrees of surprise on everyone's face suggested he hadn't told anyone but me about that initial visit at the police station. Maybe it was because we'd all been derailed by Galef's murder. I wasn't sure what it meant that he'd come only to me.

"The agent I spoke with yesterday was pretty firm that he believes the potential threat to Peyton is slim, but slim isn't none. So I wanted to bring in all of you. The more eyes we have, the better, and I'll be having a conversation with Peyton about not going anywhere alone."

Sawyer looked pensive. "Obviously we'll all help, but seems like we're a little thin on the details."

Frustration pulled Ford's brows together.

"Don't I know it? But that was all he was willing to say."

"You want me to tap Dax? See what he can dig up on Casey's former employer?"

"Who's Dax?" I asked.

"Friend of mine from the Navy," Sawyer explained. "Former Naval Intelligence, like Jace. He's been doing contract work since he retired. He's the one who tracked down the link between Roland O'Shea and that asshole doctor who fucked with Willa's head."

The guy who'd let us know exactly who the threat to Willa was last summer. He'd almost been too late, but if not for that last-minute phone call, we wouldn't have known where to even start looking when she'd disappeared. A handy man to have in our corner.

Ford nodded. "If he's got time and is willing, I'd appreciate whatever light he can shed."

"Sure. I'll message him tonight. Do you know the name of Casey's company?"

"No, but that I think Peyton probably does, so I'll ask her when she gets home."

We continued to discuss the best plan of action for keeping eyes on Peyton. Between the eight of us, it would be relatively easy to manage coverage for all the hours she wasn't in school. How she'd feel about that, I wasn't sure.

"Are you planning to tell her what's going on?" I asked.

Ford scrubbed a hand down his face. "I haven't decided. I don't want to freak her out. But I don't want her uninformed, either."

"You could explain all of this away as just caution because of the Galef murder," Daniel suggested. "And if Sawyer's guy finds something more pertinent, address it then."

Ford met my gaze across the room. "What would you do?"

It was a strange feeling being consulted like this. I understood why. I was the most like her. But it didn't change the sense that he was treating me as if I were Peyton's other parent.

"I think she's had enough challenges settling into a new life here. If we can do this without giving her cause to worry more than she already does, I think that's better. Everything's too vague right now, so telling her is only going to bring up a lot of questions none of us have answers to. She has enough unknowns."

"Okay. Then that's what we'll do."

We finalized a few more details, then everybody began filing out, heading their separate ways, until somehow I found myself the only one left. This wasn't where I wanted to be. I'd tried to avoid exactly this. My brain urged my feet to move, to carry me as far as possible from this man who still had the power to decimate me. But one look at Ford's face stopped me. His broad shoulders were slumped, the weight of this threat only adding to the responsibility and worry of new parenthood. I couldn't just walk away when he looked like this.

"Hey." I touched his arm. "We won't let anything happen to her."

His eyes met mine, raw with emotion. "I just found her. And now I find out someone could be after my kid?"

"That's not going to happen." Before I could think better of it, I stepped closer, wrapping my arms around him in the first hug I'd initiated in more than ten years.

Ford's breath caught for half a beat before those big, strong arms wrapped around me, pulling me tight against that broad, muscular chest. It was the same and somehow different. Even though we'd both changed, my body recognized his. The shape and scent of him. The steady thump of his heart, and that indefinable feeling that, in his arms, I was anchored against anything and everything the world could throw at me.

God, I'd missed this. Missed him.

His brow came down to rest against mine. Our breaths mingled, and suddenly this was no longer a friendly hug. But I didn't pull away. Callused fingers skimmed up the side of my neck, and I couldn't hold back a shiver as he brushed the hair back from my face.

"I've missed you, Bree. So fucking much." His voice had gone to gravel, as it always did when he held back big emotion. "Not just your friendship, although absolutely that, but what we might have been if I hadn't been so damned stupid."

My heart thundered in my chest as I stared into the stormy green of his eyes. What the hell was I supposed to do with that? Or with the attraction that still hummed between us? "What are you saying?"

"That it wasn't a mistake. That *we* weren't a mistake, and I wish I'd never left."

I hardly dared to breathe because this was everything I'd wanted to hear from him for *years*. But how could I believe him? This man had shattered me once before. Only a fool would allow him close enough to do it again.

But my brain short-circuited as Ford's thumb traced along my jaw. I shivered at the warmth of his touch, unable to run because every cell in my traitorous body wanted more. His eyes darkened, and I almost wept as he closed that final distance between us. The first brush of his lips against mine was tentative, careful—so different from that desperate, drunken night we'd never discussed.

This was deliberate. Intentional. And somehow that made it more devastating than anything we'd shared before.

I'd kissed other men in the past ten years. Plenty of them. I'd done a hell of a lot more. But they'd all been just physical release. Carefully managed encounters that never threatened my heart. But this... this was *Ford*. My best friend. The man who'd known me better than anyone. Who still knew exactly how to touch me to make me melt.

His tongue swept across my bottom lip, and I opened for him with a soft sound that might have been a whimper. I didn't care. One of his hands slid into my hair while the other curved around my hip, pulling me closer. The solid wall of his chest pressed against mine, and suddenly I couldn't get enough. After so many years with almost no physical contact, I needed to feel him. All of him. My fingers curled into his shirt as I rose to my toes, deepening the kiss, desperate to get closer.

All my carefully constructed defenses, my determination to hold on to my anger, my hurt, were dissolving under the heat of his mouth, the perfect fit of his body against mine. I'd forgotten how *right* this felt. Or maybe I'd just refused to remember.

God knew, there was no way I could make myself forget again.

Ford's hands slid down my back, and I arched

into him with a gasp. His mouth traveled down my throat, finding that spot below my ear that drove me crazy. I clutched at his shoulders, my body on fire, every shred of my good sense simply gone.

His voice was rough against my skin. "I've dreamed about this. About you."

My fingers tangled in his hair as I dragged his mouth back to mine. I couldn't handle talking right now. Not when he'd reduced me to a quivering mass of sheer need. The kiss turned fierce, desperate. He gripped my hips, lifting me up until my long legs wrapped around his waist. The bulge of his erection pressed against my center through my jeans, driving me a little more crazy as he carried me into the kitchen. My ass settled on a hard surface. The kitchen counter. I could work with that. I tightened my legs, pulling him closer as I devoured his mouth.

The sound of a car door slamming had us jerking apart, gasping.

Ford looked lust-addled and utterly confused.

"Peyton," I murmured.

For one more second, we stared at each other, panting. His hair was mussed where I'd run my fingers through it. My lips felt swollen, and I knew I had to look just as disheveled.

The door handle turned, and Ford backed up. I slid off the counter, shoving away from him, nearly falling in my haste to put some kind of distance between us.

Peyton bounced inside, stopping short with a look between us. "Oh, hey Bree! I didn't know you were here."

Could she see my heart thundering in my chest? "I was just leaving." My voice came out half an octave higher than normal. I couldn't look at Ford. Couldn't process what had just happened. "I've got to get back to the Brewhouse."

I bolted for the door, calling for Keeley and ignoring Peyton's confused "But I thought Monty was covering tonight?"

The cool evening air hit my flushed face as I practically ran across the yard to my house. What the hell had I been thinking? I couldn't do this. Not with Ford. Not again.

I slammed my door behind me and sagged against it, trying to catch my breath. But all I could think about was the heat of Ford's mouth and how badly I wanted to go back for more.

CHAPTER 27

FORD

As Peyton frowned at the door Bree had just run through like a bat out of hell, I snatched up the nearest thing I could use to hide my erection—the stew pot I hadn't yet found a proper home for. Mortification crawled up my neck as I struggled to get blood flow back into my brain. I could still taste Bree on my lips, still feel her wrapped around me. God, it was everything I'd dreamed of for the past ten years and nothing I expected to have again. We were still combustible, as evidenced by exactly where that little interlude would've been headed had my kid not had the worst possible timing.

Said kid glanced back at me and arched a brow. "Are you okay? You're all red in the face."

Christ, this was worse than being caught by my

moms. "Sure, I'm fine." *Redirect. Redirect.* "How did things go with Ed?"

Peyton bounced on her toes, seemingly oblivious to the fog of sexual tension still hanging in the air. "So Ed says some of the locations on this map are new to him. Like, they might've just been artistic license, but *some* of them might've been pulled from the old stories instead of the accepted history."

My pulse gradually began to slow. "Oh, yeah?" I loved that she was getting so excited about a tourist map. I could definitely appreciate a sense of adventure.

"We're going to compare it to some of his old maps. He thinks there's a possibility there could be actual pirate caches that nobody's found yet because they've been looking in the wrong places." Her eyes lit up. "Can we go treasure hunting?"

I doubted there was treasure to be found, but the excitement radiating off her made me smile. After everything she'd been through, seeing her act like a regular kid felt like a gift—like maybe I wasn't completely screwing this whole dad thing up. "Sure. Sounds fun. Did you pick which pirate you're doing your paper on?"

"Jack Rackham, I think." She fidgeted with the edge of the map that had been her constant companion the past few days, clearly bursting to share more.

"Good ol' Calico Jack. Why him?" I leaned forward, genuinely curious about what had caught her interest. These glimpses into her personality felt precious, like pieces of a puzzle I was slowly putting together.

Peyton grinned, and the expression transformed her whole face. "Pirate romance, duh. After he dumped Blackbeard on Ocracoke, he hooked up with Anne Bonny. Now *she's* who I'm really interested in, but since she wasn't from around here, she's not on the list." Her eyes sparkled with enthusiasm as she talked about the female pirate.

I grinned back, loving this glimpse of teenage sass. "Down with the patriarchy?"

"Heck, yeah." She sat up straighter, looking proud of herself, and for a moment I could see exactly who she'd be in a few years—fierce and unstoppable, exactly as a woman should be.

She finally seemed to register the stew pot in my hands. "What's for dinner?"

"Uh, haven't figured that out yet. Spaghetti maybe." I had no idea if we had pasta or meatballs or even a jar of sauce, but it was the first thing to pop into my head. Saved from mortal embarrassment, I set the pot on the stove.

"School go okay, today?" I'd picked her up myself at the end of the day, but she hadn't been in a talking mood as I'd ferried her to the Brewhouse to meet with Ed, and I'd been too focused on watching everyone we passed and wondering if they were somehow out to harm my daughter.

"It was fine."

"Want to tell me about it?"

After a moment's hesitation, Peyton hopped up on one of the barstools, and I began rummaging through cabinets to assess our spaghetti situation.

"So Madison totally likes Trevor, but Trevor's best friend Jake likes Madison's best friend Sarah, who actually has a crush on Trevor." She paused for breath. "And now Madison's mad at Sarah because she thinks Sarah's trying to steal Trevor, even though Sarah would never do that to her best friend."

Bowtie pasta. I had no idea where it had come from, but I could work with that. I set the box on the counter. "That's... complicated."

"I *know*. And the worst part is, Trevor doesn't even know Madison exists like that. He's too busy mooning over Kaylee, who's dating some high school freshman." She propped her chin on her hands. "But Madison and Trevor would be perfect together. They both love anime, and they both volunteer at the animal shelter."

I found a jar of sauce that I also didn't remember buying and some frozen meatballs. I suspected one of my moms had come by and hidden groceries when I wasn't looking. "Sounds like you've given this a lot of thought."

"Well, yeah. Madison's my friend. I want her to be happy."

I wanted the same for Peyton, and I was thrilled she'd made a friend, even if I had no idea who Madison actually was. I'd have to rectify that.

Peyton sighed dramatically. "Love is *hard*."

I bit back a smile, remembering how everything had felt like life or death at that age. "That it is, kiddo."

"I mean, look at you and Bree. You obviously still like each other, but you're both being stupid about it."

I nearly dropped the pot I was filling with water. "We're not—that's different."

"Uh-huh." She gave me a look that was pure teenager. "Sure it is."

Yea though I walk through the valley of the shadow of parenthood...

Deliberately, I turned my back and finished filling the pot with water, setting it on the stove to boil. "Did anything *else* happen today?"

"Well, not at school, but at the Brewhouse everybody was talking about how that Galef's guy's apartment was broken into."

"Really? I hadn't heard that yet." Of course. I hadn't actually stopped anywhere in town today.

"Bonita said she heard it from her cousin Danica, who's dating Chris Shelton, who's apparently a police officer in town."

My lips twitched at her recitation of sources. "We'll turn you into a small-town girl yet."

Peyton grinned again. "The gossip is kinda fun, when you're not the topic of it."

"Fair enough." Deciding this was as good an opening as I was going to get, I sobered. "Speaking of Galef, there's something I wanted to talk to you about."

For once, she didn't stiffen up at my tone, and I called that progress. Taking the time to dump the meatballs and sauce into another pan, I set them to warm on low heat and went to join her at the counter. "How are you feeling about all this stuff? Are you worried?"

"I mean, maybe a little, because everybody's wigged about it. But whatever's going on, it's got nothing to do with me, so not really?" She didn't sound entirely sure.

"Would you like to try some self-defense training? There's a class down at the community center."

"Self-defense training?"

"It's a handy thing for anybody to have. But I won't push you to do anything you're not comfortable with. I just want to do whatever you need to feel safe. And maybe a little more than that, to make me feel like you're safe."

Peyton's lips tipped into a frown. "What does that mean?"

"Nothing bad. Just that I don't want you going anywhere alone while all this is going on. As you say, it's got nothing to do with you, but I wouldn't want you to accidentally stumble into something by being in the wrong place at the wrong time. So we're gonna stick with pick up and drop off from school and from anywhere else you need to go. If I or Grandma Flo or Mimi can't do it, one of my other friends will. Okay?"

"Okay. I can live with that."

"Did you want to try the class?"

"Can I think about it?"

"Sure." With all the sexism and misogyny women and girls faced, I wanted her to be able to defend herself. But that was a longer term goal. A few self-defense classes were no substitute for consistent training. Maybe I could get her into some form of martial art. I'd have to check to see what was available.

"You wanna go dump your bag and do whatever you need to do while I finish putting dinner together?"

"Can we have garlic bread?"

"I don't think we have any bread but hamburger buns."

"So? We've got butter and garlic powder, don't we?"

"Equal opportunity bread lover. I respect that. I'll make some garlic toast."

Scooping up her backpack, she flounced out of the room. Surely that flounce meant she'd actually had a good day?

Once I heard the door to her room open, I finally let out a long, slow breath and scrubbed both hands down my face.

Much as I hated that Peyton had interrupted us, it was probably for the best. Falling back into bed with Bree would do nothing to prove to her that I'd changed. That she was actually a priority for me. That I could find a way to be there for her *and* Peyton in a way that could work for us all.

But the kiss gave me a hope I hadn't dared reach for after I'd walked out of her kitchen yesterday. She might not want to want me, might not want whatever she felt for me, but that kiss had made it abundantly clear I wasn't in this alone. Even with all her walls, all her defenses, I'd felt her melt against me, felt the way her fingers had curled into my shirt. All the years of regret and longing had poured into that moment, and I knew damn well she'd felt it too. The question was whether she'd let herself acknowledge it, or if she'd keep pushing me away like she had been since the day I came back.

Probably not, considering that the moment we'd been interrupted, the moment she'd had a chance to think, she'd fled. I knew Bree Cartwright. She was on the retreat now, scrambling to talk herself out of what she wanted because it came along with feelings. Nothing on earth scared her more than those. And I got it—after what her parents had done, after what I'd done, she had every reason to be gun-shy. But I wasn't going anywhere this time, and sooner or later, she'd have to face that.

Sawyer had said I needed to show her with actions what she needed to see. So I'd do exactly that. I was here now. And I was determined to prove to her I could be what she needed. What she deserved.

I just wished figuring out the details was as easy as figuring out what to feed a thirteen-year-old girl.

CHAPTER 28
BREE

I pulled another draft from the tap, carefully angling the glass to get the perfect head of foam. The habitual motions helped steady my hands, which had been trembling since last night. Since I'd lost my damned mind and vaulted over all my carefully constructed walls to try to climb Ford like a tree.

"—and then they tossed the whole place!" Wally's voice cut through my spiraling thoughts. "Papers everywhere, drawers dumped out. Amateur hour, if you ask me."

"Eight days after they found the body." Duck stabbed a French fry in the air between each word for emphasis. "What kind of idiot waits that long to search a dead man's apartment?"

I slid the beer across to a waiting customer, grateful for the distraction of the Gray Beards' latest theories about David Galef's murder. Anything to keep my mind off Ford's hands in my hair, the heat of his body against mine...

"Bet they were looking for money," Milt declared. "Man like that, working for the fishing company, probably skimming off the top. You know he got let go from O'Connell's because they thought he was spying for Atlantic. Fishing espionage or some shit."

"Fishing espionage? What kind of bull pucky is that? Nah, had to be documents," Cliff countered. "You don't tear apart furniture looking for cash."

"Unless the cash was hidden in the furniture," Duck pointed out.

"What do you think, Bree?" Wally called out. "You're being awful quiet over there."

I managed what I hoped was a neutral smile. "Just trying to keep up with the lunch rush, fellas."

"Speaking of quiet," Duck leaned forward conspiratorially. "Heard you were over at Ford Donoghue's place last night."

I nearly dropped the glass I was holding. Pop shot me a knowing look from his perch at the end of the bar. Recovering quickly, I focused on pulling the next pint. "It wasn't just me. Willa and Sawyer, Gabi and Daniel, and Mama Flo and Mimi were there, too. Making sure we're all on the same page about keeping an eye on Peyton with everything going on."

"Mm-hmm," Duck hummed skeptically. "That why you're blushing?"

"That's enough out of you." Pop's stern voice cut off the teasing, and I was grateful.

I grabbed a stack of menus, desperate for something to do with my hands that didn't involve resisting the urge to trace my still-tingling lips. But even that simple task proved challenging, as flashbacks of the kiss kept hijacking my brain. The tug of Ford's fingers threading through my hair. The solid warmth of him wrapped around me. The way my breath had hitched as his tongue delved into my mouth... and how I'd so desperately wanted more of him inside me.

I stumbled into an empty chair, the menus scattering across the floor. Sweet Jesus, I needed to get it together. But how was I supposed to function when my body kept replaying every scorching second?

"You okay there, sweetheart?" Duck's concerned voice yanked me back to reality.

"Fine!" My voice came out embarrassingly squeaky. "Just... clumsy today."

I gathered the fallen menus, willing my hands to steady. But it was no use. My mind kept circling back to that endless moment before Peyton walked in—Ford's hips pressing against me, his fingers gripping my ass, his tongue doing wicked things that made me forget every reason I'd spent a decade shutting him out of my life.

If his daughter hadn't interrupted us... The heat blooming in my cheeks had nothing to do with embarrassment and everything to do with exactly where I imagined those talented hands would have wandered next. Where I'd wanted them to wander next. And I'd have let him. God help me, I'd have let him do any damned thing he pleased because one touch had me ready to beg.

Because I hadn't learned a damned thing. Ford Donoghue was my personal addiction, and I'd just fallen off the wagon in a big way.

"Maybe you should take a break," Pop suggested quietly. "Get some air."

Air. Right. Because what I definitely needed was time alone with my X-rated thoughts about my former best friend and current sexy pain in my ass.

"I'm fine."

I turned blindly toward the door as it opened again. "Welcome to the Brewhouse!" My voice was entirely too bright, and the faintly amused looks on Lindsay and Astrid's faces told me they'd noticed. "Oh, hey y'all. Here for lunch?"

Of course, they're here for lunch. Why the hell else would they be here?

"I need emotional support fish tacos," Lindsay declared.

At my questioning glance, Astrid explained, "Corbin is back."

"Ah. So you'll be needing extra mango salsa and a Corona on the side?"

Lindsay folded her hands into a prayer position. "Pretty please."

Relieved to have something to do, I nodded. "I got you, girl. Astrid?"

"Burger with the works and sweet potato fries. And a Diet Coke."

As the Brewhouse was only half full, I waved at the dining room. "Sit wherever you like."

Heading back to the kitchen, I put in their order with Bonita and went to get their drinks. They'd settled at a table by the window.

"Join us for a few?" Lindsay pleaded. "I need to tell someone about the most humiliating moment of my life, and you make the best sympathetic faces."

I glanced around the dining room. The lunch crowd was thinning out, and I saw Pop sliding behind the bar. "Sure, I can spare a few minutes."

I slid into the empty chair, and Lindsay immediately launched into her tale of woe. "So I'm at my desk this morning, right? And I'd gotten there early because I wanted to organize everything before Corbin came in. New boss, first day back, wanted to make a good impression."

"Unlike high school, when you tried to impress him by falling down the bleachers."

Lindsay shot Astrid a death glare. "We agreed never to speak of that again."

Relieved to finally have something to focus on instead of my own situation, I grinned. "What happened this morning?"

"I was practicing what I was going to say. You know, professional small talk. Welcome back, here's what you missed, that kind of thing." Lindsay buried her face in her hands. "Except I was saying it out loud. To myself. Complete with different voices and facial expressions."

"Oh, no."

"Oh yes. And guess who walked in right as I was doing my best impression of his father?"

I winced. "He didn't."

"He did! Standing there in the doorway, watching me make a complete fool of myself." Lindsay groaned. "I can never show my face there again. I should just move. Maybe join a convent."

"You're Methodist," Astrid pointed out.

"I'll convert! Anything to avoid having to look him in the eye again."

I fought back a laugh. "What did he say?"

"He just smiled and said 'Good morning, Lindsay.' Like I hadn't just been caught talking to myself and imitating his family!" She slumped forward, forehead hitting the table with a soft thunk. "Kill me now."

"I'm sure it wasn't that bad." I didn't sound convincing to my own ears.

From her position on the table, Lindsay's muffled voice begged, "Subject change, please!"

"We've got you, boo." Astrid patted her on the head and turned her attention to me. "So you've made up with Ford, huh?"

I jolted so hard, I nearly fell out of the chair. "What?"

Astrid's gaze sharpened. "I mean, I just thought you were helping out with his daughter, but that reaction makes me think something else is going on with your new neighbor."

Get it the fuck together, Cartwright.

"Nothing is going on with Ford." My brain started the highlight reel of that kiss again. "As you say, I'm just helping with Peyton, because I understand her situation in a way most people don't. He asked for my expertise, as it were."

Lindsay smirked. "Is that what they're calling it these days?"

I rolled my eyes. "Get your mind out of the gutter. Just because you're crushing on your boss..."

"We agreed on a subject change!"

"Anyway, she's a really sweet kid. And she's totally crushing on my dog, so I'm seeing a lot of her."

"Well, I think it's really great of you to help him out like this." Astrid sipped at her Diet Coke. "I'm sure he's been struggling with the whole single dad thing."

Nope. I wasn't biting at that. "He's stepping up. That's all anyone can ask. I'm gonna go check on your food."

Before they could say anything else, I made my escape.

Back behind the bar, I found Pop hunched over what looked like a Xerox copy of old parchment, his reading glasses perched on the end of his nose.

"What's all this?" I leaned over his shoulder. "Something for Peyton's paper?"

His eyes sparkled. "Oh, this goes way beyond some school assignment. That little gal's got a real knack for historical research. We've been comparing these old maps to modern ones, and there are some fascinating discrepancies."

I couldn't help but smile at his enthusiasm. "So you two are cooking up a treasure hunt?"

"Maybe." He tapped the weathered paper. "These old sailing routes don't quite match up with what's documented. And some of the landmarks..." He trailed off with a secretive grin.

I could've told him her map was an artist's reproduction, but why should I spoil their fun? "You really like her, don't you?"

"She reminds me of another smart little girl who crashed into my life years ago." He peered at me over the rims of his glasses. "One who also needed somewhere to belong."

My throat tightened. "Pop..."

"I see how you look at that girl's daddy, too." His voice gentled. "It's okay to be scared, baby girl. But don't let fear keep you from something that might be worth the risk."

"I'm not—" The protest died at his knowing look.

"Bree, honey, I've watched you build walls higher than the lighthouse these past ten years. Maybe it's time to consider letting someone back in."

I traced my finger along the edge of the map, avoiding Pop's too-perceptive gaze. "It's not just about me anymore. Or even Ford. That kid has been through enough without getting caught in the crossfire if things go wrong between us."

"And if things go right?"

"Pop." The word came out strangled.

"Look at me, baby girl."

I lifted my eyes reluctantly to meet his.

"That child already loves you. And unlike the people who left you, Ford came back. He's trying to do right by his daughter. Maybe it's time to consider he might do right by you, too."

My chest ached. "I can't."

"Can't or won't?"

"Order up!" Bonita's call saved me from having to decide.

But as I swung to pick up the food, I knew the answer was both.

CHAPTER 29
FORD

Bree was officially hiding.

It had been three days since The Kiss, and I hadn't seen her once. She'd already been out when I'd tried to stop by before taking Peyton to school. If she'd come home before going into work, she'd done it with a stealth that would've made a SEAL proud. She'd been getting home late from the Brewhouse. Busy or avoiding me? Maybe some of both. I'd stayed up each night, making sure she actually got in okay, but I hadn't gone over. I hadn't wanted to leave Peyton alone. But more, I hadn't wanted to risk what might happen if Bree and I were alone together in a space where we wouldn't get interrupted.

She needed time. I also knew she'd argue she needed space, but this was as much as I was willing to give her, which was part of why I'd sprung Peyton from her algebra homework for us to go grab dinner at the Brewhouse. I also hoped to find some way to talk to Peyton about the stolen shipment of her stuff. There'd been no word from the shipping company or the police, and I knew I couldn't put this off forever. I hoped delicious food and good atmosphere might soften the blow a little.

I pulled into the Brewhouse lot, and Peyton was out of the car before I'd even killed the engine. She bolted through the front door, making a beeline for the corner booth where Ed and the other Gray Beards were settled.

"Hi Ford's daughter!" Milt called out, his hearing aid squealing.

Wally smacked Milt's shoulder. "Her name is Peyton, you old coot."

Milt cupped a hand behind his ear. "What? Who's praying?"

Was he ever going to get his hearing checked?

Peyton slid into the booth beside Ed, already pulling out her phone to show him something. My kid had adopted a whole gaggle of honorary grandfathers, and they'd taken to her like she was their own flesh and blood.

"We found another discrepancy on that map," Ed told her, leaning in close. "See here? The original survey shows..."

I couldn't make out the rest as the other Gray Beards chimed in with their own theories about whatever treasure hunting project they had going. The sight of them all fussing over her made my chest tight.

These men had been fixtures at the Brewhouse since... well, since it was still the original Tidewater Tavern. They'd watched me grow up, razzing me about everything from my first crush to joining the Navy. Now they were doing the same for my daughter.

My gaze swept the room, looking for Bree. She was behind the bar, looking harried as she pulled beers and poured drinks. As it was Friday night, the place was jumping.

The hostess appeared at my elbow, a couple of menus in hand. "We've got a table for you and Peyton over in the corner."

I didn't want to throw Bree off her game, so I followed Carly to our seat. A few minutes later, the Gray Beards dispersed, most of them heading out, so Peyton finally came to join me.

"Getting somewhere on your treasure hunting project?"

"We think so. Mr. Ed is trying to narrow down our search parameters."

I pretended to study the menu while keeping an ear on Peyton's excited chatter about the treasure map project. Despite the change in name, the core of the menu hadn't changed in years. I could recite it in my sleep.

"Did you hear about the break-in at the O'Connell Fishing Company?" A woman's voice carried from the next table.

"The place where that Galef guy worked?" her companion asked.

"Yeah. Well, used to work. I heard he got fired like two weeks before he died. Something to do with shady doings with Atlantic Fisheries. Anyway, the place was torn apart, just like his apartment. Their poor office manager, Lindsay Messina, surprised the intruder and got attacked. Police aren't sure if it's connected to Galef's murder, though."

"Wouldn't surprise me if it wasn't. Atlantic's been stealing other companies' catches for years. Is the office manager okay?"

"Yeah. Concussion, I think, but O'Connell's son showed up. He's keeping a close eye on her."

It was possible that the murder and the break in at O'Connell's weren't connected. As the woman had said, Galef had been fired a week or two before the murder. But given that Galef's apartment had also been tossed, that suggested someone was looking for something they believed Galef had. The question was what? Had that been why Galef was killed? Unfortunately, the guy seemed to have plenty of enemies. All the scuttlebutt I'd heard suggested he was a real asshole to most people. That hadn't made the police department's investigation any easier.

"Hi folks! Ready to order?" Our server appeared, notepad in hand.

"Peyton?" I gestured for her to go first.

She closed her menu. "Can I get the fish and chips? And a chocolate shake?"

"Make that two fish and chips," I said. "But I'll stick with water."

"You got it."

My gaze strayed to the bar, watching Bree move with practiced ease behind it as she served one customer after another. It was almost graceful, a kind of dance.

After the server left, Peyton propped her chin on her hand. "You know, if you want to go talk to her, you should."

I dragged my attention back to my daughter. "What?"

"Bree. You keep looking at her like a lost puppy."

Busted. Heat crept up my neck. "I do not."

"Do too." She smirked. "You're not subtle."

"When did you get so smart about relationships?"

"I'm thirteen, not blind. Plus, I read a lot of romance."

I groaned. "That's not helping your case." Shit, was that even appropriate reading for a kid her age?

"All I'm saying is, you obviously like her. And she likes you too."

I would've questioned that before The Kiss, but now I was pretty sure Peyton was right. Still. "It's complicated."

"Adults always say that when they're making things harder than they need to be." She fiddled with her straw wrapper. "I like her. She gets what it's like, you know? To not know where you belong."

My heart squeezed. "You belong here. With me. With Grandma Flo and Mimi. Always."

"I'm getting that. And I'm grateful." She glanced toward the bar. "But Bree understands what it was like before."

I followed her gaze just as Bree looked our way. I lifted my hand in a wave before I could think better of it. A blush stained her cheeks, and she quickly turned back to her customers.

"See?" Peyton said. "She's totally into you."

"You need to stop reading so much romance."

She rolled her eyes. "Never. Romance is a lesson to all women in what they ought to expect out of their future partners."

That was definitely not something I was ready to think about. I wasn't going to let her date until she was thirty. That was reasonable. Right?

"I take it you got this from your mom?"

"She was a big romance reader. Anyway, I'm just saying, if you want to date her, I'm cool with it."

I leveled Peyton with what I hoped amounted to a parental Look. "I appreciate your support." I just wished that Bree herself would be that cool with it.

From the corner of my eye, I saw Ed sit bolt upright in his booth, a pure *Eureka!* expression on his face. He shoved up from the booth, took two steps and keeled right over.

I was out of my seat, racing across the restaurant almost before he hit the floor.

"Pop!"

I dropped to my knees, reaching for him. "Ed? Can you hear me?"

Bree skidded to a halt beside us, her face sheet white. But her hands were steady. "Help me turn him over. Keep him lying down."

Ed's skin had taken on an alarming grayish cast, and his breathing came in short, uneven gasps. My training kicked in as I helped Bree turn him onto his side.

"Pop, did you take your blood thinners today?" Bree's fingers pressed against his pulse point.

Ed blinked up at us, confusion clouding his features. "What?"

"His pulse is erratic." Bree's voice remained steady, in direct contrast to the tremor in her hands. "Pop, focus. Your medication. Did you take it?"

"I... think so." Ed's words slurred.

"What's happening?" I kept my voice low, not wanting to add to the tension radiating through the now-silent restaurant.

"AFib attack." Bree's jaw clenched. "Worse than usual."

AFib. I remembered that long ago summer Ed had been going off-island for some doctor's appointments, but Bree had never said what it was all about. And then we'd imploded, so I hadn't had opportunity to ask about it again. Had she been dealing with this on her own for all these years?

"EMTs are four minutes out," someone called from across the bar, phone pressed to his ear.

I glanced over my shoulder to where Peyton stood frozen beside Monty, eyes wide with fear. Every instinct screamed to go to her, to shield her from this scene playing out. But one look at Bree's face—the terror she was fighting to contain as she monitored Ed's vitals—and I knew where I needed to be.

"What do you need?" I asked Bree.

"Keep him on his side. Talk to him. Keep him conscious." She shifted closer to Ed's head. "Pop, stay with me, okay? Help's coming."

Ed's unfocused gaze drifted between us. "Sorry to cause... such a fuss. But need to tell—"

"Hush." Bree's voice cracked. "You just focus on breathing."

I could hear sirens in the distance, growing closer. They couldn't get here fast enough.

The next four minutes felt like four years, as each tick of the clock was punctuated by Ed's labored breathing and Bree's quiet haranguing that he damned well better hang on. He was her only family, and I couldn't begin to fathom how terrified she was right now.

The EMTs, part of the Sutter's Ferry Fire Department, finally burst through the door, equipment in hand. I shifted back to give them room to work, but kept my hand on Ed's shoulder. Bree rattled off his medical history and medications with the rapid-fire precision of someone who'd done this before.

"He's on Eliquis for AFib. Last dose was this morning. His cardiologist is Dr. Matthews at Cape Fear Heart Associates in Wilmington. They have his full history."

The lead EMT nodded as his partner hooked Ed up to their portable monitors. "How long has he been experiencing symptoms?"

"Less than ten minutes. His pulse is erratic, and he's growing less responsive." Bree's voice was still steady, but her hands shook harder.

The monitor beeped a warning. Ed's eyes had drifted shut.

"Pop?" Bree leaned forward. "Pop, can you hear me?"

"BP's dropping," one EMT announced. "We need to move."

"Should we transport to Outer Banks Hospital?" the other asked.

"No, call for Medevac. With his history, we need to get him to New Hanover Regional. They've got the cardiac unit."

Bree's face went even paler. "I'm coming with him."

"Ma'am, there won't be room in the chopper. We'll need to stabilize him for transport. Best thing you can do is meet us there."

I grabbed Bree's hand and squeezed. "I'll take you."

She started to shake her head, but I cut her off. "You're in no shape to drive yourself, and you know it. Let me help."

The EMTs had Ed on the gurney now, oxygen

mask in place. If possible, his skin had gone even grayer.

"The chopper's eight minutes out," someone called.

Her eyes wide and panicked, Bree's fingers tightened around mine. "Okay. Yes."

CHAPTER 30

BREE

The fluorescent lights cast harsh shadows across Dr. Mitchell's face as she delivered the news. "The stroke was caused by a clot that broke free during the AFib episode. We've placed Mr. Cartwright in a medically induced coma to give his brain time to heal and reduce the swelling."

My hand tightened around Ford's. He hadn't let go. Not once since he took my hand at the Brewhouse. Not on the long ferry ride across the sound to the mainland. Not on the drive to the mainland hospital. Not now. And that contact was the only thing keeping me from falling completely apart as the doctor continued to talk.

My first instinct had been to pull away, to handle this the way I handled everything—alone.

But for once, I couldn't make myself do it. Couldn't pretend I was fine. The thought of facing this without support terrified me more than accepting his help.

The medical terminology washed over me in waves. Tissue damage. Anticoagulants. Potential outcomes. I caught maybe one word in three. This was everything I'd been terrified of happening since the summer he'd been diagnosed all those years ago.

"When will you know if..." My voice cracked. I couldn't finish the question.

"The next seventy-two hours are critical." Dr. Mitchell's expression softened. "I wish I could give you more definitive answers, but right now we're monitoring and waiting to see how he responds to treatment."

Ford's thumb stroked across my knuckles. "What's the best-case scenario?"

"If the swelling reduces and there's minimal tissue damage, we can begin reducing sedation. But I need to be clear—even in the best case, your grandfather will have a long recovery ahead."

I nodded mechanically, trying to process it all. Pop had always been my rock, the one constant in my life since I was eight years old. The thought of losing him left me reeling. How could there possibly be any kind of life without Pop? The Brewhouse wouldn't be the same without him in that corner booth or pitching in behind the bar.

"Can I sit with him?"

"Of course. The nurse will take you to his room. Just remember, even in a coma, patients can often hear what's happening around them. Talk to him. Let him know you're there."

Ford squeezed my hand. "I'll be right outside if you need me."

I shook my head. If he let me go, I'd crumble. "Stay. Please." The words came out barely above a whisper. "I don't think I can do this alone."

The admission cost me. I'd spent so many years proving I didn't need anyone, building walls to protect myself. But walls weren't much use when your world was crumbling.

His eyes met mine, full of understanding and something deeper I wasn't ready to examine. "Whatever you need, Bree. I'm here."

The ICU nurse led us down a maze of sterile corridors that all looked the same. The antiseptic smell burned my nose, bringing back memories of the last time I'd been in a hospital. After the AFib attack that had earned Pop this diagnosis.

Ford's solid presence at my side kept those memories from drowning me.

Room 412. The nurse pushed open the door, and my breath caught. Pop lay still as death in the hospital bed, tubes and wires connecting him to an array of beeping monitors. His weathered face looked sunken, gray. This wasn't my Pop. My Pop was larger than life, always moving, always doing. Even after he'd officially "retired," he never really stopped working.

Now he looked small. Fragile. Old.

My legs threatened to give out as we approached the bed. Ford's arm slipped around my waist, steadying me.

With trembling fingers, I reached for Pop's hand. His joints were knotted with arthritis from decades of working on boats and behind the bar, but his grip had always been strong. Now his hand lay limp in mine.

"Hey Pop." My voice cracked. I cleared my throat and tried again. "You really scared us back there. But you're going to be okay. You have to be okay."

The steady beep of the heart monitor was my only answer.

"You can't leave me, Pop. Who's going to tell me I'm working too hard? Who's going to share coffee with me in the morning and tell me stories about the old days?" Tears spilled down my cheeks. "Who's going to help me keep Monty in line when he tries to do something else outrageous with beer? I need you."

I squeezed his hand, willing him to squeeze back. "You're all I've got left. You're the only one who's never left me. You can't start now."

I don't know how long we stayed. I don't remember what else I said.

Eventually, the nurse came back. Her gentle touch on my arm pulled me from my daze. "I'm sorry, but visiting hours are over. You can come back first thing in the morning."

I stared at her, uncomprehending. Leave? How could I leave him here alone?

"Come on." Ford's voice was soft near my ear. His hand remained steady at my waist as he guided me into the hallway.

The fluorescent lights buzzed overhead. My legs felt like rubber. The weight of decisions I needed to make pressed down on my shoulders. I had to call Monty about covering the Brewhouse. Had to figure out where to stay tonight. Had to—

My breath hitched. The walls of the corridor started closing in.

Ford's arms came around me, solid and real. His chin rested on top of my head as I pressed my face into his chest. The salt and sandalwood scent of him wrapped around me like a security blanket.

God, I'd forgotten how safe he could make me feel. How he'd always been able to ground me when everything else spun out of control.

But that was the problem, wasn't it? I'd let myself believe in that safety once before. Let myself need him. And then he'd left.

My fingers curled into his shirt, anyway. Just for right now, I told myself. Just until I could think straight again. Just until I could stand on my own.

His heart beat steadily under my ear, and I wondered if he could feel mine trying to break free of my chest. If he knew how terrified I was—not just of losing Pop, but of falling back into old patterns. Of trusting. Of needing.

I'd always prided myself on being strong, on never needing anyone. But maybe real strength was knowing when to let someone help carry the load. Even if just for a night.

We stood there in that sterile hallway, neither of us speaking. Neither of us moving. His thumb traced circles on my back, and I fought the urge to melt further into his embrace.

Digging for some reserve of strength I didn't know I had, I eased back far enough to look into his face. "Thank you for coming with me. For getting me here. But you should get home to Peyton."

"Peyton is covered. Mom and Mimi have her. Right now, my only priority is you."

My only priority is you. The words echoed through my head, seeming to gather heft and weight with each repetition.

God, how many times had I dreamed of hearing that? How many nights had I lain awake wishing he'd chosen me over the Navy? Over his brothers? Over anything?

But this wasn't that. This was Ford being Ford. The good guy who always showed up when people needed him. Who always tried to do the right thing.

Except for that one time. That one devastating time when he believed doing the right thing had meant leaving.

I needed to remember that. Needed to hold on to that truth to keep from reading more into this moment than was really there. He had Peyton now. A daughter who needed him. Who deserved to be his priority.

This was just one night. One emergency. Tomorrow, everything would go back to normal, and I'd be handling things on my own again. The way I always had.

But right now... right now, he was here. His arms were around me, and I was too wrung out to pretend I didn't need it.

CHAPTER 31
PEYTON

I tapped my pencil against the page, staring at the algebra problem that might as well have been written in hieroglyphics. The numbers blurred together as my mind drifted back to Mr. Ed collapsing in the Brewhouse. The way his face had gone gray. How Bree's voice cracked when she shouted for someone to call 911.

Keeley whined at my feet, sensing my distress. I reached down to scratch behind her ears.

"I know, girl. I'm worried too."

The lighthouse keeper's cottage felt both cozy and strange. My grandmothers had made me feel welcome, but everything was still so new. Mimi had baked cookies earlier, trying to distract me, while Grandma Flo kept checking her phone for updates.

Mimi appeared in the doorway of my room with a mug of hot chocolate. "You don't have to finish that tonight if you can't focus."

I was pretty sure Mrs. Winslow wouldn't agree, but I still closed my textbook. "Thanks. Have they called?"

"Not since this morning." She set the mug down and perched on the edge of my bed.

"Is Bree okay?" But I already knew the answer. I'd seen her face when Mr. Ed fell. Like her whole world was crashing down.

"Your father's with her. That's what matters right now."

I nodded, picking up the hot chocolate. "Mr. Ed was showing me all these old maps. We were going to..." My voice caught. "He promised to take me treasure hunting when we figured out the right spot."

Keeley pushed her head into my lap, and I buried my fingers in her fur.

"I barely know him, but he was so nice to me. Like I belonged here."

Mimi squeezed my shoulder. "That's Ed. He's got a way of making people feel like they've always been part of the family."

"Is he gonna die?" The question burst out before I could stop it.

"Oh, honey." Mimi pulled me into a hug. "They're doing everything they can."

She really did give the best hugs. I tried not to cry, but tears slipped down my cheeks, anyway. It wasn't fair. I'd just found my dad, just started making friends here. Mr. Ed couldn't die. Bree couldn't lose him.

I sniffed. "I should be there."

Grandma Flo stepped into the doorway. "Your dad wanted you safe here with us, and the doctors are limiting Ed's exposure to other people right now. The best thing we can do is wait."

I needed to keep busy. Knuckling the tears away, I shut my algebra book. "I think I'm gonna try working on my history paper."

Mimi smiled and stroked a hand down my hair. "Okay. We'll leave you to it. We'll be downstairs if you need anything."

Once they'd gone, I pulled out Ed's notes. I'd grabbed them from the booth at the Brewhouse after the ambulance had taken him away. I knew he wouldn't have wanted them getting into the wrong hands. Or worse, thrown away.

I skimmed through the pages. His handwriting was a cramped sort of cursive that wasn't especially neat. Not that I could say a thing. Mom had called my own handwriting chicken scratch. Like it was my fault they'd taken cursive out of the school curriculum? I'd seen most of this before, as he'd kept me up to date on what he was doing, what lines he was tugging. But I found a page labeled "Contributing Artists" with a list of names. For a moment, I sat stumped. Then I remembered that Peter had told us that they'd been trying an experimental program where local artists made the maps for the gift shop. It made sense that, if there was an irregularity, we could ask the original artist about it.

I wondered how far he'd gotten. There were no further notations about it. If they were local artists, chances were Mimi knew them. Or at least knew of them. I could ask her about all the names on the list. But first I wanted to do a little internet sleuthing myself. Snagging my laptop, I opened a browser.

I typed in the first name from the list: "Marcus Delaney." The search results loaded, showing a few LinkedIn profiles and social media accounts, but nothing local. One Marcus Delaney was an accountant in Chicago, another taught high school in California, and a third sold real estate in Florida. None of them seemed connected to Hatterwick Island or map-making.

"Well, that's useless," I muttered. Keeley thumped her tail in response.

I refined my search, adding "Hatterwick Island" to the name. This time, the results were even more sparse—just a couple of random blog mentions that had nothing to do with art or maps.

Scrolling down, I noticed a Facebook post from the Hatterwick Island Community Center. It was from last October, advertising a local art show featuring "island talent." I clicked through and found a grainy photo of a gallery wall with various paintings and crafts. The caption listed several artists, including Marcus Delaney.

"Got you" I leaned closer to the screen.

The post didn't have much information. Just the dates of the show and a generic "thanks to all who participated" message. I clicked through to the Community Center's page, hoping for more details, but there was nothing else about Marcus or his work.

I went back to Ed's list and moved on to the second name: "Tessa Blackwood."

Keeley whined and nudged my hand with her nose.

"I know, I know. I should be doing my history paper." I scratched her ears. "But this feels important, girl. Mr. Ed was onto something, and I want to figure it out for him."

I typed in Tessa Blackwood's name and waited for the results to load, hoping this search would be more productive than the last one. Her name appeared in several local art show listings, and I found a link to the Outer Banks Summer Art Festival from last July. The event's Facebook page had albums full of photos showcasing artists and their work.

I clicked through to the gallery, scrolling past images of pottery displays, watercolor paintings, and woven baskets. Each photo had detailed captions listing the artists present. Some were candid shots of people mingling, others showed artists standing proudly beside their creations. I continued scrolling, scanning each image carefully. There were so many photos—the festival had apparently been a three-day event with dozens of participants.

About halfway through the album, my finger froze mid-scroll. My heart lurched into my throat.

"No way."

I leaned closer to the screen, studying the couple who'd been captured in candid. The guy was clean-shaven here, but it was definitely the same creepy dude I'd seen on the ferry and after. And the woman he was with here was the same one I'd seen him arguing with at school. I hadn't seen either of them since, and I'd just counted myself lucky, given everything else that was going on. But maybe that was actually weird, given how small the island really was.

As I read the names in the caption below, I sucked in a breath. "Holy shit."

Mr. Ed and I were on to something. And wouldn't it be the best get well present ever if I finished following his leads?

CHAPTER 32
FORD

A few days later, I found a quiet spot just down the hall from Ed's room in the ICU where I actually had decent signal. My phone vibrated as texts and voicemails began to roll in. I screened the lot of them, mentally filing things into what had to be dealt with and what could wait. A voicemail from Cross Country Moving had come in a couple of hours ago. I hit play.

"Mr. Donoghue, this is Mark Wheeler from Cross Country Moving. I have good news! Your shipment was recovered. We don't have a full inventory of everything we were originally carrying, but there's very little damage to what we have. As soon as the police release it, we'll have it on a truck and headed your way."

Well, that was good news. I never had told Peyton about the theft. I still would, since it was possible that stuff would be missing when we did get it, but at least not everything was lost.

Deeming everything else in my messages as things that could wait, I dialed home.

Mom answered on the first ring. "Ford?"

"Hey, Mom." I kept my voice low out of respect for anyone else in the area.

"What's the news?"

Now that I was out of Bree's sight, I let some of my own mask drop and scrubbed a hand down my face. "Well, we're past the first 72 hours. The doctor said that's the most critical. At this point, Ed's vitals are good, the brain swelling is going down, and prognosis is hopeful."

"Oh, thank God," Mom breathed.

"How's Bree?" Mimi asked.

She must have had me on speaker.

"She's holding up." That was the most positive thing I could say. In truth, she was barely holding it together, running on nothing but coffee and sheer stubbornness. Cartwrights had a boatload of that, but she was at low ebb by now. Her eyes were red-rimmed from exhaustion, and her shoulders carried the weight of all her fear. I wished I could do more to take that off her than simply putting sustenance in her hands or providing a shoulder for her to lean on and doze.

"I'm gonna try to get her to leave the hospital for a bit. Grab a hotel room so she can shower and sleep in something that isn't a chair." My own back was protesting the lack of horizontal surface the past three days.

"Is she eating?" Of course, that would be the first thing Mimi focused on.

"Ish? The hospital cafeteria here isn't bad. She's had some soup and a lot of tea. Some pudding." I rubbed at the ache in my neck. "How are things going there? How's Peyton?"

"I'm good. And tell Bree that Keeley's doing fine."

My heart squeezed. "I'll do that. I'm not sure how much longer we're gonna be over here, kiddo." I didn't want to leave Bree in her current condition, but if Peyton was struggling, I'd figure something out. Willa would probably come without hesitation. Either way, we'd make sure she wasn't alone.

But my daughter was made of tougher stuff. "We're all holding down the fort here. And we're sending all the positive vibes and stuff to Mr. Ed and Bree."

This kid was just amazing. I swallowed past the tightness in my throat. "They'll definitely appreciate all that."

"What about your work?" Mom asked. "Do you need us to bring you anything?"

"Sawyer's coming by in a bit with some overnight bags and my laptop. That'll set me up for a while longer." Feeling my phone vibrate, I checked the screen to find a text from the man himself saying he was downstairs. "In fact, he just got here, so I need to go down to meet him. I'll check in again soon."

After a quick goodbye to my mothers and daughter, I stepped into Ed's room. Bree looked up from where she sat at his bedside, her hands wrapped around one of his weathered ones. Her eyes were so shadowed, they looked bruised, and her skin had taken on that waxy, exhausted pallor that came from too many hours under fluorescent lights. I had no idea how she was still upright.

"Sawyer's here. I'm gonna run downstairs to get our bags, okay? I'll be right back."

She just nodded and turned back to her grandfather.

I hoofed it down to the lobby, where I found my friend waiting, two duffel bags and a laptop case in hand. His solid presence was a welcome relief after the strain of the past few days. "You're a lifesaver for this."

"Of course. We should've done it sooner. Willa packed Bree's bag with pajamas and toiletries and stuff. Several changes of clothes. I loaded you up with the basics: clean shirts, jeans, your shaving kit. Y'all need anything else?"

"Not that I can think of. Now that Ed's considered stable, I'm gonna try to get her to leave long enough to at least hit a hotel for a shower and a nap." Just the thought of how exhausted she looked made me want to bundle her up and tuck her into bed so she could rest. "She's running on fumes."

"That'll help, no matter what. Monty has the Brewhouse under control, so she doesn't have to worry about that. Everybody's pitching in." Sawyer shifted the bags. "The whole island's got your backs on this one."

"She'll be relieved about that when she surfaces long enough to remember life outside this hospital. Any other news from the island? Progress on the Galef investigation?"

Sawyer crossed his arms and rocked back on his heels, his expression grim. "Nothing really. Well, I say nothing. The police haven't figured out if the break-in at O'Connell's was related or not. But they totally questioned Hillary Russell in connection with the murder. You remember her from back in high school?"

I thought back through the blur of teenage memories, trying to place her face. "Cheerleader, right? Friends with Cara Conroy. I didn't realize she was still on-island." Last I'd heard, most of that crowd had scattered to bigger cities after graduation.

"Yeah. Ended up as the art teacher at the high school. One of the guys from my crew is married to one of her besties. Evidently she'd been dating Galef for a while. Not like getting married kind of serious. He broke up with her less than a week before the murder. Totally out of the blue. She'd apparently been thinking about ending it herself, so she wasn't too upset about it. At least not until the police hauled her in for questioning."

"As a suspect?" I tried to imagine the girl I remembered committing murder. Hillary had been Miss Popularity, and Galef had been... well, generally bad news. Maybe he'd grown the hell up somewhere along the way if he'd gotten her attention in the first place. Opposites attract was a thing for a reason. But murder?

Sawyer shrugged. "You know they always gotta look at the partners."

"Why'd they wait so long to question her? Shouldn't she have been one of the first people they talked to?"

"I don't think many folks knew they'd been dating. Once they found out, she got added to the list, but I think it was more procedure rather than any real suspicion that she did it. They're trying to build a timeline of what was going on in his world in the weeks before he died."

I considered everything I'd heard. "Lotta changes. Broke up with her, got fired from his job."

"I think Carson's trying to figure out who Galef pissed off enough to kill him."

"Guessing that's not a short list, given the guy's reputation. But seems like whoever it was is looking for something. Why toss the apartment after killing him if it was just a crime of passion?"

"Fair question. Either way, everybody on the island is nervy." Sawyer shifted. "It reminds me of those weeks after Gwen disappeared."

I'd been trying hard not to think about that, given I now had a child only a couple of years younger. "People want answers. The only thing that's keeping me settled is that whatever's going on with Galef has nothing to do with any of us. It seems like something that was personal, so I don't feel like we're in danger. Not from that, anyway."

"Here's hoping. There's been no word from Dax yet. But you'll be the first to hear."

In all the chaos of Ed's crisis, I'd almost forgotten that Sawyer's friend was digging into Casey's company. "Thanks. I appreciate it. All of it. I need to get on back. I don't wanna leave Bree for long."

"Sure." He pulled me in for a back-thumping

hug. "You let her know we're all praying for her and Ed."

"I will." Shouldering the bags, I headed back upstairs.

When I got back to Ed's room, Dr. Mitchell was there doing her rounds.

"His vitals are holding steady, and the latest scan shows continued improvement. He's stable, Miss Cartwright. You can take a break." Her voice was full of compassion.

Bree twisted her hands in her lap. "But what if something changes?"

It killed me to see her without her usual confidence.

"We have your contact information. I promise, the nurses will call immediately if there's any change in his condition." She glanced at the chair Bree had been living in. "The best thing you can do for him right now is take care of yourself."

I set the bags down. "There's a hotel just down the street. Half a mile, tops. You could get cleaned up, maybe catch a few hours of actual sleep."

She looked between Ed and me, clearly torn.

"Bree. Honey." I crouched beside her chair. "You heard the doctor. Ed's stable. And you won't do him any good if you collapse. Let me help."

Her eyes went glassy, but I could see her losing the battle with tears. She nodded once, and that capitulation alone would have told me exactly how exhausted she was.

I helped her up, steadying her when she swayed. Three days of hospital chairs had done a number on both of us.

"We'll call if there's any change," Dr. Mitchell reiterated. "But I don't expect there to be." She offered a kind smile. "Go rest."

Bree bent over the bed, brushing a kiss to Ed's temple. "I'll be back soon. Don't go anywhere."

When she hesitated, I squeezed her shoulder. "He's gonna be okay. C'mon."

Shouldering our bags, I led her out of the hospital for the first time in days.

The hotel wasn't far, which was good because Bree looked ready to pass out. I kept glancing at her as I drove the short distance, worried she'd fall asleep right there. Her head kept bobbing forward before she'd catch herself and jerk upright again.

Check-in was mercifully quick. The clerk didn't even blink at our obvious exhaustion or the fact that we definitely looked like we hadn't showered in three days. I signed whatever they put in front of me and took the key cards.

In the elevator, Bree swayed into my side. I wrapped an arm around her waist to steady her, and she didn't protest. I knew she'd never willingly lean on me. But I still had to resist the urge to pull her in close. I didn't want to take advantage of her mental or emotional state just because I needed to comfort.

"Almost there," I murmured as we reached our floor.

She mumbled something unintelligible as I guided her down the hall to room 317. The key card clicked. I shouldered the door open.

And stopped dead.

One bed. A king-size, but still just the one. I'd been so focused on just getting us somewhere to rest, I hadn't even thought to specify. Shit.

I stepped in, glancing around to see if there was a sofa that might fold out, but there was nothing. I set the bags down, already turning back for the door. "I'm sorry. I'll go back down and fix this."

Bree walked right past me, heading for the bathroom. "I don't care. I'm gonna shower."

The door clicked shut behind her, and a few moments later, I heard the water switch on.

Well, okay then.

I knocked on the bathroom door. "Your bag."

Bree opened it a crack and dragged the duffel inside.

While the shower ran, I settled at the small desk and opened my laptop. A flood of work emails demanded attention. I knocked out quick responses to the most urgent ones, confirming I'd remote in for tomorrow's meeting.

The water shut off. I rubbed my eyes, trying to focus on the screen.

The bathroom door opened, releasing a cloud of steam. Bree emerged wearing pink pajamas covered in... were those unicorns? I blinked, certain exhaustion was making me hallucinate.

"Your turn." She towel-dried her hair, seemingly unaware of how the whimsical sleepwear completely contradicted her usual image.

I grabbed my bag and retreated to the bathroom before she caught me staring at those ridiculous unicorn pajamas. The hot water felt amazing on my stiff muscles, and I stayed under the spray longer than strictly necessary, letting it pound away some of the tension of the past few days. God knew there was plenty of it to work through.

When I came out in sweats and a t-shirt, Bree was curled up on the far side of the bed, already dead to the world. Her damp hair fanned across the pillow, and she'd pulled the blanket up to her chin. Even in sleep, she maintained that careful distance she'd been keeping since I showed up on her doorstep for Peyton.

I stared at the floor, contemplating how badly my back would hate me for sleeping on it. But after three nights in hospital chairs, the thought was almost physically painful. My muscles twinged in protest at the mere idea.

Carefully, I eased onto the other side of the bed, staying as close to the edge as possible. Bree didn't stir. The scent of her shampoo drifted across the pillow, and I drifted to sleep and dreamed of piña coladas and getting caught in the rain with the woman softly breathing next to me.

CHAPTER 33

BREE

I woke disoriented, unsure what had pulled me from sleep. A slice of moonlight cut through the dark between curtains that weren't my own. Where the hell was I? My extra firm pillow moved, and I realized my head was resting against a broad chest that rose and fell with deep, even breaths.

Ford.

And then I remembered. Pop's AFib attack. The stroke. The hospital. The hotel room with only one bed.

Had he gathered me up in his sleep? Or had I gravitated to him like some comfort-seeking missile? I couldn't remember the last time I'd slept this deeply. My muscles felt heavy, saturated with exhaustion and relief.

Of course, I wasn't in the habit of staying up for almost three days in a row. The human body wasn't meant to run that long on coffee and pure mule-headedness, no matter what I'd tried telling myself in that endless hospital waiting room.

Ford shifted, his arms tightening around me, the warmth of his breath stirring the hair at my temple. My throat tightened. He'd been on the mainland with me for days, by my side through this whole nightmare with Pop. Handling paperwork. Fielding calls. Making sure I ate. Being exactly the rock I needed.

Putting me ahead of even his own daughter.

But we'd been here before, after the fire. He'd held me together when I thought my world was ending. Stood firm when I couldn't.

Until he didn't.

A tiny voice inside me whispered that this time was different. He wasn't some twenty-year-old kid anymore. He had Peyton to think about now, and he was committed to sinking in real roots on Hatterwick again because she needed stability. A home. He wasn't going anywhere.

The idea of that was as terrifying as it was comforting. Because if he stayed... if he *really* stayed... what did that mean for us? In the safety of the dark, I could admit that we'd been working our way back toward some form of an us from the moment I'd made that phone call and heard his voice.

"You're thinking really loud."

I jolted. "Sorry."

"You okay?" The sleepy rumble of his voice and the circles he traced on my back soothed the heart that had kicked into high gear.

"I don't know." The admission slipped out before I could stop it. Maybe because, in the cocoon of the dark, it felt safe to say that. Maybe because I was too tired to police my thoughts. Or maybe because, after everything that had happened, my carefully tended emotional walls had crumbled into dust.

"I keep waiting for the other shoe to drop. For you to leave again." The words burned my throat. "And I hate that I still care enough for that to matter."

Ford's chest expanded with a deep inhale, no doubt searching for patience, and tired of all my emotionally avoidant bullshit.

"Look, this is not the time for this, but I need you to hear this. I know I'm a package deal now. But I'm serious about proving that you're a priority for me." His fingers slid beneath the fall of my hair to cup my nape. "I can't promise I won't fuck up somehow and hurt you again. I'm human. But I won't do what I did before. I won't disappear on you."

I so desperately wanted to believe him. To let go of all my remaining defenses, because I was so damned tired of fighting everything I felt for him. And yet...

"What did you mean the other night about what we might have been?"

The question hung between us in the darkness, heavy with all the years of unspoken words and missed opportunities. I knew what I wanted him to have meant. Everything that mind-blowing kiss had implied. The promise of something real, something that could last. But I was done making assumptions about anything. I'd learned that lesson the hard way and paid for it with far too many sleepless nights and tears.

The silence stretched so long I wondered if he'd fallen back asleep. Or maybe he just wasn't going to answer.

His chest rose and fell beneath my cheek. "That you were the thing I didn't realize I'd been looking for. Right under my fucking nose." His fingers tightened on my nape. "I've loved you basically all my life, but I didn't realize until then that I was *in* love with you. Which was piss poor timing on my part, considering." A short, humorless laugh punctuated the statement. "But I was young and bone stupid."

In love with me. The words flowed over me like silk. The whisper of a promise unfulfilled. Of course, I'd been in love with him for years by then. But much as I'd wanted him, much as I'd needed him, I hadn't truly believed he'd loved me back. Not when he'd up and left.

Heart pounding so hard I thought it might burst from my chest, I swallowed past the lump in my throat. "That was a long time ago." The words came out hoarse, strained. It seemed only fair to give him the out. I hadn't planned to ambush him with any of this, hadn't meant to dredge up feelings better left buried in the past.

"Nothing's changed for me on that front, Bree." The rough pads of his fingers traced along my jaw, tipping my face up toward his. The touch sent sparks of electricity dancing across my skin. "I know it'll take time to earn back your trust, and I don't expect you to do anything with this right now because you've got too much on your plate, as it is. But it seems only fair to tell you that I'm still in love with you. I have been for the past ten years." His voice dropped lower, intimate in a way that made my stomach flutter and my toes curl.

There was pleasure and pain in hearing those words I'd waited for so long. He loved me. He wanted me back. He was willing to wait for me on my timetable. I'd wasted so many years holding him at a distance with my pain. My mind instantly began to race with all the reasons this was an absolutely terrible idea. All the ways this could go wrong. All the ways he could hurt me again, leaving me shattered and alone like everyone else in my past, save the man currently fighting for his life in that hospital bed.

But the reality was, no matter what Ford had done in the past, he was here. He'd been with me through the whole nightmare of this situation with Pop, handling my panic and grief and fear, without question, without wavering. He'd shouldered my emotional storms without flinching. He'd told me I was a priority, and he'd proved it with every quiet action and steadfast promise kept.

When would it be enough to overcome the landslide of shitty relationship examples that had led to this point? When would I believe what was directly in front of me, instead of letting the ghosts of old wounds cloud my vision? How many more times would I have to watch him show up, stay present, and prove himself before my heart would finally trust what my head already knew?

Ford loved me, and I was so damned tired of being afraid. Of fighting what I felt for him. Of pretending the magnetic pull between us wasn't strong enough to override a decade of carefully maintained distance.

My fingers curled into his t-shirt, the soft cotton bunching in my fists as I shifted, lifting my face to his, searching out the mouth that had haunted my dreams. The first brush of my lips against his was tentative. Ford sucked in a breath, his fingers flexing on my nape an instant before he pulled me closer. As he deepened the kiss, warmth spread through me like honey, and I melted against him, twining my legs with his.

This wasn't the desperate, drunken comfort of all those years ago. This was a promise. A beginning. Maybe a homecoming, too.

Ford's hands slid beneath my pajama top, skating up my spine. Trembling, I arched into the touch, desperate for more. As heat pooled at my center, I rocked against his powerful thigh, driving myself higher, searching for more friction. When that wasn't enough, I threw my leg over his hips, rolling to straddle him, until the bulge of his erection was nestled between my legs, a firm, warm pressure almost where I needed it most. My head fell back on a moan. Oh, God, that was better. I began to ride.

Ford cursed and gripped my hips, thrusting in time with my rhythm. "God, Bree. Shit. We don't— You're vulnerable. This isn't—"

I looked down at this man who'd been my rock, my comfort, my everything. The man who'd hurt me, yes, but who'd also loved me. Who'd never actually stopped loving me, despite all the years I'd pushed him away. I could feel it in his touch, hear it in his voice. And I knew I was done fighting. Done being afraid.

"This is exactly what I need. You're exactly what I need. Please, Ford."

CHAPTER 34

FORD

I wanted her. God, how I wanted her. Always had. The chemistry between us had only grown stronger over the years apart. But I hadn't expected this response when I'd crawled into bed beside her. Hell, I hadn't expected any of this. I'd assumed we'd clean up, rack out for a few hours, then head back to the hospital. But with Bree straddling me, rocking against my aching cock through our clothes, my brain was shorting out all my good intentions.

I had to be sure this wasn't grief or exhaustion or desperation talking.

Trying to hang on to some shred of control, I trailed kisses along her jaw. "Are you sure about this?"

"Don't be an idiot." She captured my mouth

again, swiveling her hips against mine as she plunged her tongue into my mouth, and whatever resistance I'd been clinging to crumbled.

My hands slid higher beneath her top, seeking the soft curves I remembered so well. "I don't want you to regret this." The words came out rough as I traced the underside of her breast with my thumb.

She pulled back just enough to meet my eyes in the darkness. "I only regretted last time because you left. You've just said you're not leaving again."

It was the absolute truth. I'd made my choice. I was staying on Hatterwick. For Peyton. And for Bree. And if she was finally ready to believe it, then I could finally, *finally* make love to her the way I'd wanted to all these years.

I tugged the ridiculous unicorn pajama top up and off. The dim glow of moonlight painted her bare breasts in silver. She was fuller now than she had been at twenty. Giving in to the urge to touch, I found each breast a perfect warm weight in my palms. Bree moaned, covering my hands with hers and pressing them tighter to her chest. I circled each nipple with my thumbs and watched them draw tight, begging for my mouth. I pulled her into reach, loving how her hips bucked to the rhythm of my suckling.

I wanted to taste every inch of her. Trailing kisses down the valley between her breasts, I savored the softness of her skin. Her breath hitched as I shifted to lavish attention on the other breast. The rhythm of her hips grew more frantic, and if I didn't want this over in the next thirty seconds, I needed her off my aching cock.

Rolling us both, I hooked my thumbs into the waistband of her pajama shorts and began to ease them down. Bree lifted her hips to speed along the process, no doubt expecting me to fast forward to the main event. But I had so much more I wanted to give her first.

I tossed the shorts aside and skimmed my hands down her thighs, feeling the soft skin and subtle tremble of her muscles. "You're beautiful."

"And you're overdressed." She managed to get ahold of my t-shirt and tugged it over my head.

The hungry look on her face as she took in my chest and arms in all their tattooed glory was beyond gratifying. But I had more satisfying pursuits in mind.

Leaning in, I pressed slow, nibbling kisses along her inner thigh, smiling as she shuddered. I could smell her arousal, and it was all I could do not to dive in like a starving man. But I wanted to savor every moment of this. Of her.

Her muscles tensed in anticipation, until she was all but vibrating with need by the time I reached her center. I paused, teasing her with my breath for a moment.

"Ford, for the love of God..."

"No, for the love of you." I leaned in to taste her with a long, slow lick.

Bree's hips bucked, and she swore a blue streak that had me grinning as I settled between her thighs to do it again and again, loving her feverish response and how her hands dove into my hair, holding me to her as I worshipped her, searching out each spot that made her gasp and moan. She was getting closer, her breaths coming in short pants, her hips rocking against my mouth. I slid one finger inside her, then another, feeling her body clench around me. I imagined that clench around my cock and almost lost my rhythm.

"Ford! I'm almost... I'm going to..."

I doubled down, sucking her clit into my mouth as I pumped my fingers. Her hips jerked. She was right on the edge as I curled my fingers just so, finding the spot that sent her over the edge with a cry. Her body convulsed around my fingers, her hips bucking relentlessly against my mouth as I slowly eased her down until she lay panting, a trembling, beautiful mess beneath me.

But I wasn't done with her yet. Not by a long shot.

I crawled off her.

"What? No. Still... need... you."

From where I dug through my bag, I chuckled. "Oh, I'm not going anywhere, sweet girl. Just grabbing a condom."

"Boy Scout. Thank God." She dropped her head back against the pillow.

I quickly shucked my sweatpants and rolled on the condom. Bree watched me with hungry eyes, and I couldn't resist stroking myself. My cock swelled in my hand. I'd waited so damned long for this. For her. It wouldn't be our last time, but I was determined to infuse every moment with pleasure for her. It wouldn't make up for the pain I'd caused her, but it damned well couldn't hurt.

I rejoined her on the bed, stretching out over her until my forearms were braced on either side of her head. I took her mouth in another long, languid kiss until she sighed against me and softened. That surrender would never, ever get old. Because I knew she gave it to no one else. Her legs parted, one of them curving around my hips, guiding me between her thighs. She lifted her hips, fitting the length of my cock in the wetness of her seam and rocking there, stroking, stroking, until my eyes crossed.

"You feel so good," she murmured, trailing kisses along my jaw. "But I know you'll feel even better inside me."

"Are you absolutely sure?" I'd taken her physical response as enthusiastic consent before. I wouldn't make that mistake again.

Her fingers threaded in my hair as she stared up at me with eyes gone dark with arousal. "I'm sure I love you. And I want this."

I love you.

I hadn't expected the words back. Not yet. Not with everything we'd been through. They were a gift I hadn't dared hope for, just like this chance with her. I wouldn't waste it.

I eased inside her with excruciating slowness, fighting every instinct that screamed to plunge deep. Her body gripped me like a fist, hot and tight and perfect. My muscles trembled with the effort to hold back, to give her what she deserved.

Bree's nails dug into my shoulders. "Ford..."

I captured her mouth, drinking in her gasps as I pressed deeper, deeper, until I was fully seated. We both groaned, and I had to concentrate on breathing, on not moving, letting her body accommodate my size.

Her hips shifted restlessly beneath me. "Please."

That breathy plea nearly undid me. I withdrew almost completely before gliding back in with the same torturous control. Setting a slow, steady rhythm that had us both panting. Her body welcomed each thrust, growing wetter, hotter.

She wrapped both legs around my hips, trying to urge me faster. But I maintained the easy pace, wanting to draw out every moment. To memorize each gasp and shiver. The way her breath caught when I hit just the right spot. How her inner muscles fluttered around me as pleasure built between us.

"You feel incredible," I murmured against her throat, tasting the salt of her skin. "So perfect."

Her hands slid down my back, urging me on as our bodies moved together, each stroke driving us steadily higher toward release.

Bree's skin was flushed and damp, her lips swollen from my kisses. I'd never seen anything more beautiful. I'd dreamed of this moment for years. Imagined having her beneath me again countless times. But reality put every fantasy to shame.

"I love you," I breathed against her throat, quickening my pace as her breathing grew more ragged. "Love you so much."

Her nails raked down my back as she arched into me. "Ford."

That breathy moan of my name nearly broke the last of my control. I'd spent years thinking I'd never hear it again. Never feel her wrapped around me, moving with me like we were made for each other.

"Let go for me, sweet girl." I shifted my angle, hitting a spot that made her gasp. "I've got you."

Her inner muscles fluttered around me. She was close. I slid a hand between us to circle her clit, wanting to watch her fall apart all over again. Wanting to feel her come around me.

"That's it. Come for me, baby. Come for me. I've got you."

She shattered with a cry, her body spasming around mine in a rhythmic grip that had lightning coiling in my spine. "Love you. God, I love you."

The words, the feel of her, dragged me over the edge into the most intense orgasm of my life.

My hips jerked against hers as pleasure wracked my body, each pulse drawing another groan from deep in my chest. I buried my face in her neck, breathing in the scent of her skin as aftershocks rippled through us both.

When I could move again, I carefully withdrew and disposed of the condom. I came back to bed, gathering her close. She curled into me, head on my chest, fingers tracing idle patterns on my pecs.

"I meant it, you know." Her voice was soft in the darkness.

"Meant what?"

"That I love you. Have since we were kids, really. Even when I was furious with you." She pressed a kiss over my heart. "Maybe especially then."

I tightened my arms around her. "I wish I'd figured my shit out sooner. Wish I hadn't wasted so much time."

"There's the small matter of me being the world's most stubborn bitch."

"You're not a bitch. You had a right to be hurt."

"Either way, we can't change the past." She propped her chin on my chest to look at me. "But we can do better going forward."

"Yeah?" Hope bloomed in my chest.

"Yeah. I want to try. For real this time."

I grinned at her. "Why, Bree Cartwright. Are you saying you want to date me?"

She thumped me against the shoulder. "Don't tease. I've never really done that before. I'll probably be terrible at it."

I brushed her hair back from her face. "You'll do fine. There are no rules here. Our relationship doesn't have to look like anybody else's, and we can take it at whatever pace you're comfortable with. Just promise me something, okay?"

"What's that?"

"That we'll talk things through the next time I fuck up or you get upset. The only way this works is if we communicate better than we did at twenty."

"I can do that." The soft, sweet expression sobered. "Do you think Peyton will be okay with this?"

I snorted. "In case you've missed it, she's been trying to match-make us almost from the beginning. She'll probably throw a party that we finally got our heads out of our asses." I paused to consider. "My moms will probably help."

"Oh, my God." She buried her face against my chest.

I tipped her chin up, so she had to look at me. "All teasing aside, you and Peyton are my priorities now. Equally. It might not always be easy, but we're going to make it work."

Her eyes softened. "I believe you."

Those three words meant almost as much as her declaration of love. Trust had always been the real issue between us. Earning it back was everything, and I was never taking it or her for granted again.

CHAPTER 35

BREE

The car tires thumped as Ford navigated off the ferry ramp and back onto Hatterwick. We'd been gone for a full week that felt more like a million years. I half expected everything to look different. For Sutter's Ferry to have undergone some kind of metamorphosis in my absence. But everything was the same. I was the one who'd changed.

Ford glanced over from the driver's seat, his thumb grazing over the back of the hand he held. "You okay?"

My fingers tightened reflexively on his, compulsively checking my lifeline. Because that's what he'd been. "What are we going to tell them?" The question popped out before I could think better of it. The status of our complicated relationship was hardly the update everybody was waiting on.

He lifted my hand and brushed a quick kiss to the back. The gesture had gooseflesh rising along my arm, even as a dozen erotic memories of how we'd spent much of our time outside the hospital unspooled in my mind.

"We don't have to tell them anything until you're ready. We have all the time in the world to figure out the details of us. Let's just take this one step at a time."

All the time in the world. Because he was staying. Building roots and a home for his daughter. And he wanted me to be a part of all that. It didn't surprise me. When Ford Donoghue made a decision, he leapt in with both feet. He wanted to be with me—something I was still wrapping my brain around—so in his mind, the rest was a foregone conclusion.

But he understood that wasn't how I worked.

I mustered a smile. "Thank you. I just don't think I'm up to your moms' reactions."

"Valid. They'll be... enthusiastic."

I slanted him a look. "Will they? I basically excommunicated you from my life for a decade."

"They never held that against you. Mimi's been waiting for me to get my head out of my ass and fix things with you for years. So, yes. But they'll all be focused on Ed, so we'll roll with that for now."

I wasn't sure what to say to that, so I lapsed back into silence as Ford turned south of the marina and headed for the lighthouse. It was strange to be going there now. It had been so much a part of my childhood and teen years. As much a home to me as the house I'd shared with Pop. But I hadn't been out here in a long, long time. I'd even avoided driving by, if I could help it, because it inevitably reminded me of Ford.

Coming back now, a trickle of unease slid through me. It wasn't rational. Mama Flo and Mimi had been nothing but kind to me over all the years I'd cut Ford out of my life. They hadn't avoided me. Hadn't interfered in any way. And, of course, over these past weeks since Peyton had come into our world, they'd treated me as if nothing had changed. But a part of me still worried about my reception as he parked the car in front of the house.

The front door opened before we'd even managed to climb out of the car. Keeley made a beeline for me, and I hunkered down and braced myself for my pup's enthusiastic greeting.

"Hey, baby girl. Who's a good puppy? Have you been a good girl?"

She barked as if to say, "Duh."

Peyton was right behind her, and as soon as I straightened, she pulled me into a big hug. It was the first contact she'd initiated. After a moment of shocked immobilization, I squeezed her back.

"Thanks for loaning me your dad."

She gave me a funny look at that. Maybe because she hadn't quite reached a point where she thought of Ford as her dad?

Mama Flo came next, wrapping me in a floral-scented hug. "How's Ed?"

"Still in a medically induced coma for another week or two, but we're past the initial crisis period, and the doctors say he's responding well. They're more confident in a positive prognosis for recovery." I was really anxious about leaving him alone at the hospital, but I needed to check on the Brewhouse and make plans for a longer-term absence, if necessary.

Mimi brought up the rear, smelling of her usual blend of baking and art supplies. "That's good to hear, sugar." She gave me a hearty squeeze, then pulled back to study my face. She stared long enough that I wanted to fidget.

At last, she nodded in apparent satisfaction. "I'm glad y'all fixed things."

In my periphery, I saw Peyton elbow Ford. "I told you apologizing would make a difference."

My mouth fell open. Was I wearing a freaking sign? Did I have some kind of invisible tattoo across my forehead? With a vague sense of panic, I looked at Ford. He just offered a sheepish shrug.

Calm your tits, Cartwright. "Fixing things" does not inherently mean "jumped each other's bones." She just means she can tell we're friends again.

Apparently not in need of my input, Mimi just wrapped an arm around me and began hustling me into the house. "Come on inside, baby. I've got a batch of cookies I made just this morning and a fresh pot of coffee."

It was ten o'clock in the morning. I didn't exactly need cookies. But that didn't stop me from asking, "Peanut butter?"

"I know they're you're favorite."

They were, and damn if that didn't make my eyes sting with emotion as I got led into the house. Ford moved close enough to press a hand to my lower back, a silent show of support as we all got settled around the table in the kitchen nook with the aforementioned coffee and cookies.

"Have the doctors indicated how long Ed's recovery might take?" Mimi asked.

I clutched one of the hand-thrown mugs between my palms, soaking up the warmth. "Not yet. There are too many factors they don't know. It'll depend on what kind of shape he's in when he wakes up. But his doctor is more optimistic now than when he came in, so that feels like a win."

"Absolutely," Mama Flo declared. "Of course, we'll help however we can."

"I appreciate that. Truly." Because they weren't obligated to help. No one was, really.

"I've been working on our project this week."

I blinked at Peyton. "Project?"

"The treasure hunt," she reminded me. "I gathered up all his notes from the Brewhouse the night he... well, when he went to the hospital. I didn't want anything to happen to them, and I figured he'd want something to talk about during his recovery."

Sweet, thoughtful kid. It took me a minute to get past the thickness in my throat. "Thanks. He'll love that."

Beneath the table, Ford settled a hand on my knee and squeezed. The touch grounded me.

"I think we could both do with a little distraction. Any news on the investigation?"

Mama Flo shook her head. "Not really. The police haven't been able to determine whether the break-in at O'Connell's offices and the attack on Lindsay Messina had anything to do with Galef or not."

I set my mug down with a clatter. "Lindsay was attacked? When? Is she okay?"

"She's fine," Mimi assured me. "A little bump

on the head. Mild concussion. It happened last week, the night before you left the island. Somebody broke in and searched the office. She apparently forgot something at work and surprised whoever it was."

"Why would that have anything to do with Galef?" I asked.

"Because he used to work there," Mama Flo continued. "They had to let him go recently."

I thought back to last month. Lindsay had said something about somebody being fired, and it getting kind of ugly. I hadn't thought anything about it at the time. "If Galef were still around, I could see him being behind it as some kind of retribution, but what would his killer want with his old job?"

Mama Flo grabbed a cookie from the plate. "That's the million dollar question. Carson hasn't found any connection yet. I think he's pushing hard for one because he doesn't want to admit there are multiple unsolved crimes going on at once in his jurisdiction."

"There's also the vandalism of the museum," Peyton added.

"What vandalism?" Ford asked.

"Somebody broke in and trashed the place. Messed up a bunch of the displays. Peter was still cleaning up when I stopped by this week to do some more research. The petty cash was stolen, and the gift shop messed up, so apparently Chief Carson is trying to say it was just kids or some off-islander who didn't know they don't really keep much money on site. But I definitely haven't heard any rumblings at school of anybody bragging about it."

"Nobody with a lick of sense would be bragging about it," Mama Flo pointed out. "Either way, the mayor has enacted a curfew in the name of public safety. With Galef's killer still out there, he's worried about how it's going to impact tourism on the island."

I huffed a humorless laugh and reached for a cookie.. "Yeah, that would be on-brand for Miles. Always concerned with how things look."

Ford leaned his elbows on the table. "Maybe so, but I don't disagree. Whether it's all connected or different groups popping up to cause problems, I'd just as soon none of you take any unnecessary risks." His gaze shifted to me. "That includes you. No closing up alone."

"Nobody's closed up alone since the fire. Not after Caroline was attacked." Not that Caroline had been completely alone. Jasper, our cook at the time, had also been there, but he'd been knocked out and Caroline locked in the supply closet by the arsonist. She would have died if Hoyt hadn't gone in after her, so we were all more cautious about safety ever since.

"No opening alone, either," Ford insisted.

"None of the things that have happened have been during the day," I pointed out. When he only arched a brow, I capitulated. "Fine. It's a moot point, anyway. Chances are I won't be around to open much. I'll be going back and forth between here and the mainland."

"I'll go with you."

"It's *not* practical for you to go with me every time. Though I appreciate the willingness."

His growl of frustration almost made me smile. Almost. He wanted to keep all of his people safe. That he couldn't be everywhere at once wouldn't sit well. But he couldn't know what it meant to me that he counted me as one of his people again.

Although maybe I was the only one who had ever thought he'd stopped.

"Either way, I do need to get on in to check on things. If you could drop me by home so I can pick up my Jeep, I'd appreciate it." Monty and Peter had moved it from the Brewhouse parking lot.

"I have food for you both to take home," Mimi announced.

"Of course you do." Ford grinned and leaned over to press a smacking kiss to her cheek. "Peyton, how about you go gather up your stuff? We'll head home, too."

"This is gonna take a minute," Mimi said. "Y'all should have more cookies."

I reached toward the plate in the center of the table. "Don't mind if I do."

CHAPTER 36

FORD

It took longer than planned to get home. We dropped Bree and Keeley at her place, then had to turn around and head into the village proper to swing by the market. Despite Mimi's casseroles, there were still some basics we needed. That led to a stop by Panadería de la Isla, the bakery owned by Marisol Gutierrez, and from there, the fish market.

I hoped we were actually home long enough to eat everything we'd bought. I knew Bree was planning to go back and forth on the ferry every few days, and I hoped Ed's condition stayed stable enough to allow it. She hadn't been wrong that it wasn't practical for me to go with her every time. I'd used up my supply of favors between the emergency leave when Peyton had arrived, and the extra

I'd managed for the few days before Sawyer had brought me my laptop.

After we'd unloaded our purchases, I dropped my keys in the bowl by the door, still trying to wrap my head around being back home. The past week felt like some bizarre dream. I kept expecting to wake up and find that Bree hadn't really forgiven me. The past several days of waking to her in my arms had helped with that, but tonight I'd be on my own, and I didn't like it.

But that was hours off. Right now, I needed to focus on my daughter.

I trailed her into the kitchen, unsurprised that she'd already gotten into the cottage loaf, which had been still warm when we'd left the bakery. "So how'd everything go while I was gone?"

She pointed the bread knife at the loaf, where she'd already cut a slice. "Want some?"

"Hell, yes."

She cut us both big hunks while I got out butter. "It went fine. I like your moms. Mimi tried to teach me to make biscuits, but mine turned out like hockey pucks."

"Yeah, that's a skill that takes practice. I still can't do it right." It was something about over-working the dough. Given she spoiled me senseless with any food I wanted when I was home, I didn't have much impetus to learn.

I accepted the slice of bread she offered. "You keeping up with your schoolwork?"

"Mostly. I got behind on some math, but Grandma Flo helped me catch up yesterday. Why does algebra have to be so *boring?*"

Kicking back against the counter, I bit into the bread and considered as I chewed. "Well, most adults will feed you this whole story about how you'll use it all the time as a grownup, but the reality is that most don't. So my theory is that it's really just a rite of passage. Sucky, but then it's done."

Peyton winced. "I hear there's more in high school."

Which she'd be in by the end of the year. Holy shit. Not remotely prepared to think about that, I decided we needed a subject change. "Sad but true. How's the pirate project coming? You said you'd been working on it while we were away."

Her eyes lit up. "I found some really cool stuff in the museum archives about Black Sam Bellamy. Did you know he was actually friends with Benjamin Hornigold? And there's this whole theory about—" She caught herself, biting her lip. "I should probably save that for my paper."

I smiled, remembering my own fascination with pirate stories as a kid. It was hard not to be a little obsessed growing up by one of the biggest shipwreck graveyards in the country. "Is any of that actually relevant to your paper?"

"I mean... it might be."

"Research whatever you want. Just don't get so caught up in it that you miss the actual point of the assignment."

She rolled her eyes. "Yes, Dad."

The easy sarcasm didn't remotely diminish from the fact that she'd just called me Dad for the first time. The sound of it was a punch to the sternum.

When I lapsed into silence, Peyton's gaze flicked up to mine, uncertain. I knew she wouldn't want me to make a big deal about it, so I bit off more bread to cover. "You need any help with anything?"

"Nah, I'm good. But..." She fidgeted with the sleeve of her hoodie. "Is Mr. Ed really gonna be okay?"

I didn't want to make any false promises, but I didn't want to scare her either. "The doctors think so. It'll take time, but they're optimistic."

She nodded, relief clear on her face. "Good. Because I still need to show him what I found in those old maps. Whichever artist made mine clearly looked at the archives."

"Artist?"

"Yeah. Peter said that a bunch of local artists were commissioned to make them, so that each one is a bit different and everybody feels like they're getting a more specialized piece of history."

"That's cool." Definitely more interesting than the mass-produced ones they'd had when we were kids.

We both continued to eat our bread in companionable silence.

"Hey, Peyton?"

"Yeah?"

"I wanted to apologize."

She tensed up, a line forming between her brows. "For what?"

"Just for being gone so long. I know you had Mimi and Mama Flo, but I should have been here."

"You were exactly where you were supposed to be. Bree needed you." The declarative statement brooked no argument.

"Yeah, she did," I conceded. "But I just didn't want you to think you weren't a priority for me."

"I got it." She paused, turning to cut another slice of bread. "So, are you and Bree dating now?"

I almost choked on the last bite of my own bread. I had no idea how to answer that. Dating was definitely not what we'd been doing on our downtime from the hospital.

While I was still fumbling to find an answer, my kid continued, "You're a total idiot if you're not, because Bree is awesome."

More with the declarative statements. Damn, did she know how much she sounded like my Mom? Amused and moved, I reached out to ruffle her hair. "Can't say I disagree."

She rolled her eyes again and smoothed her hair. "So are you?"

I thought about the promise I'd made Bree in the car, that we had time to figure this out. "We've been a little busy with Ed's situation. But things are better." That seemed a safe enough response.

Peyton nodded. "Good. That's a good start."

I needed to redirect her before she continued down this path. "You done with your homework for the weekend?"

"I've got some vocabulary in Spanish, but that's it."

"Wanna have a *Pirates of the Caribbean* marathon?"

As I'd hoped, her eyes brightened. "Hel—er heck, yeah."

"Look, I'm not gonna ride you about swearing. The deal is that you're smart enough to know when and where it's appropriate. School and in front of Mama Flo and Mimi are not it. In public, not it. But at home? I figure you should have the freedom to express yourself. Also, because I've been in the Navy for a really long time, and it's gonna take me a while to retrain myself. Fair?"

She nodded. "Deal. Want popcorn?"

"We just had bread."

"And?"

So teenage girls were also bottomless pits. Good to know.

"Fair point."

We settled in and spent the rest of the afternoon binging the movies and talking pirates. But I kept glancing out the window, watching for Bree's return. We were already into *At World's End* by the time I finally saw her light switch on. A couple of minutes later, Keeley bolted into the backyard to do her business.

Peyton was enthralled with the movie—she'd never seen past the first one before—so I murmured, "Be right back," and slipped out the back door.

Bree stood in the dark, arms wrapped around her middle.

"Hey. Any news?"

Her face relaxed at the sight of me. "No. Everything's fine. My team is incredible. I didn't have to come back at all. But I'm glad I did. I needed to check in for me, you know?"

"Yeah. Nothing new about Ed?"

She shook her head, but I could still tell something was bothering her.

I stepped into her, rubbing my hands down her arms. "What's bugging you?"

"Nothing. I just..." She glanced back toward her cottage. "I just feel a little weird being in the house alone. Which is stupid. I've lived alone for a long time. There's no reason to think I won't be fine."

"Except that there's a village-wide curfew, you just closed the Brewhouse early because of it, and there are multiple problematic people apparently roaming the island."

She winced. "Well, I mean, there's that."

"Why don't you come stay with us at our place?"

"But Peyton."

I tugged her in, linking my hands at the small of her back, savoring the warmth of her against me. "I'll have you know my daughter told me I was an idiot if I didn't date you. She was very emphatic about it."

Bree's lips twitched, a hint of amusement dancing in her eyes. "An idiot, huh?"

"In those precise words, yeah." I tipped my head down toward hers, wondering if I could steal a kiss, breathing in the scent of hops and honey that always seemed to cling to her skin.

Her fingers curled into the fabric of my shirt. "Smart kid."

"Totally smart kid." I couldn't stop the doofy grin. "She called me 'Dad.'"

The lips that had hovered half an inch from

mine pulled back, her eyes widening with delight. "Really? First time?"

"Yeah. It was in a totally sarcastic teenage eye rolling kind of way. You know, the whole 'whatever, Dad' thing. I feel like I leveled up as a parent."

Bree smiled at me, with so much more softness than I was used to seeing, her whole face glowing with warmth, and patted my chest. "Good on you, Papa."

I covered her hand with mine, squeezing gently. "So will you come stay?"

Uncertainty flickered over her face, her teeth worrying at her bottom lip in a way that meant she was trying to talk herself into—or out of—something.

"Peyton and I can come over to your place, if you'd rather." I offered the alternative quickly, not wanting her to feel cornered. "Whatever makes you most comfortable."

"That feels even weirder." She shook her head, a strand of blonde hair falling across her cheek. "Having you both in my space..."

"I want you to feel safe, Bree. Peyton won't be weirded out by the idea of that. It just shows sensible caution on your part." I kept my voice steady, reasonable, trying to channel some of my mother's lawyer-like persuasion skills.

I could see her wrestling with the notion, her

eyes darting between me and the dark windows of her cottage, so I waited, knowing pressure wouldn't get me anywhere. The last thing I wanted was to push her into something that made her uncomfortable.

With one last glance back at the cottage, her shoulders slumped in resignation. "Let me pack an overnight bag."

CHAPTER 37

BREE

Staying with Ford and Peyton was less weird than I was afraid it would be, which, in and of itself, freaked me out. It felt natural. Easy.

I didn't trust easy.

I hadn't felt comfortable just shacking up in his bed with her in the house, so we'd ended up sleeping wedged on the sofa. That way we'd have the excuse of pretending oops, we just fell asleep out here. Given Ford's height and bulk, that meant he slept on the sofa, and I slept stretched out on him. Comfortable? Not exactly. But I wouldn't have traded being wrapped up in him for anything. Ford might have, considering I'd nearly unmanned him with my knee when Keeley started barking at something in the wee hours of the morning, and I'd jolted awake, confused.

Now I was on breakfast duty and wishing for about a gallon of coffee as Peyton tried and failed to hide a delighted grin. I didn't think our ruse had fooled her one iota. Damned smart kid.

The scent of bacon filled the kitchen, and I kept my bleary gaze on the pan to make sure it didn't burn.

Ford nudged my shoulder and passed me a mug. "Here."

I inhaled deeply and sighed as my synapses perked up at the smell of dark roast. "Bless you."

He sent me a long look and a faint smile that curled my toes, before turning away to pull eggs from the fridge. "What's on your list for the day? Going in to the Brewhouse?"

"I want to check in on the lunch shift, for sure. But this morning I want to go by Pop's place to check on things. Water the plants and whatnot. I also want to pack him a bag. I know it'll be a while before he's released, but he'll want fresh clothes when he is."

Ford's hand stroked down my back. "I think that's a positive step." He glanced at his daughter. "What about you? I know you said you still have that Spanish vocab."

"It won't take long."

He nodded. "I, unfortunately, need to catch up on work."

"Peyton could come with me while you do that. Then we could bring back a late lunch after shift's over."

"Oh, yeah. That sounds good." Peyton's ready agreement had me wondering whether she was waiting for a chance to corner me about what was going on between me and her father. But I couldn't very well retract the offer because I was being a chickenshit.

So that was how I found myself loading Peyton into the front seat of my Jeep as I drove the short distance to Pop's place.

His house sat back from the road, nestled beneath ancient live oaks draped with Spanish moss. The cedar shingles had weathered to a soft gray, worn smooth by decades of salt spray and storms. It wasn't much to look at—just a simple one-story cottage with a deep front porch and white trim that needed touching up. But it was home.

"This is where you grew up?" Peyton hopped out of the Jeep, taking in the weathered wind chimes and the collection of beach glass in mason jars that lined the porch rail.

"From age eight on, yeah." I climbed the creaky steps, fishing my keys from my pocket. "Pop's lived here for over forty years. Back when this was just a working-class neighborhood of fishermen and boat builders."

Now most of those modest homes had been torn down, replaced by towering vacation rentals with infinity pools. But this little pocket had survived, probably because the owners were too stubborn to sell.

Through the front window, I could see Pop's favorite chair still pulled up to the view overlooking the water. His coffee cup sat on the side table, where he'd set it down that morning before heading to the Brewhouse. As if he'd expected to be back later. Because, of course, he had. My throat constricted.

"There's his dock." I nodded toward the weathered boards stretching out over the sound. "He doesn't take the boat out as much anymore since his heart started acting up. But he still likes to sit out there and fish."

The space felt empty without him in it. Wrong. But I pushed that thought away and focused on why we were here.

I pulled open the screen door and went to put the key into the lock, but I realized the interior door was already slightly ajar. Had he forgotten to lock it on his way out? It wouldn't surprise me. He'd been on the island since God was a boy, through all those years when people simply didn't lock up. I'd been on him the past decade to change that habit, but my success rate was spotty.

Shaking my head, I pushed the door open and froze.

The living room looked normal at first glance, but something felt off. My gaze swept left, catching on the slightly crooked drawer of Pop's roll-top desk. He was meticulous about keeping that closed.

My heart kicked up. "Stay here."

But Peyton had already followed me inside. "What's wrong?"

I moved deeper into the house, taking in details that screamed wrongness. Books pulled partway off shelves. Cabinet doors left open a crack. The throw pillows on the couch sat at odd angles, as if they'd been lifted and replaced.

"Someone's been in here." My voice came out tight. "They went through his things."

Peyton's eyes went wide. "Like at that Galef guy's place?"

Without answering, I herded Peyton back onto the porch, not wanting to contaminate any prospective evidence. Then I pulled out my phone and dialed 911.

"911, what is your emergency?"

"This is Bree Cartwright. Someone has broken into my grandfather's house." I gave the address.

"Is there any sign that the perpetrator is still on the premises?"

The house definitely felt empty, but I hadn't looked. "None obvious. We're still outside."

"Officers are being dispatched to your location. Please remain outside the residence."

I hung up the phone and texted Ford with shaking hands.

Bree: Someone searched Pop's house. Police coming.

His response was immediate.

Ford: On my way.

"Should we... should we look around outside?" Peyton asked. "See if they left anything?"

I shook my head. "Better let the police handle that. Though I doubt they'll find much." Whoever had done this had been careful, methodical. They'd either known exactly what they were doing or had been able to take their time, so as to leave little trace.

The question was—what the hell had they been looking for?

That was the same question Office Chris Shelton had after he'd cleared the house.

"Any idea what they could've been looking for? Is anything missing?"

Once I'd been given permission to look, I moved through the house, checking where I knew Pop kept anything worth anything. The spare cash in his top dresser drawer was gone, but the TV and all the easily moved electronics were still there, including his laptop and tablet.

"Possibly his spare cash, but I can't say whether Pop took that himself. I can't exactly ask him right now."

Ford wrapped an arm around my shoulders.

Chris offered a sympathetic smile. "That's tough. We're all rooting for Ed to make a full recovery."

"I appreciate that."

He rocked back on his heels, hooking his fingers into his duty belt. "There was no sign of forced entry. Is Ed in the habit of leaving the door unlocked?"

"Unfortunately, it happens more often than I'd like."

I watched as Chris considered his words and knew I wasn't going to like what he said next.

"Is it possible that Ed himself is the one who did this?"

I wanted to argue, but I hadn't been over here in the days before his AFib attack. What if he'd been having smaller episodes, and I hadn't seen?

I looked around the house again. Noting all the tiny things that were just... wrong. "No. He was meticulous about how he kept his books and his desk."

Chris just nodded. "Fair enough. We'll write up a report, but with nothing else to go on, it's looking like a crime of convenience. Somebody found the place unlocked, grabbed the cash and dashed."

"What if somebody was looking for his research?" Peyton suggested.

"What kind of research?" Chris asked.

"He was helping me with a school project on piracy in the area and found some inconsistencies between maps."

Chris flashed an indulgent smile. "Ah, yeah. Everybody on the island has to go through a pirate phase. But nobody's found anything in thirty years."

"Doesn't mean something isn't there," Peyton pointed out.

"True. Are his research notes missing?"

"No. I've got them. He had them at the Brewhouse the night he... well, when he got sick."

"I'll make a note in my report. But truthfully, Bree, we don't have a lot to go on here."

Ford's arm tightened around my shoulders. "So that's it?"

"We can pick up patrols in the area, but in all likelihood, nobody's coming back. If you find out later something is missing, we'll certainly add that in, but there's not much else we can do. I understand you're upset and probably rattled, what with everything else happening lately. Chief thinks some folks are taking advantage of everybody being unsettled to cause trouble. This is probably more of that."

I didn't like that as an answer, but I saw his point. The best we could do for now was set things to rights and lock up after ourselves.

Once Chris had gone, I began to do just that, straightening books and closing cabinets and drawers.

Ford interrupted me, taking me by the shoulders. "I think you should move in with us until all this is sorted."

"Ford..."

"Seriously. I'll worry less. Please."

"Yeah, if it's safer for me to be with somebody all the time, the same is true for you," Peyton insisted.

I split a look between them. "Really? You're both going to railroad me?"

"Railroad is such an aggressive term," Ford drawled, but I didn't miss the hint of a smile at the edge of his mouth.

"Sorry. Not sorry," Peyton announced. "Is it working?"

I could fight them on it. I lived right next door, after all. But the idea of being alone in my place still left me a little unsettled. I didn't expect that would be any better after finding out that Pop's place had been searched. Maybe Chris was right, and it was a crime of opportunity. But in the wake of the murder and all the other vandalism that had happened around the island, it just didn't feel right.

I blew out a long breath. "Fine. But when you see how much stuff Keeley comes with, I'm going to remind you that you brought this on yourselves."

CHAPTER 38
FORD

The moving van pulled up to the curb at the front of the house, its diesel engine rumbling in the quiet neighborhood. It was here far sooner than I'd expected, but the company manager had expedited delivery as soon as the police were finished processing everything. My stomach clenched as I wondered exactly what we'd find inside. How much was damaged? How much was missing entirely? How much of Peyton's childhood remained intact?

My daughter appeared beside me, bouncing nervously in her scuffed-up Chucks. "Is that it?"

"Yeah. Just remember what we talked about. Some stuff might be..." Gone? Destroyed? Ruined beyond repair? I'd warned her of all that, but I couldn't make myself say it again, not when I saw that flicker of hope in her eyes. She'd already lost so much.

"Yeah, I know. But at least we got most of it back." Her voice carried a forced brightness that had me clenching my fists against an outcome I couldn't control.

I didn't even know what "it" was, not really. Some furniture, which we desperately needed to fill the house with more than just the bare essentials we'd cobbled together. Books, clothes, and the precious pieces of the life Peyton had led before her mother's sudden death. Pieces, too, of the woman I'd made a child with but hadn't really known at all.

The timing was less than ideal. Bree was next door, packing the essentials to move in. Well, no. Just to stay for a while. I had to remind myself this wasn't a permanent arrangement. Not yet, anyway. Bree wasn't ready for that. I'd need to ease her into the idea slowly, like coaxing a skittish cat from beneath the porch. She was still learning to trust what was between us. To trust that I wouldn't break my promise again, wouldn't leave her behind like everyone else had. I'd give her as long as she needed. And in the meantime, I should probably hunt for a bigger house for the three of us. Something with a yard for Keeley and enough space that Peyton could really spread out and make it her own.

One step at a time.

The driver hopped down from the cab, clipboard in hand. "Mr. Donoghue?"

"That's me." I signed where indicated, accepting delivery.

"I'm afraid we don't have a full crew, but you have the two of us to help," the driver said, jerking his thumb toward his companion, who'd slid out of the passenger side of the truck. "Just let us know where you want us to put things."

I had no idea what kind of state things had been in before the theft, and I didn't expect boxes to have been properly sorted and labeled after. We'd be going through things long after these guys left. "Let's get started."

The driver rolled up the door on the back of the truck with a metallic rattle that echoed through the morning air. My heart sank at how little was inside. It barely filled half the space, leaving a stark emptiness. I spotted mostly cardboard boxes in various states of wear, but also at least a couple of dark wood bookcases, a bed with its frame partially dismantled, a weathered dresser with brass handles, and what looked like part of an overstuffed chair in faded blue peaking out from behind everything else.

Peyton clambered inside the truck bed with the energy only a teenager could muster this early in the day. I watched her carefully for drooping shoulders or other signs of disappointment or shock, knowing this represented all she had left of her old life. But she only pounced on the nearest box with determined focus, her fingers already working at the tape. Maybe there hadn't actually been that much in storage to begin with? Or maybe she was just better at handling loss than I'd expected.

She paused with a box balanced against her hip. "What should we do with this stuff?"

"For now, probably pile the boxes along that empty wall in the living room until we get the furniture placed wherever it's going to go. Then we can shift around boxes as needed." I gestured toward the house, already mentally rearranging the space to accommodate everything.

Bree emerged from her cottage. "What's all this?"

"The rest of Peyton's stuff." I watched her face carefully, knowing she'd understand the weight of what that meant.

We exchanged a long look, the kind that came from years of history and shared understanding. Bree knew about the theft and recovery, so she'd also be prepared to handle whatever the fallout from this was for Peyton. My kid might seem okay now, but seeing all her possessions like this could trigger something deeper.

"Then let's get it inside." Bree leapt in to help.

Between the five of us, we got the boxes unloaded in fifteen minutes, making quick work of the smaller items with everyone pitching in. Then came the furniture, which required more coordination and careful maneuvering through doorways. There were three bookcases. Solid wood pieces that spoke of quality and permanence. One went to Peyton's room, while the other two were tucked into a corner of the living room. Once we cleared away the boxes, they'd stand side by side along the back wall, creating a proper library feel. Turned out there was a loveseat hiding back there, upholstered in a soft blue fabric, as well as a patterned area rug that would pull the room together. After some finagling to move the sofa we'd gotten from Beachcomber Bargains, we got the rug down and the sofa and loveseat in place. The cushy reading chair, worn but still comfortable-looking, also went to Peyton's room, where it would give her a cozy spot to curl up with a book. That left the bed and dresser, the two heaviest pieces we'd need to tackle.

"Do you want to swap these out for the ones in your room?" I wasn't sure where they'd go otherwise. The third bedroom had been turned into my office, and there wasn't room to shoehorn a bed in there between my desk and filing cabinets. Worse case, we could store it in the garage out at the lighthouse until such a time as we had a place for it.

Before she could answer, my phone rang, the vibration buzzing against my hip through my jeans pocket. I glanced at the screen, expecting it to be Mom or Mimi checking in. The sight of Dax Shepherd's name kicked my pulse into high gear. Did he have some answers for me at last?

"Sorry, kiddo. I need to take this. Y'all figure out what you want to do with the bed and dresser."

I stepped out to the backyard and answered. "Dax. Tell me you have news for me."

"I do. Sorry it took me so long. I've been digging between assignments, and I was out of the country for most of the past week. Things got a bit complicated down in South America, or I would've gotten back to you sooner."

I didn't ask doing what. Since he'd left the Navy, he'd taken on a lot of contract work in arenas where it was best no questions were asked. The less I knew about his activities, the better for everyone involved. I didn't know him well enough either way, having only met him through Sawyer a handful of times at various gatherings and celebrations. His reputation for getting answers was what mattered. "No worries. I appreciate whatever you can tell me. Anything you found would help at this point."

"Northwest Global Logistics looks clean on paper," Dax said. "Import/export business, specializing in Pacific Rim trade. But dig deeper and you find a pattern."

My fingers clenched around the phone. "What kind of pattern?"

"Employees who ask too many questions tend to disappear. Five in the past three years. Local police wrote them off as voluntary departures, but their families say different."

I paced across the back patio. "And Casey was looking into this?"

"She was working with the FBI, gathering evidence of whatever illegal shit they're into. That evidence vanished after her death. Company's hired multiple PI firms to track it down, but so far, nobody's had any luck. So they're taking... some more aggressive measures."

Everything in me tensed at the sound of that. "Do they know about Peyton?"

"That's why I called. They started in Portland, but they've widened the search. Word is they've discovered your paternity claim."

The blood drained from my face. "How sure are you?"

"Two of their known contractors were spotted in Norfolk day before yesterday. These aren't the kind of guys you hire for legitimate business."

"You think they know she's here?"

"If they don't yet, they will soon. The paternity claim creates a paper trail."

I glanced through the sliding glass door, my hand pressed against the cool surface. Peyton and Bree were sorting through boxes of what looked like old photos, both laughing at something, their heads bent close together. The sight of them together squeezed my heart so tight I could barely breathe. They were my family—the one I'd never known I needed until now. I'd just found them. Just brought them together. The thought that someone might try to take this away made my throat close up. I wanted to be able to hold them close without fear of some amorphous threat hanging over our heads, wanted to protect this fragile new happiness we'd stumbled into.

"What do I need to do?" My voice came out rougher than I intended.

"Keep her close. Maybe up security on your house. I'm working on getting more intel about their operations, see if I can't help the feds along some. But Ford? These people are dangerous. If they think she knows anything..."

"She doesn't. She's a child."

"Doesn't matter. I doubt they'd take that chance. I certainly wouldn't risk it if it were my kid."

I scrubbed a hand down my face, as if that

would erase the horror from my expression. "Yeah, no. Of course not. Do you have pictures of the contractors who were seen in Norfolk?"

"Emailing them your way."

"Good. Thanks, Dax."

"No problem. I'll be in touch."

I stood in the backyard long after I'd hung up the phone, wrestling with what I'd just been told and what to do about it. So long as the information Casey had gathered was out there, Peyton was in danger. But what could I do? I wasn't law enforcement. And while I'd burn the world to keep my girl safe, that wasn't enough for the feds to take the company down. Maybe there was something still hidden among the stuff that had just been delivered. I'd talk to Peyton about it. And I'd share the pictures of the two men Dax had emailed me with her and the rest of my friends and family. Maybe I should pass them on to Chief Carson as well, so island PD was on the lookout.

It wasn't much, but it was something.

Locking down the panic that wanted to take hold, I shoved my phone in my pocket and went back inside to deal with the immediate chaos.

Bree was on the phone, one arm wrapped around her middle as she listened to whoever was on the other end and made the occasional "uh huh" noises in reply. I recognized tension in her posture and crossed the room to join her, even as my already jangling nerves stretched tighter.

"I understand. Thank you."

She hung up, and for a long moment didn't move. Then she lifted her face to mine. Tears clung to her lashes and my gut twisted. It had to be news about Ed. I braced to catch her, to weather the storm of her devastation. And then... she smiled.

"He's waking up."

Before the words had fully penetrated my brain, Bree threw herself at me with a laugh. "He's waking up!"

As Peyton whooped, I caught Bree close, spinning to keep us from toppling over. "That's amazing."

Amid all the uncertainty, it truly was a beacon of desperately needed hope.

She eased back and framed my face between her palms, those gray eyes lighter than they'd been in days. "He's going to be okay."

In that moment, held captive by her touch, it felt as if everything else would be, too.

Then she released me, tugging back with fresh frenetic energy. "I have to get to the ferry. I don't want him waking up alone."

Of course she didn't. And I didn't want her going to the mainland by herself, just in case there was some unexpected turn for the worse. But there were details to sort. A daughter to protect.

"I know you're excited, but slow your roll. You've got another hour until the ferry, and you should pack a bag this time, for the just in case."

"Right. Right." She turned a circle, as if half expecting all her stuff to have materialized amid the boxes we'd just taken off the moving truck.

I nudged her toward the door. "Next door."

"Right." She bolted.

"Don't leave without me!"

A backward wave was my only reply.

CHAPTER 39

BREE

The late afternoon sun slanted through the hospital windows as Ford and I made our way through the now-familiar corridors toward Pop's room. It had taken so much longer to get here than I'd wanted. Peyton had begged to come along, those big eyes of hers doing their damnedest to break my resolve. But the doctors had been clear about limiting Pop's contact with others while he was coming out of the coma, and I couldn't risk anything setting back his recovery.

In the end, she'd stayed with Willa and Sawyer, a choice which had caught me by surprise until Ford explained that he'd arranged for them to keep Keeley, too. No question, my pup would enjoy a playdate with her best pal, and the prospect of romping with two dogs had brightened Peyton's mood considerably.

My hand found Ford's without conscious thought, our fingers lacing together. The contact steadied me, helped keep the wild hope in check. I knew this was far from the end of his recovery. It was just a tiny first step. I needed to remember that it was no guarantee he'd go back to being the Pop I remembered. But it was so hard not to jump ahead to when everything was okay again.

Ford's thumb stroked along the back of my hand. "You're practically vibrating."

"I can't help it." The words tumbled out. "After everything that happened, just having him wake up means everything." Because one of the fears that had been stalking me since his AFib attack was that he'd never wake up again. That I'd never get the chance to say goodbye.

Ford's grip tightened. "I know."

The comfort of his presence still felt new, like a gift I wasn't quite sure I deserved. But I was grateful for it, especially now.

We rounded the corner to Pop's floor, and I caught sight of his regular nurse, Sarah, coming out of his room. She broke into a smile. "Perfect timing. He's been in and out, but more alert each time."

My heart leapt. "Has he said anything?"

"Not yet, but he's responding to commands—squeezing hands, wiggling toes. All good signs."

I barely remembered to thank her before pulling Ford toward Pop's room. The steady beep of monitors greeted us, along with the whoosh of the ventilator they'd kept him on while reducing his sedation.

Pop lay still against the white sheets, but some of the gray pallor had faded from his skin. His chest rose and fell in a steady rhythm.

I dropped into the chair beside his bed, keeping hold of Ford's hand as I reached for Pop's with my free one. "Hey Pop. I'm back."

His fingers twitched against mine.

"Did you see that?" I twisted to look up at Ford, who nodded.

"Talk to him some more."

"So Monty's got this wild idea for spring break." I stroked Pop's hand, sharing the gossip like I always had. "He wants to do a pirate-themed promotion. Says we should dress up the staff. Peter's already designed him this elaborate costume with a fancy tricorn hat." The memory of Monty's enthusiastic demonstration made me smile. "He was prancing around the bar in it the other day, making everyone call him Captain Montgomery."

Pop's fingers twitched again, and I swore I caught a hint of amusement around his mouth.

"Oh, and you should see what he wants the rest of us to wear. I told him there was no way I was putting on a corset, but he's determined. Says we need historical accuracy." I shook my head. "I reminded him we're a microbrewery, not a renaissance faire."

Ford chuckled beside me. "I'd pay good money to see that argument."

"You missed the best part. He's commissioned Peter to paint a new sign with a pirate ship on it. Claims we need proper ambiance." I leaned closer to Pop. "But between you and me, I think he just wants an excuse to wear the hat full time."

The corner of Pop's mouth twitched upward.

"And get this—he's already ordered these plastic doubloons to hand out as drink tokens. Special rum drinks, naturally. Says we're going to make a fortune off the college kids for spring break." I squeezed Pop's hand. "I told him you'd probably have some opinions about historical accuracy yourself when you saw his getup."

Pop's lips moved, and though his voice was raspy and slurred, I caught, "No... swords. Insurance... nightmare."

The laugh that burst from my throat was half sob. I squeezed his hand harder, struggling to keep my voice steady. "Hey there, Pop. Good nap?"

His eyelids fluttered, fighting to open against

the harsh fluorescent lights. When they finally cracked, his gaze was unfocused, drifting around the room before settling vaguely in my direction.

"Wha..." He licked dry lips. "Where?"

"You're in the hospital. Had a bit of an AFib episode." I kept my tone light, though my heart was hammering against my ribs. "Scared the hell out of everyone at the Brewhouse."

Ford's hand settled on my shoulder, a quiet anchor as Pop processed this information with glacial slowness.

"How long?"

"About two weeks." I stroked his hand, noting how his fingers curled weakly around mine. "The doctors had to keep you under while they got everything sorted."

His brow furrowed. "Tired."

"That's okay. You just rest. I'll be right here."

Pop's eyes started to drift closed, and I thought he'd fallen back asleep when they suddenly snapped open again. His gaze sharpened, focusing on where Ford's hand was still linked with mine.

A smile tugged at the corner of his mouth as his eyes moved between us. "About damned time," he muttered, voice gravelly but clear.

Heat rushed to my face. Trust Pop to notice that particular development even through a fog of medication. But before I could stammer out any kind of response, his eyes had already slipped shut again, breathing evening out into the rhythm of sleep.

I sagged against Ford, relief making my knees weak. Pop had woken up. He'd spoken. He'd even managed to be a smartass about my love life. The tightness that had been living in my chest for two weeks finally began to ease.

Ford's arm slid around my waist, supporting me. "You okay?"

"Yeah." I swiped at the tears tracking down my cheeks. "Just... yeah."

We sat with Pop for another hour, watching him drift in and out. Each time he woke, he seemed a little more present, though he didn't manage more than a few words at a time.

Dr. Mitchell's arrival pulled us into the hallway for an update.

She consulted her tablet. "The initial signs are very encouraging. He's responsive, oriented, and showing good comprehension. His speech is a bit slurred, which is normal at this stage, but he's able to form complete thoughts."

"What's next?" I asked.

"We'll continue to monitor him closely as we decrease sedation. Once he's more consistently awake, we can better assess what deficits we're dealing with and develop a rehabilitation plan." She looked up, her expression kind but serious. "I want to emphasize that we're still very early in the process. It's too soon to make any definitive predictions about recovery time or exactly where his baseline will be. But what we're seeing so far gives us reason to be optimistic."

I nodded, processing. "When can we bring others to see him?"

"Let's give it another day or two, see how he does with extended periods of consciousness. Then we can start allowing brief visits from immediate family."

Dr. Mitchell tucked her tablet under her arm. "I need to check on my other patients, but the nurses will page me if anything changes." She touched my shoulder. "Try to get some rest yourself. You look exhausted."

Not exactly flattering, given I'd actually been home and slept. But the sleep hadn't been actual rest—just fitful tossing and turning, punctuated by anxiety-fueled nightmares. I managed a nod, holding myself together until she disappeared around the corner, her footsteps fading down the sterile hospital corridor. Then my legs gave out, my whole body trembling with exhaustion now that the wave of excitement had passed.

Ford caught me before I hit the floor, gathering me against his chest with those strong, steady arms.

The dam broke. Two weeks of terror and stress and hoping poured out in great, heaving sobs I couldn't control. I buried my face in his shirt, clutching handfuls of the fabric as the tears came, my whole body shaking with the force of my relief and fear and bone-deep weariness. That salt and sandalwood scent surrounded me as I finally let myself fall apart.

"I've got you." His breath was warm against my scalp. "Let it out. He's gonna be okay. You did everything right."

My whole body shook, wracked with sobs I couldn't contain. "I was so scared. When he collapsed, I thought..." I couldn't finish, the words catching in my throat as fresh tears spilled down my cheeks. The memory of Pop's face going slack, his body crumpling, was still too raw.

"I know." His arms tightened around me, one hand moving in slow, soothing circles against my back. "But you heard the doctor. He's already being a smartass about us. That's our Ed. He's too damn stubborn to let this keep him down for long."

A wet laugh escaped me. "We're never going to hear the end of it."

"Wouldn't have it any other way."

Ford held me until the storm passed, until my breathing steadied and the tears slowed to occasional hiccups.

When I finally lifted my head, his shirt was soaked. "Sorry about that."

He brushed the tears from my cheeks with his thumbs. "Don't apologize. You've been holding that in for two weeks."

"I had to stay strong. For Pop."

"And now you can let go a little. He's coming back to us."

I sagged against him, suddenly bone weary. "Yeah. He is."

Ford's thumb traced along my jaw. "Let me take you to dinner. You haven't eaten since breakfast."

"I'm not really hungry." The words came automatically, though my stomach chose that moment to growl in protest.

"Yeah, that's convincing." He pressed a kiss to my temple. "Come on. We'll grab a hotel for the night, get some proper food in you."

"But Peyton—"

"Is having the time of her life with Willa and Sawyer. She texted me pictures of the dogs earlier." His phone appeared, showing Peyton sprawled on the floor between Roy and Keeley, her face split in a wide grin. "We can figure out longer term arrangements tomorrow, but for tonight, she's good."

I studied his face, searching for any hint of uncertainty. "You're sure?"

"Bree." His hands framed my face. "I know

you're used to taking care of everyone else. But let me take care of you for once. Okay?"

The tender concern in his voice undid me. I nodded, not trusting myself to speak.

"Good." He grabbed our coats from the visitors' chairs. "I know this great little Mexican place downtown. Real food, not hospital cafeteria mystery meat."

"Sounds perfect." I paused long enough to brush a kiss to Pop's weathered cheek. "I'll be back tomorrow. Love you."

Then I let Ford guide me toward the elevator.

CHAPTER 40
FORD

Ed was more lucid today. His eyes tracked between Bree and me, his expression shrewd despite the lingering effects of medication. "So, I didn't dream that. You two are speakin' again."

One corner of Bree's mouth hooked up. "Yeah, we are."

His gaze shifted to me. "Reckon since you're here with my girl again, you two finally got your heads straight and are doin' more than speakin'."

Bree's cheeks flushed scarlet. "Pop!"

I was still trying to find some kind of response.

"What? I'm old, not blind." He shifted in the hospital bed, wincing. "Been watching you dance around each other since you were kids."

Deciding the best defense was a good offense, I

tugged Bree closer, sliding an arm around her waist. "To be fair, sir, that was mostly my fault. Took me way too long to realize what was right in front of me. But I promise you, I'm done being an idiot. Your granddaughter is my priority now, and I'm going to spend however long it takes proving that to both of you."

Ed's eyes narrowed, studying me with the same intensity I'd seen him use when staring down belligerent drunks at the tavern. "About damn time." He looked at Bree. "This what you want, baby girl?"

Cheeks fading from fire engine red to a pretty pink, she leaned into my side, her warmth seeping through my shirt. "Always has been."

"Well, alright then." He settled back against the pillows. "Just remember I've got a shotgun if you mess this up again."

"Pop!" Bree's face flamed again.

I tightened my hold on her. "Message received, sir. But you won't need it. I learned my lesson the hard way. I'm not letting her go again."

Ed nodded, apparently satisfied. "Good." His eyes began drifting closed again, and I wondered if he'd worn himself out already. Then they snapped wide again. He struggled to sit up. "The map. Where's the map? Shit, I left it and all my notes at the Brewhouse when I fell out."

Bree gently pressed him back. "We have it. It's fine."

His gnarled hand gripped hers with strange urgency. "You have to keep everything safe. Hidden."

Frowning, Bree glanced at me.

I shrugged. Did he think it was a real treasure map instead of a souvenir? That they'd legitimately found something someone would want? Maybe he was still confused because of the coma.

"Nobody else has the map, Pop. It's fine."

"There's an irregularity in the map," he insisted.

"Peyton found it." Surely that would calm Ed down. "She gathered up all your notes when they took you to the hospital."

His fingers tightened on Bree's hand. "Keep her safe. If anybody finds out, they'll come after her."

My spine stiffened. I'd had about enough of vague threats to my daughter. "Who'll come after her?"

But Ed's eyes were glazing over again, medication or exhaustion pulling him under again.

"Pop, what are you talking about?" Bree smoothed his hair back. "Who's going to come after Peyton?"

His head lolled. "Keep... safe." The words slurred together as he drifted off.

I exchanged a look with Bree. "You don't think..."

She shook her head. "It's just a souvenir map. Something fun for tourists."

"But he seems really worried about it." And about my kid. The one I was this close to putting in a bubble until the world quit losing its collective mind. "And someone did break into his place."

Not that we'd told Ed that. The doctor had been clear he didn't need to get overexcited or exert himself.

"Crime of opportunity, like Chris said." But she didn't sound convinced.

"You said yourself that nothing was taken, though." I ran a hand through my hair. "What if there's something to this treasure hunt of theirs? It's been ages since there's been a find of any significance, but we've both heard the stories. Treasure hunters are still a cutthroat lot."

"You think there's any chance they've found something for real?"

"I don't know. But Ed seemed pretty adamant about keeping Peyton safe. And he's not usually the type to get worked up over nothing."

Bree chewed her lip. "No, he's not."

I looked down at Ed's sleeping form. What did he know that had him so worried? And more importantly, was my daughter in danger because of it?

Probably not. And yet I couldn't shake a lingering sense of unease, probably just because I hadn't actually seen my kid today.

"I'm gonna go check in with Sawyer." I stroked a hand down Bree's ponytail. "Be back in a bit."

Out of respect for the other folks on the floor, I took the elevator down to the cafeteria level and found a quiet corner.

Sawyer picked up on the second ring. "Hey man. How's Ed?"

I gave Sawyer the rundown on his improved condition. "He's definitely more with it today. Recognized both of us. Knew what was going on."

"That's great news."

"Yeah. And he definitely cottoned to the change in my relationship with Bree."

"Oh, yeah?" Sawyer's amusement carried through the phone. "How'd that go over?"

"Seems pleased. He offered the expected reminder that he can still kick my ass if I fuck it up again."

"Well, that all seems about right." There was a pause. "How *are* you and Bree?"

I leaned against the wall, watching people drift in and out of the cafeteria. "We're good. I mean, we've hardly had a chance to figure out what we are, with everything going on with Ed, but we're a we. And right now, that feels like a damned miracle."

"I'm happy for you, man. I know what she means to you."

My throat tightened. "I just wish it hadn't taken me fucking up for so long to figure that out myself."

"Better late than never."

"How's my girl? Was she a good guest?"

"She's great. She and Willa had a grand old time with the dogs. Which, for the record, is where she'd have preferred to spend the day. But I delivered her to the school doors myself first thing this morning."

I let out a breath I hadn't realized I was holding. "Thanks, man. I really appreciate you and Willa taking her."

"Anytime. You know that. And there's been no sign of either of those guys Dax warned you about. Willa's notified all the ferry staff company wide, so if they board anywhere, we'll hear about it. Everything's good here, brother."

My shoulders loosened another fraction. Peyton was safe. That was the important thing. "Thanks for keeping an eye out."

"You know we've all got your back. Willa's picking her up after last bell."

I glanced at my watch. Two more hours until school let out. "You're no doubt in the middle of a job and do not have time to indulge my over-protective parenting."

"No worries. You've had a lot on your plate. Let us know how Ed progresses and what your plans are. We're good with keeping Peyton as long as you need. Although I expect your moms are gonna want some more grandma time."

I'd no doubt have an earful from them when they found out everything I hadn't told them when I'd left the island yesterday. But that was a problem for Future Ford. "Will do. I think we'll have a better idea by end of today or maybe tomorrow. We'll keep you posted."

I hung up the phone and stared out the window at a patch of green space with winter-bare trees. I knew Ed was far from going home, but now that he was out of the worst danger, I felt better about the idea of leaving Bree for a little while if I needed to. Which I probably would soon. There was only so much of my work I could do without the secure internet connection of my home network, and I was woefully behind. My superiors would be on my ass soon enough if I didn't catch up. And that didn't cover my duty to Peyton.

More than a little tired, I dropped my brow to the glass. I really needed life to stop coming at me like a bullet train so I could catch my breath. Thank God for my friends and family. I didn't have any idea how I'd be able to do all this without help.

The call with Sawyer should have put me back

at ease. There was nothing to be worried about. And yet I couldn't shake the sense that something was wrong. Or maybe it was my own guilt for having to split my time between Bree and Peyton. Either way, I was still tweaked.

I could call the school. Not to talk to Peyton. That would be ridiculous. But just... to be absolutely sure she was where she was supposed to be.

Feeling ridiculously over the top, I looked up the number and dialed.

"Sutter's Ferry Middle School."

"This is Ford Donoghue. I'm calling about my daughter, Peyton Walsh."

"Oh yes, of course." The secretary's tone warmed with recognition. News traveled fast on Hatterwick. "Is everything alright?"

"Yeah, everything's fine. I just..." God, this felt ridiculous. "Could you check that she's in class? I don't need to speak to her. Just want to make sure she's where she's supposed to be."

"Certainly, Mr. Donoghue. We can send someone to check." A pause. "Would you like us to call you back?"

Too late, it occurred to me how this must sound —like I thought my kid was skipping or getting into trouble. Which wasn't it at all. But explaining my paranoia about shadowy corporate threats would probably make me sound certifiable.

"That'd be great, thanks." I rattled off my cell number, already planning my retreat to Ed's room. "I appreciate it."

"Not at all. We'll call you right back."

I hung up, feeling both relieved and slightly foolish. Peyton was fine. She was exactly where she was supposed to be, probably bored out of her mind in whatever class she had this period. And here I was, acting like one of those helicopter parents I'd always secretly judged.

But Ed's words kept echoing in my head. Keep her safe.

Shaking it off, I headed for the elevator. Time to get back to Bree and see if Ed had woken up again with any more cryptic warnings.

But he was still sleeping when I made it back.

Bree rose and joined me in the hall, sliding her arms around me. "Everything okay?"

"Yeah. It's fine. I'm being ridiculously paranoid."

"Understandably."

"I called the school to check on her." I winced. "Is that terrible?"

"Under the circumstances, no. What did they say?"

"They're checking to see she's properly in class and supposed to call me back."

It took a lot longer for the call to come than I

expected. A full twenty minutes had passed, and I was wondering if I ought to call back, when my phone finally began to vibrate.

"Hello."

The voice on the other end sucked in a breath, and in that moment of silence, I knew the news wasn't good.

"Mr. Donoghue. This is Principal Carpenter. Your daughter isn't in class. Neither is her friend Madison Daniels. They haven't responded to hails over the intercom, and no one has seen them. Is there any viable reason for her absence? Does she have a history of skipping at her old school?"

I had no idea. But everything in me shouted that something was wrong, wrong, wrong. "No. Call the police. I'm on my way."

CHAPTER 41

BREE

The ferry couldn't move fast enough. I paced the deck despite the whipping wind, scanning the choppy waters as if I could somehow make us reach Hatterwick faster through sheer force of will. The cold spray stung my face, but I barely noticed, too focused on the distant shoreline that seemed to taunt us with how slowly it grew larger.

Ford stood at the railing, knuckles white where he gripped the metal. It was the only thing keeping him from crawling out of his skin. The set of his jaw spoke volumes about the terror he was holding back. I knew that feeling. The helplessness. The what-ifs crowding out rational thought.

He'd made call after call as we'd rushed from the hospital. To Sawyer. To his moms. To Chief

Carson. Carson had for sure given him grief about where he'd gotten the information about the guys he believed had taken Peyton. Ford had insisted it didn't matter, that everyone simply needed to be on the lookout. And based on all the reports that kept popping up on my phone, they were. Hatterwick was out in force, despite the dark clouds looming on the horizon. The whole island had mobilized. Even the tourists were joining the search parties. After Gwen, no one wanted to take chances with missing kids.

The thought of Peyton out there somewhere, maybe hurt or scared, made me want to scream until my throat was raw. She wasn't even my daughter, but these past weeks... God, when had she burrowed so deep into my heart? When had I started thinking of her as part of my weird little family?

The ferry horn blasted, long and mournful, signaling our approach to the dock. Ford's shoulders tensed further as the island's outline emerged through the gathering gloom, a dark smudge against darker clouds. Red and blue lights flashed near the pier—police coordinating the search efforts. I spotted Coast Guard vessels out beyond the marina, their white hulls stark against the churning gray water. A helicopter buzzed overhead, following the coastline.

"They'll find them." My voice shook with the

fear I was trying desperately to hide, undermining the comfort I was trying to offer. "The whole island's looking. You know how Hatterwick takes care of its own."

"Before the storm hits?" His words were barely audible over the wind that whipped my hair around my face. "Before whoever took them—"

I grabbed his hand, squeezing hard enough that my knuckles went white. We both knew what he wasn't saying. That this wasn't just two kids skipping school for an afternoon adventure. Not with everything else going on. Not with the shadows that had been gathering around the edges of our lives these past weeks.

Thunder rumbled in the distance as we docked, the hollow sound echoing across the water like nature's warning bell. Time was running out.

I white-knuckled the steering wheel as we pulled off the ferry, Ford vibrating with tension beside me. The late afternoon sky had turned an ominous gray-green, the kind of color that made my stomach clench with dread, and I knew the first fat drops of rain wouldn't be far off. The air felt thick enough to chew.

The school parking lot had transformed into a command center, with Carson's cruiser serving as the hub, its lights cutting through the murky twilight in steady red and blue pulses. Clusters of people huddled around maps spread across car hoods, marking off areas already searched, their fingers tracing desperate patterns across the paper. Parents clutched their own children close, as if afraid they might vanish too, while teenagers pointed out favorite hangout spots to officers, their voices carrying notes of barely contained panic.

My throat closed up at the sight. God, it was just like before. The same faces wearing the same worried expressions. The same mix of determination and fear. The same helpless feeling that we were already too late, that history was about to repeat itself in the worst possible way.

I killed the engine, and Ford was out before I could unbuckle my seatbelt. He made a beeline for Carson, who stood barking orders into his radio, his face lined with the kind of tension I hadn't seen since Gwen disappeared.

"Chief." Ford's voice cracked. "Any sign?"

Carson lowered his radio, his weathered face grim. "Last confirmed sighting was at lunch. Security cameras show both girls heading toward the cafeteria, but not coming back. Their backpacks aren't in their lockers or anywhere else we've found. We've tried pinging their phones, but they're either dead or turned off." He shook his head, the gesture heavy with the weight of too many similar conversations.

"What about—" Ford started.

"We're checking everywhere, son. Got teams combing the whole island. Coast Guard's got boats in the water. But this storm has damned shit timing." Carson glanced at the darkening sky, where angry clouds were gathering like bruises. Thunder rumbled in the distance, a low warning of what was coming.

I stepped closer to Ford, needing the contact as much as wanting to offer support. My fingers brushed against his arm, feeling the tension thrumming through his muscles. The same hollow feeling I'd had twelve years ago opened up in my chest, that mix of dread and helplessness threatening to overwhelm me. But this time had to be different. We had to find them. We wouldn't let more teenagers vanish into thin air on this island, not again.

"Ford!"

We spun toward the voice to find Sawyer hustling up to the command center, Willa right behind. His face was ashen.

"I'm so sorry. I should've—Well, I don't know what I should have done. Maybe kept her home from school entirely. But she seemed fine this morning. I thought..." His voice trailed off, thick with regret.

Ford shook his head. "This isn't on you, brother." But I could hear what he wasn't saying. That it was his fault. He was Peyton's father. She was his responsibility. The weight of that settled visibly on his broad shoulders, making him look older than his years.

By that token, it was on me, too. Because Ford had been taking care of me instead of her, spending precious hours helping me deal with my own issues when he should have been focused on his daughter. None of which was productive thinking under the circumstances. We needed clear heads, not guilt.

"Mama Flo and Mimi are out as part of the first wave of searchers," Willa said.

"Where are the dogs?" I asked.

"We thought it was best to leave them back at the house. Just in case."

Probably sensible. Neither Roy nor Keeley were trained to search, and they'd probably just get in the way.

Carson began describing where they'd started the search and how it had fanned out from the school, his weathered face set in grim determination as he gestured toward a map spread across the hood of his cruiser.

Willa wrapped her arms around herself, her voice barely above a whisper. "What if this is like Gwen? Roland O'Shea's office was broken into last month. We know he wasn't working alone. What if it's starting again?"

Her words sent a chill down my spine, voicing the fear we'd all been trying to suppress.

The blood drained from Ford's face. I grabbed his arm to steady him, feeling the tremor that ran through his muscled frame. My fingers tightened instinctively, offering what little comfort I could.

Carson cut her off, his weathered face hardening. "Now hold on. Let's not get ahead of ourselves. Two teenagers skipping class is a far cry from what happened with Gwen Busby." He tapped the map with thick fingers, as if trying to physically ground us in reality.

But I saw the fear flash in Ford's eyes. The same terror that had gripped the island thirteen years ago when Gwen vanished without a trace. That collective nightmare still haunted us all, lurking beneath the surface of every missing person report, every delayed return home.

"Chief." Ford's voice was rough, like he had to drag the words past a barrier in his throat. "The guys I told you about, from Northwest Global—"

"We don't have any evidence connecting them to this," Carson interrupted, his tone brooking no argument. "No proof they're on-island. Right now, we treat this like what it likely is—two kids who decided to play hooky and lost track of time."

But we all knew that if that's what it was, the entire island wouldn't be out searching. The gathering darkness and growing crowd of volunteers told a different story. One that tasted of old fears and fresh panic.

Thunder cracked overhead, making us all jump. The first heavy drops of rain splattered against the pavement, dark spots blooming on the concrete like bruises spreading across skin.

"We need to find them before this storm really hits," Sawyer said. "Exposure will up the risk of hypothermia."

Ford turned toward the nearest search quadrant, his jaw clenched so tight I could see the muscle ticking. Sawyer grabbed his shoulder, anchoring him in place. "I've got extra rain gear in my truck."

I followed Ford and Sawyer to his truck, parked at the edge of the lot. The wind whipped harder, pelting us with stinging drops of rain that felt more like ice than water. Sawyer yanked open the crew cab door and pulled out a pile of bright yellow slickers and rubber boots, the kind fishermen wore when the weather turned mean.

Ford's hands shook as he tried to pull on the rain gear, fumbling with the snaps like a man who'd forgotten how his own fingers worked. The tremors spread up his arms until his whole body vibrated with barely contained panic.

I caught his wrists, stilling his fumbling fingers.

"Let me help." My own heart was racing, but I forced myself to stay calm, to be the steady one for once.

His eyes met mine, wild with fear, the usually vibrant green now dark with desperation. "I can't lose her, Bree. I just found her." His voice cracked on the last word.

"We won't lose her." I helped him into the slicker, zipping it up with steady hands. "The whole island is looking. We'll find her."

"What if—"

"No." I gripped his face between my palms, forcing him to focus on me. His skin was cold from the rain, but I could feel the tension thrumming through him. After all the times he'd been my rock, it was time for me to return the favor. "No what-ifs. We need you present and thinking clearly. Peyton needs you thinking clearly."

He drew in a ragged breath, then another. Some of the panic faded from his eyes, replaced by determination. He covered my hands with his, pressing his forehead to mine. "Thank you."

"Always." The word slipped out before I could stop it, heavy with meaning neither of us could afford to examine right now.

Sawyer cleared his throat and held out flashlights, tactfully ignoring our moment. "Sun's gonna set soon. We'll need these." The beam of his own light cut through the growing darkness.

I released Ford to take one, checking the batteries. Thunder boomed closer now, and the rain fell harder, drumming against my slicker. We needed to move fast before the storm got worse and any traces of Peyton's path disappeared completely.

Ford squared his shoulders, jaw set in that stubborn way I remembered so well. "Where do we start?"

CHAPTER 42

FORD

We caught a break when the police received a tip from a tourist who'd been taking a selfie video from the parking lot of the park that led into the maritime forest at the center of the island. On reviewing the footage prior to posting, she spotted the girls ducking into the woods, seemingly alone. Having seen the news of the girls' disappearance, she'd brought the footage to Carson. The video had been taken around two o'clock, and was the latest confirmed sighting. So the search had been moved to the park.

Carson was now certain that the girls were simply playing hooky and that we'd find them in the woods, maybe with a sprained ankle or broken bone that was preventing them from making it out on their own. I'd never hoped so much for normal teenage delinquent behavior in my life, but my gut said this was nothing so simple. I didn't know if that was based on anything real or if it was because the parking lot was right near Osprey Beach, where Gwen Busby had disappeared. My brain bombarded me with memories of that other search all those years ago. Never mind that the lowering dark and the frigid rain were nothing like the bright, sticky heat of that early summer day.

I remembered Miles Busby's panic as we'd searched and searched for his sister. The same panic bubbled beneath my skin. A desperate determination to burn the world to save my child. Had Miles been making fevered deals with whatever deity might be listening? Or had he been thinking about the looks on his parents' faces if they failed to find her? Anticipating the blame that they'd heap on his head for failing to protect his sister? The blame he'd no doubt lived with for thirteen years.

The beam of my flashlight cut through sheets of rain, searching for any sign of my daughter. Every shadow looked like a body. Every rustle of leaves in the wind sounded like a cry for help. My heart hammered against my ribs, threatening to burst.

"Ford." Bree's voice anchored me, her hand squeezing my arm. "We're going to find her."

I nodded, not trusting myself to speak. She'd

insisted on staying with me when the search parties split up, probably sensing I was close to losing it completely. The steady pressure of her touch kept me focused, kept me moving forward instead of spiraling into panic.

Somewhere in these woods was my little girl. My daughter, who I'd only just found. Who I was only beginning to know. Who trusted me to keep her safe. And I'd failed her.

"Left," Sawyer called softly, redirecting our line to maintain the search grid.

I adjusted course, scanning the ground for any trace. A footprint, a scrap of clothing, anything that might tell us which way they went. But the rain had turned the forest floor into soup, obscuring any tracks that might have been there.

Frustrated, I lifted the beam, panning it ahead to check my course. And I saw something. A quick glint where no glint should be. I swept the light back, trying to find it again.

There. A hint of reflection from a dark knot in an old oak tree.

"Hold up." I approached the tree, heart in my throat. Nothing natural would catch light that way.

I reached into the hollow, and my fingers touched smooth plastic. Pulling it free, I found a zip-top bag in my hand. Inside, I could make out a notebook and something else folded beside it. My hands shook. I didn't need to open it to know that this was Peyton's map. She took it everywhere, keeping it close like some kind of security blanket or talisman.

"What is it?" Bree asked, moving closer.

"Peyton's map. And I think these are Ed's notes. Her notes." I held the bag carefully, not wanting to damage the contents. "She wouldn't have left these behind willingly."

Bree called out. Sawyer, Willa, Daniel, and Gabi converged on our location.

I held up the bag. "She was here. This was stuffed in the knot of that tree."

Daniel frowned. "Why'd she shove it in there?" Concern deepened his Louisiana drawl.

"Hiding it from somebody. Nothing else makes sense." I turned a circle. "If they were on their own up to this point and then heard someone coming, she could have shoved it in there in a hurry." My kid was nothing if not resourceful. Her cross-country trip from Oregon proved that.

"She must have thought whoever was coming was a threat, otherwise why hide it?" Gabi said.

"And she hasn't come back for it, so maybe she was right." Daniel's tone was grim. "Fan out. Maybe we'll find some sign of which way they went."

"Can I see that?" Bree held out her hand for the bag.

I was reluctant to let go of this last connection to Peyton, but did as she asked before turning back to the search.

"Over here!" Sawyer's voice cut through the drumming rain.

My heart seized as I splashed through puddles toward him. He stood beneath a massive live oak, examining something caught in the lower branches.

"What is it?" My voice sounded strange in my own ears.

He pointed his flashlight at a scrap of purple fabric snagged on rough bark. "This looks like the shirt Peyton was wearing today."

I reached out with trembling fingers to touch the torn cloth.

"There's more." Sawyer swept his beam across the ground. Broken branches. Churned mud. Signs of bodies hitting the ground hard. My stomach lurched as I pictured my daughter struggling against whoever had grabbed her.

"Two sets of adult-sized boot prints." Sawyer crouched to examine the mud more closely. "Looks like they came from that direction." He gestured toward the deeper woods. "The girls' tracks stop here."

I braced myself against the oak's trunk, bile rising in my throat. This was my nightmare made real. Someone had taken my daughter. Those federal agents had been right. She'd been a target all along.

"Ford!" Bree's sharp voice pulled me out of the fear spiral. "You need to see this."

I hustled back to where she huddled with Gabi and Willa, the notebook open. Their faces were lit by the harsh glow of phone flashlights, casting deep shadows across their worried expressions.

"Read it." She thrust the book toward me with trembling hands.

"I don't think now is the time to review her thoughts on a treasure hunt." My blood beat a frantic rhythm, urging me to *act*, even though I didn't know where or how. Every second we wasted here was another second my daughter could be getting further away.

"It's not her thoughts on the treasure hunt."

I scanned Peyton's neat handwriting. The pages were filled with her careful observations, each entry dated and cross-referenced like she was building a case.

"Look here." Bree's finger landed on a page headed 'Island Crime Timeline.' Her nail tapped against the paper with increasing urgency.

Below it, Peyton had meticulously documented every break-in and search that had occurred since David Galef's murder. She'd drawn arrows connecting seemingly random events, creating a pattern I hadn't seen before. My daughter, it seemed, had been paying far more attention to the island's troubles than any of us had realized.

> Theory: Someone's searching for something specific. But what?

On the next page, she'd noted:

> The map was created by Hillary Russell. Signature hidden in the artwork. She was David Galef's ex-girlfriend. Coincidence?

My hands shook as I turned to the last entry.

> Compared treasure maps in museum archives, as well as to the other maps made by Hillary in the gift shop. All match except one location, which does not fit the art style of the rest of the map.
> Why would Hillary mark something different? What if she didn't? What if _he_ did?

What if X doesn't mark treasure at all?
What if it marks information/evidence, and
the map accidentally got mixed up with the
batch destined for the museum gift shop?
Maybe that's what they were arguing about
when I saw them at school.

I frowned, trying to process what Peyton was suggesting. "It's a huge leap." Surely my thirteen-year-old hadn't just solved the motive for a murder that had been stumping police for weeks. It was just that she had a big, active imagination. Then again, kids sometimes saw things adults missed, their minds not yet trained to dismiss the improbable.

"Except someone broke into Pop's place looking for something. And remember, he was insistent that she needed to be kept safe. We didn't know why. What if they stumbled on all of this while they were doing their treasure hunt?" Bree insisted. "People knew the two of them were working on this map. If she's right, this location could lead to the reason David Galef was murdered."

And if someone was willing to murder Galef over that information, they likely wouldn't bat an eye at adding to the body count. The idea of it made me break out into a cold sweat.

"The location is remote by island standards, but it isn't far." Willa's finger traced the path on the map. "We can check it fast, just in case. Everyone else will continue the grid search."

It still felt like a long shot, but it was action. In this moment, I needed to move like I needed to breathe. And if there was even the remotest chance that this was real, then I had to follow up.

"Let's go."

CHAPTER 43
BREE

The beam of my flashlight swept across the ground, barely more than a red glow through the filter I'd attached. I hadn't asked why Daniel had a collection of them in his pocket. Every step had to be careful, deliberate. The last thing we needed was to alert anyone to our presence.

Sand shifted beneath my feet as we picked our way toward the coordinates Peyton had indicated didn't fit. The storm was dying down, but thunder still rumbled in the distance.

"There." I pointed to a cluster of rocks ahead— one of the few spots on the island where they existed naturally. Most had been brought in over decades for various building projects.

Ford surged forward, but Sawyer grabbed his

arm. "Slow. We don't know who might be watching."

He nodded, forcing himself to match our measured pace. As we drew closer, my heart sank. A hole gaped in the sand near the rocks, maybe two feet deep. Empty.

"Dammit." Ford dropped to his knees beside it, hands fisting in the sand. "They're not here. Where the hell are they?"

I crouched beside him, studying the churned-up sand around the hole. There were traces of footprints, but the storm had already begun to erase them.

"Where now?" The desperation in his voice cut straight to my heart. "What do we do?"

"Hey." I gripped his shoulder. "These maps are never exact, you know that. The coastline's constantly changing. That's why following old treasure maps is almost impossible. This isn't the only potential location."

"We don't even know if they're following Peyton's lead."

"They must be. Think about it. She hid that map for a reason. If she claimed to know where this evidence is hidden, that's leverage. That's what's keeping her alive."

I winced at the fear that flashed across Ford's face. *Way to go, Bree. Remind him there are more reasons his daughter might be in danger.*

"I'm sorry, that was a terrible thing to say." I grabbed his hand. "But your kid is smart and resourceful. Look at how she made it here from Oregon all on her own."

He squeezed my fingers, taking a shaky breath. "You're right. I know you're right."

We all hunched over the map together, studying the faded markings.

"Wait." Willa leaned in, pointing to a formation marked on the paper. "I think I recognize those rocks. They're past Pelican Inlet, maybe another quarter mile from here."

"You sure?" Ford's voice held desperate hope.

"Pretty sure. There's this weird formation that looks like a fish if you catch it at the right angle. Not many spots like that on the island."

Ford was already on his feet, but I caught his arm. "We stick together this time. No splitting up."

The determination in his eyes matched my own. We weren't letting anyone else disappear tonight.

We picked our way through the maritime forest, staying low and quiet. I wished we had more light than the red-filtered beams of our flashlights.

"When we find them," Sawyer whispered, "you three hang back."

"Like hell," Gabi hissed.

"We're trained for this," Daniel said. "You're not."

"And what happens if you get shot?" Willa demanded in quiet steel.

"Better us than you," Ford said.

For a moment I shut my eyes, my brain offering up exactly that scenario. Ford rushing in blind, taking a bullet to save his daughter. Breaking his promise again and leaving me for good this time.

Panic helps no one.

I wanted this over. I wanted him safe. Under no circumstances did I want this to turn into a hostage situation. I just needed my family home. So I shoved down my resentment at being left out of this plan of rescue.

"He's right," I murmured. "We can't help if we become liabilities."

Gabi shot me a look of betrayal. "So we're just supposed to stay back while they play hero?"

"We're supposed to be smart," I said. "None of us are trained for this kind of situation. The best thing we can do is stay out of their way and be ready to help once it's over."

I didn't like it any more than they did. The thought of Ford walking into danger made me physically sick. But charging in without a plan would only make things worse.

Willa's shoulders slumped. "I hate that you're right."

"Me too." I squeezed her hand. "But Peyton needs us thinking clearly right now."

Through the trees, pinpricks of light appeared. Daniel held up his fist, and we all froze, clicking off our own flashlights.

The three men moved ahead, hands flashing in what I assumed were military signals. I had no idea what they were saying for sure, but I assumed the gist was that they'd continue through the trees and circle around behind whoever was out there with those lights. Then Ford caught my eyes and pointed firmly at the ground. That signal was crystal clear. *Stay*.

I nodded. I didn't want to make this worse.

They disappeared into the shadows, and the wait began.

I managed approximately two minutes before I began to creep forward, toward the edge of the trees. I wouldn't get involved, but I needed to see for sure if Peyton was there. Gabi and Willa flanked me, moving as quietly as possible. Our footsteps were masked by the sound of the surf and the lingering patter of rain.

Where the trees gave way to sea oats and sand, we crouched down, close enough now to make out the scene ahead. Two men with guns stood over two smaller figures, flashlights trained on the hole being dug in the sand with their hands. I recognized the dark blonde hair plastered against Peyton's head.

My heart leapt into my throat. They were alive. But for how long? What happened when they found whatever they were looking for? Or worse—what if there was nothing to find?

One of them jerked his weapon. "Dig faster."

Peyton's shoulders hunched, but she didn't look up. Smart girl. Keep them focused on the ground, not their surroundings.

Madison whimpered, and the second man kicked sand at her. "Shut up and keep digging."

My fingers dug into the wet bark. Every instinct screamed to rush out there, but I forced myself to stay put. The guys knew what they were doing. We had to trust them.

Please let this work. Please let them all be okay.

One of the men began to pace, his agitation growing with every step. "This is the last place." He kicked more sand at the girls.

"I don't have the map anymore, okay?" Peyton's voice cracked. "I'm doing my best. Remember, things change along the coastline with tides and storms and stuff. This isn't an exact science. Do you know of any other rock formations besides this one and the other we dug out?"

"This is the only other one. It has to be here somewhere," the second man growled.

I recognized these men. Oh, not their faces or voices. But their type. In her pursuit of drugs, my mother had exposed me to plenty of their ilk. They tended to fall into two camps—desperate or dangerous, always operating under someone else's hierarchy. As a child, I'd learned how to avoid them, become invisible because I knew how quickly they could turn.

The girls worked their way around the sides of the massive rock formation, hands raw from digging. As the rain finally began to ease, my eyes caught a dark shape offshore. A boat running dark.

That couldn't be anything good.

Please let Daniel see it. Please let him already be calling this in to the Coast Guard.

"Charon is going to be pissed if we come back empty-handed," the first man muttered.

His partner's eyes raked over Peyton and Madison in a way that made my skin crawl. "The profit will offset his irritation. If we don't find it... Well, at this point, nobody else is gonna find it either."

Bile rose in my throat as his meaning became clear. These monsters planned to traffic the girls.

Willa's hand found mine in the darkness, squeezing hard. I returned the pressure, acknowledging the horror of what we'd just heard. We had to trust the guys to handle this, but God, waiting was torture when those bastards were threatening children.

Gabi tapped my shoulder and pointed. Through the drizzle, I could just make out Ford, Sawyer, and Daniel spreading out to flank the men. They'd left the cover of the trees and were creeping closer to the gunmen. The roar of the ocean would cover the sound of their approach, but if either gunman turned to look toward that boat, they'd be sitting ducks. Did the boat even have anything to do with what was happening here on the beach?

I strained to hear what the men were muttering about, but their words were lost in the crash of waves. One of them shifted, starting to turn toward the water.

My heart stopped. He was going to see Ford.

I burst from the trees before I could think twice about it, forcing a relieved laugh. "Oh thank God, you found them!"

Both men whirled toward me, but I kept moving forward, arms outstretched toward the girls. "Everyone's been so worried. The whole island's been searching."

"Lady, stop right there."

"The radios are down from this nasty weather." I kept my voice bright, pretending I didn't see the weapons they were trying to conceal. "I guess that's why you haven't called it in yet. But seriously, you guys are going to be heroes. Finding these girls in weather like this?"

These were definitely not the two men we'd been on the lookout for because of Dax. No time to think about that right now. I reached for Peyton, who was staring at me with wide eyes. "Come on, sweetie, let's get you home."

The distinctive click of a safety being released stopped me cold. One of the men had given up trying to hide his gun and now had it trained directly on my chest.

I raised my hands slowly. "Whoa, what's going on here? I promise I'm not trying to hurt them." I gestured toward Peyton with my chin. "I'm dating her father. We just want to take them home. Everyone will be so relieved to see them safe."

The gunman's eyes raked over me in a way that made my skin crawl. "You're not going anywhere."

"Look, I don't want any trouble." I kept my hands raised, shifting my weight to move fast if I had to. Behind him, I caught glimpses of movement in the darkness. Ford, Sawyer, and Daniel were getting closer. Just a few more seconds.

"What are you doing?" The second man stepped forward, agitated. "We need to get out of here."

"Relax." The first man's smile turned predatory. "She's a little long in the tooth, but I'm sure they can find a use for her too."

"Dude, I don't—"

Three dark shapes launched from the shadows.

I grabbed both girls' arms. "Run!"

We sprinted across the sand as the sounds of fighting erupted behind us. Peyton stumbled, and I hauled her back to her feet, pushing them both ahead of me.

A gunshot cracked through the night.

I didn't hesitate. I threw myself over both girls, driving us into the sand. My heart hammered as two more shots rang out.

Then silence fell, broken only by the crash of waves and our ragged breathing.

My ears rang from the gunshots, blood pulsing so loud it drowned out the surf. I kept both girls pinned beneath me, afraid to lift my head. Afraid of what I'd find if I looked.

Hands grabbed my shoulders, and I tensed until Ford's voice cut through the chaos in my head. "Bree! Are you hit?"

I shook my head, still protecting the girls.

"Let me see. I need to see you're okay."

He dragged me up, and I fell into his arms. His hands ran over me, checking for injuries.

"You're fucking insane." His voice broke. "And I love you so much."

He yanked me against his chest, then reached for Peyton. Madison got swept up too, as he pulled us all into a crushing embrace.

Peyton burst into tears, clutching Ford's shirt. "I'm sorry. I'm so sorry, Daddy. We just wanted to find—"

"Shh." He pressed his lips to the top of her head. "You're safe. That's all that matters right now."

I couldn't stop shaking, the adrenaline crash hitting hard. Ford's arm tightened around my waist, holding me up.

Madison sobbed against my shoulder. "I want my mom."

Over Ford's shoulder, I spotted Sawyer and Daniel securing the gunmen with zip ties. The men cursed and struggled, but they weren't going anywhere.

Then movement on the water caught my eye. "The boat!" I pointed toward the dark shape lurking offshore. "There's a boat running without lights!"

Daniel's head snapped up. He squinted through the darkness, then grabbed his radio and took off running down the beach.

Ford pulled back just enough to look at Peyton's face. "Are you hurt? Did they touch you?"

She shook her head, wiping at her tears. "No, we're okay. I knew you'd find us."

"Always." He pressed another kiss to her hair. "But please, never do anything like this again. You scared years off my life."

"I'm sorry." Her voice wobbled. "We thought we could figure it out ourselves. I didn't mean for any of this to happen."

"I know, baby." He gathered her close again. "Everything's going to be okay now. They'll be locked away where they can't get to you anymore."

Madison sniffled against my shoulder. "Are they really going to jail?"

"Yes." I smoothed her wet hair back. "They absolutely will."

Gabi materialized with a bright smile. "Police are on their way, but how about y'all let me check you over while we wait?"

"But we're not hurt," Peyton protested.

"Humor us," Ford said. "Please."

She burrowed deeper into his embrace. "Okay, Daddy."

CHAPTER 44

FORD

Though exhaustion dragged at every cell of my body, sleep wouldn't come. I still felt cold down to my very core, as if I'd never be warm again, despite Bree's comforting weight curled against me in bed. I simply couldn't let go of the fear of what could have happened to Peyton and Madison. In the course of giving initial statements to the police, I'd heard Bree report what the kidnappers had said.

They'd intended to traffic my daughter and her friend.

If we'd been any later...

If I hadn't found the map...

If we hadn't given credence to Peyton's theories and followed it...

I'd been a father for barely more than a month,

and I was already facing down my worst nightmare. If I wasn't fully gray by Christmas, it would be a miracle.

Bree's fingers flexed against my chest. "Can't sleep?" Her voice was a quiet rasp in the dark.

"No." On a sigh, I turned to brush my lips against her temple. "Every time I close my eyes, I think about what could have happened to her. To you."

I'd seen combat during my years in the Navy. There'd been a few close calls, times I hadn't been sure I'd come out the other side. But nothing had ever terrified me more than seeing Bree bolt from the cover of the trees, deliberately drawing the focus of two men with guns.

"You could have been shot."

Her hold tightened on me. "So could you. That's why I did it. Y'all had no cover. They'd have seen you."

That didn't make it any easier to convince my panicked heart to settle back in my chest.

She pressed a kiss to my pec. "It all turned out okay. We got to them in time. Peyton and Madison are both safe."

For now. As the on-hand doctor, Gabi had checked them out and cleared them both. Other than abrasions on their hands from all the digging and general exhaustion and shock, neither girl had any permanent damage. They hadn't been assaulted. I was beyond grateful for that. And yet...

"This was a threat we didn't even know to look out for. There are still the men connected to Northwest Global. Am I gonna have to start keeping my kid under lock and key for her own good?"

Bree was silent for a long moment. "We're gonna figure it out."

I made some sound of disagreement.

"We are," she insisted. But she didn't follow the assertion by blowing smoke up my ass about how. It was something I'd always appreciated about her.

"I don't think I can sleep." Gently detangling myself, I sat up.

"Me neither. Maybe a snack or some tea will help."

I dragged on a T-shirt as a concession to Peyton. Not that I thought she'd likely wake. She'd been exhausted by the time we'd gotten home and showered. But I was trying to make changes, so she'd feel comfortable.

In the kitchen, Bree turned on the light over the stove and filled a kettle with water. I didn't actually like tea, but coffee was hardly a good idea at two in the morning. It really wasn't about the tea, anyway. It was about having something to do with our hands while our minds were too busy.

"Feels weird not to have Keeley to let out."

It had already been so late by the time we'd gotten home we hadn't wanted to drive all the way to the north end of the island to get her from Sutter House.

I skimmed my hands down Bree's arms. "We'll pick her up tomorrow."

She smiled a little. "Hungry?"

We hadn't stopped long enough to have any sort of dinner last night beyond a protein bar during the search.

"I could eat."

She dragged out the carton of eggs and a bag of shredded cheese. I found the last third of a loaf of sourdough from Panadería de la Isla and cut off a few slices for toast. The oven door groaned as I pulled it open.

A minute later Peyton shuffled in looking hollowed eyed and a little haunted.

"I'm sorry, baby. Did we wake you?"

Her hands knit together. "No. I wasn't sleeping great."

I opened my arms without thinking. But she walked straight into them and burrowed in for a hug. I wrapped her tight, feeling something in me settle at the contact.

"Having nightmares?" Bree asked softly.

Nightmares. Because of course she would be. I

mentally moved therapy higher on my list of priorities.

But Peyton shook her head. "No, it's not that. Well, not really." She tucked her head a little tighter against my shoulder. "There's something I need to tell you."

Nothing in that statement boded well. I fought my instinctive need to tense. Peyton needed to feel like she could share anything with me. That I was a safe space.

I stroked a hand down her hair. "Okay."

She sucked in a breath. "I found it."

"Found what?"

"The thing those men were looking for. At least, I think I did."

Now I did pull back to look at her. "What are you talking about?"

Peyton fidgeted, hooking one bare foot behind her ankle. "You said you saw my notes about that Galef guy's murder and what I thought was going on."

"We did."

"It was at the first site we dug. But the guys who had us were distracted. They kept looking around, I guess, in case anybody stumbled on us. I knew once they had it, we'd be expendable, so I shoved it in my pocket and lied that it wasn't there."

All the blood drained from my face at the risk

she'd taken. At the fact that my thirteen-year-old knew what expendable meant.

"That was risky but really smart," Bree told her. "It bought more time for us to find you."

I was glad she, at least, could speak. Horror still had me by the throat.

Her fingers knit again. "I know I should have given it to the police, but honestly, in all the chaos with the rescue and after, I kind of forgot about it until we got home."

Swallowing down my emotions, I tried to manifest a calm I didn't feel. "That's okay. We'll turn it over to the police when we go in to make your full statement later today." They'd no doubt have things to say about fingerprints and chain of evidence, but I absolutely didn't have the bandwidth to think about that right now. "What is it, anyway?"

"A flash drive."

"Have you looked to see what's on it?" Bree asked.

Peyton shook her head.

I scooped a hand through my hair. "Okay, bring it to me."

"But I want to see."

I didn't have a clue what kind of information might be worth killing for, but my imagination was happy to provide a multitude of terrible options.

"Baby, we don't know what's on there. It may be a thing you don't need to see."

Her expression took on that mulish cast I was starting to recognize. "Well, can you open it and see first? It may just be files or information or something. But I've come this far. I want to know."

"Peyton—"

Her shoulders squared in a defiant stance that would do Mom proud. "I put together what the police didn't even manage. You can't argue with that."

"Nobody's questioning your intelligence, kiddo."

Bree laid a hand on my arm. "She's not wrong, Ford."

I split a glance between them, recognizing I was outnumbered. "Fine. Okay. Bring it here. I'll screen it."

While she retrieved the flash drive, I grabbed my laptop from my office. She came back into the kitchen with a thick zip-top bag rolled around a flash drive.

With the notion of fingerprints fresh in my own mind, I grabbed a pair of the latex gloves I kept in the kitchen for cutting jalapenos. Then I carefully extracted the drive and plugged it in. There was a single folder with only two video files inside.

"You go to your room for a few minutes while

we screen whatever is on here. If it's okay for you to see, we'll call you back."

With an epic teenage huff, she turned on heel. "Fine."

We waited until we heard her bedroom door shut. Bree went to check to make sure she was there just in case.

Then she returned to stand beside me. "What do you think this is?"

"I have no fucking clue."

I clicked on the first video file. The footage was grainy, obviously captured on an old cell phone. My breath caught as I recognized a much younger Miles Busby wearing a faded t-shirt with the logo of his family's old marina.

"Have you considered my offer?" The question came from a male voice off-screen.

Miles shifted his weight. "I can't do it."

"Come on now. We both know your family is struggling. This would provide a much needed influx of cash."

Miles glanced around nervously, as if checking for witnesses. "It's dirty money, and I'm not gonna use my family's business to launder it for you."

A fist shot into frame, catching Miles in the gut. He doubled over with a grunt. The attacker's tone remained casual, almost conversational. "I don't think you understand the situation here. I was being nice, giving you the illusion of a choice. But either you say yes and take the deal, or someone you care about is going to pay the price."

Miles straightened, wiping blood from his split lip. He spat on the ground. "Fuck you."

"You're going to regret that, Busby."

"Oh, my God." Bree's fingers dug into my shoulder. "This has to be about Gwen."

My stomach churned as I processed the implications. This video had to be from right before Gwen disappeared. Someone had been blackmailing Miles, threatening his family. And now, over a decade later, people were willing to kill to keep this evidence buried.

Without a word, I clicked over to the second video file. The footage was even grainier than the first, but there was no mistaking the terrified face of fifteen-year-old Gwen Busby. Her dark hair hung in tangles around her face, duct tape covered her mouth, and her wrists were bound behind her. She huddled in what looked like the hold of a boat, metal walls visible behind her.

Bree's fingers dug deeper into my shoulder as a voice spoke from off-screen. "You were warned, Busby. We own you now."

The camera panned across Gwen's trembling form before cutting to black.

My heart thundered against my ribs. That

video had to have been taken right after Gwen disappeared. She hadn't run away or been killed on the beach like everyone assumed. She'd been kidnapped to force her brother's compliance.

"Jesus Christ." I scrubbed a hand down my face. "This was why Galef was killed. Peyton was right. Whoever did all those break-ins was looking for this. It proves there's been some kind of human trafficking going on, probably all this time."

"Ford..." Bree's voice shook. "What it proves is that Miles was somehow involved. Coerced certainly, but involved. No one else is specifically implicated."

I stared at her. "What are you saying?"

"What if Galef was blackmailing Miles? What if Miles saw getting rid of him as a way of finally getting out from under this?"

If that was true, then there was still a very desperate man out there who'd already killed once to try to get his hands on this information.

"We have to get this to Chief Carson immediately." I started to reach for the laptop but froze as I heard the sound of a gun cocking behind me.

"I wouldn't do that if I were you."

CHAPTER 45

BREE

I was dreaming. I had to be. Because Miles Busby, the mayor of Sutter's Ferry, was standing in the doorway to the kitchen, a gun aimed at Ford's back. But the smell of burning toast from the oven told a different story. I was very much awake, and we were all still in danger.

Every muscle in Ford's body was tensed, ready to act, to defend. But he didn't move other than to flick his eyes toward me in warning to let him handle this.

"Turn around slowly." Miles murmured the order, as if he didn't want to wake anyone still sleeping. Not that any of us were.

Oh God, Peyton! What if she heard something and came out of her room? If she startled him...

Ford did as he was told, hands raised.

Miles was desperate. Gone was the usually polished, golden boy who'd worked his way into local politics so he could leverage his position for the alleged betterment of Hatterwick and Sutter's Ferry. In his place stood a man with disheveled hair and shadows under eyes that had seen far too much. Obviously, he was here for the evidence. It was about him, after all. The hows and whys of it didn't matter. The only thing that mattered was that gun and stopping him from using it.

We needed to buy time. For what, I had no idea. I had no fancy skills, no training in how to fight. All I had was years of experience behind the bar, listening to people. I knew how to get them to talk. So I'd get him to talk.

"What are you doing here?" Look at that. My voice only quavered a little bit.

The look of desperation on his face turned almost feral. "I've gone to an enormous amount of trouble to get that flash drive. You're going to hand it over and forget everything you just saw."

Or else what? But I didn't voice the question. The last thing I wanted to do was antagonize him.

"I cannot imagine how difficult it has been for you." I kept my voice sympathetic, the same tone I used with drunks who just needed to have their heartbreak validated so they wouldn't get rowdy.

"To hold on to this secret and have a piece of trash like Galef throw it in your face." I watched Miles' fingers tighten on the grip of the gun. "Because that's what he did, right?"

Miles' face twisted. "That little pissant." Spittle flew from his lips. "My life has already been a living hell for the last thirteen years, and that little asshole thought he could get more by dangling that over my head." His voice shook. "My family has suffered enough. I have suffered enough."

Ford shifted beside me, and Miles jerked the gun toward him. "Don't move."

I pressed my hand against Ford's arm, willing him to stay still.

His muscles vibrated with tension, just waiting for the chance to spring. But Miles was too on edge, too reckless. One wrong move and that gun would go off.

"Nobody would blame you," I said softly. "Killing him was justified."

Miles shook his head, the gun wavering. "I'm no cold-blooded murderer. It was an accident." His voice cracked. "He threatened me. Said he was going to publicly release the videos." He dragged a trembling hand down his face, the stubble along his jaw rasping against his palm. "I don't even know how he got his hands on it. Apparently, it was hidden somewhere in O'Shea's office."

"How did it happen?" My heart pounded against my ribs as I watched those fingers flex on the butt of the gun.

"We got into a fight. I shoved him. He fell and cracked his head." His eyes took on a haunted look. "The fall killed him. So I had to get rid of him."

"It was self-defense," I agreed, nodding. The words tasted like ash in my mouth, but I had to keep him talking, keep him from doing something worse. Keep buying time until... until what? What was the endgame here? Distracting him enough to give Ford an opening?

Ford remained statue-still beside me, but I could feel the tension radiating off him. One wrong move and this could all go sideways fast.

"Yes." Miles' voice was hoarse. "So, hand over the flash drive."

"Okay." Hands lifted, I edged slowly toward the laptop. But I couldn't stop myself from asking the question that had been beating like frantic wings in my brain since I saw that last video. "Did you ever find out what happened to your sister?"

The gun trembled in his grip. Pain and grief twisted his features into something almost unrecognizable. "It's my fault." His voice cracked. "They took her and did God knows what with her. And it was my fault."

The words seemed to pour out of him now, as if

they were a tide he'd been holding back for years. "All this time I've had to live with that." His gaze shifted to Ford, and something like relief flickered across his face. "I'm really fucking glad that your kid didn't suffer the same fate. These are really bad people."

"Look—" I wondered if Miles could see the flutter of that muscle in Ford's jaw that betrayed the calm, measured tone of his voice. "—if you take this to the police—"

"No." Miles' face contorted. "No. I have a wife. I have children. My parents are still living." He began to pace, the gun jerking with each agitated movement. "I managed to convince them to sell the marina. Thought that would get me out of this shit. But they just kept coming back, wanting more." Sweat beaded on his brow as his words tumbled out faster. "You don't understand. This is so much bigger than anything our tiny ass department can handle."

I watched Ford's hands slowly lower, though his body remained coiled and ready. "Then let us help you figure out another way."

"There is no other way!" Miles' voice cracked. "As long as that evidence exists, my family will never be safe. I won't let anyone else I love get hurt because of my mistakes."

The likelihood that this was the only copy of these videos seemed slim. But I wasn't about to bring that up.

"What about the feds?" Ford's voice remained steady.

Miles let out a bitter laugh that held no humor. "The feds are too busy chasing their own tails. I'm doing what I have to do to protect my family." His shoulders sagged, the manic energy draining from him. "I don't want to hurt either of you. Just hand over the flash drive."

The gun lowered slightly, no longer aimed directly at us. My heart leaped into my throat as I caught movement behind him.

Oh God. Peyton stood in the hallway, her face pale but determined.

Every maternal instinct I possessed screamed at me to do something, anything, to keep her safe. I tensed, ready to throw myself between Miles and his target if he spotted her.

But Peyton moved on soundless feet, stepping up right behind him. "I have to protect my family, too."

A sharp, electric crack split the air, followed by Miles' body jerking and convulsing. The gun went off with a deafening bang, and I flinched back as drywall dust rained down from the ceiling. Ford sprang, tackling Miles. The gun clattered to the floor, and I kicked it out of reach. In seconds, it was over, the mayor face-down, arms twisted behind his back.

From where he knelt, knee pressing Miles' still twitching body into the floor, Ford stared at his daughter in sheer disbelief. "Where the hell did you get a stun gun?"

Despite her pale face and the way she still clutched the device in her shaking hand, Peyton shrugged. "It was Mom's. She always said you could never be too careful."

My legs turned to jelly as the adrenaline drained away. I staggered over and wrapped my arms around Peyton. She slumped into me, and we sagged to the floor together. I squeezed her tight, pressing a kiss to her temple. "You did good, kid."

"Somebody grab the duct tape from the junk drawer," Ford ordered.

Peyton managed to scramble up to retrieve it, tossing it over to her father. He used it to bind Miles' hands and legs. Then he called 911.

While he made his report to the dispatcher, I dragged myself back to my feet and finally turned off the oven. The toast inside had burnt to a crisp. I carried the stink of it out the back door and set it on the patio table. Then I pulled out a bowl and began cracking eggs.

At Peyton's curious look, it was my turn to shrug. "Might as well have breakfast. It's going to be a long night."

CHAPTER 46
FORD

My kid was officially fourteen.

I wasn't ready. I hadn't been ready for so many things around fatherhood. The constant worry, the way my heart seemed to live outside my body now, the crushing weight of responsibility that came with every decision I made.

Peyton had bounced back from the events of the past couple of months with shocking ease, but I hadn't been able to do the same. I was having a hard time letting her out of my sight, jumping at shadows and checking her bedroom door three times before going to bed myself. Thankfully, she was tolerating it well, only rolling her eyes a little when I insisted on taking her to school or picking her up from friends' houses. Bree and Mom and Mimi had helped with that, creating a protective circle around her that made me feel less crazy for being so vigilant. As had Ed, who'd been released from the hospital in plenty of time to be here for today's birthday party, his presence another anchor of stability in our newly reformed family unit.

He still had a long way to go with his recovery, but we were all circling around him like protective satellites, making sure he didn't overdo it while still letting him maintain his dignity. He'd get through it, and his doctors were confident he'd make an almost full recovery as long as he stuck to the program and kept his stress levels down. That was going a lot better since he found out the Galef situation had been resolved. Turned out he'd made the same connection Peyton had right before his AFib attack. The shock of the whole thing sent him over the edge. If Peyton hadn't grabbed his notes, we might never have known about any of it in time.

Right now, a promised deep sea fishing trip next summer was the carrot on a stick getting Ed through the year or more of rehab ahead. He was determined to catch a replacement for Marv, the marlin that had burned along with the original tavern, though we all knew nothing could truly replace that fish. It had been his pride and joy for over twenty years, mounted over the bar like a mascot. His own personal Moby Dick.

I scanned the yard again, taking in the cheerful chaos of the party. Picnic tables dotted the space between my cottage and Bree's, festooned with balloons and streamers in Peyton's favorite colors. The late afternoon sun cast long shadows across the grass, and the breeze carried the scent of Mimi's massive German chocolate cake. Keeley and Roy were playing a spirited game of keep away with a lime green frisbee.

My daughter's laughter rang out as she and Madison huddled over something on Madison's phone. Probably some social media thing I was too old to understand. Turned out there was nothing like acquiring a teenager to make you feel old in your thirties. Mom was deep in conversation with Gabi and Daniel about some environmental initiative, while Sawyer and Willa helped Mimi arrange the food spread, and Ed snuck appetizers off the platters of food near his chair of honor.

Bree caught my eye from where she was setting out plates, raising an eyebrow in silent question. She knew me too well. Knew I was still struggling to relax, even with Miles Busby behind bars and the flash drive safely in the hands of law enforcement. The two men who'd taken Peyton and Madison had been arrested, and Daniel's team had managed to snag the boat that had been running dark that night. I wasn't privy to the details, but things were slowly being dismantled. I should have been satisfied with that.

But I wasn't.

I forced myself to take a deep breath. This was Peyton's day. She deserved to have it be perfect, unmarred by my lingering paranoia.

But I couldn't shake the feeling of waiting for the other shoe to drop. Maybe it was the dad thing —this constant awareness that my kid could be hurt or taken from me. Or maybe it was the military training that had kept me alive all these years.

"Earth to Ford." Bree's hand slipped into mine. "She's safe. We're all safe."

I squeezed her fingers, grateful she understood without me having to explain. "I know. Just can't seem to turn it off."

"Then let me help distract you." She stretched up to press a kiss to my jaw. "Come help me with these plates before Mimi decides we're being antisocial."

That was definitely an appealing offer, but before I could take her up on it, my phone rang. I checked the display, and my stomach bottomed out at the sight of Langston's name flashing across the screen.

"I need to take this. Be back."

With a quick squeeze of Bree's hand, I ducked into the house and answered. "Langston?"

"I guess celebration is in order."

Not at all what I'd expected from the federal agent. "Is it?"

"It's Peyton's birthday today, isn't it?"

"Yeah. Is that why you're calling?" I knew I sounded borderline rude, but this man never came with good news. Every time his number popped up on my phone, my stomach twisted into knots, dreading whatever fresh hell he might be bringing to our doorstep.

"Yes, and no. I have a rather unconventional gift."

"What's that?" My fingers tightened around the phone, bracing for impact.

"We took down Northwest Global. The key players have already been arrested, and we expect their operations to be shut down within the month. We got the evidence we needed through another informant, so there is no longer any plausible reason for anyone connected with the company to have any interest in Peyton, no matter how remote. It's over."

"What about the two goons they hired, who were spotted in Norfolk?" I hadn't stopped looking for them since Dax had brought that potential threat to my attention.

"Pinched last week on another job. They're out of commission. Oh, and I happened to touch base with the police who handled the recovery of your moving pod. Yours wasn't the target. One of the other units was being used for drug trafficking. Idiot who was supposed to pick it up couldn't remember which one it was, so he stole the whole fucking truck. Seriously. It's over."

"It's over," I repeated, not entirely believing it. The words felt foreign on my tongue.

"Your daughter is safe."

"She's safe." I let out a shuddering breath and covered my eyes, fighting back the sting of tears I hadn't expected. "She's actually safe. Truly?"

"Truly."

"Oh, thank God." The tension that had been dogging me for weeks finally released at the confirmation, leaving me light-headed with relief. My knees actually wobbled, and I had to press a hand to the wall.

"Thought you'd want to know."

"I appreciate it. And Langston?"

"Yeah?"

"With all due respect, you'll understand if I say I hope I never hear from you again."

The other man laughed. "Understood, and no offense taken. Though from what I hear about how your kid pieced together what happened with the murder on your island, she could have a future in the Bureau down the line."

"Hopefully, she'll decide to be something nice and safe. Like a podiatrist."

Langston chuckled again, the sound warm with understanding. "Hope springs eternal. Have a nice life, Donoghue."

I was still standing there several minutes later, staring at my phone and trying to process everything, when Bree came to find me. Her footsteps echoed softly in the hallway as she approached.

"Everything okay?" she asked.

I pulled her into my arms and beamed, unable to contain the joy bubbling up inside me. "Everything is fantastic. That was Agent Langston. They took down Northwest Global. Peyton is safe."

Those gray eyes I loved so much brightened, hope and relief washing across her face. "Truly?"

"Truly."

I spun her in a giddy circle. Finally, finally, the dark cloud hanging over us had lifted. As Langston had said, that was something worth celebrating, and I knew exactly where I wanted to start. I captured Bree's mouth in a kiss, pouring out all my relief and happiness. She tasted of strawberry lip gloss and the promise of a tomorrow I hadn't been free to imagine. But now I could. There'd be no more looking over our shoulders. No more wondering if today would be the day someone came for my daughter.

Bree melted against me, fingers sliding into my

hair. God, I loved this woman. Loved how she'd stepped up to protect my kid without hesitation. Loved how she called me on my shit but supported me, anyway. Just... loved her.

"Dad! Bree! Come on, I'm starving, and Mimi won't let us eat until everyone's out here!"

We broke apart at Peyton's voice. Bree's cheeks were flushed, her lips curved in a soft smile that made me want to kiss her again just to coax out more of that softness she hid so deeply beneath that prickly exterior.

She gestured toward the door. "We should probably..."

"Yeah." I caught her hand, threading our fingers together. "Let's go celebrate."

Outside, Bree got pulled away from me and into the divvying up of food. But that was okay. We had time.

"You're looking a lot less like a guy on a gallows walk," Sawyer observed. "What turned that attitude around?"

I gave him the update from Langston, watching the tension ease from his shoulders as well. He still hadn't fully forgiven himself for what he considered losing Peyton on his watch.

"Damn, that's awesome. Seems like things are finally settling down."

"Thank God. I'd like some time to just be, you

know?" I felt like I'd been in the middle of a hurricane since January, caught in an endless cycle of one crisis after another. The thought of a quiet evening with Bree and Peyton sounded like heaven.

"I hear that." He glanced over, his eyes thoughtful. "You talked to Rios since the arrest?"

News of Miles Busby's arrest and the contents of the video had swept the island like wildfire. The Busby family was, of course, utterly devastated. But the one good thing to come out of all of it was that Rios was, at last, unequivocally cleared of suspicion in Gwen's disappearance. Thirteen years was a long time to carry that kind of weight.

"I don't think he knows how to feel about it. And I'm not sure he'll believe people are really over blaming him until he's come home and seen it firsthand." I'd talked to him briefly, but the conversation had been stilted, weighted with too many years of distance.

"Hope he'll do that soon. I miss our boy."

"Same," I agreed. Despite all the chaos and danger, being home around family and friends had been fantastic, and I wanted the same for all the Wayward Sons. Maybe then our circle would finally be complete again.

Across the yard, Bree fell into a fit of laughter with her grandfather. I couldn't help but grin. It was so damned good to see her smile. So damned good to be a part of it, when I knew I'd caused so much hurt.

"It's good to see you two happy," Sawyer observed.

"It's good to be happy. I never thought she'd forgive me."

"And now that she has?"

I understood what he was really asking. "I want something real and permanent with her. But with everything that's happened, I'm not sure Peyton is ready for that."

Sawyer rolled his eyes. "That girl's been in match-making mode with the two of you practically from the beginning. She'll be on board."

"He's totally right," she whispered behind me.

I jolted, uncomfortably reminded that my kid could walk like a cat. "You'd be good with that?"

She looked at me with far more wisdom than a fourteen-year-old almost high school freshman ought to possess. "Dad, if you don't lock that down, I will forever question your intelligence."

I looked from her to Sawyer, who only grinned.

"Well, I guess you told me." I snagged her around the neck and pulled her in so I could ruffle her hair and press a smacking kiss to her head. She squirmed in mock protest and giggled. "But today is for you. We can plan the asking for later."

"I'm holding you to that," Peyton declared. "Right now, I'm having more cake."

Sawyer and I watched her trot over to the picnic table.

"Priorities," he said.

I grinned. "Priorities."

EPILOGUE
BREE

"I can't believe I let you talk me into karaoke night again." I crossed my arms, watching Monty set up the equipment.

"It's because I brought home another shiny award for Dark Moon Rising. And it'll be fine this time. Promise. We have our list of banned singers, and there's a firm two-song limit."

I gave him the side eye. The last karaoke night had devolved into an epic disaster involving three fistfights and someone trying to perform an entire Broadway musical. But Monty had earned his victory lap with that gold medal from Brewgaloo, North Carolina's biggest craft beer festival. We were offering samples to everyone in celebration.

The bar was packed tonight, mostly with locals

getting their fun in before the tourists descended for Memorial Day weekend. This was how I liked it best. These were my people. The ones who'd supported me and Pop through his recovery, who'd come out to help search when Peyton had disappeared, and who'd raised a toast in our honor when Ford and I had gone public with our relationship. I was feeling a little squishy in the heart region and so incredibly grateful for how things had turned out.

School would be out next week, and Peyton couldn't wait. She currently sat with the Gray Beards in their corner booth, surveying the crowd and listening to their usual cutting up. Pop's color was good, and his rehab had been progressing faster than the doctors had anticipated. They had no idea how stubborn Ed Cartwright could be. My Pop was gonna be around for a good long while. Thank God.

My gaze swung toward the door, and my heart lifted as I spotted Ford. I started to raise my hand in a wave and stopped as I saw who'd come in behind him.

Rios paused just in the entryway, his dark eyes scanning the room, cataloging the occupants and every tactical detail of the place. At least until his sisters saw him.

"Rios!" Caroline's joyful shriek cut through the babble of voices. She scrambled up from the table where the McNamara clan was holding court, trailed by Gabi.

I grinned as I watched the pair of them converge on him, trapping him in excited hugs. I couldn't actually hear them from this distance, but I suspected they were both peppering him with questions in rapid-fire Spanish. It took a while for him to run the gauntlet of hugs and greetings from family and friends. But eventually he made it to me.

I came out from behind the bar and pulled him in for my own hug. "Good to see you."

"Great to see you, too." He pulled back, dividing a look between me and Ford. "Glad you two got your heads out of your asses."

Ford cheerfully flipped him a middle finger.

I shook my head in amusement. "We've heard that often enough, we're considering putting it on a t-shirt and selling it at the bar."

"It would be a best seller."

At this point, I wondered if everybody had known how we'd felt about each other. It hardly mattered. We were together now, and we were happy. That was the only thing that was important.

"You want to try the new beer? Dark Moon Rising just won a gold at Brewgaloo."

He glanced around, clearly taking in the sample glasses we usually used for taster flights. "Sure, I'll have a sample."

"Don't be silly. As a welcome home, you get an entire glass on me."

Rios laughed, and the sound was a little rusty. It didn't quite make it all the way to his eyes. I wondered what he'd been up to, and what had precipitated this surprise visit home.

Back behind the bar, I took my time building Rios's pint, letting the head develop properly. Behind me, voices drifted over from a nearby table.

"Did you hear about Madden Reilly?"

The name caught my attention. I hadn't heard it in years.

"Miles and Gwen Busby's cousin? The one who moved out to Washington?"

"California. She was some big deal prosecutor out there. Emphasis on was."

"What happened?"

"Lost her job."

"Over what?"

"Helped convict an innocent man. New evidence came to light, and the conviction was overturned. Guess the guy had connections 'cause next thing she knew she was out."

"Ouch."

I risked a glance at Rios. His expression hadn't changed, but his shoulders had gone rigid. The irony wasn't lost on me. Madden had been one of the loudest voices condemning him after Gwen disappeared. She'd never forgiven him for being the last person to see her cousin alive.

My hands tightened on the glass. After everything that had come out about what really happened to Gwen, I wondered if Madden felt any remorse for how she'd treated Rios. For helping drive him off the island. Somehow I doubted it. Some people couldn't admit they were wrong, even in the face of overwhelming evidence.

I topped off his beer and slid it across the bar. "Karma?"

He sipped at the beer and jerked one shoulder. "Maybe now she'll learn to think before she acts." Lifting his glass in a toast, he headed over to join his family.

I watched Rios settle in beside his niece and Gabi, noting the way he kept his back to the wall, maintaining clear sight lines to all exits. Ford's gaze tracked him too, his expression thoughtful.

"Is he okay?"

"Something's stuck in his craw. If he's here long enough, Sawyer and I will get it out of him."

The screech of feedback made me wince as Monty tapped the mic. He bounded onto our makeshift stage, beaming at the crowd. "Welcome, welcome to karaoke night at the OBX Brewhouse! Now, we've got some ground rules. Two-song limit per person. And if you're on the banned list

—you know who you are—don't even think about it."

I relaxed slightly. Maybe this wouldn't be the disaster I feared.

"To kick things off, we've got a special treat. Please welcome Ford Donoghue and Bree Cartwright!"

My head snapped up. "Excuse me, what? I don't karaoke."

Ford turned that devastating smile on me—the one that had talked me into everything from sneaking onto fishing boats to midnight swims since we were kids. He held out his hand. "Come on."

The crowd started chanting my name. Pop and the Gray Beards were the loudest, though Peyton and Mimi's voices rang clear above the rest. I hadn't even seen her and Mama Flo arrive.

I shot Ford a look that promised retribution. "Fine."

The bar erupted in cheers as I came out from behind the counter.

Ford's hand closed around mine and he tugged me up onto the stage.

"What are we even singing?" I demanded.

He handed over a microphone with a grin. "A classic."

The opening notes of "I Got You Babe" filled

the bar, and I shot Ford a look. "Really? This is your idea of a classic?"

He just grinned and launched into Sonny's part. I couldn't help laughing at his exaggerated gestures and dramatic facial expressions. What the hell? In for a penny.

I channeled my inner Cher, complete with hair flips and hip swaying. The crowd ate it up, particularly when Ford and I played up the cheese factor, facing each other and gesturing dramatically. Pop was practically falling out of his booth laughing.

Peyton had her phone up, no doubt recording the whole mortifying spectacle for posterity. I'd have to get her to send it to me later. Not that I'd ever admit that out loud.

We finished with a flourish, and I took an exaggerated bow, ready to escape back behind the bar. But Ford's hand tightened on mine when I tried to step away.

I turned back. "What are you..."

The words died in my throat as he dropped to one knee.

"What?" My voice came out as a squeak.

The entire bar went dead silent.

Ford grinned up at me, still on one knee. "Bree Cartwright, I've loved you most of my life. First as my best friend, then as the woman who stole my heart, and now as this amazing bonus mom to my kid. You're the missing piece I didn't even know I was looking for until I lost you. I was an idiot to ever let you go, and I don't want to waste another minute. Will you marry me?"

My heart threatened to burst right out of my chest, hammering so hard I could barely hear anything else over the rush of blood in my ears. My vision blurred as tears welled up. I blinked hard, desperate not to cry in front of half the island. Ford still knelt before me, his green eyes filled with so much love it made my chest ache.

This was Ford. My Ford. The boy who'd held my hand through every thunderstorm. Who'd snuck me candy bars when I was stuck in detention. Who'd taught me to swim and climb trees and throw a punch. The man who'd come back into my life and proved that sometimes dreams really did come true.

My throat closed up. I couldn't speak past the knot of emotion.

The silence stretched. Someone in the crowd—probably Duck—called out, "Say something, girl!"

I managed a watery laugh. "I will marry you on one condition."

His eyes sparkled. "What's that?"

"You never, ever get me up here again."

The bar erupted in laughter. Ford's grin widened. "Deal." He slipped a ring on my finger—

where had he been hiding that?—and surged to his feet.

His mouth claimed mine in a kiss that had the whole place whooping and hollering. When we broke apart, I spotted Peyton giving us an enthusiastic thumbs up from her spot with the Gray Beards. Pop wiped suspiciously wet eyes with his napkin.

"I love you."

God, I'd never get tired of hearing that. "I love you too."

"You're stuck with me now."

I tipped my head back to look at him. "Promise?"

The entire bar raised their glasses in a toast as Ford wrapped his arms around me, both of us grinning like idiots. Which, I supposed, we were. The happiest kind of idiots, who'd finally found their way back to exactly where we were supposed to be.

Together.

OH MY GOSH, they really *do* need to print t-shirts with the date they finally got their heads out of their asses! But I had so much fun writing this book, and I hope you enjoyed it as much as I did. Be on the lookout for *Night Moves*, Corbin and Lindsay's novella that runs alongside this book. And, of course, don't forget the enemies to lovers story of Rios and Madden coming next year! That's gonna be explosive...

Meanwhile, don't forget to get your bonus epilogue with more of Ford and Bree's happily ever after. Sign up here to land it straight in your inbox: https://harperjacksonbooks.com/all-along-the-watchtower-be/

OTHER BOOKS BY HARPER JACKSON

Wayward Sons

- *Smoke on the Water* (prequel novel)
- *Won't Back Down* (Book 1)
- *Against the Wind* (novella)
- *All Along The Watchtower* (Book 2)
- *Night Moves* (novella) Coming 2026
- *On the Other Side* (Book 3)
  Coming 2026
- *Bad Moon Rising* (novella)
  Coming 2026
- *Carry On Wayward Son* (Book 4)
  Coming 2027

ABOUT THE AUTHOR

Harper Jackson has rescued her co-workers from a hostage situation, battled ninjas, and stopped international espionage—in her head anyway. Now that she's no longer busy devising ways to make staff meetings more entertaining, she's pouring that imagination into tales of breath-stealing, small-town romantic suspense. She believes that peach cobbler with ice cream is the best dessert ever and has a black belt in taekwondo to back it up. She lives in the Deep South with her husband and canine furbabies. Find out more about Harper and her books at https://harperjackson.com or explore the lighter side of her catalog as Kait Nolan at https://kaitnolan.com.

www.ingramcontent.com/pod-product-compliance
Lightning Source LLC
Chambersburg PA
CBHW060301100726
47907CB00002B/240